THE BOOK OF WATER
THE DARK LIBRARY SERIES
BOOK ONE

MORGAN REILLY

LIBRA'S INK
PUBLISHING

Copyright © 2024 by Morgan Reilly

Cover art by germancreative

As this is a work of fiction. Any resemblance to actual events, locales, or persons, living or dead, is entirely coincidental.

All rights reserved. No part of this book may be reproduced, distributed, or transmitted in any form or by any means, including photocopying, recording, or other electronic or mechanical methods, without the prior written permission of the author, except in the case of brief quotations embodied in critical reviews and certain other noncommercial uses permitted by U.S. copyright law.

Unauthorized reproduction or distribution of this book, or any portion of it, may result in severe civil and criminal penalties, and will be prosecuted. Additionally, this book is not authorized for data collection and/or usage in Artificial Intelligence (AI) platforms and technologies.

Published in the United States of America.

To Ariel & Savannah
I love you to the moon and back.

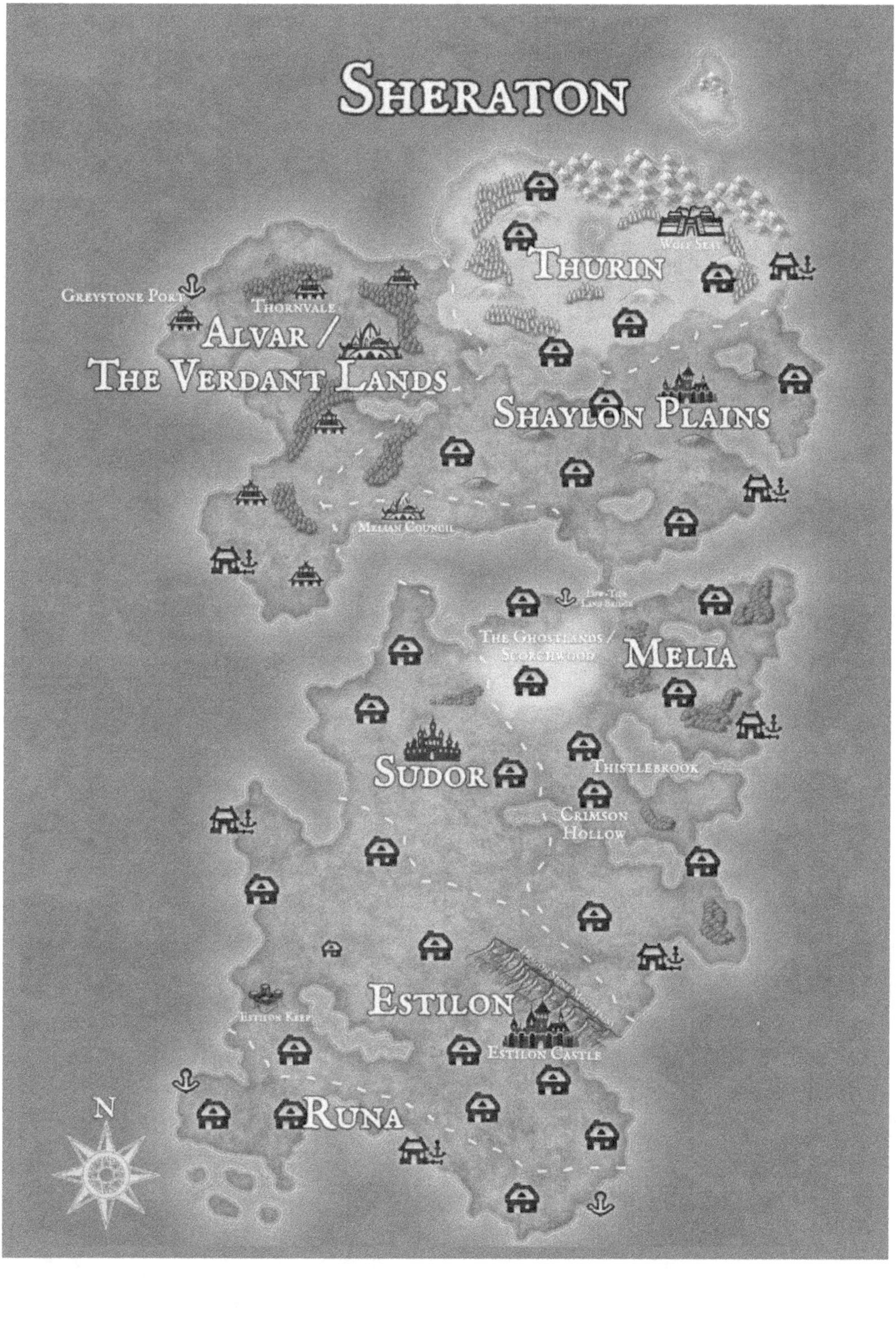

Sheraton
Thurin
Greystone Port
Thornvale
Alvar /
The Verdant Lands
Shaylon Plains
Melaan Council
The Ghostlands /
Scorchwood
Melia
Sudor
Thistlebrook
Crimson
Hollow
Estilon
Estilon Keep
Estilon Castle
Runa
N

To Shanna, goddess of water, patron of sea and magic,
  To Brena, goddess of fire, patron of artistry and creation,
  To Erys, goddess of air, patron of storms and rain,
  To Rhiann, goddess of earth, patron of land and fertility,
  To Anya, goddess of order, patron of life and justice,
  To Aishlin, goddess of chaos, patron of death and crossroads,
  We swear our undying fealty.

CHAPTER 1

Watching rain fall through the water was like watching the world upside-down. The drops shattered through the surface like shooting stars, their trails of liquid stardust falling short as the sea absorbed their magic and power.

Celine's fingers combed through the water, weaving magic around each shimmering star through her underwater sky. She hummed her shadows to life, their shades flickering darkness against light.

One tendril of darkness for her father, Janis, the former merking. Another for her mother, Queen Elynda. The coils of shadow magic entwined. Celine tried to remember them smiling, her father's brilliant purple eyes next to her mother's sea green. But their images came in flashes, laughter without sound. She couldn't remember their voices until she dreamed, even as they said her name.

Celine pulled at the shadows for them, her will and determination fixed upon her targets. Dathan, the Usurper King, and Santus, First Commander. A true pairing of brawn and brain, of destruction and cunning. Where Dathan was the fist, Santus was the elegance of how the hand should hit.

Her father had been first, of course. Janis, the merking whose throne Dathan wanted more than anything else Shanna's sea could offer. Her mother, Elynda, had been later, after she'd tried to poison him on their arranged wedding night.

Think of Dathan instead. Usurper King. Dathan planned a third anniversary celebration with Santus and his league of sycophants. The celebration would be the perfect place to haunt them, to have her shadows make them relive their darkest nightmares.

Dathan and Santus. The king and his commander. What terrors would her shadows make them see?

"Go, my beautiful dark," Celine whispered. The shadows moved from her hand through the sea water, swaying to her delicate melody. "Give them my regards."

The shadows would reach them, affecting their conscious thoughts and focus. What did the merking and his first commander see when the shadows seeped into their mind? Did they relive their sins and their past mistakes? Or was such a fate only reserved for those in possession of a conscience?

She'd called Santus *king killer* only once, earning her a week in merfolk prison where she was nearly starved and tortured with iron. But she smiled at the idea of saying it again, thrilled by the gleam of loathing in his eyes. "But where is the lie?" she would say. "*King killer.*"

She moved her hands through the water, picturing the first commander, wishing for a stroke of dark magic to wipe the smugness from his mouth. She called to the forces of shadow, as Kasindra had taught her, and shadows were eager to do her bidding. Daily, the shadows served, tireless and hungry.

"Don't let Dathan win, my dear," Kasindra had said, her lavender eyes filled with hatred toward her brother. "He will destroy himself soon enough, but don't let him destroy you."

But grief already destroyed her. The version of her that existed now was Celine remade, the aftermath of love and loss and the thirst for vengeance. This new, reborn Celine crafted spells to haunt and torment. Her revenge wasn't set in death but life-in-death, building her magic to send Dathan and Santus straight to Aishlin and the bottom of the seven hells.

May the Chaos Realm welcome them both, she thought. *Take them, and free my parents from your hellscape. I will gladly send their despicable souls in exchange for those whom I love.*

But if Aishlin was listening, she gave no sign. Still, Celine hoped. Still, Celine prayed.

"Go to him," she whispered to the second wave of shadows, smiling at their obedience. Some tendrils of shadows combed through her teal hair, bringing her to laugh. "Fill their minds, little ones. Fill their dreams. Keep them from rest."

The shadows moved to their work, but with the anger simmering deep within, this spell wasn't enough. She needed more. She needed something *stronger*. Arcana crystal would help, but it was rarer by the day as merfolk and humans farmed it greedily. Even in Estilon, bearing no hospitality for magic or magic folk, arcana crystal still found its way into eager human hands. So, when the familiar iridescent shimmer of arcana crystal caught her eye, Celine raced up from the sea floor, dusting up sand and seaweed. The node was small, only about the size of her palm, but she could do something with it.

She summoned one dagger, the handle filling her waiting hand as magic pulsed from her palm, using and manipulating the water to form a blade thin and sharp, delicate enough to separate the gem from the node without damaging the root system or cracking the glass surface. Small barnacles twisted up the length of the hilt, her index finger grazing one as she prepared her grip.

But as quickly as hope filled her, disappointment fizzled out the fire. The break on the far side of the crystal revealed someone's crude farming, the broken remnants held fast by the coral. Swimming closer, Celine could see correctly how small the node truly was, the width and span deceptive at the angle she'd seen before.

She carefully farmed what was left, a mere fraction of what she'd thought, the crack giving her two small pieces instead of a larger one. She slipped the pieces into her bag, the strap barely pressing any weight against her chest. Though useful, the crystal was devastatingly light.

A boat-shaped shadow consumed her own, stretching over the coral and sea floor. A commercial fishing vessel, by the look of the hull, one privately owned. Only the king's sanctioned ships could legally fish for merfolk, a barbaric decree made as the war between nations escalated. But the crown's laws at sea didn't stop fishermen from accepting whatever quarry their nets fetched. Buyers paid dearly for rarities of the sea, be they made of stone or scale.

A man jumped off the side, diving into the water with ease before swimming toward the sea floor. A mass of bubbles surrounded him like sea foam before they cleared, but he was too far away to notice any details beyond the contrast of his white shirt and dark brown trousers. His bare feet and broad hands pushed through the water.

Celine summoned her second dagger as she watched, glancing upward for any sign of a falling net. But nothing else came, and the man continued to swim for a stretch of coral she had yet to explore.

There, barely perceptible until she swam closer, hiding in the shadows: another arcana crystal.

No.

What she'd gathered wouldn't be enough to cast and reach Santus. The physical cost of dark magic was steep, but one arcana crystal helped to pay it. Celine's fingers strangled her daggers as she crept slowly, the man a skilled swimmer as he reached the coral in a series of strong, practiced strokes.

I'd prefer not to kill you, she thought. If only humans could hear merspeak. *Let's hope scaring you off is enough.*

But the nearer she swam, the stronger his magic pulsed from him, like a delicate heartbeat only detectable by those who shared it. Celine dispelled one of her daggers, cutting through the water as she raced to stop him, blocking his utility knife just in time. Her rich teal hair billowed around her as she met his startled eyes, as bright as the afternoon sky.

Bubbles escaped his mouth as he cried out, unleashing a wave of force magic. The pulse hit her in the chest and pushed her back, giving him time to retreat. He abandoned the crystal, working his arms and legs to swim for the surface.

But he was too late. Voices carried ethereal, haunting grace through the water seconds before the merfolk appeared, five swarming the fishing vessel in a shimmering rainbow of color. One maid, her coloring a rich orange, reached the man before Celine could pull him to safety. The maid's deceptively delicate hands cupped his face, her full lips parted, preparing for a kiss.

His cries for help erupted in bubbles. His hands and feet pushed with strength waning beneath her magic, the maid's singing wrapping around his mind as she drew nearer.

"This isn't a sanctioned ship," Celine said, her voice strong in the maid's mind. "He was only after the crystal."

"King Rolf doesn't have to give his emblem for ships to fish for us." The maid's hands untied the thin cord binding his hair, and she stroked the freed blond tresses as one would for a lover. There was still some fight in him, his hands trying in vain to push hers away. "And this handsome one is already here. A delicious little treat."

Celine poised her empty hand to cast, her will summoning the shadows to her call. "And what was his crime?"

"*Existing.*"

"Charlie!" Muffled voices cried overhead. The men had stayed, risking their lives to save his. "Charlie! Grab the rope!"

A rope hit the water and uncoiled slowly. Charlie turned forcefully, his eyes watching its steady sinking. Fear braced his gaze as two merfolk surrounded him.

Celine aimed both shadow and blade at the mermaid, meeting flesh and scale at the maid's arm. The pain was enough to loosen her grip, and Charlie broke free. But the boat spun with the influence of the swimming merfolk, the rope pulling a lazy trail through the water.

Another merfolk came fast, his twin swords gleaming in his hands. Celine used her daggers to block his aim as she dodged, using his own momentum to guide her through the water.

"You'll only live long enough to regret that." The mermaid summoned her own weapon, a long, thin sword that cut through the water with ease. Her murderous gaze pierced through the water, her orange eyes burning like twin flames.

Celine moved to Charlie, more bubbles escaping his mouth in panic as her hands pushed hard against his back. He flailed, instinctively fighting, but Celine didn't relent.

No, he wasn't fighting. He was *drowning*. His body struggled and chest convulsed as more air escaped.

She pressed her mouth to his, holding on as he jerked weakly in protest. She held his head with both hands, parting his mouth with her tongue and pushing air into him. Her gills fluttered as her body became a vessel to help him live. His hands tried to push her waist before his body accepted her offering, his hold relaxing at her sides, though his touch remained firm.

The kindness cost her. The mermaid slammed into Celine, her sword blade slicing a neat line up her tail. Charlie sailed back with her but had gathered his bearings enough to swim for the surface. The rope glided away, following the track of the whirlpool.

"Of course you would cause trouble." That voice—a smooth tenor, echoing in her mind.

Santus.

Right hand of the king, and a self-righteous prick.

He mocked her with a quiet chuckle. "Leave it to you to risk your life for the scum of the earth."

Celine sneered, every muscle clenching at the sound of his voice, at the sight of his green hair and fin. His face was perpetually locked in arrogance, dancing the midline between smugness and disgust.

I could kill him now, she thought, the wistful dream becoming a reality as the thought set in. *I could kill him right now and be one step closer.*

There would still be Dathan, the royal brawn to Santus's brain. But once the head was removed, severing the hand would be easy.

"You've been in their nets before, Celine." Santus's green eyes were almost luminescent in the watery dark. "You know what monsters they are."

"And what monsters are we?"

Another voice, a gentle female mezzo soprano that was no less sharp. Jessa, Dathan's daughter. Her snow-white hair, eyes, and fin startled even the merfolk as they beheld her in the deep blue of the sea.

"This isn't a sanctioned military ship, Santus," Jessa said. "They're just fishermen."

Dathan's own daughter, telling Santus to stand down. Her dislike of him wasn't exactly unknown among the merfolk, but the daughter of the Usurper King coming between the first commander and his human prey? Celine didn't bother to hide her shock, her stepsister an unlikely ally in defense of humans.

"There's no such thing as a mere fisherman with humans and their greed." Santus looked up at the ship with a disgusted curl on his lips. "Your father would be disappointed in you, Jessa."

An ice-white eyebrow arched higher. "I'd be worried if he *wasn't* disappointed."

Screams broke through, and the merfolk scattered. One net fell, the taste and smell of iron already seeping through the water as the laced hemp sank. It made no catch, but it offered the men enough time to sail away to freedom. The vessel pushed forward, the sails catching wind.

Charlie was nowhere in sight. He must have made it. At least Celine wasn't surrounded by angry merfolk for nothing.

Getting under Santus's skin was an unexpected perk.

"You traitor," one merfolk hissed at her.

"You stupid fool," said another

Santus smirked. "You're always so adept at making friends, Celine. Really, how *do* you do it?"

"I won't sacrifice my principles." A weak reply, but all other words failed her. "No one is worth that, Santus. Least of all, you."

Somewhere in the fight, a blade had sliced through Celine's arm, blood feathering freely into the water. The wound didn't close as it should have.

"Leave this, Santus," Jessa said. "The waters of Shanna don't deserve further bloodshed."

Santus glowered, the deep green of his gaze flashing dangerously before he glanced at the surface of the water. The boat had made significant distance, removing them from any equation he may have tried to calculate.

"Let's go," Santus said to his company, and they followed him back to whatever hole he crawled from.

"The absolute loathing I feel for that waste is unfathomable," Jessa said before regarding Celine with concern.

Celine snorted a laugh despite the burning and aching over every inch of her body, especially her arm. "Something we have in common."

Jessa held sympathy beneath her chilled veneer. "He was out of line before. About your capture."

"It's—" But she stopped. What was there to say?

"Human weapons aren't enough?" Jessa shook her head, her white hair like snowfall. "Merfolk have to use them, too?"

After a moment's silence, Celine said, "Thank you. For your help."

"Just doing the right thing." Then, with the hint of a smile, she added, "Anything to get my father's fin in a tangle."

Jessa had always said *my father*, not *our father*, which Celine had appreciated. They would hardly call their union *family*, but there was an unspoken understanding between them. That, and Jessa had honor where Dathan did not. Jessa had been kind since Celine's parents died, a surprising kindness that impressed Celine into trusting that Jessa would do the right thing, despite her father. As her step-sister swam away, Celine was grateful for at least one boon from Dathan's cursed reign.

The cut on Celine's arm burned with an aching heat, blood still seeping from the thin red line. Celine pressed her hand to the wound, fevered and bleeding, and whispered healing into her skin. She groaned through the searing ache as the toxin burned its way out, her magic pulling it from muscle and blood and skin. With cool relief at last, her wound slowly sealed itself closed.

"Damn you to the Seven Hells." She imagined Santus and his goons twisting into the unknown tortures awaiting them in each layer of the Kingdom of Chaos. "You and your Usurper King."

King Dathan, who played at being a king when he was nothing more than a tyrant with a child's temper. But his tenure on the throne wouldn't last much longer.

Quickly, Celine swam for the coral, her hope fleeting as she sought the crystal Charlie had risked his life to get. But what remained was broken, the crystal harvested crudely and quickly by inexperienced or hastened hands. Charlie had harvested it, after all, unless one of the other merfolk had taken it for themselves.

She fished out more pieces, adding them to her bag before swimming for home.

CHAPTER 2

Human artifacts filled Celine's reef, all of them in and around the living coral and stone. Pieces of art, various tools, clothing, and jewelry, things she and her friends had collected after ships collided with rocks or lost their duels with storms, finding their way to the bottom of the sea.

The most precious among them were the books.

The brine and sea life were cruel to the paper and binding, so she and her friends read them before they dissolved to nothing. Zander and Quinn enjoyed reading passages back and forth to one another, both of them blushing deeply at scenes of romance.

Alone, Celine tucked herself against the curved alcove at the base of a sea stack, a book in hand.

"Typical."

By the gods, again? "What are you doing here, Santus?"

He flicked his fin toward a small pile of shiny bobbles nestled on the seafloor. A few of them toppled down, clinking and clattering in the sand.

Killing you will be easy. But a silent warning tingled the back of her neck. He would know better than to travel alone, especially to see her, the royal orphan.

He hovered several feet away from her, sneering at the book in her hands before glaring at the human objects that filled the reef. His long, green hair floated around him like tendrils of seaweed. "Have you nothing better to do?"

She had no patience for him. "What do you want, Santus?"

At this, he grinned. "You honestly don't know why I'm here?"

She raised an eyebrow to appear bored, hiding the churning in her stomach. "I could take a guess, but why deprive you of the joy of telling me?"

"You not only released a ship full of humans trespassing through our waters," Santus said, his tone gleeful, "but you also injured your own people."

"They weren't trespassing," Celine said heatedly, "and my actions were in defense of myself and the humans they were going to kill."

"You are a *disgrace* to your people," Santus looked around at the reef with a smirk. "What do you expect from someone who lives in a trash heap?"

"What law have I broken?" Celine challenged. "The ship wasn't sanctioned by King Rolf to fish for merfolk. The human dove into the water to farm arcana crystal, which is not illegal." She waited. "They would have murdered a human simply for swimming in the sea. What law have I broken?"

"You've broken our *trust*," Santus said. "Your love and sympathy for humans is troubling."

He expects me to want their trust? Celine's lips curled in disdain. *He is delusional.*

"Anyone who finds joy in murder is troubling," Celine said, her words sharp. "As you well know."

He sneered.

"What do you have to prove, Santus?" She tilted her head, doing little to hide the pleasure at his annoyance from her teal gaze. "What do you have to prove, and to whom?"

He swam to her in a flash, hand grabbing her chin and holding her face inches from his. She manifested one dagger, aiming the point at his ribs.

"Let me make this very clear," Santus said, his voice low in her mind. "All I need is one reason. Just one."

"To do what, Commander?" Celine didn't drop her dagger, nor did she drop her eyes. Her free hand conjured carefully in the water, the shadows surrounding them with their cooling touch. "How badly do you want to see me dead?"

"You have this strange notion that you can speak to me however you'd like."

"I find it fascinating," Celine went on, "that I have this effect on you." It was difficult with his hand holding her chin, but Celine managed a satisfied smile as the shadows climbed higher. "Do I keep you up at night, Commander?"

He pushed her back, and she landed hard against a pile of books that went toppling. But she laughed at Santus's vulnerability, dispelling her magic.

"I didn't know you felt that way about me, Commander. I'm flattered."

"Watch your back, Celine," he said, his tone dangerous. "One more misstep, and you will know its consequence."

"Promise?"

But he didn't turn to see her coy expression, the competitive challenger within her too proud and stubborn to back down. Within seconds, Celine was alone once more.

I should have killed you. The thought was a whisper to the empty dark. *Who would have saved you, Commander? Who would have fought to come to your aid?*

The bitterness of the missed opportunity soured on her stomach as she settled back into her space, her body not fitting as well as it did before. But the darkness was cool, the sand comfortable, and the book a welcome distraction.

Until...

"My dear."

From around the reef came a stunning mermaid, her lavender tresses streaked with gray as her matching tail glistened. Seaweed adorned her hair as though it grew from her scalp. For the Sea Witch, perhaps it did. The gray in her hair was the only sign that time had touched her.

The Sea Witch did nothing that wasn't a benefit, and that included venturing out of her lair to make a personal visit unannounced.

"I saw something interesting today when I peered into my cauldron." Kasindra's broad smile shimmered. "Would you like to hear it?"

Celine closed her book. "What will it cost me?"

"Oh, this comes at no charge." Mischief shone in her lavender eyes. "Santus has been toying with magic again."

Celine almost laughed. When was Santus *not* playing with magic? But for Kasindra to bring it up... "Should we be worried?"

Kasindra steepled her fingers. "There will be fallout. That much is clear. But the danger will consume him, along with those unlucky enough to be too close."

"Could that include Dathan? Or would that be asking too much of Fate?"

"Fate is considered fickle by those who don't know how to touch her." She brought her hands to Celine's hair, smoothing the teal strands with a loving touch before kissing her forehead. "The wise know that Fate obeys the diligent, which we are."

Diligent. "But my magic still doesn't feel strong enough."

"We're close," Kasindra said. "The Usurper King will fall in the coming days. It is inevitable." Then, after a moment, sensing Celine's growing distress, she added, "He and his first commander will know who they've crossed. The moment they took your parents was the moment they signed their warrants for death."

Celine didn't meet Kasindra's eyes, glad for someone who understood and shared her bitterness and anger.

Kasindra took Celine's hands and squeezing her fingers. "My brother never should have taken the throne for himself. He's damned our people to turmoil, especially while we war with the humans of Estilon." She rubbed her thumbs across Celine's knuckles. "Both Dathan and Santus will pay for their crimes against us."

Kasindra's confidence was fortifying. "Thank you."

"Keep trying, my dear. Janis and Elynda would be proud of their strong, beautiful daughter. But be careful of your alliances."

Celine met her gaze, curious. "Who—"

"I watched Jessa help you earlier," she said. "My cauldron shows me everything." She kissed Celine's hands before letting them go. "Trust is as precious as arcana crystal and just as fragile."

Celine stared, tempted to ask the Sea Witch to explain herself, but she left before Celine could utter a word.

"Just a moment's peace to read. Just one. That's all I ask."

She opened the book blindly, eyes skimming the black letter shapes across the wet pages, stopping at one line in particular.

"We can't change who we are," he went on. *"Nor should we. But we can change what they've turned us into. What we've turned ourselves into."*

Celine touched the words with her fingertips. *What we've turned ourselves into.* After everything, and with still more to do, what has *she* become?

A vessel nearly filled, she thought. *A weapon nearly ready.*

As Santus and Dathan will soon see.

"She just *showed up*?"

Beneath the blooming dawn, Celine watched the Estilon shore with Quinn and Zander, Quinn's blonde hair a beacon beneath the growing sunlight, where Zander's was a deep red.

"She warned me about my alliances and left," Celine said.

"She didn't mean us, did she?" Quinn's eyes darkened, their golden hue a contrast to her confrontational mood.

"She meant Jessa."

"Jessa's alright," Zander said, confused.

"She's also Dathan's daughter and his captain." But Celine didn't believe in Kasindra's caution, either. If Jessa had a goal relating to Celine's downfall, she could have seen to it a dozen times over. "She's just concerned."

"Concerned about you having *friends*?" Quinn only raised a single eyebrow, offering nothing else. But she didn't have to. Her suspicion was clear.

"Trust is fragile. Like arcana crystal." Celine shrugged, self-conscious and very aware of their disapproval of her relationship with the Sea Witch. "That's what she said."

Quinn grimaced. "She seriously compared trust to arcana crystal? Or did you just do that?"

"It was her, but I never shy away from a simile."

Zander laughed. "Of all the things to learn from those human books, *simile* is what sticks."

"A lot of things have stuck," Quinn said, crossing her arms. "Though I am flummoxed by *dancing*."

Celine gave the painted sky one more glance before diving, the sunlight just enough to shimmer off of the flecks of arcana crystal buried in the coral. The first crystal of the morning belonged to Zander, its pristine shape filling the length of his hand. He sang a steady melody, the unseen feathers of magic becoming visible within its clear walls. He sang until the crystal filled, augmented, glowing iridescent pink with magic, and he set it inside his shoulder bag, fastening the flap closed.

"Why do you think she came all this way to tell you that?" Quinn asked at last. "It makes little sense. She must see outcomes all the time—mine, the king's, her own." She stopped working, squinting at Celine. "But she took time to tell you directly. No warning, *no payment*." Quinn blinked three times, her facial expression exaggerated. "I don't trust it."

"Well, trust *is* as fragile as arcana—"

Quinn interrupted with a playful jab at her side. "I'll show you *fragile*!"

But the fun ceased with shouts from the land, loud enough to reach them through the water. The merfolk surfaced again, eyes alert as a team of knights escorted one man into Estilon Castle, their hooves thundering against the earth. Men shouted, gates opened, and they soon disappeared from sight.

"What in the seven hells?" Zander swam closer. "To be escorted by so many knights, and at the speed they were going..."

"Has King Rolf finally died?" Quinn asked. "Assassinated in his sleep?"

"Perhaps, but what of his son?" Zander sank into the water. "We don't know if Prince Owen will be any worse. At least with Rolf, we know our enemy."

"We haven't had good luck learning about the prince," Quinn admitted. "Information has been thin."

"I heard he's pretty reclusive," Zander said.

Reclusive, but Celine had seen him walking along the shore alone beneath the night sky. Secret escapes in the dark, with Celine in the distance, watching.

"You're not going to see Kasindra today, are you?" Quinn's question, like a bolt from the blue.

"Yes." Celine braced herself for an argument that didn't come.

"Are you any closer?" Zander asked, even though the subject made him uncomfortable.

His sympathy warmed where Quinn's dislike had cooled. "I'm learning a lot."

And it was true. Dark magic was difficult to master, but the shadows came when she called. With each passing day, she was getting stronger. But she still wasn't strong enough.

"You fight as well as the two of us," Zander said, though the compliment was generous. Quinn was formidable with her blade, and Zander was strong with his magic. Celine was mediocre, at best. "You don't have to—"

"I do." She met the gaze of one friend, then the other. Deep red eyes, followed by light golden ones, both of them matched in their concern. "After what he did. What they *both* did." Celine stopped, grateful that they already knew. She didn't have to explain herself. The words remained understood, even if unspoken. "They left me little choice."

"Celine—"

"I'm alright, Quinny," she said, though her voice betrayed her. "We all have our parts to play, and I have mine."

"Revenge is a path that doesn't end well," Zander said. "It will take a piece of you that you will never get back."

Guilt and shame slipped down her chest to settle in her core, icy and hollow. But she wasn't ready to stop. She wasn't ready to let go.

"Be careful." Quinn touched Celine's arm, a gentle anchor to keep her grounded. "Kasindra will use you, Celine. Please don't forget that."

"I know." But Celine wouldn't stop. She used Kasindra, too.

"Let's keep looking," Zander said, hands wrapped around the strap of his satchel.

The three swam through the coral, the ambience of the sea filling the silence.

CHAPTER 3

Kasindra's dwelling was an underwater cave, thick with overgrown seagrass and kelp. Bones littered the sand, some of them fish, some merfolk, and some human. Celine set her jaw against the sickly sweet scent of decay as she slipped into the large stone mouth, fighting the turn in her stomach.

There was no sound in this part of the sea. The deathly silence amplified the sound of her body cutting through the water as she swam, eyes tracing the shape of every object. She had nearly every inch memorized, from the clear bottles awaiting potions and corks to the enchanted parchment bearing pearlescent ink. But what fascinated Celine was Kasindra's garden, magically made and magically kept. Tall, lush plants thrived on the fertile ground, flora that did not exist but through Kasindra's magic and remained a source for her power. What Celine would give to explore those plants, to tap into the magic they possessed. Perhaps one day, when Kasindra was well distracted…

"You're late." Kasindra's smooth alto eased its way into Celine's mind. "I was beginning to think you weren't coming."

"I tried casting today." Celine swam around stalagmites, turning deeper into the cave, dark but for the bioluminescent fungi and algae that thrived in the mineral-rich stone. "My magic is strong, but it isn't strong enough. Not yet."

The bright green of Kasindra's cauldron gave her lavender hair and eyes a gray hue. "You're still gathering yourself, my dear. Dark magic requires everything you have."

What more did Celine have left? "I'm giving everything."

Kasindra swam around the cauldron, the lights painting sinister shadows in the valleys of her face as she settled in front of Celine and took her hands, softness and gentleness in her touch. "There is always more, my dear. There is still a part of you that hasn't let go. You must trust the magic more than you trust yourself, and you'll let go."

Celine looked toward the garden, her curiosity growing by the second. "You said this was a great source of power." If Celine's hands weren't in Kasindra's grip, she would have reached for one of the nearest fronds of green and purple, eager to know its waxy-looking texture beneath her fingers. "Not even arcana crystal could compare."

"It is a powerful conduit," she said with suspicion in her voice.

"What of my own?"

"We've been over this, my dear."

"I'm not strong enough." Celine focused her teal eyes on the Sea Witch, willing her to understand, to give in, to see things as she saw them.

"This garden thrives off of living things." Kasindra caressed a nearby purple-green leaf. "Even as we speak, it helps me to maintain even the most powerful of spells. But it requires a lot to maintain. If your shadows struggle–"

"I'm not struggling." Celine had been too easy, too vehement, to interrupt Kasindra like that. Why was she still having to prove herself? "I can do this."

"You can, in time." Kasindra moved back to her cauldron. "Trust in the arcana crystal, until then."

But arcana crystal was fleeting. Short-term. Celine wanted *permanence*. Something that would eternally be hers and no one else's. Her magic would drive Dathan and Santus into Chaos. Her parents would be free. They deserved a far better afterlife, and Celine would give it to them.

She closed her eyes, imagining what part of herself still held on, but came up with nothing. Her heart was in. All in.

Kasindra cupped Celine's hands in hers. "Let us begin."

And they each pulled at the shadows, using both water and darkness in a strange union between Shanna's magic and Aishlin's. The Sea with Chaos. Water with Death.

Celine practiced with her teacher, willing any resistance to fade away as the magic worked through her blood. But the shadows wove themselves around her, sinking into her skin, filling her with their cold.

"Good." Kasindra swam toward her cauldron, reaching toward a shelf of stone for the glass orb she kept close by. The purple and green smoke swirled as she lifted her hand to it, the magic within reacting to her. She moved her fingers around the smoke-filled orb, the colors moving together until they coalesced. "Very good, Celine."

Celine pushed harder, encouraged by her teacher, by the power that coursed through her blood.

She heard him screaming, his jaw clenched tight as he tried to muffle the sound. But his voice ripped through his throat, and Celine swore she could smell his blood in the water.

Then he was quiet. His breathing had slowed, deepened...then stopped.

"Father!"

Sadness gripped her chest, the memories too vivid despite the years between then and now. Five years, but the sights and sounds were still as fresh as the minute he suffered his last beneath Santus's cruelty. Santus, who toyed with magic, who harvested toxins from the Coral Deeps, who preyed on those Dathan told him to hunt.

It took her father nearly a week to die. And as the memories of his death flashed in her mind, as her ears heard his screams and her tongue tasted copper in the brine, resolve hardened her heart. She wasn't aware any softness remained. Every practice with Kasindra brought more of her anguish to the surface, fueling her casting and her rage.

She would make sure Santus felt every inch of her father's suffering.

"You're strong enough, my dear," Kasindra said, her voice a soothing whisper. "You only have to believe it."

She believed it. With every pounding thud of her racing heart, she believed it.

She would make Santus and Dathan believe it, too.

Celine left the Sea Witch with anger still burning in her blood, her determined eyes scanning the coral landscape for any glimmer of arcana crystal. Before the heat simmered, before her resolve faltered, she would find enough arcana crystal and reach Santus this very day.

Her journey took her to the northeastern coast, the cliffs of Estilon hundreds of feet above sea level. A few humans, be they brave or foolish, jumped from those heights to tempt the hands of nature, all for a few moments of adrenaline and ecstasy. But there was an inlet through the cliff side, reachable on foot without causing harm to life or limb. Tucked away beneath the water's surface was a small cave of porous stone where fungi and algae thrived. Among them, *arcana crystal*. Celine protected this secret, visiting as infrequently as possible.

So, when a loud splash disrupted her thoughts, her keen teal eyes searched through the clear water, finding bubbles and movement near the inlet. Celine drifted closer, watching the man move with great form, his long and lean body pushing through the water with ease. He skirted the edge of land toward a corner easily missed by untrained eyes, and he slipped out of sight.

Not again.

She reached the entrance, slipping through the water behind him. He propped his legs against the stone incline to steady his torso above the surface, leaving enough room for her to come up behind. She watched, hands ready to defend herself.

"Damn." He rubbed his forehead, his voice echoing off of the wet stone. Water slicked his short, dark hair from his face. He ran his hands through the dripping locks. "What do I do now?"

He was familiar, but where—

He spun before she could blink, and he cried out, flailing backward onto the stone, crawling up and out of the water. He hissed, lifting a bare foot cut by the sharp edge of a stone. Blood welled in the cut but didn't ooze. His crystalline eyes, wide with shock, were bright in the blue-green bioluminescent light of the fungi and aura sprouts, and he stared into her eyes with wonder.

"Don't kill me!" He raised his hands, pleading, his body unsteady where it lay, still somewhat inclined into the water. "I mean you no harm. I swear it."

Celine studied him, blinking slowly, trying to remember where she'd seen him before. "I know you."

He gulped. "I swear on my life, I'm just searching for arcana crystal."

"Your life is what you risked coming here." But something nagged at her the longer she stared and the more he spoke. His bright eyes. The satisfying symmetry of his face. His voice, a pleasant, smooth baritone. "Who are you?"

He hesitated, eyes flashing to the exit behind her. The only way out.

She tilted her head, curious. "I can feel your magic."

"You—" Flickers of panic tugged at his mouth and sharpened the tightness around his eyes. "You can tell that?"

"You can't feel mine?" She swam closer, amused that he tried to scramble higher up the incline, only to slide back down.

"I'm still learning how to use it."

"A difficult feat, in a kingdom like this."

Celine's eyes wandered over him, his shirt clinging to his heaving chest and stomach. A strong body, even in its leanness. His legs were long, noticeable even in the haphazard bending and steadying against the rock that kept him out of the water. He had the body of a fighter.

When their eyes met again, he jumped as though startled. Celine allowed a hint of a smile to show through, taking a bit of pride in the power she held over him. "You didn't answer my question."

His eyes darted toward the exit again. "Please."

"I'm not interested in killing you." Hopefully, he could tell she spoke the truth. "I'm interested in who you are and what you want."

"I told you. Arcana crystal—"

"Which is also what I want." She narrowed her eyes. "Something about you is so familiar."

He held out a hand as a defensive plea. "If you'll let me."

Then he shifted, his dark hair lightening, his skin tanning, his frame widening just enough to appear like a different man. The only thing that remained were his eyes, bright blue and piercing.

"*Charlie*?" She stared, almost dumbstruck. "You can't be serious." *This infernal human.* "Do you genuinely have a death wish?"

He smiled, a hint of a dimple appearing on his cheek. Did he add it for his second identity, or was it a small piece of him that remained? "You remember my name."

"It's not often a human survives hungry merfolk and comes back for more."

"You have me at an unfair advantage." He relaxed, letting his legs extend. The wound on his heel was inflamed and angry. "You know my name, but I don't know yours."

"Celine." She studied the brightness of his eyes, captured by them.

"*Celine.*" He smiled. "It suits you."

But his current mission had her worried. "You're after more arcana crystal?"

"More?" Then he realized. "I didn't get any last time. As you well know, I was interrupted."

"But the crystal's gone." With a sinking feeling, she knew. "Santus."

Goddesses damn him and rid us of his pestilence.

"Santus?"

"The one who almost killed you." She gestured around her own face as she described, "Green hair. Murderous eyes."

"Oh, right. *Him.*" He quirked a brow. "Though the orange mermaid left a stronger impression."

"Not enough for you to value your life and stay out of our sea."

She reached a hand toward his injured foot. When he recoiled, she said, "I can heal that, if you'll let me."

Relaxing once more, Celine held his ankle and touched the cut across his heel. He jerked with a grimace, a light flush painting his cheeks.

"Apologies." He cleared his throat. "I'm ticklish, not afraid."

"Being afraid can help you survive." She pushed magic into the wound, even though her skill in healing was rudimentary. A cut was easy enough, and the red line sealed in seconds.

"Thank you, Celine." His gaze pierced into her, as though the biological light of the surrounding algae and aura spores wanted to aid his stare in reaching her. "I'm here because something's happened to my father. Some malady. I can heal, but what I can do isn't strong enough.

Hence–" He gestured vaguely to the cave that surrounded them. "*Arcana crystal*."

He aimed to heal where she aimed to hurt. Funny how opposites collided. But if Celine could have saved her father, she would have done anything, no matter the risk.

"I'll help you." Her own foolishness washed over her as the words left her. Damn those eyes of his. "But you have to do exactly as I say."

Stupid, stupid, stupid.

He blinked. "You'll find arcana crystal?"

"No. Any arcana crystal I find is mine."

One eyebrow rose, his expression somewhat sardonic as though he'd been duped. "Then how?"

"Medicine." Celine pulled a layer of algae free from the stone, letting it rest across her fingers. "We can make something to help him heal. But I need to know what he ails from."

Charlie shrugged a shoulder. "The doctors are baffled." He traced his fingers down his neck with a clawing action. "Black veins beneath his skin."

Black veins. The same that her father had suffered. "Caused by a toxin—hell's touch. A fungus that grows here."

"Hell's touch. And it grows *here*?"

"Deep in the sea." She stared, questions flowing too fast to track. "Do humans typically venture into the deep and dangerous sea to farm?"

"No human I know would dare venture so deep and trespass on the merfolk."

"Present company excluded." She met his gaze unwaveringly. "How did your father become poisoned with a merfolk toxin?"

"A question I was just asking myself." After a beat, he asked. "Is there a cure?"

"No."

Anger and disappointment mingled on the handsome features of his face. His eyes focused as they looked around the cave, desperate for some unknown answer.

She went on. "The only thing we can do is ease his suffering with sedatives and pain relievers." She scraped more algae from the wall. "Do you have any skill making medicine?"

"My teacher does."

She held out her hands, smeared with algae and holding bits of stone-grown fungus. "See that he makes the strongest sedative he can. That's the only relief your father can have." With a grimace, an ache pinging in her chest, she said, "I'm sorry. Truly. No one should go through this."

"Thank you."

He shifted to his other form and, with her help, swam back to the base of the inlet. The algae coated his hands like a second skin. "Oh, by the gods, *the smell*."

"These can make something topical or be brewed—"

"Prince Owen!"

Charlie winced, looking back toward Celine.

She stared, agape, remembering the shape of him, silhouetted in the dark beneath the various phases of moonlight. The heir of the throne of Estilon. "You're Prince Owen?"

"Hello, Celine." With his sheepish but satisfied grin, the dimple was there. "A pleasure to meet you."

"You could have said."

"You didn't ask, and I didn't want—"

"*Prince Owen!*"

He turned and called, "On my way!"

"Your father. King Rolf." She stared at the ingredients in his hands. "I don't know how merfolk toxin reached him."

"You must regret helping me now."

His voice was meek, but the keen brightness in his eyes was not. He'd gotten aid for his father, even so from an enemy. Though Celine doubted she would have done differently had she known who she was helping.

"Your king and mine have made monsters of us both," she said, "but my father also suffered the same toxin. I meant what I said before. No one should go through that."

"Prince Owen!"

"You have magic," she said, looking toward the grassy incline. "Does your father know?"

Whoever beckoned Owen at the top of his lungs walked closer, his footsteps trudging down the land toward the inlet. "By the goddesses, holy and divine, *Prince Owen*!"

"Tyrion, for gods' sake, I'm here!"

As his back faced her, she sank into the water, her stomach curdling with being so easily led. The few times she'd seen him on the shore by the castle, he'd taken to walking near to midnight. Whether by cover of darkness or beneath the white light of the moon, the night changed everything it touched, and the restless prince had been no exception.

But now, swimming away from the inlet, Celine chastised herself. The shimmer of nearby arcana crystal assuaged her feeling of foolishness, hands eagerly plucking a modest node from the coral at the base of the cliffs. If only the piece were bigger to allow her to cast stronger and longer.

But, if she had her way, the dark would never let go.

She swam toward home, leaving the magical prince behind for the promise of a wish fulfilled. The cold dark of the sea surrounded her as she moved deeper, reaching the sea floor with her arcana crystal safe in her hands.

"I shouldn't be surprised."

She stopped, her hair billowing around her as she turned, the familiar green appearing from the coral.

"Helping the human prince of Estilon." Santus shook his head, disgusted. "You're a disgrace to your people."

Two more merfolk appeared behind him, neither of them Celine recognized.

"Take her to the king."

A pair of hands seized Celine's arms from behind before she could react. She screamed, thrashing, until a summoned blade met her throat.

"Your father will want to hear about this."

"He's not my father, you gutless murderer," she snapped, hands trying and failing to summon the dark magic made to kill him. "You left my father to suffer so that his death would be a mercy. You *coward*."

"You seem to be under the impression that—"

But movement interrupted him as a flash of pale gold and blood red came in a flurry, Quinn and Zander armed and furious.

"She will see the king," Santus said, his tone official and dangerous. His own pair of broadswords appeared in his hands, poised to strike. "She will face the consequences of helping humans and the royals of Estilon."

"You've resorted to stalking her, now, have you?" Quinn spat, snarling. "You sick bastard."

"Arrest them all," Santus ordered. "Let's see what King Dathan has to say." He smirked. "The perfect entertainment for his celebration."

"His anniversary isn't for another week," Celine said.

"Why not celebrate now, with the arrest of his rebellious stepdaughter?"

Quinn and Zander didn't go without a fight, even as Celine tried to break free from the stone grasp of the hands that held her. She thrashed hard, her muscles and skin and bones aching and burning. She tasted blood on the water and saw that one of Santus's men bled from his arm.

"Enough!" Santus's booming voice carried force magic, pushing everyone back with a sonic clap. "To the king!"

CHAPTER 4

The journey was long, with the three of them fighting until, at last, Santus summoned more magic to subdue them. Subtle magic crept into their ears, dulling their minds, making them easier to lead.

Merfolk built their structures from stone made from the offerings of the sea—from animal bones to seaweed—all of it fortified with magic. Kelp and coral brought life to the inanimate, and merfolk thrived in the expansive structures their ancestors had built.

Dozens of gem-colored eyes watched as Santus and the others escorted them to the palace. They swam toward Dathan's stolen throne, surrounded by stone and coral structures that thrived with life in a rainbow of colors. The buildings were beacons of iridescent white, pink, and gold, symbols of opulent luxury to any outsider who didn't know the cruelty they represented.

"It's high time the king dealt with this nonsense," one guard said. "Such behavior should not go unpunished."

"He's too soft with her," another said. "But that generosity has run out."

Too soft? Generosity? Celine wanted to spew a string of curses and prove their stupidity, but she kept her mouth closed, her lips aching as they formed a tight white line.

"Gods above and below. What now?"

Celine focused through the gathered crowd to find the snowy white crown of Jessa, moving her way to the procession.

"Celine was caught helping the human prince of Estilon," Santus said. "She will face Dathan's judgment."

"What?" Jessa's icy stare met Celine with disbelief. "Is that true?"

"I didn't recognize him, but yes." She squared her shoulders in defiance as the guards pulled harder on her arms, leading her forward. "And I would do it again, even while knowing who he is."

"We do not suffer traitors in this court," Santus said, posturing in importance and grandeur.

"Whether in this life or the next," Celine said, her voice in his mind alone, "you will know what it means to suffer. You will never stop paying for what you've done."

Santus's deep green gaze focused on her, but he said nothing, swimming the long path of pearl, clamshell, and stone to the seat of King Dathan.

The merking waited as though he expected of her arrival, his wide, strong body consuming the breadth of the throne as his long blue tail draped over his seat of bone and coral. His matching hair, graying to silver, only emphasized the depth of his dark stare, eyes almost black in their reach of blue.

Celine couldn't bear to be very close to the Usurper King without her stomach churning. She silently cursed him, praying that her repulsion would magically turn his stomach.

The merman gripping Celine's arms finally released them. She glanced back at Quinn and Zander, glad to see that they were still with her, unscathed.

"Celine." Dathan's deep voice rested with familiarity in her mind. This wasn't her first time before his throne in discipline, but it may very well be her last. "I'd hoped to not see you come before me this way again."

"Didn't you?" She met his eyes unwaveringly. "I thought you rather enjoyed our time together."

"You test him," Jessa said, her words a warning. "Guard your life, Celine."

Celine was tempted to do the opposite in favor of embedding herself further beneath the Usurper King's skin. But Jessa was right. She needed her parents freed from Chaos. Dying or going to prison would complicate that plan. Considerably.

"The cause of all your troubles, Celine, is your sickening infatuation with humans." Dathan looked at his hands as though bored. "Your reef is a garbage heap, stepdaughter."

She bared her teeth at the title. "So is the throne sullied by your scales."

Pain stabbed her mind, and she screamed through clenched teeth. His voice boomed, echoing within her mind. "Your insolence will cost you everything that you hold dear. Do not test my patience further."

Quinn and Zander suffered, too, their pain resonating in Celine's mind and body. Dathan's magic joined them on purpose, grounding Celine in what was truly at stake. Fear gripped her then, at last. "Leave them alone, Dathan. Or do you wish to further alienate your people?"

The pain ceased, curiosity flickering in his dark eyes. "My people respect me."

"What you stole may yet be stolen," she said. "You haven't earned their love. Your leadership hangs by a thread."

He growled, the rumble like thunder. "What you have done, Celine, what you *continue* to do, warrants a traitor's death."

The merfolk gasped, Quinn and Zander the loudest of them all. Their terror filled her, Celine's mind swimming with their angered shock.

"Father." Jessa stared. Somehow, she hadn't seen this coming. "You can't be serious."

He leaned forward, his smile dangerous. Even toward his own daughter, any resistance would not be tolerated. "What about me, daughter, tells you otherwise?"

He leaned back, arms lazily draped over his throne, pleased with the effect of his announcement. He gestured with his hands, showing off. "But I am a kind and benevolent king, and there is a way to redeem yourself, Celine. You may yet be a benefit to your people in the fight against humans, rather than a nuisance."

Celine waited, silent, feeling the burning stares of the many eyes that watched her.

"We have been in talks with the king of Estilon, and an arrangement has been reached to bridge the rift between our peoples."

Murmurs from the crowd, and Celine glanced at Quinn and Zander, confused.

"I knew nothing of this," Jessa said quickly, worry lining her forehead. It was true. "He said nothing to me."

"After so many years of fighting and bloodshed, King Rolf and I have agreed to form an alliance between our kingdoms."

The murmurs graduated to voiced disagreements and cries of outrage.

"We've allied with that murderer?!"

"He's sanctioned the deaths of our people!"

"What can we hope to gain from—"

Dathan floated up from his throne, anger sharpening his already severe features. "*SILENCE.*" His maddened eyes stared unblinkingly at his stepdaughter. "It is done. And you—" He pointed, his arm trembling in rage. "*You* will be just the piece we need. You are so eager to help the son of a murderer, then you shall marry him."

Celine was dumbstruck, staring at the merking, his victorious grin full of malice.

"You are betrothed to the crown prince of Estilon as a sign of peace to end this war between our kingdoms." Dathan grinned, his eyes wide with malice. Then, he spoke to her, *only* her, as the murmurs rose once more. "Kill him, Celine. Kill him and his father. You will meet the son of Jesper, another human king from an enemy kingdom. Work with his son to end the bloodline of Estilon." With a laugh, he added, "Then you will kill Jesper and his son and send their nation into political turmoil." He regarded the gathered merfolk, his demeanor theatrical. "I would gladly sprout legs just to watch them fall!"

Celine closed her eyes, rubbing her ears to rid them of Dathan's voice. Refusal was death, and so was this mission.

He intended for her to fail.

He was sending her to die.

"You have three days," he said. "Prepare to depart these seas, never to return. The prince will see to your arrival at Estilon Castle, and you will be his wife." Then, quietly, he added, "And his murderer."

Three days.

She stared at the Usurper King. Dark magic simmered beneath her skin. Her palm itched to cast.

Three days to kill you.

Hands grabbed her and forced her back. It wasn't until she, Zander, and Quinn were far from the coral palace before they were released.

"Good riddance," one guard said. "Good bloody riddance."

CHAPTER 5

Celine peeked above the surface, eyeing the empty shore and the silhouette of the castle against a darkening sky, the setting sun burning orange, red, and yellow on its way down. Was Prince Owen blissfully ignorant to the arrangement their monarchs had made, or did he know that his future bride would sprout legs and emerge from the sea?

She sank, letting the water take her. Her arms floated and hair fluttered around her like blue-green smoke. If only the current would sweep her far across the distant seas and to lands where no one knew her.

"*We cannot change who we are, nor should we. But we can change what they've turned us into. What we've turned* ourselves *into.*"

And Celine wanted nothing more than to change what she'd become—a pawn in Dathan's twisted game. *I will see his end.*

"*Revenge is a path that doesn't end well. It will take a piece of you that you will never get back.*"

How much of herself would she lose? How much had she already lost?

She swam down, spotting the familiar red of Zander's hair and fin. He stayed close, with Quinn busying herself around the reef, farming for whatever was edible or useful.

"What are you feeling?" he asked. Not *how* but *what*. *How* was obvious enough.

"Bitter and pissed," she said. "With a healthy dose of *powerless*."

"Dathan is a fool and a tyrant."

"With a personal vendetta," Celine said. "I'm the last piece. It's amazing he let me live this long."

"Celine—"

"It's true, Zan." Still, the flash of hurt on his face pierced through whatever stone wall she'd tried to build around herself, caging in her emotions to limit the satisfaction of those eager to see her falter. "But I take comfort in knowing that I'll haunt him long after I'm dead."

"Don't talk like that."

She met his melancholic eyes, the deep red shadowed by everything that happened. "There will be no alliance. This is a king's game, and we're the pawns."

He rested a hand on her shoulder. "I should never have taught you human chess." Then, more seriously, he said, "Say the word, and we swim to the edge of the world."

"Wouldn't that be lovely?" A new battle swelled in her chest, an emotional tide wishing that they could flee with no consequence. "Going as far as Kema, or even the other side of Ileden."

Celine had seen a map of the world in one shipwreck she explored. There was so much water she hadn't seen, that her parents hadn't seen. Where would they go, given the chance? *Likely to a beach somewhere*, she thought with a small smile. *Father couldn't stand the cold.*

"Running away won't help," Quinn said, joining them. Her satchel hung around her chest, weighted by whatever she'd harvested from the reef. "There's nowhere to go. Death in the sea or death on land." She gestured with her hands, flat like the plates weighing a balance. "Choose your fate."

"The only choice we have," Zander said, "and even that is a mask. Fate plays us on its whim."

The wise know that Fate obeys the diligent, which we are. Kasindra's words were a reassurance. Even with this wrinkle, Celine's plan could still work. She still had three days.

The trio returned to their reef, an unspoken truth weighing on them that the time they shared bled like an open wound. It wouldn't be long before they were separated, whether by magic or death.

They shared a small meal of shellfish and seaweed before turning to their hoard of books. Celine's hand reached for the top volume on the nearest stack, opening its cover to inspect the blank ink crisp on brown pages. The title, *Keepers of the Dark*, filled the page in clean, sharp letters.

Zander pulled another book and flipped haphazardly to the middle. Slowly, clumsily, he read, "*One must always look to the past for answers to the present.*"

Quinn adopted a regal voice, the fake accent exaggerated in its importance, and repeated the words. "*One must always look to the past for answers to the present.*" Then she dissolved into a fit of giggles as she toyed with a nautical spyglass. "Did they have a philosopher on board?"

"Every sailor's a philosopher," Zander said. "The way they talk about the sea as a living thing makes me wonder if they all worship Shanna."

Zander chose another book. "De—" He tilted his head, squinting. "Decorum."

"Oh." Celine nodded. "Read that. That's helpful. *Decorum*. This might help me pass as a human."

"You won't have any problem passing as a human," Quinn said. "Just call any royals you meet, *your highness*. Humans are obsessed with it."

"*Your highness.*" Celine washed away the notion of amnesia. Only in Quinn's favorite stories would that plan work. "Go ahead, Zan. What does it say?"

They passed the hours with Zander reading slowly and Quinn helping to pose with Celine as instructions on bodily posture were presented, both when walking and when eating.

"A lady must never be alone with a potential suitor," Zander read. "The pair must always be in the company of a ch–chap–chapper-one." He squinted, looking at them both. "What in the seven hells is a chapper one?"

"Chaperone," Quinn corrected. "A guardian of sorts. A chaperone makes sure they don't get into any trouble." She wiggled her eyebrows at the suggestion of *trouble*.

"How do you know all that?" Celine asked.

"You would be surprised to learn that sailors and merchants alike enjoy romantic stories." She gestured behind her to her collection in the coral. "*Several* books later, I feel well versed in the romantic presentations of humans. They almost ritualize it."

She looked over the spines and covers of each book, curious. "What sort of stories have you read?"

"Loads." Quinn pirouetted through the water toward her, picking one book at a time. "This one is a pirate story. Here's one where a witch kidnaps an infant princess. And this–" Quinn looked at Celine with wide eyes. "This is *poetry*."

"Poetry?"

"Songs without music. It's—" She held her hands open, searching for the word, before sighing heavily, her exaggerating breath defining poetry's quality.

"How could it be a song without music?"

Quinn was already flipping through the pages with eager eyes and hands. "Trust me." When her finger landed on the right place, she straightened, holding the book aloft, dark blue eyes focused intently on every word.

The wind is the breath of the dead.
Sunlight, the warm touch of souls to soothe the living.
Thunder, their voices to bed remembrance.
Rain, their grief for those left behind.

Celine stared, hearing the words echo in her mind as they drifted to her heart.

"It's good, right?" Quinn beamed, turning to another one. "Listen to this one."

Take the dark and swallow it,
For it cannot survive
The fire of your soul.

Zander swam closer to look over Quinn's shoulder, reading as her fingers passed over the paper. "Where did that book come from?"

"I don't remember if it was a fishing vessel or not. But I'm always surprised by what I find." She looked over the book once more, closing it in her hands, before replacing it on her shelf. "Who knew those jerks liked to read?"

Their families probably knew, but Celine kept that to herself. Merfolk missed their lost loved ones as much as the humans likely missed theirs. No one side was without grief in this war. And there was still darkness ahead.

Perhaps this would be the last stretch of darkness before, at last, she would see light. Before her *parents* would see light.

"Here's one of my favorites. *Stowaway.*" Quinn presented a book with a deep red cover. "A young woman hides on board a merchant ship. She's running away from home, desperate, and meets a sailor with a past he'd rather keep hidden. He helps disguise her as a man to keep her safe on board until they reach their next port, but *someone catches them.*" Quinn squeals, spinning in the water. "Stolen kisses in dark corners, the risk of being found out any second. By the gods, I wish I could read it again for the first time."

Celine met eyes with Zander, who watched Quinn with unconditional love. To him alone, she said, "Still think reading is boring?"

"Not when Quinn does it."

Celine laughed to herself. "Good answer."

"It's good you're having fun."

The three turned, eyes and mouths wide with shock, as Kasindra approached.

"I don't mean to interrupt," she said, her smile soft as she looked at Celine. "I only wanted to speak with you. See how you were."

"What do you expect?" Quinn said, her tone sharp. She crossed her arms. "She's been sentenced to death. How could she possibly feel?"

"Quinn—"

But Kasindra held up a hand, stopping Celine. "This isn't the end, child. Nowhere close." To Celine, she asked, "Do you have a moment?"

Celine moved to her but stopped as Quinn's hand gripped her wrist.

"Whatever you say to Celine, you can say in front of us." Quinn looked from Celine to Kasindra. "We already know everything, anyway."

Kasindra looked to Celine, who nodded before proceeding. "Very well."

Quinn released Celine, crossing her arms again. Zander swam closer to her, sweeping her golden hair back and saying, "It's alright, Quinn. She can help."

"I can," Kasindra said. "Nothing has changed, Celine." She rested her hands on Celine's shoulders. "Your path is still very much before you."

"Of course things have changed!" Indignant, Quinn looked from Kasindra to Zander, then Celine. "She's going to live on land among humans who hate us!"

"Quinn." Celine looked over her shoulder. "Please."

Quinn's mouth closed with resentful fury.

"Go to land, child," Kasindra said. "Marry the prince. Protect your life. You will still save your parents. This *detour* doesn't change the outcome you will bring to the Usurper King."

Detour felt generous, but Kasindra's confidence was reassuring.

"Here." Kasindra moved a hand in front of Celine and conjured a beautiful necklace, the golden chain thin and the charm delicate—a spiral seashell. "Keep this safe, my dear. If you need to return to the sea, break the shell, and you will be transformed."

"But my magic—"

Kasindra shook her head. "This has everything you'll need. You won't need your magic or any arcana crystal to change back. But it's only good for one use." Kasindra dropped the necklace into Celine's palm and closed her fingers around it. "Follow Dathan's order and keep working in secret. We'll catch Dathan and Santus off their guard." She embraced Celine. "I am still with you, child, no matter where you are."

Celine closed her eyes, almost melting into the Sea Witch's embrace. The maternal touch was almost cruel in the need it stirred up within her, so long had she been without her mother. But Kasindra wasn't anything like a mother, and Celine would not want her parents to see the work she'd done to free them.

"Visit me every night at midnight," the Sea Witch said, pulling back and smoothing Celine's hair from her shoulders. "We will keep one another informed. I will help you in any way I can."

"Don't let Dathan send her to land," Quinn said, bitterness thick in her voice. "That would be really helpful."

Kasindra didn't spare Quinn a glance, smiling only at Celine. "Trust me, and trust yourself. Your hard work will not be in vain."

After a brief kiss on Celine's forehead, Kasindra left.

"The absolute *nerve!*" Quinn's hands balled into fists. "Celine, please—"

"Quinn." This time, it was Zander. "She's got enough pressure from everyone and everything else."

Pressure from Dathan. From Kasindra. From Quinn and Zander.

From herself.

But Kasindra was right. This was a detour, one that would still lead Celine in the same direction she's been working toward for three years. It was only time that would change, not the outcome.

Zander took Quinn's hands, but she jerked them away. "You can't possibly—"

But Quinn stopped as Celine embraced them both, wrapping her arms around their shoulders and holding them close.

"I love you," Celine said. "I'm sorry this happened. I'm sorry I brought this on all of us."

"You didn't." Emotion was thick in Quinn's voice. "It's Dathan and his stupid minion."

Even with the weight of everything, Celine laughed. "*Minion.*"

They parted, returning to their books, but the happiness from moments before had dissolved to thoughts of worry.

CHAPTER 6

Celine and the others rested in their favorite places among coral, stone, and algae. It had been nearly half a day since Celine had conjured her shadows, her palms itching to bring them to her again.

She shivered with the blast of cold as the shadows swept across her skin. They swirled around her fingers, palms, wrists, and arms, up to her shoulders and throat.

"Hello, my loves." She laughed quietly as they continued to dance and sway. "It's time, isn't it?"

Dathan and Santus, unsuspecting of the dark touch to come. What she would give to see...

The idea grew, taking root, spreading through her mind until she manipulated the shadows to show her. The dark curled until it formed something like a glassless mirror, the portal within shimmering. But Dathan did not come into view.

Strange. She tried to push the shadows further, sensing their contact with Dathan. But the shadows moved through his mind, as though it were intangible.

Magical protection, likely from Santus. Would Celine have similar luck with the first commander?

She reached with her shadows. Relief unfurled within her as his green hair and fin came into view. He didn't look pleased, despite Celine's sentence supposedly being the highlight of his day. Rather, his furrowed brow enhanced the wrinkles on his forehead and around his eyes.

"You're looking old, Commander," Celine muttered. "Old and tired."

"I don't *care* what it takes," Santus snapped.

Who received the brunt of his frustration? But as she tried, Celine couldn't shift the gaze of the shadows as they scried. It showed only the subject she wished to see, nothing more.

"Commander—" A voice she didn't recognize. "He's growing impatient."

"He will have to wait." Santus punctuated each word as its own sentence. "Or he will become our next meal."

Who? But as Celine waited, nothing more was said.

"Begone." Santus waved his hand in dismissal. "I've had enough. I need to rest."

But which human? The human king colluding with Dathan to end the monarchy of Estilon? Someone else?

Celine broke the spell, the scrying lens dissolving like black ink in the sea.

"Go to the commander," she said to the shadows, sending them on. "Find out his secrets."

If only the shadows could bring his secrets to her. While they couldn't fill her mind with someone else's thoughts, they can toy with the thoughts in someone else's head. And Santus's mind was a glorious playground.

Dathan was unimaginative and careless, his brawn the only real opposition from him. But Santus apparently had layers yet to be explored. Tearing Dathan from his throne may prove more difficult than first expected.

"Seep in through the cracks," she whispered to the shadows, even as they disappeared from view. "There's always a way in. Find it."

They were as eager, leaving her with vigor and purpose. And she reclined on the cool sand, looking up at the seemingly limitless dark.

Bring them Chaos, she prayed. *Give them a taste of what's to come.*

She flexed her fingers, wondering how her magic could become stronger without the crystal, without a garden of her own.

Thriving flora, purple and green, with arcane power eager for use and purpose.

Her curiosity had gotten the better of her.

CELINE PEEKED into Kasindra's cave, listening for any sign that the Sea Witch was home. Slowly, carefully, Celine swam in, navigating around stone and seaweed with familiar grace. The cauldron casting its eerie, sinister glow. Beside it, perched on its stone shelf, was the orb filled with magic that matched the garden's colors. One powered by the other? Or one an extension of the other?

What would it take for Celine to find out?

She was careful as she approached the garden, the power radiating from each stalk and frond like a pulse. And that power reached for her, urging her to tap into the reserves it held.

She extended her hand, feeling a familiar call, sensing a familiar presence. There was something about this garden that she knew, that she *really* knew. Magic? Strength? Power? Or something else?

"I know you're curious."

Kasindra's voice made Celine recoil as though she'd been burned, the shock of being caught surging through her muscles and bones like a lightning strike.

"But the garden will only answer to me." Kasindra passed by her cauldron, looking over its smooth surface. What did she see, other than her own reflection? "I'm sorry for my brother. My foolish brother."

"Fate obeys the diligent," Celine said, echoing Kasindra's words. "It's as you've said. My path has changed, but the destination remains the same."

"That it does." Her smile was comforting.

"I tried scrying on Dathan," Celine said. At this, Kasindra raised an eyebrow. "I couldn't see anything."

"The same problem I've been having." Kasindra rubbed her chin, lips pursed. "His magic has gotten stronger, probably thanks to Santus's tutelage. I wonder..."

When Kasindra didn't finish her thought aloud, Celine asked, "Are my shadows not reaching him?"

"It's possible," she said with a quiet hum, her mind still in motion. Her eyes flashed to Celine, brighter, her smile widening. "He's smarter than he looks, which is saying something." There was the low rumble of a laugh deep in her throat. "I do love a challenge."

"How will I break through?" Celine asked. "Being on land will make it that much harder."

"Don't doubt the shadows, my dear. He's blocked himself from merfolk trying to watch and see, but has he considered what the *shadows* watch and see?"

She looked more confident than Celine felt.

"Now, my dear, I've been thinking." Kasindra floated to her shelves, her hands passing from one bottle or jar to the next, plucking ingredients from the shelves and holding them in her arms. "We must meet every night to keep one another posted on the goings-on above and below."

Celine waited, watching Kasindra arrange her reagents before opening them and sprinkling a bit from each into the cauldron. Then, Kasindra turned to her garden, her thumb and index finger poised to pluck leaf or petal from the flourishing plant life. What did the garden feel as Kasindra took from it? How did it replenish itself? She had her suspicions, none of them pleasant.

Life requires life. Life cannot thrive from the dead, but from the living. It is the way with all things.

Had Kasindra said that, or did the words find Celine on their own? After years under her study, she couldn't be sure.

Kasindra sang softly, the power of her voice lulling the garden as she plucked a single green leaf from one vine stretching up the cave wall. That was the last ingredient, and the cauldron's usual bright green color shifted to a beautiful purple, its glow amplifying and darkening the lavender of her hair, scales, and eyes.

"Getting to the shore may prove troublesome, depending on how much the guards watch and patrol." Kasindra wove her hands through the water, the mixture spinning faster. "This should help make you undetectable, albeit for a short time."

"Invisibility?" Celine's mind turned at the possibility.

"No. Potions do not create invisibility. But your presence will be... *foggy*, we'll say. It'll be as though you pass through in someone's peripheral vision, even if you're right in front of them."

"Will it be something they take?"

"No, it'll be something you *wear*." She conjured the liquid into a bottle, the purple floating through the water as though it had a life of its own, and it filled a vial held in her fingers. Then, when the vessel was full, she pressed a cork firmly into its mouth. "Dab this on your throat and wrists." Kasindra indicated on her own body the area right below the earlobe and at the center of her wrist. "The aroma will make whoever smells it a little dazed. And this—" Kasindra produced another vial, already mixed and filled, this color a dark green. "This will protect *you*. Dab a small amount under your nose to block out the smell of anything else."

Celine looked at the vials, their colors complimentary. "This should be perfect."

"You'll only need a small amount of each, so these should last you as long as you need them." Kasindra grinned. "Meet me at midnight every night without fail. If I don't see you, I'll assume the worst and bring the Sea of Kings upon Estilon."

"I'm honored, but that would risk everything," she said. "I will reach you."

"Very good, my dear."

Celine met her gaze, sadness coming to the corners of her eyes at last. "Are you alright?"

"It's just—" Kasindra stopped, pressing her lips together. Then, "You've worked so hard, Celine. You're close to the outcome you've waited for."

Happiness and pride surged through her chest, warming her from the inside out. She'd felt it too, but hearing Kasindra say it made it *real*.

"Enjoy your remaining days at sea," Kasindra said.

Two days, then Celine would have to leave. Two days was nowhere near long enough to be with Quinn and Zander, to view the sea with fresh eyes as though seeing it for the first time.

Two days, then everything would change.

"Be with your friends and take these tools with you." She looked from the vials to the shell necklace Celine wore. "You will be just fine."

"But Dathan and Santus won't be. Unless Santus has figured out a way to block the shadows." The worry still wormed around in Celine's mind.

"Don't stop trying," Kasindra said. "Because you can't scry upon him, you can't know for sure. Unless you plan on casting in his presence?" She chuckled. "I wonder how he'd react."

Celine left her mentor, swimming through the dark waters for the flourishing reefs rich with life. She took her time returning home, hands brushing against seaweed and anemones, fingertips gliding across coarse coral and stone.

The sea. Calm beauty. *Home.* And the human world would be so different from all that she knew.

Quinn and Zander were there, mixing algae and undersea herbs to blend homemade tonics and medicine. Celine watched them, their actions complementary in every way. They were two halves of a whole. Knowing they would have each other when she was gone...

You're not dying, she thought. But it felt like a great enough change that she was avoiding, as though to postpone grieving a loss.

Celine made sure to smile as she swam to them, Zander working a green paste into his mortar with the pestle as Quinn added the next ingredient.

Quinn glanced Celine's way, a knowing look in her eyes. "Learn anything useful?"

"No." Celine hugged Quinn from behind, resting her head on her shoulder. "These two days are going to go by too fast."

"They already are," Quinn said, resting her hand on Celine's. "What should we do first? Visit the Coral Deeps?"

"And risk getting lost while inhaling all of those spore clouds?" Zander shook his head. "Out of the question."

"It's good practice for holding your breath." Quinn grinned. "You'll know your gills are working if you don't see any hallucinations."

"My gills work just fine, thank you very much." Zander set the pestle down and used a wooden tool to scrape the viscous green liquid into a lidless jar. "And that's enough of that."

"Spoil sport." Quinn spun, leaning back to look at Celine. "What do you want to do?"

Celine answered with a shrug. "Read?"

"We already read." Quinn slipped from her arms and swam around the reef, eyes looking toward the distant, dark horizon of the sea floor. "If not the Coral Deeps, then we could swim south and farm for sun shells."

"Warm waters, bright sunlight." Zander nodded. "That's much more the ideal."

"Anything with you two is the ideal," Celine said. "I don't care what we do. We don't have to do anything."

As she spoke, the growing distance loomed before them. Quinn's lips quivered slightly, and she widened her smile to fight the emotion that welled within. But as she moved to speak, her eyes moved to something behind Celine.

"What's—" Celine stopped mid-question as her eyes found the snowy-white hair, eyes, and tail of Jessa swimming toward them.

"Sorry to interrupt," Jessa said. "I was just—I wanted to check..." She winced, sweeping her hair aside. "I wanted to see if you were alright."

"Yes and no," Celine said. "Which answer do you want?"

"The real one." Sympathy and sadness filled Jessa's white eyes. "It should have been me, Celine. I'm Dathan's daughter. Any deal he strikes should include me. Even a political marriage done right under our noses."

"It shouldn't have been you," Celine said. "It shouldn't have been anyone. None of this should have happened."

None of this. Dathan's rule, Celine's parents...

None of this.

"I wanted to say I'm sorry."

Celine managed a smile edged with sadness. "You shouldn't apologize for someone else's mistakes."

Jessa moved to take Celine's hand but reconsidered, crossing her arms instead. "I hate his nickname. The Usurper King. And I hate even more that he's earned it. Everything he does—" She stopped herself, closing her eyes. "Everything he does pushes me further and further away."

It was Celine who reached for Jessa, resting a hand on her shoulder. "Perhaps when he's gone, your leadership will change all that."

"*My* leadership?" She shook her head. "Your father was the throned king before mine. It should be you."

"Even with all the lessons and training," Celine said. "I don't think I could fill that seat now. Not after he filled it. Not after…"

Not after my father's death. How could Celine express that her taking the throne was thievery of a different kind?

Jessa said nothing, the silence between them rife with thoughts unspoken. Until…

"Celine of the merfolk."

They all turned at the official tone of the approaching guard. Celine met the eyes of one, her heart sinking. She knew why they were here.

"What?" Jessa looked from that guard to another that approached. "What is going on?"

"You have been summoned before the throne," one guard said. "It is time to send you to the shore."

"What?" Jessa's shocked white eyes met Celine's.

"He can't mean—" Quinn is awash with disbelief. "You still have two days!"

Jessa, with her shoulders back, approached the guards. "What has my father done?"

"Condemned her to death." Zander glared at the guards, the crimson shade of his eyes deepening. "His hands are already stained with so much blood."

Defeat swirled in Celine's gut, but in all of her racing thoughts, none of them held a solution to the king's summons. She was going to the shore now, ahead of his promised schedule. Another show of power to express his control over her.

But that would end soon enough.

Celine swam to the guards, even as Quinn and Zander reached for her hands. Celine clasped theirs, kissing their fingers.

"I'll be alright. This isn't the end." She met their gazes with what she hoped was confidence, masking the cold storm of emotions that raged in her gut. "This is far from over."

Jessa remained at her side as Celine released Quinn and Zander and went with the guards. Her friends followed, their silent rage vibrating through the sea, and all of them continued in silence, the suspense too oppressive for sound.

CHAPTER 7

The coral palace glistened beautifully at Celine's approach, even though the sun couldn't reach such depths in the sea. The ocean was alive, Shanna's gifts glowing with their own joy and power, the life of the sea thriving.

What would life on land look like? What would it *feel* like? Even as she swam between the guards, surrounded by everything she held dear, she was already homesick.

"Celine." Dathan grinned from his royal perch. He swished his fin, knocking a loose bit of stone. It bounced and clattered as it fell down the coral incline. "Sorry to cut things short."

Quinn and Zander's faces were grief stricken. Shame lined Jessa's eyes and mouth. Celine's racing heart pounded harder, eyes itching and tingling.

Don't show him. She stilled her face, forcing her muscles to be as stone. *The bastard king doesn't know what's coming. His fate is sealed.*

"Our people are waiting patiently for the alliance between our kingdom and Estilon."

Murmurs in the crowd rose, but Dathan's dark gazed silenced them.

"Go to the shore. Do right by your people." His self-satisfied grin shot a surge of white-hot anger through her blood. Her fingernails stabbed her palms. "Report back when human blood stains your hands."

He raised his hand with a flourish, and something unseen took hold of Celine's body. Pain pulsed at her back, reaching down her hips, down the long bones of her tail, all the way to the edge of her fin. She met Dathan's manic eyes before her muscles and bones seized, her body throwing itself back, her lips thrashing beyond her control.

"Celine!" Zander and Quinn, their voices filling her mind even as Dathan laughed.

"Father, stop this!"

"Celine!"

But her body was under his control, his magic tracing hate through every muscle and down every bone. She screamed as her scales retreated into skin, as her muscles snapped and bones reformed to become a pair of legs.

"No!"

"Celine!"

It was taking far too long. Dathan took his time reshaping her. Celine would die from the agony.

Coherent thought was a luxury. Celine could only form flashes of emotions as thoughts, but she had a vague imagining of Dathan suffering in Aishlin's chaotic darkness, paying dearly for every crime committed against the merfolk. Against *her*.

Strength, she prayed, hoping Aishlin was listening. *Stay with me.*

"Ah, ah, ah." Her voice, that soothing alto. Kasindra. "You're taking this too far, brother."

Magic snapped, and Celine's body changed with some of her strength returning.

"You dare interfere with my judgment!"

"I absolutely dare." Kasindra laughed. "You dare take away her magic, playing as Shanna herself? Brother..." Her voice adopted a sing-song teasing. "You don't think you're a *god*, do you?"

Dathan screamed at her, no words or coherent argument. Just rage.

"Such blasphemy will warrant penance. I *saved* you, brother. Shanna's wrath is formidable."

When the transformation ended, her body throbbed as though

her remade bones vibrated with futile resistance. She remained limp in the water, fatigue battling with the pulse of pain that kept her conscious.

But Kasindra was there, protecting her from Dathan. She would be all right.

But water burned her nose, and her open mouth struggled with the brine that filled it.

"Celine!"

"We're coming, Celine!"

"By the gods, she's drowning!"

Hands gripped her arms and pulled her quickly up and away. She barely saw Zander's fin before her vision blurred, and his mouth met hers, hastily breathing air into her mouth. It was difficult to accept at first, her mouth navigating around the sea that tried to drown her so she could accept his breath. But her lungs eased as she inhaled from him and exhaled into the water.

She surfaced, breathing freely, coughing out sea water and pain. Quinn and Zander's hands didn't leave her, their arms holding her close.

"Celine?" Quinn swept hair from Celine's face.

"I just need—" Celine groaned through a searing wave of pain. *"Seven hells."*

"You can still hear us." Zander let her lean against his shoulder as she breathed, her eyes closed. "You're still merfolk."

"I think that's thanks to Kasindra," Celine said. "She stopped Dathan from taking it from me."

"What? Your magic?" Quinn stared, horrified. "He was turning you into a human?"

Celine nodded. "He wanted me powerless here."

Quinn sneered, anger darkening her sunlight-colored eyes to a dangerous amber. "I can't wait to celebrate his death."

In a startling rush, Jessa surfaced. "Celine!" She looked from Celine to the others. "What the hells happened?"

Quinn and Zander explained as Celine still worked to catch her breath. Her *breath*, for she had a nose and mouth to fill her lungs, not her gills. She released Zander and touched her neck, feeling the smooth skin there.

"He tried to take her magic?" Jessa closed her eyes, turning her face away. "I'll never be able to apologize enough."

"I told you," Celine said. "Don't apologize for someone else's mistakes."

"He's my father."

"That doesn't make you responsible for him." Celine reached out for her hand, which Jessa accepted. "You're not your father. And he's nothing compared to you."

Tears welled in her frosty eyes. "I don't know what to do."

"Be there for your people," Celine said.

"Help us, Jessa," Zander added. "This has to stop."

"It should have been me," Jessa said. "By the gods, Celine, he should have sent me."

"He wants me to kill them," Celine said, damning Dathan and his malicious goals to the seven hells that awaited him. "There's another king and a son. I've forgotten their names, but I'm supposed to kill them and the royal bloodline of Estilon." She shook her head, water dripping faster down her face. "He wouldn't have sent you, Jessa, even if I didn't give him a reason. He's always wanted me dead."

"Celine—"

"Gods know why I was spared when my parents weren't," Celine said. "Kasindra, perhaps? But that doesn't matter." She looked down into the water, seeing her aching legs alongside their glistening tails. "I'll die there, or I'll die here."

"No." Quinn shook Celine by the shoulders. "Not as long as you have us."

Jessa looked beyond the three of them, unable to meet their eyes. "I don't want him to die."

A meek confession of a daughter wanting to save her father, despite him being the bastard Usurper King. Celine's heart ached for the daughter who loved him.

"There has to be a way to remove him from rule without this ending in his death," Quinn said. "A toxin, perhaps?"

"Something to figure out later," Jessa said, eyes scanning Celine. "She's in a lot of pain."

"I have medicine in the reef," Zander said.

"And clothes?" Jessa raised an eyebrow. "She'll gather a lot of attention if she's on the shore, naked."

Zander sank beneath the water without another word. Quinn and Jessa rested their hands on Celine's back and hips as they hummed a soothing melody. Relief seeped through her skin, her muscles relaxing as the throb of pain eased.

"Jessa!" Dathan's voice, booming through their minds. "Where the devil have you gone?"

Jessa looked at the water, alarm widening her eyes. "I have to go before he sends someone here." She squeezed Celine's hand. "I'm sorry."

She swam off quickly, leaving Quinn and Celine to hold on to one another.

"We should get you closer to shore." Quinn spoke with her mouth this time, her voice choked by the emotion that tightened her throat. Celine felt the same grip hold her voice hostage. She could barely breathe, her chest tightening as Quinn's tears fell. "Celine—"

Celine held her close as she cried, biting against her own tears. She wanted nothing more than to dissolve into sea foam and be remade into anything but this.

Celine reached a hand to the water, curling her fingers, willing the shadows to come. They arrived as summoned, swirling around her fingers. She could almost feel their sympathy.

Go to him. Make him suffer Aishlin's chaos. Bring him darkness.

The shadows obeyed, soaring through the water as bidden. Celine said nothing of this to Quinn, still trying to soothe her as she sobbed. Zander returned minutes later with his satchel strap across his chest and a bundle of soaking wet fabric in each hand.

"A shirt and trousers," he said. "We have little else."

"It will do."

With their help, Celine dressed and swam closer to shore.

"There's medicine in my bag." Zander ducked under the satchel strap and draped it across Celine's shoulders. "And some food."

They reached the incline of land, too shallow for Quinn and Zander to swim. Celine hesitated for only a second before she crawled forward, fire blazing in her back, hips, and legs.

"Can you stand?" Quinn asked.

"Give her time," Zander said. "It's like she's a newborn."

Celine crawled to the shore and moved to stand, the sand giving way beneath her weight. As soon as she reached her feet and straightened, the trousers slipped off of her hips. Reaching to catch them pulled at her back, and pain throbbed in her thighs. She crumpled to the ground like an empty sack.

"Celine!"

"I'm all right, Quinn," she lied. It was nearly impossible to deceive with her real voice. She couldn't control it and keep it steady as she breathed through the pain. Her voice was the sound of anger caged in. Anger toward Dathan, toward her new body, toward the man she would marry. "I promise, I'm all right."

Celine repeated the lie to herself to make it true. She crawled to the shallow hillside that rolled up to the main road to Estilon, one hand holding her clothes as the other held her weight. She growled, every movement making it worse, but she turned to her friends as they watched her from the water.

"See?" Celine's wide smile felt more like a grimace, betraying the veneer feebly hiding her agony. "You both need to go before someone sees you, and I need to tighten these infernal trousers."

Quinn didn't argue, but Celine could feel the resistance pulsing from her stare.

"We should have stolen one of those waist things." Zander made a motion around his hips.

"A belt," Celine said, trying to keep her tone light. "Humans wear belts with their trousers. That's what the books say, anyway."

Zander pulled Quinn close, the pair of them matched in their grief. Celine's heart shattered into a million pieces.

"I love you both." She glanced down the shore for any sign of a human approaching. "Now go while it's still safe."

"I love you, too," they each said.

Celine didn't turn from the water until her friends were out of sight, and only then did she let her body crash against the sand at long last. Her legs were as limp as seaweed. With hurried hands, she found the jar of healing salve and rubbed it all over her hips, legs, and back, reaching into the borrowed clothes much too large for her.

Closing her eyes, she focused on her breathing, focused on the dark magic swirling around Dathan and Santus both, sweeping them into the void, together.

Where had Santus been when Dathan cursed her to an early transformation and exile? Was he the one behind the magic while Dathan remained the face of her punishment?

Where are you, Santus? She reached her hand toward the water, summoning shadows to find him. *I'm not finished with you yet, Commander.*

She looked toward Estilon with tired eyes. If she survived to become Prince Owen's arranged wife, what could he do about bringing the Usurper King to his destruction?

An army following his command...

Secret magic at his disposal...

The human prince could prove a powerful ally, indeed.

CHAPTER 8

When Celine opened her eyes, morning had progressed to afternoon, but her body felt frozen in time. She stirred, pushing herself up, propped against sun-warmed stone.

"*Ah–*" Her hips and legs throbbed. The sensation, having distanced itself in sleep, came rushing back in waking. Her bare feet dug into loose, coarse sand as she tried to situate her body more comfortably. The textures of sand and stone were rough against her salt-dried skin.

Her clothes, with dampness lingering in the fabric, chilled her skin against the sea breeze. She'd never been *cold* before, with the puckering of her skin and the slight shivering in her bones. She was slow in getting to her feet, every shift in weight a reminder of her painful transformation, all made worse by her incessant shivering.

Celine balanced precariously, covering her hips and legs with more of Zander's healing balm while she stood, one hand balancing on stone as it held the open jar, the other reaching into her trousers to touch skin. *Skin*. So foreign, when the texture of scales was natural to her. Skin was too soft, too vulnerable. How had humans survived this long as a species, when they were so squishy and easy to kill?

Her eyes, adjusting to the afternoon light, spotted something just out of reach of the water as it stretched onto shore. Was that–was that *rope*?

Celine hobbled toward it, her balance unsteady. She winced at every aching step as her feet sank into the sand, but her right step landed on a round rock, tilting her foot to one side. She fell, hands bracing her fall as pain pulsed up her elbows and shoulders like lightning strikes.

"Come on, Celine."

She blindly reached back for the steep wall of the hill, but she'd gone too far.

"Get up." She took a deep breath through her nose. "*Get up*."

On all fours, she tucked her legs beneath her as her feet pressed against the ground. With quivering limbs, she stood, one arm out to help with balance as the other hand held onto the trousers. One step, then another, and one more as she reached the small stretch of rope waiting for her in the sand. Beside it, the lines fading were the letters Z, Q, and C. *Zander, Quinn, and Celine.*

They'd been here and checked on her, bringing her a makeshift belt. Tears warmed her eyes as she bent to take the rope and tied it clumsily around her waist, cinching the trousers in place. Flakes of dried salt fell from her still-damp clothes. She reached her hand into the water, a quivering smile on her face as she sent her thoughts to them, knowing that they couldn't hear her. But maybe they could *feel* her.

She settled back down, panting, exhausted while also rejuvenated. She opened her satchel and searched through the medicine and healing herbs until she uncovered something wrapped in damp fabric. Pieces of raw fish and seaweed, enough for two conservative meals. She ate slowly, savoring the rich saltwater taste, and exhaled in luxurious peace. Her body was healing, albeit slowly. Her friends were alright. For now, she was alright, too.

Eventually, she would need to travel to Estilon. Eventually, she would need to meet Owen as his promised wife.

Celine wanted to curse Dathan for his selfish deals, but her thoughts had run as dry as her clothes and skin. Instead, she ate slowly, grateful to Zander and his kindness, grateful to Quinn and her healing. She leaned against the sun-warmed stony incline that was a blend of a hillside and a cliff, hearing the sounds of humans and horses above and behind her. The horizon offered a soothing calm–so soothing that, in the dream, she wandered through the dark, walking on her human feet, feeling with human hands, but she couldn't see. The pitch darkness was so thick, she could almost feel it against her skin. Each step was tentative and slow. Cold wind swept across the back of her neck.

Not, not cold wind. *Breath.*

Something was there with her. Something alive.

"Celine?"

She bolted awake, her body curled on the beach, nestled against the foot of the hill. The sun had set past the horizon to make room for the waning moon and stars, but the night sky still provided enough light to silhouette the man before her. Her heart pounded with such force that it pulsed in her ears, nearly drowning out all other sound.

"Are you alright?"

That voice.

She blinked, eyes adjusting, staring straight into Prince Owen's striking blue eyes.

Celine stared, mouth open and eyes wide, the pulse of energy surging through the air like the aftermath of a lightning storm.

He was the prince of Estilon, soon to be its king...soon to be *her husband*, if the wedding came to pass.

If. The tenuous nature of her being here, among humans, alongside the prince of Estilon, consumed every thought. *If the wedding came to pass, should Celine live to see it done.*

"Are you alright?" Prince Owen tossed aside a piece of driftwood and brushed his hands on his trousers before offering them to her. "Do you need help?"

Celine pushed herself up, scrambling, her body still a foreign entity. She fumbled forward and fell as he caught her, her feet and legs precariously bent as he held her up. His warmth reached her immediately, his touch holding the gentle power of a knight's strength.

He helped her as she corrected her stance, the reassuring pressure of his arms steadying. She held his biceps as he gripped her elbows, either of them letting go. "What happened to you?"

"I–" A very large part of her wanted to feign ignorance, saying *I don't know* and letting Owen fill in the blanks. Another part of her wanted to take this chance to run, but her body was far from capable.

The truth was the safest route. At least, for now. Owen had met her before. He knew what she was and likely already concluded what she was going to say.

"Are you injured?" He looked her over. "What happened to your clothes?"

Celine looked down at herself. "It was all I had." She swallowed hard, bracing herself for what was to come. The urge to flee had never been stronger. "King Dathan sent me."

With ice-cold panic, Celine harbored a dangerous thought: What if Dathan had lied? What if there was no alliance to be forged by marriage? What if he sent Celine to the very people they fought against to have them do away with her, keeping Dathan's hands clean?

"King Dathan." He studied her, the moonlight emphasizing the focus in his eyes. "You're—"

Clearing his throat, he let her go and stepped back. She rocked on her feet unsupported but stayed standing.

"Apparently, if the merking is to be believed—" The legs beneath her were far too fragile, like her bones were cracked glass. "—we're to be married."

He stared, his face a visible war between selves—the diplomatic prince seeking the right thing to say and the shocked human betrothed to a mermaid. "We were going to send someone for you later this week."

"Dathan changed me suddenly. I had to hurry to the surface. I—" She swallowed saliva that went down like shards of glass, scratching their way down her throat. "I didn't know what to expect."

She hated being this vulnerable. She hated revealing such weakness. But what else was there to do but tell him the truth?

"I—" He licked his lips, likely trying to think of something to say. "I just wasn't expecting you yet."

"To be fair, I wasn't expecting you yet, either." She winced, her hips and back struggling to support her weight. She widened her stance, which helped. "I'm sorry to push up your timeline, your highness." Her tone bit as severely as the pulsing ache in her legs. "May I sit down?"

"Your highness?"

Past Owen came a tall man in chain mail with the Estilon tabard draped over him. Behind him was a shorter man, similarly dressed.

"Celine," Owen said, "this is Tyrion and Liam, my guards. Tyrion, Liam—" He partially turned to them, gesturing a hand toward Celine, "this is Celine. My betrothed."

He said it so easily, whereas Celine had considered lying about her identity. Both men shared the same perplexed expression, so she settled her gaze on Owen, who stepped closer.

"Let's get you inside," he said, draping her arm across his shoulders. "Can you walk?"

"I think so." But her footsteps were unsteady on the coarse sand.

"Here. Allow me." With that, he scooped her up and turned for the path back to the castle. His chest was solid, his arms strong. "I apologize for my abruptness, but this will be much faster. I would like my court physician to examine you, if that's alright."

She adjusted Zander's bag to keep it from dangling awkwardly as Owen walked.

"I will go ahead, your highness," Liam said with a bow. "Geoffrey is likely with a patient."

"Thank you, Liam."

Tyrion stayed as Liam jogged on, nodding at the guards stationed at the castle gate as he moved forward, undeterred.

Celine's arms found Owen's neck, reassured that she was safe for now.

"I'm afraid your chambers aren't ready yet," he said. "The maids will prepare something while we wait for the physician."

She liked the sound of his voice, the subtle musical timbre rich with depth. The more she listened, the more she wanted to unravel the layers of its sound.

"Thank you." It was all she could think to say.

"I didn't mean to be so abrupt before, about meeting you earlier than expected. I almost didn't take a walk." His tone was light until he said, "I haven't been able to rest for days. The king's condition has worsened."

"I'm sorry." How long did Rolf have before his body could fight no more? "Did the ingredients help?"

"Some."

He watched his feet as he ascended a short set of wooden steps leading up from the beach to the grassy land. And there, tall and impressive, was Estilon Castle. Even silhouetted against the evening sky, painted with the blue shades of the cooling hour, it was magnificent to behold. She was so small beneath its towering presence.

"You must still be in a lot of pain," he said. "Am I hurting you?"

"No." She tightened her hold around his neck as though to prove herself. "I'm fine."

"I wouldn't be fine." He glanced down at her as he continued walking toward the castle, his bright blue eyes catching moonlight. "I would be anything but fine."

He passed through the castle gates with an affirming nod toward the guards, Tyrion still trailing behind him. Was this the only way out of the castle? Should things prove troublesome, how would she get out?

"Your highness." The guards at the gate spoke and saluted in unison. Then one asked, "Has something happened?"

"My betrothed has joined Castle Estilon," he announced. "Liam is on his way to Geoffrey now. Would one of you bring in the head lady's maid?"

"Right away, your highness." Another salute, and one guard hurried ahead of them toward the castle while his second remained at his post.

Celine eyed the expanse of the massive courtyard, noting guards all patrolling in pairs along the grounds and the parapets.

She studied what she could of the layout, counted as many guards as she could see, and now braced herself for the crossing of the threshold.

"Celine?"

"Hm?" She blinked up at him. "I'm sorry, your highness. I've only ever seen it from the water."

"It can be rather overwhelming," he said. "We're preparing chambers for you, as I've said, and we'll see about a bath and a change of clothes."

"You don't have to go to such trouble, your highness."

"It isn't any trouble." His words were genuine. For a pair of strangers committing to a task they neither asked for nor wanted, he didn't deviate from kindness. "And you can call me Owen."

She blinked, eyes tracing his profile as he watched his steps.

"I'm sorry for not telling you who I was earlier," he said, "but I enjoyed—I don't know—how *casual* you were. Now, it's *your highness*."

"Soon to be *husband*." She shrugged a shoulder. "It's a lot to take in."

"That, it is."

Dathan's words echoed in her mind, their bloodlust curdling on her stomach. If only Owen knew what the merking wished of her.

The foyer of the castle was busy despite the late hour, and those passing through stopped at the sight of the prince, their eyes going from Owen to the woman he carried in his arms.

"Miss Helen is on her way," a young woman announced. Her dress was simple, nothing like what Celine spotted in the paintings that adorned the walls.

"Thank you. And the physician?"

"He's with a patient," came a voice deeper than Owen's, the sound much more through the nose than the throat. "Trouble with indigestion."

The man was tall and lithe like Owen with a similar physical build. But he was almost opposite in every other way, with light hair and beard, dark eyes, and something sharp at the edges of his eyes and mouth. Traits that would have looked less sinister on someone else. "What's happened?"

"I'm not sure." Owen adjusted his hold on Celine, holding her so that she could face the man approaching. "Uncle Graham, this is Celine, my betrothed, sent from King Dathan this morning. Celine, this is Prince Graham, Captain of Estilon Guard and brother to my father, the king."

The introductions rolled off his tongue so easily, and his hold didn't waver.

"The woman on the beach. The mermaid from the sea." Prince Graham bowed his head to her. "Word has already reached me. Liam wasted no time in sharing the news. I hope you are well."

She smiled weakly, nodding back, tightening her hands to keep hold of Owen's neck. She wished she had more strength and control over this body. This body that was *not* hers but someone else's. "Thank you."

"We're headed upstairs for Geoffrey," Owen said. "Have him come to my chambers."

Graham bowed his head. "As you wish, your highness."

The large stairs before them were wide and curved to the left and right. Celine stared up, watching the movement of servants and knights passing through. "Your chambers?"

"Just until yours are sorted," he said. "It'll be much more comfortable than Geoffrey's infirmary."

A middle-aged woman hurried from a corridor at the top of the stairs, her graying black hair tied neatly back, her hazel eyes finding them at once.

"Miss Helen," Owen said. "We'll have her in my chambers until hers are ready."

"The maids are nearly finished," she said.

"Excellent," he said. "Would it be too much trouble to have a bath drawn?"

"I should say not, your highness." Helen looked Celine over. "Poor child. What on earth happened?"

"Transformation," he answered. "I found her on the beach, and she's still in a lot of pain. I've called for Geoffrey already."

"Rightly so," Helen said.

Celine looked around the foyer as Owen ascended the stairs, catching sight of Tyrion still behind him. She nearly gasped, forgetting he'd been there with them since the beach. He didn't bother hiding his suspicion, made more ominous by the amber light of the sconces lining the walls.

"You were sent by your king," Tyrion said. "Transformed and rushed to the surface."

She waited, seeing the disbelief in his eyes. What more could she say? The Usurper King sent his stepdaughter in his daughter's stead? And Dathan wanted Celine to shed blood in his name?

"At least we've met before now," Owen said as he reached the top of the stairs. "You're not a *total* stranger."

"You've met?" Tyrion asked.

"A few times," Owen said. "We both have a common love of deep-sea diving."

Tyrion did not look amused.

"I'm also relieved that we know one another." But she said nothing of their last meeting. Did any of them know Owen had magic?

"Allow me." Tyrion walked ahead, leading them along with Miss Helen to the left corridor. Celine stared at the tapestries and drapes, at the shining suits of armor by large paintings of old Estilon kings and queens, all of them cast in flickering shadow from Tyrion's torch. Their footfalls moved from stone to something lush and soft, their steps quieting as they passed down wooden walls with closed doors.

Owen's chambers were the last door on the right, which Tyrion opened and entered with practiced ease. Owen stepped in sideways and carried her toward the bed. The room impressive in its simplicity, the bed modest for a king's son. What impressed her more were the stacks of books on one side while an easel stood with a painting on the other.

"Geoffrey will be here shortly," Miss Helen said. "I'll fetch you some clothes."

"Thank you, Miss Helen." Owen set Celine down to sit upright at the foot of the bed.

"I'll see to the fire, my lord." Tyrion crouched at the fireplace.

"That won't be necessary, Tyr. I can—"

"I insist. I wish you to not be alone together, your highness." He looked up from Owen to Celine. "Forgive me, my lady. Your appearance is sudden, and I will ensure my prince's safety."

Celine's toes curled as she tucked her feet beneath the bed. "I understand." She gripped the strap of Zander's bag with both hands, her heart pounding beneath her fingers. "I would do much the same."

Two swift knocks on the door preceded Miss Helen's reentry. "Her chambers are ready, your highness."

"Already?" Owen exhaled. "It was really no rush."

"She is a guest of Estilon and must be treated as such." Helen swept into the room and offered Celine her arm. "Shall we?"

Owen moved to take her up into his arms again, but Celine raised a hand, reading the tension coming from Tyrion and Helen. Neither of them was pleased to meet her. Neither of them likely agreed with this arrangement between their king and hers. And here she was, an interloper, a stranger, to be welcomed as a guest within their walls.

She stood, taking Helen's proffered arm, and moved with shaky steps as Helen led her out.

"Geoffrey is already waiting inside," Helen said. "After his examination, we'll see to your bath and clean clothes."

Examination, but there wasn't anything wrong with her. And what could a human physician do that merfolk medicine couldn't?

But she, with Miss Helen's support, walked across the hall to an open door, where a pair of maids passed in and out with buckets. Firelight already flickered in the room, but Celine could feel the lingering coolness that the fire steadily warmed away.

When Celine stepped inside, an old man stood looking through the window, his hands clasped behind his back. A large bag rested open on a small table, two small chairs tucked beneath it. He turned, his warm smile deepening the wrinkles around his mouth and eyes.

"Welcome to Estilon." He bowed at the waist. "I am Geoffrey, at your service."

"Celine." She bowed as well, helped by Helen's hand. She recited a line she'd read in several books: "It's a pleasure to meet you."

Helen helped her to the bed, the same size as Owen's with similar dressings. But the moonlight was absent from the windows, Owen's having the full view of the eastern sky. But if she faced west, she could look out to the sea...

"Shall we?" Geoffrey approached. "You've been transformed into a human. I can only imagine how that kind of trauma has affected you."

"It was very painful," she admitted, "and I still feel the aching. But —" Apprehension nearly shielded her from speaking up, but she met his kind eyes. "I'm not sure I need to be examined."

"As you wish, my dear," he said. His acceptance of her wishes washed over her in cooling relief. "Any bleeding or bruising?"

"No bleeding, as I've seen," Miss Helen said. "I'll know more with her bath."

"And you're not having trouble walking?"

"No. It hurts, of course, but I can move."

"Full mobility. Good, good." He went to an open bag on the table, pulling a vial of clear amber liquid. "A simple pain reliever that will also help you sleep. One sip should do it." He showed the bottle between his thumb and index finger. "If you don't like the taste, add some to a cup of tea. Just a small amount."

He held the medicine out to her, and she accepted it with both hands. The glass was warm from his touch.

Two sharp knocks came, and Miss Helen carefully opened the door. "Yes, your highness."

She moved to let Owen step in, his look cautious as he glanced from Geoffrey to Celine. "Is all well?"

"I should say so," Geoffrey said, closing his bag. "Have a bath and a clean change of clothes, Celine, and rest well tonight. You'll be presented before the king and queen tomorrow."

She didn't dare ask him to repeat himself. "The king and queen?"

"Yes," Owen said, the dimple shadowing his cheek as he half-smiled, amused. "You're to be my wife. We should present you to my parents before our wedding."

Miss Helen cracked a smile, but the swirling storm in Celine's gut prohibited any kind of amusement. King Rolf and Queen Adella, the monarchs of Estilon. And Celine of the merfolk would stand before them and do what? Curtsy and thank them for the opportunity to marry their son and heal this political wound?

Yes, she thought. *That's precisely what I have to do, unless I want them watching my every move.*

...Which they may already plan to do.

Geoffrey bowed once more. "Send for me if there is any need."

"I offer my services as well," Owen said to Celine. "I'm just down the hall."

He nodded toward Miss Helen before leaving with Geoffrey as two maids stepped in, each of them carrying buckets that now held steaming liquid within.

"That should do, ma'am," one said to Miss Helen. "We have the soap and brushes ready."

Celine ducked out of Zander's satchel strap, hearing the gentle tinkling of the glass vials from Kasindra. "My friends gave me healing medicines before I left. They're in this bag."

"That's fine, miss," one maid said. "Would you like them in the bedside table drawer?"

"That would be best," Miss Helen said, offering Celine her hand once more. "Let's start your bath, shall we? You'll be wanting to rest, I'm sure."

She was, but *rest* seemed elusive in this strange place with these strange people.

This is only a detour on your path. She took a deep breath. *Remember what you're going to do.*

THE BRUSHES WERE harsh against Celine's skin as the maids bathed her. She cried out as the bristles scratched, causing the maids to recoil.

"By the gods," one said, running a hand across her back where the bristles had been. "You're as soft as a newborn."

"Is salt water good for the skin?" one maid asked, eyes keen as they looked her over.

"Silly." The other maid slapped her arm playfully. "It's the seaweed."

"How do you know so much?"

"Ladies." Miss Helen's reprimand was soft and short. "Let's finish before the water gets cold."

They switched to washcloths, which Celine much preferred, and their steady rhythm of washing soothed much of her aching muscles in her back and shoulders. The hot bathwater did a lot to ease the remaining ache in her hips, back, and legs, and when bathing was done, they dried her and wrapped her in a soft towel as Helen brought a pile of garments, all covering a pair of leather boots.

"Wear these tonight." Helen passed her the pile of white. "Take the medicine from Geoffrey and rest well. We'll see about dressing you first thing in the morning."

She looked at the array of fabric that Helen carried to a tall wooden cabinet. She opened the doors, revealing a bar at the top with a platform at the bottom, and lifted a lilac dress with white trim to hang.

"What is that?" Celine asked, pointing.

"A wardrobe," one maid answered with the barest hint of a giggle.

"A wardrobe for your clothes," Miss Helen said. "And we use hangers for dresses and the like." She set the other bits of white fabric on the platform. "Things folded go here. Small clothes, trousers, that sort of thing."

Small clothes and wardrobes. Celine had read about them enough know their purpose.

At least I have some *knowledge of what's going on.*

"Now." Helen gestured toward the tub. "Away with this, and away with you. Our guest must rest."

The maids curtsied and took bucketfuls of Celine's bathwater and toss them from her window. She watched, intrigued, finding herself listening for the *splash* from outside.

"Once, I doused a knight unfortunate enough to walk under after training," one maid said, grinning wickedly. "He was *fuming* when he crossed my path, but I said I saved him the trouble of washing!"

The other maid cackled, but no trace of amusement found Miss Helen's face.

When they emptied the washtub, the maids curtsied before leaving with it and their buckets.

Unaffected at the challenge, she asked, "Do you need help getting dressed?"

"No," Celine said quickly. "I know small clothes and dresses."

"Very good." Miss Helen gave the room one more glance before leveling her eyes at Celine. "I will see that you receive the utmost care, young lady, but I warn you. Owen is very dear to us."

Celine blinked.

"The announcement of his betrothal shocked us all," she said. "Many of us believed it was a delusion from the king's malady." She pressed her lips together, as though she'd said too much. "If you have any designs on our prince, know that everyone in this castle will stop you. Myself included."

"I don't–"

"If you *don't*," she interrupted, "then we will get along just fine." Helen bowed her head and left, the door latching quietly behind her.

Alone, Celine exhaled so fully that her body deflated and collapsed onto the bed.

She'd hoped the hardest part was over, but the uphill climb had only just begun.

Uphill, with legs still unsteady.

CHAPTER 9

When Celine's eyes blinked awake, golden sunlight flooded the room. She stayed there, frozen, remembering the hours that led to her finding rest, her mind practically collapsing into dreamless sleep.

Rising was a challenge, her body stiff and aching from sleep. She used the bed for balance as she put her weight on her legs and feet. She shuffled toward the table, toward Zander's satchel, and pulled his medicine from within. The jar was damp from the moisture lingering in the fabric, salt flakes falling to the tabletop like white sand. Her hands were careful with the clothes as she massaged the translucent green ointment to her legs, hips, and back. Her throat tightened as she breathed the familiar, briny scent of home.

Two sharp knocks came before the door opened. Celine stood straight, balancing by the table with the jar of medicine still in her hand.

"Oh, you're awake." Miss Helen stepped in with a smile as her two maids followed. "Prince Owen has asked to take you to market after meeting the king and queen. If you're feeling up to it, of course."

"Market?" Celine had read about *markets*, and she'd seen so many humans passing in and out of Estilon with carts and animals. "That sounds lovely."

Helen raised an eyebrow. "Yes, I'm sure it does." Then, more casually, she added, "Market meets once a week, so your arrival is timely." She went to the wardrobe and pulled out the lilac dress. "Let's get you ready, then."

Ready to meet the king and queen.

Many hands passed over Celine's body, wrapping her in layer after layer of fabric. From the band around her chest to the stockings on her legs, once they pulled the dress over her head and tightened the straps in the front, she felt like a fish caught in a net. The aches flared, but Celine grit her teeth to hide as much discomfort as she could. She was glad for the healing balm making this bearable.

"Oh, splendid," Helen said. "Everything fits beautifully. Though I may have to take out the bust a bit." She pulled lightly at the shoulder seam. "Are you uncomfortable?"

She wanted nothing more than to strip free and run back into the water, but she didn't dare speak the truth. "No, Miss Helen. Thank you. Everything is lovely."

"Excellent. The boots are just there. They should slip right on." She had set them at the foot of the bed, the calves of the boots having flopped over. "If they don't fit, I can see about getting a different size."

Celine stared at the footwear, unsure. She glanced at Miss Helen's feet and those of the two maids. They each wore boots of a similar style to the ones presented. "I'm sure these will be fine."

They would have to be fine. The last thing Celine wanted was to ask anything of the severe and watchful woman assessing her every move.

Cautiously, Celine slipped one foot into the boot, feeling the heel and arch of her foot rest comfortably. The toe of the boot was too close. Without a word, she slipped on the other boot and stood, wobbly and unsure. She couldn't feel the floor with the boots on, but something told her that moving around in only her hosed or bare feet was against the rules.

"They feel nice," she lied. "Thank you."

"I will have some food brought," Helen said. "Prince Owen will come to collect you shortly."

"Thank you." That was all she could think to say. *Thank you...yes, thank you,* when every second in this castle led to another growing in awkwardness and discomfort. She didn't know how to navigate this very human terrain. She felt the scrutinizing eyes of everyone she met, as though they waited for her to slip up.

Celine was alone for only a few minutes before a different maid brought a tray full of food. Aromatic smells of spices and flavors filled the space, and Celine's mouth watered. She sat at the table, tempering her eagerness, and ate delicately. Everything tasted delicious, though the meat was regrettably cooked. A large side of raw fish sounded absolutely *divine*.

"Um. Miss?" The maid's look was tentative, as though she waited for an imminent reprimand. "May I?"

"What?"

"The utensils, Miss." The maid approached the table and picked up one of the three metal tools next to her plate. "Fork and knife for the meat, Miss, and a spoon for the soup."

Fork, knife, spoon. Celine remembered those words from the books she'd read. And sailors had used these tools to stab or scoop food. Somehow, Celine had missed them entirely, her eyes and hands going straight for her quarry to sate her hunger.

She was clumsy at first, dipping with the spoon and stabbing with the fork, but she understood well enough. The maid smiled, and Celine, once again, felt as though she'd done something wrong.

"I like your style, Miss," she said with a beaming smile. "One tool in each hand."

"Isn't this how you use them?"

"No, Miss. They make us put one down and pick up the other, using the same hand."

Perturbed, Celine put down the spoon. "That's ridiculous."

The maid laughed, though not in jest. It was appreciative, even comfortable. "I agree, Miss."

She thought of Zander and Quinn. How would they use these strange tools? How would they cope with such a strange eating custom?

But, as she smiled to herself, imagining them eating with a fork or spoon, the pang of sadness struck hard. She breathed through it, willing the tears away, her heart throbbed.

There was a quiet knock, and the maid answered it promptly before bowing at the waist. "Your highness!"

Owen stepped in tentatively, smiling. A night's sleep had done him well, by the brightness of his eyes and the healthy glow to his skin. "Oh, splendid. Breakfast."

Celine moved to stand, unsure of what to do, but Owen stopped her.

"Please, don't stop. I only wanted to check in and make sure you were alright."

"Yes," Celine said, settling back down. "They've taken excellent care of me."

"Marvelous. And I've spoken to Geoffrey about giving you a tour of the castle." Owen bent his tall frame to rest his hands on the back of the chair opposite Celine's. His long fingers reached down the back panel, nearly reaching its rounded edge to curl under. "It's alright if you're not up to it, but if I were you, I would be bored to tears if I didn't have something to do. And—" He paused for dramatic effect. "It's Market Day."

His excitement increased her curiosity. "A tour would be nice." Celine tried to poise her fork correctly, preparing to take another bite of food, but her fingers didn't communicate with the instrument well enough. The metal clattered against the plate, startling all three of them. "Oh! I'm so sorry!"

"No need for apology." Owen tilted his head, and Celine would swear there was a hint of mischief in his eyes. "Do I make you nervous?"

"No." She hesitated. "*Yes.*"

Celine looked up at him, eyes tracing the shape of his curved shoulders and elongated arms as his hands still rested on the back of the chair. But his posture didn't read *superior* with hers as *inferior*. It was two people finding themselves amused with one another, one of them in a purely jovial mood while the other hid her open vulnerability beneath a practiced veneer.

Celine let her amusement show as she asked, "When shall we leave, your highness?"

"As soon as you've finished."

With that, Celine took up the spoon and used both utensils in tandem. "Oh, yes, this is much more efficient."

Owen watched in awe.

"Two utensils do seem better, my lord," the maid said.

He nodded slowly. "Indeed."

CHAPTER 10

Thanks to medicine and rest, Celine was better on her feet, though she preferred to feel the floor beneath her. The boots pinched her toes, and the soles confined every bend and step of her foot. She couldn't wait to remove those offensive things at the first opportunity.

"I don't want to overwhelm you," Owen said as the pair left Celine's room. He clasped his hands behind his back, walking close to her. "Is a trip to the market too soon?"

"The prospect of a walk sounds pleasant. I've never been on one before."

He showed a hint of wonder at the truth of it. "We'll go as frequently as you wish."

The prince's guards waited at a respectable distance, their chain mail and tabards complimented by the bright morning sun. She nodded to them both and said good morning, which they returned.

Taller than Owen by about four inches, Tyrion carried himself with a confidence that didn't seep into arrogance. His light brown hair was nearly blond in the morning sun beaming in from the tall windows, and his dark blue eyes missed little as they watched Owen and the world around him.

But the other, shorter knight carried himself differently, like one ready to prove himself. He ran his hand through his short, dark hair, his light brown eyes following her.

"Forgive me," Celine said to the other knight. "I've forgotten your name."

"No need for apology," he said. "I imagine things have been a bit of a whirlwind."

She appreciated his leniency. "Yes, it has."

"This is Sir Liam," Owen introduced. "One of our newest and bravest knights."

"Thank you, your highness." Liam bowed his head. "That means a lot."

In the daylight, the foyer was grand and rich with color, from the tapestries to the paintings to the colored glass in the windows.

"After the market," Owen said, "I should like to take you—"

"Ah."

A voice interrupted them as they moved to descend the stairs—Prince Graham, walking from the other side of the stairs, smiling at his nephew.

"I see our guest is cared for." Graham nodded his head at Celine in greeting. "How are you faring, young lady?"

"I am well, thank you." Celine mirrored his posture, nodding her head. She clasped her hands in front of her and watched as he and Owen greeted one another.

"Giving her the grand tour?" Graham didn't wait for an answer. "I highly recommend having tea in the butterfly garden, especially on a day like today."

"Thank you, Uncle. We should have time this afternoon."

"Wonderful." He paused before asking, "Your highness, may I have a word?" Graham's eyes darted to Celine before returning to Owen. "Just for a moment."

"Of course. Celine?" Owen gestured a hand toward the stairs. "Would you mind waiting downstairs for a moment?"

She nodded in assent and slowly stepped down, Tyrion and Liam remaining with him. The first step down jarred her equilibrium, forcing her to bring both hands to the banister as she continued down. Losing balance stirred her attention, which she quickly regained, tuning her ears to Owen and Graham. But neither spoke until Celine was downstairs.

She listened intently, lamenting the loss of her merfolk hearing. The echoing off of the stone walls hindered more than it helped. She locked eyes onto Graham and watched his mouth. *"Don't trust just anyone."* When his eyes fell on her, she bowed her head, hoping to appear meek.

"Thank you, Uncle," Owen said, his voice carrying more loudly than Graham's. "Trust that I will be fine."

"Jesper is cunning," Graham said.

At the mention of his name, Celine shivered. *Send their nation into political turmoil.* Jesper was the human king aiding Dathan. But where was Jesper's son? How did Owen meet her before he did, if their plan was to take down Estilon together?

She breathed through the rising panic, her stomach lurching.

"I wouldn't put it past him to try *anything*." Again, Graham glanced toward Celine. "Be careful."

Graham moved past Owen to continue down the corridor of rooms as Owen stepped quickly down the stairs to join her.

"Shall we?" He grinned, but the edges around his eyes remained sharp. He gestured to the right of the stairs toward a closed wooden door. "The Great Hall is just there."

"The Great Hall," she repeated. "What makes it great?"

Tyrion chuckled.

"It's where the king and queen sit and receive guests," Owen said. "Where we host parties and dinners."

And where I will be weighed and measured.

Owen offered Celine his arm, which she took gratefully. His strength helped her to step forward as he opened the door into the Great Hall.

The floor was checkered white and blue, with each square large enough for one person to stand in. There were shields lining the walls painted with images and emblems that Celine didn't recognize, with similarly styled tapestries as the foyer hanging between them. Following the walls down, she studied the throne set, two ornate chairs of wood, gold, and embroidered fabric in the middle of a dais with a rich, crimson carpet beneath them. Behind them were tapestries bearing the symbol of Estilon.

The king and queen sat at the far end of the room, their clothing regal, though their heads bore no crowns. Gold bands, instead, wrapped around their heads in modest adornment. Modest for a monarch, at least, even as they sat in intricately carved thrones.

The natural light highlighted the natural colors of wood, the arranged flowers by the thrones, the beautiful fabrics that made up the royal outfits. Tapestries and banners adorned the tall walls between dressed windows, and they walked down a carpeted path toward the royal seat.

Owen stopped them several feet in front of the thrones, bowing his head at his parents. Celine mirrored his bow, nervously looking from king to queen.

"Mother," Owen said with a smile. Then, more solemn, "Father. This is Celine of the merfolk."

"How do you do, Celine?" Queen Adella said, bowing her head slightly. "Welcome to Estilon."

"You're rather early, aren't you?" King Rolf coughed quietly. "Was Dathan impatient?"

"I should say so, your majesty," Celine said. "It caught me by surprise, as well."

"I thought we were getting the other one," Rolf said, looking at Adella. He waved his hand, trying to recall. "The one with white hair."

"Jessa," Celine said, offended by him calling her *the other one*. She set her shoulders back, swallowing a more biting response in favor of something more diplomatic. This human king could have her killed, if he chose. "I apologize if I am not to your liking, your highness."

"Nonsense," Owen and Adella said at once. Then, Adella added, "We are pleased you're here."

Owen rested a hand on hers, curling her fingers against his arm. "I would very much like to show Celine our castle and our market."

"We'll discuss the details of your ceremony soon," Rolf said before another coughing fit seized him, this one more severe. Celine watched the edges of black veins peek from beneath his collar. Hell's Touch. "Damn it all. Where is that tea?"

"On its way, dear." Adella smiled at Celine, then Owen. "Enjoy yourselves. I'll see to your father's tea."

They bowed once more before turning from the great hall, the passage out somehow shorter than when they'd entered. But Celine couldn't trust her eyes, only her feeling of relief that it was over.

Once the wooden door closed behind them, Celine could feel herself breathe again.

"Did you see?" Owen leaned close to keep his voice low. "The marks are worse than before."

"I did." She brought her other hand to his arm, sympathy in her touch. "I'm sorry, your highness."

"Please, call me Owen. We are to be married soon." He exhaled a quiet laugh. "I enjoyed your informality from before, remember?"

She only smiled in response, the notion of marriage still so foreign, even as it loomed over her. "Before, with your uncle." Her palms had perspired, a strange sensation. "Have I caused a problem?"

"What do you mean?"

"I didn't mean to proceed ahead of schedule," she said. "I don't want to be a burden."

"You're not a burden." His voice was low, a reassurance just for her. "Our parents have thrust us into a situation without our consent."

Celine bit her tongue. Dathan was no parent of hers, but disputing would raise more questions and alarm. What if she wasn't enough for the deal and they sent her back? Or, rather than send her back, what if—

"My uncle has the kingdom's best interest at heart," Owen went on. "And he and I see eye to eye on a lot of serious points."

Celine refrained from asking what *points* those were.

"He's loyal to Estilon," Owen said. "And he is one of the few people who is completely honest with me. Such a gift is invaluable."

Celine looked down at her aching feet as Owen took her hand to lead her down the front steps. His hold was gentle, open as though to let her sweep her hand away if she wished it. But she was grateful for his warmth, her fingers resting comfortably in his palm.

Whispers met her ears, the servants watching as they walked together

"Ignore them, Celine." He offered a kind smile, holding her hand tighter. "They'll gossip about anything." Then, with a flash of mischief, he added, "We can at least give them something to talk about."

Tyrion let out a discrete chuckle before clearing his throat.

"Is there anything you're curious about?" Owen asked, the two of them moving through the courtyard. "The human world is probably very different from that of the merfolk."

He rested her hand in the crook of his arm as he led her toward the entrance gate. Celine could already hear the sellers and patrons from the market, the fabric tops of the stalls visible through the bars of the iron gate.

"I have hundreds of questions," she said, "and I can't remember a single one of them."

The lie was casual enough. Every question she wanted to ask related to the sea, to Dathan and Santus, to continuing her magical tasks without any restraints or prohibition. But there were dozens of ears and eyes listening and watching. Besides, would Owen understand?

Be careful of your alliances. Kasindra's warning. Did her cauldron show her this, too?

A word of warning would have been nice.

"This market has some of the best sweets," Owen said. "There's peach crumble from the baker that will send you reeling."

Though Celine didn't know *peach crumble*, the way Owen's voice changed emphasized its power over him. "Is that your favorite?"

"There is no equal."

"Peach crumble in summer, cinnamon bread in autumn." Liam looked from Owen to Tyrion. "My mouth's watering just thinking about it."

"Autumn is approaching," Owen said. "You'll have the joy of knowing both desserts very soon."

As they stepped beyond the gate, Celine watched humans mill around stalls of wood and fabric that lined the dirt path from the castle gate down into the city. *Market Day.* "Oh, my."

"Our economy is surviving," Owen said, "though the wars have taxed a lot of our kingdom's resources."

Wars, plural. A war on land, a war at sea. The fringes of Dathan's command came to her, but she brushed them away. She wanted no part of his ruse, no part of his crackbrained plan. She knew it wouldn't succeed, and, if she had to guess, so did he.

He didn't expect her to win, so she wouldn't play his game, least of all by his rules.

"War often does," she said. "The merfolk have paid, as I'm sure the humans have, too."

"I feel I should say this." He put a hand over hers, edging her closer. "I don't agree with this war between our people, nor do I condone any actions my father has taken against the merfolk. A large part of why I agreed to this marriage was to have the power to stop it, to form an alliance between our people and end the bloodshed."

Noble, if it worked, but as the eyes followed them downhill toward the stalls, Celine doubted if every human here would agree with letting go.

"Then our alliance is on common ground," she said. "I only hope there are others who share your vision."

"You and me, both."

There were a few whispers among the vendors and patrons, all of them speaking in remarkably indiscreet ways about the prince and the young woman on his arm.

"The king is giving him away to the merfolk," one said.

"Will their children have *gills*?"

"Looks like she's got legs to me." A crude chuckle. "And *nice ones*, I'd wager."

"Good morning, your highness," several greeted, bowing respectfully, then they eyed Celine and offered her a small courtesy bow, which she returned.

Nearby stalls were filled with smoked meats, raw goods, livestock, bundled herbs and mixtures in glass jars. There was so much to take in as Owen led her through the crowd toward a covered table of herbs and tinctures below a wooden sign reading *Smithson Apothecary & Tea*. The man waiting there was tall, lithe, and with an otherworldly beauty in the symmetry of his face. And, just as with Owen, she sensed the magic coming from him. One of the godborn?

Between them was the common thread of magic that pulled, and as she and Owen neared him, she could better see the iridescence in his hazel eyes. He blinked once, with intent, telling her without words that he understood what she recognized within him.

"Smithson," Owen said. "I trust you've been well."

"I have, your highness. How is your father?"

"Not good," he said. "Thank you for helping to prepare the medicine from the sea. It helped him have some peaceful rest."

Celine studied the apothecary and his wares, his skill evident in the products on the table.

"This is Celine," Owen said. "She helped me farm those ingredients for the medicine."

"Ah." Smithson smiled, bowing his head. "A pleasure to meet you, Celine of the merfolk. I hope your transition to land has been smooth."

She smiled, veering away from the truth. "It has been, thank you."

"I'm giving her a tour of the market," Owen said. "And I wanted to thank you for your help."

"Of course, your highness. And welcome, my lady." Smithson bowed respectfully. "I hope you enjoy your time with us. Our shop is actually just there." He gestured to his left, down the stretch of the path leading into town. "Just around the corner. We have some remarkable tea blends that you may enjoy. All our ingredients are naturally sourced, even from the sea itself."

"I should like to visit soon." All of this *decorum* was exhausting. Humans spent so much time making a show of politeness. But Smithson's kindness seemed genuine, and she was relieved to know another person of magic. "It was lovely to meet you."

"Likewise, my lady."

How many other magic folk lived in Estilon, unknown and undetected? How much did King Rolf know about his kingdom, where even a magicborn in hiding could run a business in his own kingdom?

Owen had said that he didn't condone the war, that he wanted to end the bloodshed. Perhaps he would keep his word and work to repair what had been broken for so long.

"Smithson is my teacher," Owen whispered, leaning close to her. "I'm sure you could sense that he isn't human."

"I did." She looked up, caught by the amusement framing Owen's eyes and mouth. It made her smile warily. "What?"

"I didn't expect to feel this way," he whispered. "I can share this part of myself with you without hesitation. The freedom, it's—it's like I can breathe."

She brought her other hand to his arm, caught by their unexpected camaraderie. Future husband and wife, as decreed by their kings, but friends? If so, what an expected grace to be gifted by the powers that be.

"He is a favorite of my mother's," Owen said of Smithson. "He even sends her new blends of tea to try. Upon her word, a blend will either go to market or be erased from memory. Such has been their friendship for as long as I can remember."

"He must be very skilled," Celine said, eyeing the vendors as they passed. Some looked at her with curiosity, others with malice.

"It's just here," Owen said, signaling one of the farther stalls. "The peach crumble that will change your entire world."

"My entire world *has* changed," she said with a nervous laugh, but she stopped as she caught the luxurious fragrance from the baker's stall. Her lips parted in wonder. "That smell..."

"It's good, isn't it?" Owen extended a hand to the young woman at the stall. "Four peach crumbles, please."

The young woman lifted four palm-sized cups made of paper, the vessels holding golden brown confections with slices of peaches and sugary crumble adorning the tops. Owen passed one each to Tyrion and Liam before giving the third to Celine. "Tell me this isn't the best thing you've ever tasted."

She took a tentative bite, breathing in the fragrance before her mouth finally tasted it. She closed her eyes, the tanginess of peaches and mingling with the creamy sweetness of the soft cake, and the crumble topping perfected the texture.

"You've had nothing like it, have you?"

"Never, your highness." Celine blinked up at him. "This is delicious."

Owen, satisfied, took a large bite of his portion. He thanked the young woman at the stall before leading Celine further into the market, where vendors sold richly dyed fabrics, curated perfumes, and raw textiles.

"Your highness," one female perfume vendor greeted with a wave.

She was a middle-aged human with graying hair and kind eyes. Her smile was broad as she looked from Owen to Celine. "A sample for your highness and his betrothed. Made from the finest roses in Estilon."

The woman, meeting Celine's gaze, gave a subtle wink before Owen moved forward to the next stall.

Owen accepted the small bottle, labeled Rose Oil with the name *Estelle's Fine Perfumes and Scents,* handwritten in fine letters. He passed the bottle to Celine. "Thank you. That is very kind."

Further on, they reached stalls adorned with richly dyed fabrics and clothes sewn with impressive skill. Celine reached a hand toward a brilliant purple bundle, the fabric some of the softest she'd ever touched. "There is so much here."

"And there's more." Prince Owen smiled, lips closed, and glanced up to the parapets. "Tell me, Celine. Are you afraid of heights?"

Heights? She imagined the tall cliffs to the north, only, this time, she tried picturing the world from the grassy top of its very tall wall, rather than from the sea. "I'm not sure."

Eyes alight, he grinned. "I have something to show you."

Behind her, she caught Liam and Tyrion sharing a look. What it meant, she couldn't tell, except for the subtle tightening within her stomach.

Onward and, apparently, upward.

CHAPTER 11

Prince Owen led Celine to a door in the wall that surrounded the castle.

"This will take us to the top," he said, holding the door open for her. "You can see for miles from up there."

Celine entered and stepped up carefully, the passage narrow enough for only one person to ascend comfortably. In a frenzied situation, she imagined the trouble the guards would have ascending or descending to face a threat or crisis. Did they practice running single-file? Or did they let urgency and adrenaline move them?

The wooden steps creaked beneath her weight. The toe of her boot caught the hem of her skirt as she stepped up, propelling her forward into the stairs.

"Whoa!" Owen's hands and arms were quick, taking hold of her arm and waist and pulling her upright. He stepped up quickly, balancing her against his chest, steadying them both in the narrow passage. His hand was firm at her side. "Are you alright?"

Breathing quickly, they stared, eyes wide and lips slightly parted. Celine held tight to Owen's arm, her other hand gripping his shirt, his muscles strong and taut as they held her steady. Even as his body was strong, his eyes were gentle, studying her face for any sign of pain or discomfort.

"Yes," she said quickly, a flush burning her cheeks. Her hold loosened on his arm and shirt, but he didn't let her go. Not yet. With a light laugh, she added, "A dress and boots are strange when you're used to water and scales."

"Would you be more comfortable back at the castle?"

"No, your highness." Celine took one tentative step up, wanting to meet the challenge of experiencing *heights*. "If I may be straightforward once more, I am determined to see this remarkable view."

"I would ask that you remain straightforward with me, Celine, at every opportunity."

The sparkle in his eyes held her gaze as she slipped her hand into the crook of his elbow. She gathered up her skirts with her free hand. Movement, though tight in the narrow space, was easier now, as Owen's steadiness reassured her every step.

Soon, after two short sets of stairs joined by a landing, the pair reached the top of the castle wall. The stone portal was without a door, bathing them in sunshine. Celine didn't blink as she took in the landscape outside of the castle, the reaches of the kingdom she'd never seen before. To the right, she glimpsed the golden sand of the shore, but the rest of the expansive landscape was new—trees, clouds, rolling hills, and the mountain range reaching far in the distance.

"It's incredible." Things Celine had only read about were finally shown. "I never imagined it would look like this."

"Look like what?"

"Descriptions in books can certainly paint a picture, but you have to have seen the image first, I think." She looked from left to right, scanning the horizon, taking everything in. "I only had a partial view from the sea. Nothing like this."

He was quiet, allowing her to take everything in. His eyes augmented the thrill of the moment, and she enjoyed the touch of his eyes.

"Over there is the sawmill." He pointed ahead, a bit to the right, where the rolling hills curve into trees.

He went on. "And further down are farmlands. Dozens of farmers with fields full of crops and livestock. The kingdom is thriving, thanks to them."

Celine smiled to herself, a part of her enjoying how much Owen took pride in his people. If only Dathan would speak with such reverence.

"Beyond is Estilon Forest." He pointed toward a thick gathering of green-topped trees. "Not a very exciting name, I admit." He leaned against the parapet with his torso toward her, a casual stance that didn't detract from the intensity of his gaze. "What do the merfolk call the sea?"

"Your highness?"

"We call it the Sea of Kings. Again, not very exciting. And we've titled the docks Estilon Harbor. Pretty on-the-nose."

Celine touched her nose, confused, prompting Owen to smile.

"The merfolk don't have a special name for the sea?"

"No." No name ever crossed her path, at least. "The sea is vast, far more and far greater than any creature living within or without."

"Such devotion. Are you a worshiper of Shanna?"

"The merfolk were created by Shanna," she said, "but we aren't exclusive in our worship. We embrace the pantheon as one. Each goddess complements another—earth, fire, water, sky."

"Even death and chaos?"

It was Celine's turn, mischief toying with her features. "Have you ever seen an anglerfish?"

Owen burst out laughing. Even Tyrion and Liam chuckled, doing their best to maintain their composure as they stood guard. Celine nurtured the swelling pride within her core until a scream cut through the air with a knife-edge sharper than her dagger. They all turned toward the sound, scanning what they could see to determine its source.

"There." Celine pointed toward a village in the distance where humans were running, frantic. More screams peeled through the air. "What's happening?"

One human wore clothes different from the others–a black shirt, dark brown leather trousers, and a white belt around his waist. "Raiders," Owen said. "By the gods."

"Raiders?"

"Mercenaries?" Tyrion asked, his body language having shifted instantly from *peace* to *war*. "Hired by Jesper, perhaps?"

Humans killing other humans. The magic folk may not have needed to lift a finger in this war if they saw fit to destroy themselves.

Owen turned quickly, going for the stairs and jogging down them. Celine held her skirt away from her feet, trying to keep up.

"I'll have my men escort you to your room," Owen said, reaching the foot of the stairs and continuing through the hallway within the wall of the castle. There, near to the stairs, was a small room filled with armor and weapons.

Instead of waiting to be shown outside, Celine followed him. "I'm coming with you."

He looked at her as though she'd grown a third eye. "I beg your pardon?"

"You're at war with Sudor," she said. "And you've agreed to undergo marriage to a mermaid to seal an accord with the merfolk kingdom. The merfolk kingdom can help." She gestured to herself. "You've seen me fight. Having me with you would not be a detriment."

He read her face, his refusal forming his lips. But, surprising those present, he said, "Alright, warrior maiden. You help the women and children. Keep them and yourself out of danger."

"Your highness," Tyrion said, stepping forward. "Your armor is with the smithy."

"I'll wear what's here." He already slipped into a padded shirt, hastily tying what he could at the shoulders. Celine, understanding, helped him fasten as Liam fetched him a mail shirt.

With the ties finished, she looked around at the weapons neatly organized on the wall. Several were recognizable, identical matches found in a ship's wreckage. Prince Owen reached for a shield and short sword, but her eyes found the collection of daggers, all of them nearly identical in make and style. Summoning her own would likely cause a stir among already panicked people, so she pulled two off the wall and took up the corresponding belt, fastening it to her waist. Slipping the sheathed blades into the holding straps, she looked at Prince Owen, ready.

"You know your way around weapons," Liam said, his brow furrowed.

"Daggers are a favorite." She eyed each of them, stopping at Owen. "Ready?"

He nodded. "Let's go."

She followed Owen out, turning to follow the wall further into the castle grounds. Liam jogged behind Celine as Tyrion left to rally more forces.

"The stables are just here." Owen looked ahead, jogging faster. "The horses won't be ready."

But Liam was sure. "We'll work fast, your highness."

Horses. Celine hadn't expected riding a large animal. She'd seen the knights traveling back and forth on the main road, their control and balance impressive. But Celine, with this new body, was anything but controlled and balanced.

She heard whinnying as they ran close, the stableman blanching at the sight of the prince's fast approach.

"Raiders," Prince Owen said succinctly. "Are two horses ready to ride?"

"Absolutely, your highness." The stableman worked fast, pulling a beautiful brown mare up to Owen. She was massive and broad, her muscles flexing beneath a shimmering coat. "Matilda's just had a brushing, sir."

"There's a good girl." Owen smoothed the mare's long nose, kissing her face before helping the stableman ready the horse and strap on a saddle. Glancing over his shoulder at Celine, he said, "I assume you don't have any experience."

"None whatsoever."

"Here." Once the saddle was ready, Owen guided her. "Put your left foot in the stirrup and swing your right leg over."

"Your highness." The stableman looked scandalized. "Shouldn't she ride side-saddle?"

"We're already taking too much time, as it is." He waited, ready to help Celine climb into the horse. "Once you're seated, I will climb up and sit behind you."

"Will Matilda be alright?"

"She's a warrior maiden, too."

Celine followed Owen's directions implicitly, stepping into the stirrup and hoisting herself up. He gripped her sides, his broad hands curved at her waist, helping her up without issue. Her right leg cleared Matilda's back with a burning flare of pain, but Celine growled through it, finding her seat in the saddle. Owen climbed up behind her, reins in his hand, his arms tightening slightly against her sides to hold her in place.

"If you feel you're about to fall," he said into her ear, "hold on to me."

Then the pair thundered down the path toward the city gate.

CHAPTER 12

Celine's heart pounded in her chest as she rode, the thrill of speed surging the energy in her blood. Only hours into her human form, and she experienced such thrill and adventure that had only existed within ink and paper.

The wind combed through her hair with the wild affection she expected from nature, her torso secure in Owen's hold as he steered his horse and urged her faster.

"Are you alright?" Owen asked.

"Yes."

And she was, save for the aching in her hips and legs. But the moment's urgency and the adrenaline in her veins pushed that aside.

The village was far on foot, but Matilda's speed made the distance feel small. The cries of children opposed the sinister laughter of men, which joined with the screams and whimpering of women.

In the time it had taken them to reach the village, someone had set the fire to a home, smoke billowing out of every door and window.

"There." Owen pointed toward a field of grain untouched by the raiders. "Take the women and children there. As many as you can."

"Yes, your highness."

Reaching the edge of the village, stopping at the nearest house,

Owen dismounted and helped Celine down. But her legs failed her as she landed, causing her to buckle among the dust and dirt. Owen called for her immediately.

"I'm alright," she said, her tone urgent. "*Go.*"

He took up sword and shield and ran for the nearest sound of distress. Thunderous hoofbeats behind her signaled the coming of more men.

As Celine stood, she pulled both daggers free from the belt, the blades glistening in the sunlight. While this human body was not her own, and while she was not fighting in water, at least the weight and grip of the daggers were familiar.

Someone cried in one of the nearby houses, the backyard filled with logs, a stump and ax for chopping wood, and an empty wheelbarrow. Celine went to the door and tried the locked handle. Inside, someone screamed.

Grimacing, she kicked against the door twice before the wood splintered and the hinges squealed, the door swinging in. One raider stood in front of an old woman with two young boys tucked beneath her arms. With the clatter of the breaking door, the raider turned, his perplexed look shifting to enjoyment.

"A lovely doe wanders in." His raspy voice sent shivers down her back.

"Leave or die." She stood defensively, the daggers ready.

"Are you prepared to kill, my *deer*?" He laughed at the joke. "I won't kill you." He edged closer. "I'll make sure you *live*."

Celine worked fast, trusting her body. He'd tried to dodge, but she was faster, her merfolk swiftness still very much a part of her, even in this new shell. She shoved the first blade into his gut and the second into his side, spinning on the balls of her feet to move behind him and keep his hands from reaching her. But her ankle didn't accommodate the spin, buckling beneath her and bringing her to the wood floor. The raider followed, landing on top of her.

The smell of blood was different out of the water, still rich in copper and iron but salty on its own, a sickly sweetness that toyed cruelly with her stomach.

"Go!" she shouted to the woman and children, pushing the man off of her. "Go to the field!"

But the woman stayed, offering her aged hands to help Celine push the dead raider off of her.

"Get to the field," Celine repeated. "Prince Owen and his knights are here. Get to safety."

The woman hobbled, one of her legs lame, as the boys rallied around her. "Come on, Gran!"

"Use the barrow, Gran." One boy ran out and pushed the wheelbarrow to the door.

"Oh, that's brilliant," Celine complimented, trying not to breathe too deeply. The smell of blood and sweat was all over her.

Sheathing her daggers, Celine helped the old woman settle in as the boys heaved her forward. Celine hurried around the front to reach the next house, glancing at Owen fighting alongside his men, their mail and swords glistening in the sunlight as the red flame of their tabards danced with the black shirts of the raiders.

A hand pulled her back, fingers rough in her hair, and she slammed against the ground hard. The raider didn't say a word as he brought a sword to her throat, his look deadly.

"Stay quiet now," he said, his voice low, pressing a dirty finger to his lips. "Those daggers will fetch a pretty price and save your life."

"Yes, they will."

She didn't hesitate, pulling one free and shoving it into his arm. He howled, the edge of his sword grazing her throat near her shoulder, but she let the stinging pain fuel her anger as she righted herself and stabbed him in the chest. With a kick, she sent his body to the ground as she moved to the next house.

Empty, and so was the next one. But a mother and her three children huddled behind their wagon, sobbing next to the body of a lifeless man.

"Get to the field," Celine said. "We have to go now."

The two littlest ones filled the woman's arms, and the third reached up for Celine. Mirroring the mother holding her children, Celine lifted the child up. "We have to hurry."

They ran, the children crying, as a raider charged them, blade high in the air. But an arrow shot through his neck, spraying blood on the mother and one of her children. They screamed, but they didn't stop running.

Celine looked to the source of the shot and found Tyrion perched on the roof of one house. He nodded at Celine once before taking aim at the next raider.

Reaching the field, Celine found the old woman and two boys. "If something happens," she said, setting the child down, *"run."*

More voices and more screams, the panicked sounds of livestock pulling her attention. Several villagers were in a large barn, trying to calm the animals as the building next door burned.

And there, in the heart of the village, Owen fought unarmed, the raider beating the seven hells out of his upraised shield. Owen's sword lay in the dust several feet away.

Celine ran, her body hating every second, but the world slowed as she watched a figure appear, his own dagger ready to stab Owen in the back. His body moved differently than the other raiders, more precise, more practiced in stealth and grace.

Celine's voice froze in her throat, but her hand moved of its own accord. She was so far from home, so far from her own body, but her hand knew its work when a dagger's handle was in its grip. The weapon sailed through the air, blade turning over hilt, flying straight for the raider who moved with the elegance of an assassin.

The blade met its mark in the man's back. He wheezed a groaned before his knees buckled and his body fell.

Owen turned, awestruck, his eyes finding Celine before his target landed a hard blow against his shoulder. He wailed, almost falling to one knee, but he brought the shield up as his attacker recoiled, shoving him hard until he stumbled back. Then another arrow, compliments of Tyrion's bow, pierced through the raider's chest, killing him instantly.

Several villagers were already fleeing toward the field, likely seeing the others gathered there. The few remaining raiders tried to run, but they didn't get far. The knights of Estilon dispatched them quickly, their swords and tabards bloody.

Blood and sweat all around her, manure and livestock close by in the barn…

Celine swallowed hard, tasting bile, the overwhelming stench covering her face like a hot, suffocating mask. She pulled the dagger from the man's back, his body latching sickeningly as his muscles resisted.

Owen stared, breathless, his crystalline eyes bright beneath the sun. "You saved my life."

Celine ran from him, her stomach already lurching, and she fell to her knees as she heaved. She gathered her hair with one hand, heaving once more before the tide ebbed. She wiped her mouth, desperate for something to drink, her throat burning as she gulped to breathe.

"Taking a life is no small thing," he said from behind her, "even in defense of yourself or someone else. I'm sorry."

Shame soured her already sickened stomach. This wasn't the first human life she'd taken during her survival in the sea against greedy fishermen, but she'd never smelled death before.

"I'm alright." She composed herself, wiping her mouth again. "Thank you."

He helped her to her feet, and she kicked dirt and dust over her sick as Owen shouted commands to help the villagers.

"We'll have food and medical supplies brought from the castle," Owen said to one of his guardsmen. "They will need help burying their dead and repairing their homes."

The men were quick to follow Owen's orders as villagers returned from the field, their hands and voices reaching out to their prince in gratitude.

"Thank you, Prince Owen."

"Thank you, your highness."

As he received each of them, Celine knelt beside the assassin and turned him over. There was nothing unusual about his clothing, matching the other raiders in style and color. She searched him without ceremony, finding a silver necklace around his neck with a charm–a crescent moon crossed with a dagger–and a letter in his pocket, along with a small piece of gorgeous blue-green crystal.

"Arcana crystal?" But the color was too different. Yet, cradling it in her fingers, power pulsed from it. A magical heartbeat. *Power*, living and thriving in a delicate, iridescent shell.

She laid the crystal on the assassin's still chest and read the letter:

"Raid the village. Owen will show. Make sure he doesn't return home."

Owen approached, his arm looped through the holds of his shield as he wiped the blade of his sword with his tabard.

"I found these." Celine yanked the necklace from the dead man's neck and showed it to him, along with the letter. "He was sent specifically for you."

"Jesper. I'm sure of it." He sheathed his sword and held the necklace by its chain, the sun catching its charm. "He prides himself in his network of spies."

"And this." Celine touched the crystal again, its power reaching her fingers before the made contact. "Have you ever seen this before?"

The lines on Owen's face smoothed. He dropped the necklace into her palm and took the crystal between his fingers. "By the gods, how does he have that?"

"What is it?"

"It's like our precious arcana crystal." Owen kept his voice low, his crystalline eyes bright as they stared into hers. "Apparently, it's mined from the earth, and there are rumors that Sudor has one of the richest mines in Sheraton."

"There's more of it?"

"Not here, but yes." With a hint of mischief, he closed his fingers around the crystal. "I'll let you keep it if you teach me magic."

Alarmed, she looked around them for any ears listening in. "Your highness."

He grinned, inching closer. "I could learn a lot from you."

Celine didn't expect to find it difficult to look away, the brightness and symmetry of his face pleasing. She let the necklace dangle, the charm oscillating from its chain. "You're in a splendid mood for someone who's just survived an assassin."

Tyrion and Liam approached, eyes alighting to the note and necklace.

"What's that?" Liam asked, watching the charm spin while it dangled from Celine's fingers.

"Moonblade," Owen said.

Celine looked at each of them. "What is Moonblade?"

"A guild of spies and assassins. Itinerant. Ruthless, yet they supposedly live by a code amongst themselves." Owen turned the letter over, seeing that the reverse sign held no other markings. "Had he been waiting long before my arrival?"

"How did he know you would help this village?" she asked. "Isn't that expecting a lot from the prince to come here, personally?"

"In some kingdoms, perhaps," he said, "but I have a bit of a reputation."

"*A bit of a reputation*," Tyrion repeated with a scoff. "If there's a fight in Estilon, Owen's out to meet it head-on."

"I think it's brave," Liam said.

"It's foolish." Tyrion shook his head. "The prince doesn't have to show up to every skirmish. That's what his knights are for."

"I don't send my men where I wouldn't go, myself."

"You're the heir to this kingdom," Celine said, only to retreat as soon as the words left her mouth. "Forgive my impertinence, your highness, but the line ends with you."

"So, I should do what? Stay in my chambers all tucked in, safe and sound, while the world folds in around me and my people?" He folded the letter and tucked it into a pocket. "My father and Graham will need to know about this as soon as possible."

With his knights helping the villagers pick up the pieces of their lives, Owen readied his horse and waited for Celine to mount first. As she climbed, she patted Matilda's neck, lamenting the extra weight on the mare's back. She bent down to her and said, "I will have to learn to ride on my own, it seems. Thank you for carrying me."

Owen climbed up and urged Matilda on, her movements easy despite carrying two.

"You fight well on land and in the sea," Owen said, leaning close, his breath brushing through her hair around her face and neck. "I'm impressed."

She couldn't hide the smile or the blooming flush on her cheeks. "You as well, your highness."

CHAPTER 13

Upon their return, Owen and Celine brought the horses to the stables with Liam and Tyrion, the four of them striding back to the castle.

"You two should clean up before your evening watch," Owen said. "I'll see Lady Celine to her chambers."

Lady Celine. Such a human title. But Celine enjoyed it as Owen's voice gave it shape.

"Our orders are to remain with you, sire," Liam said.

"There are a dozen other knights at every inch of the castle," Owen said, gesturing vaguely around them to those in chain mail and red tabards circulating around Estilon Castle. "I'll be fine."

"You stay with the Prince," Tyrion said to Liam, "and I'll bathe first. Then we can switch."

"Alright," Liam agreed.

But Tyrion blinked at him, confused, which then made Celine confused.

"Alright?" Tyrion echoed. "*Alright*?" He tilted his head to look down at Liam, his brow furrowed. "Are you well, young knight? You hate it when I bathe first."

"Because you take an hour and leave everyone else to clean up your dirty water." Liam grimaced at the thought. "But taking turns is a good idea."

Owen looked between them, the conversation unfolding as though he wasn't there. "Have I no say in this, as your prince?"

"No," Liam and Tyrion said together. Tyrion added, "King's orders, I'm afraid."

Tyrion didn't let up in his suspicious look of Liam, but he conceded. "Alright. I'll go first, and I'll even clean up after myself. You stay with Owen and Lady Celine until I've finished."

Tyrion left them, glancing over his shoulder back at them twice more before fully committing to his walk toward the barracks.

"I'd like to speak with my father about what's happened," Owen said, looking from Celine to Liam. "Then we'll each return to our chambers."

Liam stepped closer to Celine, hands clasped behind him. "You fight well, my lady. I didn't expect a merfolk to be so well practiced with daggers."

"Thank you," she said, pleased. "Though my own daggers are more familiar, these served me well."

"And served *me* well," Owen said. "I'm quite grateful for your practiced skill, my lady."

Owen led Celine up the stairs and, this time, stepped to the right, down a different corridor that opened to a large sitting room before wide, bare windows and three closed wooden doors, two near each other and one off to itself. He walked the length of the room without stopping, Celine at his heels, going to the leftmost door, nearest to them.

"Where are we going?" she asked.

"My father spends his days in his solar," Owen said. "Stubbornly staying out of bed. He needs to—"

Glass shattered. "I don't *care* what it takes!"

"Rolf, you have to stop this!"

Graham? Arguing with the king?

The three froze, listening, staring at the closed wooden door to their left.

"Your sickness is taking over, brother," Graham said. "Your stubbornness is making it worse."

"My *stubbornness* is what's keeping Sudor from sweeping over Estilon like a storm!" Something wooden clattered to the floor. "And they're mining this special new mineral? Something rare and extravagant that will make Jesper and Sudor beyond rich?" She heard Rolf's growl through the closed door. He coughed furiously. "I want that bastard's head on a pike! I want him *dead*!"

Rolf's coughs were unending, and Celine grimaced at the sounds of him struggling to drink.

"Damn it all, Graham. Just get me to my room."

The three hurried around, hiding behind a thick wooden pillar as Graham emerged, holding Rolf's arm across his shoulders.

"I will see to everything, brother," Graham said. "And Owen—"

"Tell Owen nothing." At this, Celine's eyes darted to the prince's face, reading the lines on his brow that controlled the presence of shock. "He is about to be married. Let's wait to tell him how Estilon will fail beneath the weight of Sudor's new export once he secures allegiance with the merfolk."

The two shuffled out of sight, and Owen waited the span of two breaths before speaking. "I already know we're economically weak. How could I not, with the way our people struggle? What can be expected when we're fighting two wars?"

"Which should, hopefully, only be one now," Celine said. "But I can't imagine what financial gain he expects from our marriage. Is the wealth of the merfolk the same as that of humans?"

"Gems and pearls," Owen said. "And apparently arcana crystal."

Dathan's demands echoed ominously in her mind. The merking wouldn't honor any human agreement, but with Celine in Owen's corner, with her plan's culmination coming closer, maybe...

"We should get cleaned up," he said, looking down at her. "I'm sure you would like to rest."

By the gods, yes. "I appreciate that, your highness. This new body is a lot to get used to."

He took her hand and placed it in the crook of his arm. They walked toward the corridor of rooms at a steady pace, which allowed Owen to fully notice how Celine limped slightly with every step.

"You *are* injured," he said.

"No, your highness." She lifted her skirt to show the boots. "These things pinch my—what are they?"

"Toes?" He managed a small smile. "I'll see to some well-fitting boots."

"I'd much rather go without them, altogether. Feeling the floor as I walk is much more reassuring."

"Something you and I have in common."

Celine felt Liam's silent presence behind them as they continued to her side of the castle, the side she shared with Owen.

At her door, Owen paused. "Let the maids know when you're hungry, and they'll have food brought up from the kitchen." He pointed to a door down the hall, the one she first entered upon her arrival. "I'll be there, if you need anything."

"Something to read?" she asked with a quiet laugh. "Do you have books here?"

His expression lightened as he grinned. "We have a *library*."

She nearly gasped at the notion–a room solely devoted to books, something she'd longed to see with her own eyes. "A *library*?"

Beaming, he said, "I can't wait to show you. But have Miss Helen help you with something to wear. And reassure her that she will have replacement clothes as fast as our tailor can make them."

Owen moved the short distance to his room with Liam and, with one final look at her, he slipped inside. Liam remained outside, one hand clasping the opposite wrist, and nodded to her once. He would remain there, as he'd said to Tyrion, and wait.

Celine opened her door and gasped, staring at the maid already inside. But, where Celine was startled by an unexpected presence, the maid was startled by the amount of blood that stained Celine's clothes.

"Gracious, miss!" The maid, who'd been with her at breakfast, pressed a hand to her heaving bosom. "By the gods, what's happened?"

Celine looked down at herself again, ashamed. "There was a raid at a nearby village."

"I'll fetch Miss Helen, then, miss," she said, going to the door with hurried steps. "That was one of her favorite dresses."

Of course it was. Her muscles tightening as dread washed through her. *Of course it was.*

"Heavens above." Miss Helen stared at the bloodstained state of the dress.

"Please," Celine said, trying to remove the garment with little success until Helen's hands reached for the fastening behind Celine's neck. "Please, what can I do?"

"Remove the infernal thing first."

Helen grumbled quietly, and Celine couldn't make out what she was saying. She wasn't sure she wanted to. She helped Celine further undress and hung the soiled garment over her arm. "I'll have another dress brought, my lady."

"I'm sorry, Miss Helen."

"A raid, you said?" Miss Helen shook her head. "That was no place for a lady. I'm surprised Prince Owen agreed."

Celine said nothing, keeping her defense to herself.

"I'll see to some new clothes at once, my lady."

Once Helen left, Celine waited, sitting on the edge of her bed in her small clothes, grateful that the bloodstains hadn't soaked beyond the dress. She pulled off those wretched boots, stretching and flexing her feet and toes as she reclined back onto the bed, closing her eyes.

Exhaustion finally reached her as her body remembered the fights and the lives she'd taken. Those raiders had tried to turn those villagers into victims, burning and terrorizing and killing. Celine wasn't new to defending herself and others, but familiarity didn't make the aftermath any easier.

Two sharp knocks preceded her chamber door opening, a lady's maid bowing as she hastily announced, "Her majesty, the Queen."

The lady's maid stepped aside as Queen Adella entered. Tall, with a frame that showed the opposite of fragility, Queen Adella's presence was simultaneously impressive and intimidating, her earth brown hair pulled tight, emphasizing the angles of her ageless face. This was not the same woman she'd met in the Great Hall—the Queen of Estilon, caring for her ailing husband. This was Owen's mother, her look sharp and her gaze fierce.

But what was the most impressive was the sense of awareness that tingled the back of Celine's neck. She was in the presence of something not altogether human.

Queen Adella had magic, and narrowed her eyes at Celine. How could Celine not notice her power before? Was it distance? A magical shield?

Behind the queen stepped in another woman, early in middle age with a kind smile.

"Our tailor, Lady Cynthia," Queen Adella announced. "She needs to measure you. She won't take long."

"Hello, my lady," the tailor said with a small bow. "Forgive the intrusion."

"It's no intrusion," Celine said quickly beneath the pressure of the queen's gaze.

The tailor instructed Celine to stand and pose as she used a ribbon marked with numbers to assess Celine's height and roundness. She finished by noting the length of Celine's legs and arms.

"I've been instructed to create three dresses for you, my lady," Lady Cynthia said.

"What about trousers?" Celine smiled weakly, her hopes thin.

"You mean like what you were found in?" the queen asked, an eyebrow lifted.

"These clothes are nice," Celine said, cowering a bit, "but they're hard to move freely in."

"I'm sure," Queen Adella said. "As you wish. Dresses and trousers, then."

Cynthia took one more measurement down the inside of Celine's legs before she bowed to exit. "I will get started right away, your majesty."

"Thank you, Cynthia."

After the tailor left, the queen remained silent as she side-glanced toward the lady's maid lingering by the door.

"Thank you," the queen said to her. "You may wait outside."

"Yes, your majesty." With a hastened curtsy, the maid left the room.

The queen, without a word, sat down in one of the dining room chairs, her eyes finding the iron tools by the fireplace. "I apologize that they haven't removed those yet." Blinking once, her eyes settling on Celine, she said, "You may ask me anything you wish."

What?

"For example," Queen Adella said, "you may be curious about my own heritage, which you've likely sensed."

Celine nodded. "You're elven?" It was purely a guess, after meeting the apothecary in the market.

"Earthborn. Fae. Elven. Whichever term suits you. My husband often remarks about the human need to label things." Her level expression carried within it a warning. "This is a truth only you know."

"And Owen?"

The queen waited the span of three heartbeats before she shook her head. "He doesn't know."

"He is half earthborn, half human," Celine said, "raised under a father waging war against magic folk."

"The deal was precise," the queen said, the warning in her voice returning. "Both in planning and in timing."

Celine kept further questions down that thread to herself. "Why did you marry King Rolf?"

"We have our reasons." *We* being *the earthborn*. So their marriage must have been arranged, just like Celine's to Owen. "My question to you: Why did the merfolk agree to this insane proposal?" But before Celine could answer, the queen added, "Is my son in danger?"

"Yes, your majesty. I think someone tried to kill him today."

"Was that someone you?"

Celine's danger sense flared, caught in the grip of the queen's stare. "No. I swear it."

"Was he supposed to find you?"

Celine flinched. She hadn't expected that, though she probably should have. "Your majesty?"

The queen spoke quickly, her tone and behavior disarming. "Your arrival was earlier than agreed upon. You were in a pitiable state, and Owen was quite concerned. Clever, catching him in a way so that his guard was lowered. So, I will ask you again: Was he supposed–" she repeated more slowly, her tone predatory. "–to find you?"

Celine shook her head, fear chilling her insides. "No, your majesty. I didn't expect him to." She shuddered to take a breath, feeling as though what little clothing she wore had tightened itself around her. She couldn't deny the sudden urge to tell Queen Adella everything. "This new body came with a lot of pain. I wasn't given any instruction beyond *change*, and I was changed suddenly."

"You *were changed*?"

"King Dathan." Celine swallowed, the nervous gesture painful. "It was sudden."

The queen's lips flinched in a snarl, but she held her composure. "I'm not sure anyone expected this to actually come to fruition."

"The marriage?" Celine was confused. Dathan was quite specific. "What *was* expected, your majesty?"

The queen studied Celine for several moments, the severity of her look lessening as she did. "My husband viewed the arrangement between your people as an insult. He'd hoped to rile up your king to the point that he would become reckless, giving my husband an edge in this stupid war."

Celine didn't want to tell the queen the whole truth in all its darkness, but the words poured out of her mouth before her mind had any reckoning to stop them. The truth was pulled from her, and her heart raced in panic as she spoke. "I was sent here as punishment." She winced, hearing the insult of her own words. "I was accused of being a traitor and was sent here to unite our people, or I would die."

She intentionally left out her additional direction to kill the royals of Estilon and Sudor. Queen Adella would see to Celine's disposal swiftly.

The queen narrowed her eyes. "Traitor?"

"Any who dare tread our waters are risking their lives when they do so. But I—" She looked down at her hands, the queen's piercing gaze seeing through every layer. "I'm not a murderer."

"Dathan sent us a merfolk charged with treachery?"

"He sent his *stepdaughter*, charged with treachery." Taking a fortifying breath, Celine met the queen's gaze. "I think he assumed you would kill me so he wouldn't have to."

"Stepdaughter." The oppression from the queen worsened. "Who are you, child?"

"Celine," she answered, the words coming against her will. "Daughter of Janis and Elynda."

"Janis." Sitting back, Adella released her magic, the oppression leaving Celine breathless. "The former merking." Her gaze didn't waver. "The one Dathan killed."

Celine didn't answer.

"You've been through a lot in your young life," she said quietly, resembling the queen Celine had met in the Great Hall—kind, warm, maternal. "I apologize for the questions."

Interrogation, but Celine kept that thought silent.

"I will have some medicinal tea brought for you. A blend made by Smithson, our apothecary."

"Thank you, your majesty."

"Thank *you*, Celine. For protecting my son." Then, after a beat, she added, "I would like that to continue. For you to protect him. His coronation will be soon, and the threats won't stop coming."

Celine nodded. "Having someone with magic on the throne of Estilon will be a benefit to both our people."

"Indeed."

"May I ask?" Celine paused, gauging the queen's reaction before she continued. "Was it a blood pact with Rolf? Is Owen the promised first born of a deal sealed with magic?"

"He is. Rolf knew what he was getting into regarding the bargain. The deal was also his security in maintaining rule over Estilon."

"What was the deal?"

"Rolf's father wanted power," she said simply. "They were an aristocratic family with no royal connections, and this deal won him a throne in a country formerly war-torn within themselves and with neighboring kingdoms."

"And you've been here ever since?" Celine asked. "Rolf's *father* made the deal?"

"The deal has been set for over fifty years," Adella said. "Rolf's father would have the throne, as would his son, and then the heir would be magicborn. I've been in Estilon ever since Rolf was old enough to marry, and I have been his only wife."

"Fifty years," Celine said. "What of your life before?"

At this, Adella's eyes hardened. "My family understood the price we would pay for a throne under magical rule. But–" Tension spread to her mouth, neck, and shoulders. "I miss them terribly."

"I'm sure they miss you, too." Celine swallowed, her throat painfully dry. "Was he cruel?"

Adella waited the span of a breath before answering. "No. He didn't dare risk any cruelty toward me."

There was a dark gleam in her eye that told Celine everything. Queen Adella was powerful. No human king would cross her and live.

"How do you stand all of this iron?" Celine rubbed her arms, her eyes finding the fireplace tools she hadn't moved yet.

"I've grown used to it," she said. "But it still bothers me. Here."

The queen stood, gathering up her many skirts and taking the iron rack by its top. Slowly, grimacing, she walked it down to the other side of the fireplace. "Is that better?"

"Yes, your majesty." Celine exhaled as relief swept in. The presence of iron was still there but much more tolerable. "Thank you."

Adella stood by the fireplace a moment, thinking. "I would like you to remain by my son's side. You protected him today, and you are magic folk. You will sense more than he will, I think." She paused, something of a pained look tightening around her eyes. "I haven't had the chance to train him with his magic. It's one of my lifelong regrets. Which, I must remind you—" The warning tone returned again. "Should the truth of my son and I come out—"

"I will not say a word." Celine knew the power seated before her. "Magical allegiances are needed now more than ever, your majesty."

"Will you protect my son?"

"Yes, your majesty."

"Because he is of the magic folk?"

"Because he's not his father," Celine said. "Because he's kind."

"That, he is." Satisfied, the queen turned for the door. "I apologize for my intrusion, especially in your state of undress."

Self-consciousness reached Celine then, but the damage had been done. She bowed to the queen and said, "Thank you, your majesty."

Upon the queen's exit, Celine stared at the closed door, her legs and arms and body growing restless. She paced the room, going from bed to window before stopping at the dining table, pulling the daggers from their sheaths and seeing the dried blood still on the blades. Cleaning them would give her a task, and her hands and mind required something to keep them busy.

Prince Owen. *Magicborn*. The half-human son of an earthborn mother in a kingdom that harbored no friendship with magic or magic folk.

Now, keeping Owen alive–that was a far heftier task. At least she had an ally with the queen, as far as the prince was concerned. And such an alliance was already helping her to return to her path, where Dathan and Santus waited.

She grimaced at the blades she cleaned at the idea of them escaping her, getting away with what they'd done.

May he never enjoy a full night's rest until his heart stops beating.

She was careful with the blades, taking them to the wash basin and rinsing them carefully before rubbing the blood free from the metal. She didn't have any fabric, so she used the tips of her fingers, careful around the sharp edges.

This water was fresh, no trace of salt within it. Her mouth remembered the taste of the sea, her skin remembering its coolness, and with an aching in her heart, Celine longed to return home.

"Quinn," Celine whispered into the empty room. "Zander." Her voice quivered, as did her intake of breath. "Are you alright?"

She exhaled, collapsing onto the bed as the energy of nerves slowly receded. She imagined their voices in memory. Zander, giving reports from the patrol. Quinn, reading poetry or a romantic scene from a novel. Celine closed her eyes. She was with them in the water, her body back the way it was. The way it should be.

"I'm safe," she said to them, the friends captured in her memory. "I miss you."

Celine breathed deeply and slowly, the comfort and cushion of the mattress and blanket enough to pull what remained of her consciousness as her body finally relaxed.

CHAPTER 14

What Celine noticed first was the cold. She'd stayed on the blankets rather than beneath them, and even the fireplace did little to stave off the chill of the room. She rose, seeing clothes laid out for her—a white dress, thin and loose. In the wardrobe, doors open, was a new dress hanging.

"Kasindra." She whispered her name in the empty, quiet room, wondering how close to midnight she was.

Celine selected the white dress, the most comfortable and the easiest to put on. The sleeves cinched at her wrists, and the dress draped around her knees. Not exactly warm, but at least she had clothes.

The merfolk medicines and potions were in the drawer of Celine's bedside table. She opened it, the glass tinkling, and pulled out the purple and green vials. She uncorked the green, her shield against the other potion, and dabbed a small amount under her nose. It was oily and smelled of the sea, but there was something *off* about it. Not old or decayed or stagnant, but something *other*. As though it was from a sea that was not her home.

With a quick swish of the purple potion, Celine dotted her neck beneath her ears and her wrists, just as Kasindra had shown her. Potent flowers assailed Celine's senses, even with the green protection doing its work, so she applied more green beneath her nose. With any luck, she would slip out of the castle and all the way to the sea unseen.

But what if someone caught her, despite Kasindra's protection?

"I just wanted some air," Celine said, nodding to herself, trying the fib on for size. "I miss the sea."

It wasn't completely untrue. The best lies always had a touch of truth in them.

Satisfied, she stepped out, the corridor dark and empty. The floorboards groaned and creaked beneath her footsteps as she crept forward, moving around the corner toward the stairs.

Still, no one was in sight. Was Estilon Castle so weakly protected?

But Celine started as someone coughed, clearing his throat. A guard appeared downstairs to her left, coming from a hallway beneath. His steps were measured and routine, body language relaxed, though his hand rested on the pommel of his sheathed sword. She waited for him to pass before continuing down, her toes and the balls of her feet touching down with each step to test her weight. The stairs remained silent, and she passed unheard and unseen as she descended the final stair.

When the guard was gone, she hurried to the main door, careful with its operation. It took strength to push open in the struggle to remain silent, and as soon as she opened it enough to step through, she danced out as though the floor burned her feet. Two guards stood outside, near enough to the door that one glance would catch her. She hurried to the side, eager to slip past without a trace.

So far, no one had seen her, and she followed the exterior wall, staring at the gate where four guards waited on patrol. How had Kasindra described the potion's effects? A *little dazed*? That wasn't enough to risk getting caught.

She backtracked, following the wall further to the side of the castle, seeing an archway glowing with amber firelight. Carefully, she peeked in, hearing voices but seeing no guards. To the left was a passage, and to the right were stairs leading up.

Up the wall, from the inside. And then she could climb down.

But how would she get back in?

She navigated behind the castle to more dirt than grass, with wooden fencing and cross-staved figures wearing clothes filled with straw. Curiosity nearly won until her eyes spotted another archway further on. The portal was dark, and as she edged closer, she listened to the pleasant sound of flowing water.

But her nose scrunched up at the stench. The castle's sewage system? Her next step closer made her recoil, the familiar pull of iron siphoning magic and warmth. The archway housed an iron gate, locked shut.

It was this, or nothing. Unless she asked Owen to take her to meet Kasindra in the middle of the night, there would be no visiting her mentor.

"A key…" She hoped for something hanging nearby in the archway, but there was nothing, not even a shimmer of light on the stone. The reflection of the moon on the flowing pulled her gaze, the undulations almost mesmerizing.

Instinctively, she pulled at the water with her magic, feeling it bend to her will.

The water…

Could it…?

A thin stream of water obeyed her will, rising it to the iron lock that held the gate closed, and filling it. Through the water, Celine touched the mechanism inside. The construction was fascinating and easy to understand. With a satisfying *click*, the lock hung open from its loop. Now, all that remained was her *touching it* to open the gate.

She pulled her gown's sleeve as a makeshift glove, wincing and gritting her teeth through the painful push of the repellant metal. The fabric was too thin, and the iron burned where she held it. Every inch of her body fought against its proximity, and she tried to move her hand faster and faster. She fumbled with the lock, catching it before it dropped, but the metal touched her bare skin. She hissed in pain, hanging it on a horizontal bar in haste to get rid of it, and with careful steps and covered hands, she pushed the gate open and, from the other side, pushed it closed.

Sweat beaded at her hairline, but she made it out. The quiet night outside the castle was peaceful in its organic beauty, a welcome reprieve from the iron hell she just experienced.

She wasted no time hurrying to the sea, her bare feet cold against the grass and sand, sloshing a little as they touched down on the tide-moistened shore.

There, in the distance, Celine could make out her familiar shape. Even in the partial moonlight, Kasindra's lavender hair was a beacon. And as she hurried, Kasindra neared the shore until both were close enough to speak.

"Hello, my dear." Kasindra's voice was a comfort. Celine fought the urge to step into the water and reach for her. "What have you learned, child?"

"The king is suffering from Hell's Touch," she said. "But how did a merfolk toxin reach the king of Estilon?"

"How, indeed." Kasindra grinned. "A blessing, as far as I'm concerned. Poetic justice."

Celine stared at the Sea Witch, her expression almost unreadable. "Did you know?"

"I know a great many things, child."

But even in her smugness, Celine couldn't be sure. *How*? And *who*? Kasindra, herself? But Celine didn't find that likely.

"Anything else?" Kasindra asked.

Celine opened her mouth, but closed it almost immediately. Adella and Owen having magic…

Something internal urged her to keep that information from the Sea Witch. Something dark had touched King Rolf. What would happen to Owen?

Celine had sworn to protect him, even if that meant from Kasindra.

"Getting out isn't easy," Celine said, hugging the blanket tighter around her. The breeze from the sea blew right through the fabric, and she stood, feet soaking in wet sand. "I'm not sure I can meet you every night."

"Do your best, child," Kasindra said. "I will try to come up with something stronger to help you pass by unnoticed."

"The only secret way out that I've found is made of iron." Celine grimaced. "I almost didn't make it."

Kasindra's lavender eyes flashed with a challenge, as though she read Celine's concerns as defiance. "You will meet me tomorrow night, Celine."

Celine blinked, too shocked to speak.

"Now, go back to your prince." Kasindra poised her arms to rest her chin on one hand, that arm supported by the other. "When will you be wed?"

"I'm not sure." Celine shivered, the cold from Kasindra's demeanor competing with the cold of the night. She turned toward Estilon Castle with a staged suggestion of urgency. "I should go."

"Rest well, my dear."

Celine stepped back for the shoreline, watching Kasindra drift back to the depths before disappearing altogether.

Her steps were unsteady in the shifting, wet sand as she moved with trembling legs. In all of her shock and haste, she failed to ask about Quinn and Zander. Guilt soured on her already uneasy stomach.

You will meet me tomorrow night. No room for anything other than Kasindra's will. But Celine understood the costs when she agreed to learn from the Sea Witch. Quinn had warned Celine that Kasindra was using her, but Celine wouldn't deny the opportunity before her. And the dark power she'd learned so far hadn't been wasted or done in vain.

This was the last thought to pass through her mind before something rushed behind her, an arm encircling her waist as the other reached her head, a hand gripping a cloth pressing hard against her nose and mouth. The stench was sharp, assaulting her senses, blurring her vision.

"I don't know your angle," the man said, his voice familiar. "But you're not who I was expecting. What is your merking playing at? What are *you* playing at?"

She tried to turn, tried to glimpse his face, but he held her firm, pressing the fabric harder until she almost couldn't breathe at all.

...She struggled to fight back, to scream, strength fading from her muscles, her body falling limp...

...When she awoke, cold, dark stone surrounded her. Stone and *iron*.

The world spun, the dim space a blur of black, gray, and amber. She blinked slowly, consciousness fleeting until a clang of metal stirred her, a fright jolting adrenaline through her blood.

"She's awake." A man's voice echoed off the stone, far too loud and far too strong. She winced, too weak to bring her hands to her ears. She knew the voice, but her mind couldn't conjure the face to match. Her eyes and her mind were far too bleary to generate anything that made sense, except for how *tired* she was.

The metal clanged again, louder this time. She jolted in shock.

"Open your eyes, Celine."

She forced her awareness to sharpen as she traced the dark stone walls leading to thick iron bars and the man who stood on the other side of them.

Liam, hands clasped behind his back, his expression smug. "You are under arrest on suspicion of subterfuge as a threat against the crowned prince of Estilon."

"*What*?" Celine worked to push herself upright, her head swimming and pounding with pain as she moved. She should have stayed lying down.

From out of view stepped Prince Graham, still wearing his mail and tabard, as was Liam.

"It was upon my order," Graham said.

"Your order?" She blinked through the fog clouding her mind, remembering his glances toward her when he spoke to Owen. "Does the prince know about this?"

"Liam has a right to find you suspicious, young lady," Graham said, ignoring her. "He posed interesting questions that require answers before we move forward."

"Move forward where?" Celine snapped, crawling back away from the iron bars. But the window above her had iron bars, too. Her breath came short as the very air she breathed was poison. "Back to the sea? Or to my execution?"

Dathan may have his way after all. *Damn him.*

"You're stronger than you look," Liam said. "I was worried the sleeping blend wouldn't work."

"We're both full of surprises," Celine said, her tone biting. "I didn't take you to be an asshole, but wonders never cease."

"Watch your tongue," Graham chastised. "You speak to a knight of Estilon."

"Those words mean nothing to me." Celine glared at Graham, her throat tightening. She should use her voice magic and render them useless, blubbering idiots.

Something silver glimmered in Liam's fingers...a thin chain, something round and familiar there...

She reached for her throat, only to find it bare.

"Your necklace?" Liam held it up by its chain, the shell catching the limited firelight from the torches. He watched the pendulum swing of the charm. He didn't know the power that he let dangle from his fingers. "An interesting design. Where did this come from? Sudor? Runa?"

"What does it matter?" She sneered. "You seem determined to find fault with it and with me, no matter what the truth is."

"What does King Jesper hope to get out of this little mission of yours?" Graham asked, ignoring this exchange.

"Who?"

"Don't play coy. Why are you here? What does King Jesper want?"

"Who is King Jes—"

Graham slammed his hand against the bars. Celine hated that she reacted, jolting against the cold stone, legs kicking at the blanket. "Don't lie to me!"

"You're diluted," Celine snarled. "Do you always arrest people simply because one of your knights tells you to?"

"His evidence was sufficient," Graham said. "No one has seen you as merfolk. No one watched you become human. How do we know you are who you claim to be?"

"Owen saw me as merfolk," she screamed. The fringes of her voice magic were so close, so easy to conjure. "Have you bothered asking your own nephew, you stupid man?"

"Sir Liam said that you struck him," Graham said. "That is a punishable offense, all on its own."

Celine couldn't believe what she was hearing. "He's lying. How could I strike him when he had me bound and drugged?"

"Knights of the realm do not lie."

"Oh, of course not." Her sarcasm was biting. "They're sworn to always tell the truth, even if telling a lie benefits them. Especially when the one who hears them is stupid enough to blindly trust them." She glared at Liam, her look deadly, then she moved those fatal eyes to Graham. "And they would never lie to protect one another."

"Mind your tongue, wretch. You speak to a prince of Estilon."

"A prince who wishes to be king?" She lifted an eyebrow. Her bones trembled, eager to escape the reach of iron, but there was nowhere to go. "A prince who would take advantage of his dying brother and his trusting nephew when the promise of power is so close? Perhaps you only pretend to be unintelligent. Perhaps you're more cunning than you look. But you're not the only one who can spin words like gold."

Graham growled, slamming his hands on the bars again. "Spread your lies and see how useless they are."

With a gesture, he led Liam out. Liam, who looked back at her with a sinister smirk as he twirled the necklace around his fingers.

It was Celine's turn to scream. "You cowards! You bastards!"

The iron pulled harder, a parasite made of metal, soaking every ounce of magic within her, drinking of her strength like a leech on her skin.

At least I have magic to take. At this, she almost smiled. *I'm still merfolk, after all.*

The dungeon was quiet and cold. The straw scattered on the floor did little to stave off the chill as she curled there, shivering.

COLD. So cold. And no energy left. But every trace of sleep that her body longed for was desperately out of reach. Her body trembled, keeping her awake, her breathing labored and shallow as the toxic air continued to poison her.

Sweat gathered at her hairline, under arms, against her palms. She laid on her side, one arm tucked against her as the other stretched out across the floor. At the coming of the dawn, they would find her dead, and only then would they know the truth of who she was and what they had done.

"Zander," Celine said with her thoughts, pushing with all of her weakened might that they might hear her. "Quinn. I love you. And I'm sorry."

CHAPTER 15

The stone floor sapped all warmth from her body, but she couldn't shiver. She could barely feel herself breathing. How much longer before the iron would take her? Before its sickness would stop her heart?

Would she go to the Chaos Realm? Likely, after all the dark things she'd done, after the shadows she'd tried to give to Dathan and Santus. All of that, only to end up dying on the floor in a human prison.

I'm sorry, Mother. I'm sorry, Father.
All of that work, wasted.
All of that work, only to follow you to hell.
I tried. I promise, I tried.
I'm so sorry.

With the squeaking of the hinges, the door opened, and in came someone with warm hands that smelled of roses. Celine couldn't open her eyes, the weight of her eyelids far too heavy.

"What is the meaning of this?" A stern female voice, maternal, angry. The queen. Her hands stroked Celine's clammy face. "How dare you imprison her!"

"There were suspicions, your majesty." Graham, his voice much different now than it was when he was interrogating her.

"Suspicions of what?" She snapped her fingers. "Get her to her chambers at once. Call for Geoffrey and Smithson. She needs medical attention immediately."

"I don't understand—"

"The *iron*, you fool," Adella said as hands and arms raised Celine's body. "Can't you see? She's nearly dead. You could have killed her."

"The iron?"

"Because she's *magic folk*." Adella sounded at her wits' end. "She's *exactly* who she said she is, and you've condemned her to iron sickness. She'll die if we don't help her."

"Geoffrey is still with the king, your highness." That voice, so close to her, belonging to the arms that held her…Tyrion?

"Then have Smithson come immediately." Her tone was curt and resolute. "In naught but her nightgown in this damp hellhole. And that *iron*."

The arms carrying her were careful, holding her close to his chest. "You're going to be alright. Her majesty is *furious*."

"Tyrion?"

"Yes, my lady. I've got you."

"Liam—"

"What did she say?" the queen asked.

"It sounded like Liam."

"Liam—" It was a labor to inhale, to give breath to her words. But for this, she made the effort. "Liam is an asshole."

Tyrion chuckled. "She's not far off, your majesty."

"I'll see to his punishment," Adella promised. "Let's get you settled and seen by the physician."

"I'll fetch Smithson personally, your majesty."

"Thank you, Tyrion. I trust you'll be quick."

"Yes, your majesty."

Celine's body was heavy, and consciousness fluttered with her eyelids. Tyrion carried her upstairs, turning the corner toward her room.

"Helen," Adella said. "No one is to come in until I give express permission. Is that clear?"

"Yes, my queen."

Tyrion laid Celine carefully. Her eyelids fluttered open as Adella covered her with thick, soft blankets. But she couldn't keep her eyes open.

Then came the softest, sweetest music that rivaled the power of the merfolk, a beautiful mezzo soprano speaking the language of magic with warm hands touching Celine's face, chest, stomach, legs, and finally, her hands.

"Your majesty—"

"Sh." Adella held Celine's hands in both of hers. "Rest. I must finish the magic quickly."

She continued singing, crossing Celine's arms across her chest and touching her forehead, chin, and each cheekbone. Pain coursed through her muscles, but Celine had no strength or voice to cry out. But Adella's power swept over and *through* her, pulling every ounce of poison from her skin and blood until it was over.

With the final trace of it gone, Adella sang more softly, straightening Celine's arms and tucked them beneath the blanket, the song's end carrying her into peaceful dreams where a man's voice was far in the distance, where the sensation of magic in the room buzzed as she heard him speaking to the queen. Smithson? He had an affectionate tone when speaking to Adella.

Then, at last, she sensed his magic as he came in. *Owen*.

She said his name, reaching up, her arms still beneath the blanket. She felt him move the blanket to free her, his hands gentle against her skin.

"I'm here." He took one of her hands, his warmth unparalleled by any other. He pressed the back of her hand to his cheek. "You're so cold. What have they done to you?"

"The iron in the cells," the queen said. "It almost killed her."

Owen pressed her hand between both of his. "Thirty lashes to them both." His voice was dangerous.

"I've seen to Liam's punishment," Adella said. "I have not done so with Graham."

Owen growled. "I can't believe Liam would do this, that he would act without telling me."

"It is my understanding," the queen went on, "that Graham was convinced by Liam to act. That the nature of Celine's introduction to Estilon was questionable."

"Because she didn't show them her fin first?" His words were knife-edged.

"I believe that's precisely it. Graham said that Liam's primary argument was that Celine is a plant from Jesper. Graham said that Celine claims you two have met while she was in her natural form."

He took a deep breath. Celine's eyelids fluttered, trying to see him. "She saved my life. I was swimming and—"

He hesitated, and she could feel the truth burrow deeper into himself. His mother didn't know that he farmed arcana crystal.

"Shark," Celine muttered.

"Did she say *shark*?" Adella's surprised voice bordered on scolding. "Owen Charles, heir to Estilon, you faced a *shark*?"

Celine would have smiled, would have laughed at such use of his name, but any additional effort beyond remaining conscious was impossible.

"Our meeting was quite special," he said, rubbing small circles in the back of her hand.

"At any rate," the queen said, returning to the topic at hand, "Liam thought this was potential proof." The gentle tinkling sound of metal caught her ears. "Her necklace."

Celine's fingers moved at the word *necklace*. "Please."

"Celine?" She felt Owen lean closer. "Are you alright? Are you in pain?"

"Necklace—" The power to return home, secured within the shell.

"It's safe," Adella said, putting chain and charm into Celine's other hand, curling her fingers around it. "Shall I put it on the bedside table for you?"

Their voices were far away, swept by the wind of the sea, reaching far into the blue-sky horizon, sailing fast into the reaches of nowhere and everywhere all at once.

"Celine?" She felt Owen lean closer. "Celine?"

She opened her mouth to answer, but the fringes of consciousness faded, the soft embrace of fatigue pulling her heavy body deeper into the bed until she floated into nothing.

CHAPTER 16

Celine opened her eyes, the weight of rest lifted. She didn't stir as the voices continued, Adella and Owen murmuring.

"You tend to her personally," Owen said. "Do you already care for her?"

"The poor girl was dying."

"But to wait at her bedside, and to summon Smithson to help her. *Personally*." His tone was light, curiosity threaded throughout. "It has raised a few eyebrows, Mother. Especially with Father now bedridden."

"Everyone else's eyebrows are not my concern."

Owen chuckled, keeping his voice down. "And what of mine? May I be let in on this little secret you two seem to share? This special bond that has seemed to sprout quickly?"

"What secret, son?"

"You have taken a special interest in her, is all."

"She saved your life in that village, and apparently in the sea, as I have come to learn. Liam acted too rashly to call her a danger. A spy of Jesper." The queen said the Sudorian king's name like a curse.

At this, Celine moved to sit up, her arms trembled as they bore her weight.

Owen went to her immediately, resting a hand on her back as he readied her pillows to support her. "Take it easy."

She looked up at him, sleepy but alive.

"How do you feel?" Owen asked. "Are you in any pain?"

"No," she said, her voice weak but present. Iron sickness had almost taken that from her, too. "What did that asshole say?"

Owen's jaw dropped. The queen, unperturbed, clarified. "She means Liam."

"I apologize," Celine said, rubbing her face. "I forgot myself for a moment."

"You've just survived a sickness deadly to your kind." Adella's tone indicated *our kind*, and the camaraderie therein fortified Celine's heartbeat. "You've earned your words."

Celine restated her question, meeting Owen's eyes. "What did Liam tell you, your highness?"

"He didn't tell me anything. Graham reported to me this morning, and I come to find my mother has already rescued you from the cell and is caring for you."

"They didn't report my arrest?"

They'd left her in that damned cell, withering away, surrounded by all that iron.

Her shadows would have their work cut out for them.

"That was the same concern I had." Adella gave Owen a pointed look.

"I couldn't fight back." Celine touched her nose and mouth. "He made me breathe something. And the iron…"

She looked at the queen, hoping she knew, hoping Adella understood the depth of her powerlessness.

Celine touched her throat, feeling the absence of the chain.

"It's here." The queen lifted the necklace from the bedside table and handed it to her. "I know it is precious to you."

"Yes." But after the hell she'd emerged from, she hesitated to tell them why.

"Here." Owen delicately took the chain from her fingers. "Allow me."

He readied the clasp. Celine's hands swept aside her hair as he brought the chain around her throat, leaning over her and embracing her without touching her. His cool breath swept over her neck and shoulder, his fingertips careful with the clasp until it was set. When he let go, the chain fell against her skin, the weight of the charm comforting against her chest.

"Thank you."

Owen sat on the bed. "I'm sorry that happened. I'm sorry I didn't know."

"It's over now." But Celine's body was devoid of any energy. The iron had stolen so much from her.

"Perhaps we should protect one another," he said. "Never let the other out of our sight."

"Didn't Liam and Tyrion say the same thing about guarding you?" Celine remembered vaguely the orders from the king. "They are your shadow."

"The easiest solution is to wed," the queen said nonchalantly. "No one would dare strike against the queen consort unless they bore a death wish."

"Which may need to happen sooner than expected," Owen said, his voice and eyes both soft as she took both of them in. "Would that be alright?"

"As you wish, your highness."

"As *you* wish, too, Celine," he said. "Your choice matters in this."

Does it? But she had no strength left to fight, even as her thoughts raced around the prospect of marriage to a man who was still nearer to stranger than friend.

His finger touched beneath her chin to lift her face, his expression kind. "I look forward to the moment you call me Owen."

Her smile was soft, her face and neck warming. She reached for the hand that held her chin, fingers curling around his wrist, learning the shape of him as he looked at her.

"Rest," he whispered. "I will have a guard stationed outside."

Liam won't dare enter here unless he wishes to die. She kept the threat unspoken, finding that the borrowed daggers remained where they were on the table. Good.

"Drink this." Adella gestured to the cup at her bedside. "This is a blend from Smithson. It will help you recover your strength." The queen rose. "I've instructed the maid to bring you two more cups, two hours apart. Drink every last drop."

Smithson, the magicborn apothecary, the gentle voice speaking with Adella. Some of the memory returned as Celine reached for the cup, and, with Owen's help, she delicately sipped the warm tea. Bitter, but it tasted *right*. The herbs sank into her blood and muscles almost instantly. "Thank you. That's perfect."

"Smithson knows his work," Adella said, with a touch of pride. "Now rest. We will discuss your wedding tomorrow."

"Will she be up for it?" Owen asked.

"The tea will help. I trust she will feel more like herself soon."

Celine took another sip of tea. "You said the king is bedridden." She looked from Owen to Adella, seeing their expressions darken with faint shadows. "Has his condition worsened?"

"I'm afraid so," Adella said. "Owen tells me it's a toxin called Hell's Touch." Her lips pursed slightly. "I'm concerned about how this has happened when there are eyes everywhere in the castle."

Celine thought of the potions from Kasindra, those that hide and mask from others, even when in plain sight. If the toxin came from a merfolk assassin, did they have the same protection in place? And if they did...

Celine fought the urge to glance at her bedside table. Saying something would light suspicion to her, and she did *not* want to revisit that prison cell. But thoughts turned, thoughts of whose hands sent the king of Estilon slowly to his death.

"Get your rest," Adella said, standing. "Call for us if you need anything."

Celine thanked them, and once they left, she tried to move from the bed, but her body refused, the effects of the tea already working over her body. She let them take her over, falling once more into the arms of sleep.

As promised, twice, two hours apart, a maid brought Celine tea. With each successive cup, her strength of body returned and hunger rumbled in her stomach.

Celine was grateful for the interruptions. Her dreams were riddled with flashes of her parents burning in the pits of Chaos. Celine couldn't remember their voices, except in their screams. She rubbed her ears, trying in vain to banish the sound. She sat up, eyesight bleary but mind fully conscious. Even after nearly dying, rest remained elusive.

The room was dark and cold, though the hearth fire blazed as she snuggled into the blankets. Clean clothes lay on the bed beside her, likely from the maid while Celine slept, including a fresh white dress like the one she'd worn before. Celine slipped it over her head. If only all human clothes were this comfortable.

The fabric helped, but she was still cold. And *hungry*. Owen had mentioned a cook in the castle. But where?

Celine pulled the blanket off of the bed and wrapped herself up before venturing out of her room, opening and closing the door quietly before looking up and down the hall. She'd remembered where in the hallway her chamber door was when she returned from the village, so she was *fairly* certain she'd find her way back. The only worry now was finding *food*.

But before she left, she eyed the daggers still on the dining table. What if she ran into Liam during her late-night search? Celine took one sheathed blade, curling the handle with the blanket in the curve of her fingers.

She crept downstairs, finding her way in the dim lighting with the cold stone sapping warmth through her stockinged feet. She shivered, hugging her blanket closer as she crossed to the wide head of the grand staircase. Tall windows allowed the moonlight to cast its blue-white light into the space as the wall sconces burned their small orange fires. She stepped downstairs carefully, one hand still holding the dagger as the other touched the banister.

Should she go left or right?

She turned right, eyeing the tapestries and paintings and full suits of armor on display. King Rolf was deliberate about showing his wealth, but the grandeur of the space warranted the richly dyed fabrics, the delicate paintings, and the shining metal in human shape.

The first door she reached wasn't locked, but when she peered inside, the dark space was expansive and empty. The Great Hall. Silly that she didn't remember.

"Celine?"

She turned, spinning fast on the balls of her feet, her shoulder landing hard against the door jamb as her wide, panicked eyes met Graham's. The nearest sconce cast a warm light across his features, emphasizing how they were jagged and sharp like the edges of stone.

"Are you alright?"

"I'm not in trouble again, am I?"

He shook his head. "No, of course not. I am sorry, Celine." He bowed at the waist. "I hope you'll forgive me. I acted in haste before I had proper information to do so."

She remembered what he'd said, how he'd believed Liam implicitly. But it was the same among the merfolk. They would more readily trust one of their own over a human, should the situation ever arise. If it was a matter of choosing a human over Quinn or Zander, Celine's loyalty and allegiance were unshakable.

Still, she took Graham's apology for what it was, nothing more.

He straightened, looking over her shoulder through the open door. "What are you doing here?"

"I–" She gulped, tightening her hold on the dagger's sheath, still wrapped in the blanket's edge. "I was looking for food."

"In the Great Hall?"

She glanced behind her, embarrassed. "I'm still getting used to the castle."

He pushed past her, moving closer than she would have liked, and closed the door. "I will have someone–"

"Uncle?" Owen moved down the steps at a jogging pace. "Is something wrong?"

"I found a wanderer in the castle." Graham's tone was light, but his expression was not.

"I'm not *wandering*," Celine said, sticking up for herself. "I'm *hungry*."

"I'm hungry, too." Owen offered his uncle a smile that didn't reach his eyes. "Uncle, if you would excuse us, I will show Celine the kitchen and choose something from the pantry."

Owen offered Celine his arm. The pair moved across the foyer, turning left at the stairs to a small corridor with a door at the end.

"Are you alright?" Owen asked quietly as he stopped in front of a closed door. "Did he say anything to upset you?"

"No." But after a beat, Celine added, "He doesn't trust me. Not that he should trust a stranger, especially one walking around the castle at night."

"He errs on the side of caution with most things. Strangers, especially. But after all that you've endured, I feel you've earned some trust."

He turned the handle and pushed the door open, revealing a large room filled with moonlight shining off of copper pots and pans. Copper–and *iron*.

Celine took a half-step back, eyes searching the space and spotting several pans cast in iron hanging from hooks on the wall at the opposite end of the room. Then, looking to the left, the massive stone hearth took up the length of the wall and held a large cooking pot, iron cast, from its hook. Further down was the roasting spit, cleaned of any meat that had been cooked there.

"Let's see what's here," he said, stepping in.

Celine moved right, following Owen, her body hyper-aware of the dangerous metal in the room, and watched him stop at a door in the nearest corner of the kitchen. For being Adella's son, iron didn't seem to bother him. His human side must protect him. Perhaps, like his mother, he was used to it.

"This is the pantry," he said, opening the door. Celine inhaled a luxurious scent that mingled both sweet and savory. "What do you feel like?"

"Anything," she said candidly, hugging the blanket tighter as her stomach grumbled. "I could eat a whale, at this point."

Owen laughed. "Understood. Let's see what's in the larder, too." He pulled a basket of small breads out of the pantry and passed them to Celine. "Hold this. I bet there's some cheese that will taste excellent with these rolls."

Adjusting her hold on the blanket, she used her free hand to hold the basket, the other protecting the dagger out of sight.

Rolls. Celine eyed the balls of bread as Owen closed the pantry door and opened another very close to it. This space was dark and composed entirely of stone, the temperature much cooler within.

Slabs of salted meat and fish rested directly on dark stone shelves covered in thin fabric. The smell of raw meat wafted out of the larder, but it wasn't unpleasant. Owen moved in and out quickly, holding a block of yellow cheese with a satisfied smile.

He moved further into the kitchen as Celine stepped back, the reach of the iron stronger in the middle of the room. He opened a drawer and rifled through its contents, stopping as he noticed her inching back. "Is something the matter?"

"Are we eating in here?"

His brow furrowed, confused, eyeing her hands as they clutched the blanket. "My idea was to take you to the library."

"The *library*." Excitement swallowed the repulsion. "I've read about them." Then, worried, she asked, "How much iron does the library have?"

"Very little." Realization dawned on him. "Oh, Celine, I didn't even think." He looked around, seeing now the very tools and cookware that had her edging closer and closer toward the door. "Let's hurry, then."

With their food collected, Owen retrieved a dark bottle from a wall shell and moved for the door. "You've read about libraries?"

"My friends and I have a lot of books in our reef."

The tug of iron halted as Owen closed the door behind them. Quietly, the pair ascended the stairs, stopping at the first door on the right. With neither word nor hesitation, Owen opened the door and waited for Celine to step inside.

"Welcome," he said, "to my favorite room in the castle."

Even in the dark, the library was impressive. Shelves upon shelves of books in the middle of the room that were framed by shelves built into the walls, spanning from floor to ceiling and filled with volumes of all shapes, sizes, and colors. The tall windows let in moonlight, but there was much of the room that remained in shadow, casting it in a romantic hue where Celine wouldn't mind getting lost.

The fireplace in the library was small, and with a long rug stretching out in front of it, two cushioned chairs sat close together with a small table between them, everything facing the fire. On the opposite side of the fireplace was an iron holder filled with tools.

"What is with the human obsession with *iron*?"

Owen chuckled. "Here." He tucked the cheese in the basket with the rolls and placed everything on the table between the chairs. "I'll build us a fire and put those away."

Owen pulled the flint and stone from the small pocket set into the frame of the fireplace. He arranged kindling and fresh wood before pushing the stone down the length of the flint to make a spark. Fire caught the kindling in seconds, and warmth radiated toward Celine in the most pleasant, welcoming way. He used the tools to set the wood and fire together, then moved them around to the other side of the hearth, away from her.

"Thank you," she said, sinking into a plush cushioned seat.

Satisfied, Owen sat on the rug in front of her, his shadow stretching long against the light of the fire. "Bread and cheese, please." He grinned at the rhyme.

Celine obliged. As his fingers curled around the browned top and bottom to pull them apart, Celine asked, "Should you cut the bread, too?"

"I didn't think to do it when we were in the kitchen," he said. "And I didn't bring a knife."

"I did." She presented the dagger to him, hilt first. "I haven't returned them to the armory yet."

He raised an eyebrow, taking the proffered blade and unsheathing it. Seeing that the blade was clean, he carefully cut the roll and asked, "Do you always take evening strolls so armed, my lady?"

"It seemed like a good idea," she admitted. "And I didn't want to hide it from you."

"Hide that you were armed?"

She nodded.

"You took *two* daggers from the armory," he said. "Do you have the second one with you?"

"No. It's in my chambers."

"Pity." He chuckled, glancing back toward the shelves filled with books. "We could have had a mock duel in the stacks." With the first roll cut, he laid a slice of cheese on the top half and presented it to Celine. "The top is the better half. I hope you like it."

Celine took a slow, tentative bite. The soft texture of buttery bread and the savory taste of rich, salty cheese was luxurious. She closed her eyes as she chewed with slow deliberation.

"It's good, right?" Owen said with a chuckle, taking his own bite. "We were very lucky in our find, raiding the kitchen."

Celine smiled. "Raiding the kitchen." She took another bite. "We can go on another raid tomorrow night, if there's more."

"I think that's an excellent idea." He leaned back on one hand, chewing his second bite. One more remained in his hand, poised to serve. "Did you get any sleep?"

"Some." She popped the last of her snack into her mouth and chewed. "I was too exhausted to do much else."

"Me too." He readied a second roll with cheese and extended it to her. "Are you alright, Celine?"

She tilted her head, curious. "Your highness?"

"You've been through a lot in a short amount of time. From the raiders to the dungeon, and having iron sickness." He spoke softly, likely afraid to upset her and the jovial air between them. "I'm genuinely sorry for all that you've endured. You've been under my roof for such a short period and have already been through the gauntlet."

"None of what I've been through was at your hand."

"But my hand should have protected you."

She studied him, gripping the blanket around her as she leaned forward, seeing him clearly. "After we are married, our hands will protect each other's." She extended hers from the blanket, open as she'd seen humans do as she watched from the sea.

Owen shook it, their accord sealed.

"If you are ever in distress, Celine," he said, still holding her hand, his thumb skating across her knuckles, "I hope I will earn your trust so that you may call upon me. And confide in me."

Warmth filled her as her heart fluttered. "Likewise, your highness."

At this, he smiled, lips closed as the wrinkles around his eyes deepened. Slowly, he released her and made them both another snack of bread and cheese. "What happened yesterday in the village was no small thing. I'm the prince of Estilon, soon to be its king. I've been in battle and survived. I've fought raiders, just like yesterday. My blade has taken lives." He looked up, honesty in his light blue eyes. "But it never gets easier."

"No," she said, before catching herself. She took a breath and added, "Nor should it."

"May I ask?" He was careful, but also deliberate. "You are skilled with a blade. This didn't seem like your first time."

"It wasn't," she admitted. "Only, I'm more used to *fin* than *feet*."

She waited, fighting the pulling opposites of wanting to tell him everything while also wanting to shield parts of herself that should remain in the dark.

At last, she said, "I've killed before. Fishermen, with merfolk in their nets." She swallowed. "Like you said, it doesn't get easier."

He winced. "I'm sorry, Celine."

"You shouldn't apologize for faults that are not your own. And let's hope this union is exactly what our people need." She played with the seamed edge of the blanket nearest her thumb until Owen passed her another bit of bread and cheese. "I didn't realize our kings were in talks until mine made the announcement. At my trial, no less."

"*Trial*?" His eyebrows rose. "What happened?"

"The first commander was waiting for me when we finished at the cave. When I learned you were Charlie."

Owen remained silent, watching her speak as firelight flickered over his face and eyes.

"I was brought before the king and given the task of marrying the human prince of Estilon to unify our kingdoms." She took a small bite, chewing slowly. "I'm his stepdaughter. His marriage to my mother is a forced custom of one king defeating another."

"By the gods."

"Dathan told me to betray you," she said, meeting his eyes. "The man who ordered my parents' deaths charged me to commit murder, or I would die." She took a slow breath through her nose, looking at the food in her hands. "He mentioned the king of Sudor and his son.

Dathan said that once the line of Estilon is ended to betray them and whatever trust they've forged."

"Dathan and Jesper?" Owen's eyes darkened. "How long have they been in league together?"

Celine shook her head. "I'd never heard of Jesper before, not until then."

"And Jesper's *son*?" Owen leaned forward. "He doesn't have a son."

"I was supposed to meet him," Celine said. "But I showed up ahead of schedule, it would seem."

"How did that happen?" Owen asked, pulled suddenly with this new line of questioning. "You already on the beach, waiting?"

"I was to have three days to prepare, to say goodbye to my friends, but after the first day, he—" She swallowed, ears catching the memory of Quinn screaming.

He put his hand on hers, bringing her to realize that she'd clenched her food in her fist. Her fingers relaxed, the bread and cheese in a solid, pinched mass.

"I am not a threat to you, Owen," she said. "I want you to know that. But I—" Anxiety and anger were at war with what force would strangle her first. She rubbed her empty hand on her throat. "I want to see Dathan dried to a lifeless husk and burned to ash for what he's done. He and his first commander. They destroyed my family. They tried to destroy *me*."

"Celine." His tone was both calm and urgent. "I think you and I want the same thing."

Perhaps it was the way he held her hand, for she slipped down from the chair to sit beside him on the rug, their knees touching.

She read the anger and cunning that passed over his features as he spoke. "What you said before, about the Hell's Touch being a merfolk toxin." His brow furrowed. "I think Dathan somehow had my father poisoned. And what you said about Jesper and the merking..."

"I never imagined Dathan had someone on land, a human willing to do his bidding," she said. "Unless it was one of the merfolk, transformed?" She shook her head. "I didn't know his destruction was so far-reaching."

A moment of silence passed between them. Celine moved her

fingers, settling into Owen's hold. "Thank you for listening, your highness. That wasn't easy to say."

"Owen." He covered her hand completely. "Call me Owen. You did before. After that confession, I think we've earned some informality."

"*Owen.*" She managed a small smile. "Why does it mean so much to you? We're strangers, you and I."

He opened his mouth to speak but stopped himself. "I know our marriage is sudden. I know *all of this* is sudden. But I feel very good about the two of us working together. What I think we're planning is no small thing, and the more we get to know one another, the better we can help achieve our mutual goal."

"A mutual goal of revenge?"

His bright eyes blazed as they reflected the firelight. "Yes. A mutual goal of revenge."

"I'll need your help to go to the shore at midnight," she said. "My teacher asked to see me each night to make sure I was doing well."

"Midnight?" He gave her a confused look as he took a bite of his food. "Specifically midnight?"

Celine shrugged a blanket-covered shoulder. "She's particular. But I barely made it out last time, and Liam…well, you know the rest."

"You *made it out*?" He handed her another roll with cheese. "How? Through the northwest gate?"

"*Northwest gate.* Locked iron door over fetid water?"

He chuckled. "That's the one." After a moment, he said, "We'll go to the sea together tomorrow night. I'll meet this teacher of yours. As long as she doesn't turn me into a frog or something."

The pair ate with contented silence. Then, satisfied, Owen got to his feet.

"I'm still not tired enough to sleep," he admitted, offering his hand to her.

She stood with his help, his hand comfortably warm. "Neither am I."

"Reading helps me rest." He pivoted on his heel to stand beside her and look at the shelves before them. "I'll show you my favorites."

She followed Owen down the center aisle between two columns of shelves, three on each side. But instead of being overwhelmed, Celine found herself in a sea of another kind, one of words and images and ideas, all of it shaped by ink and paper.

Eagerly, she stepped forward.

"THE CORRIDOR WAS *dark as he stepped through, his bare feet quiet against the wooden floor. But when his foot touched something wet, he recoiled.*"

Celine gasped, listening intently as Owen read to her. "What is it?"

He laughed quietly and kept reading, his voice low for dramatic effect. "*He stared, eyes adjusting to the dark, ears keenly aware of the sound of someone breathing.*"

Wood creaked at the door, and Celine's wide eyes stared, waiting to see someone coming inside. She hugged the blanket tighter around herself, leaning closer to the fire, closer to Owen, closer to the dagger.

Owen closed the book, marking the page with his finger. "I'll stop there. I didn't mean to truly frighten you."

"I'm not frightened." But Celine didn't blink as she looked from Owen to the door. "I thought I heard something."

He leaned closer to her, grinning. "The sound of your beating heart?"

She shoved his shoulder, bringing him to laugh again.

"Would you like me to keep reading?"

"Yes." She eyed the book in his hand, then looked at him directly, determined to prove her mettle. She set her shoulders and sat up straighter. "Please, Prince Owen, do go on."

His amused smile was relaxed as he opened the book and continued. But more than wanting to know how the story goes, she watched him read, eyes studying the shape of his mouth as they formed the words. The smooth tenor of his voice soothed her, and she relaxed near him, wrapped in the blanket by the fire.

CHAPTER 17

Celine would see them whenever she would dream about Chaos. Two merfolk silhouettes, moving through blue-black shadows, illuminated by something unseen. The closer she moved toward the dim light, the more detail she could see hasty, jerking movements, as if something in the water stunned them over and over.

She knew this was a dream. *The* dream. The looping nightmare that had made its home in her mind whenever she slept. She'd had one night's reprieve from this recurring nightmare, one glorious night where her body, exhausted beyond reckoning, could do nothing but rest.

But her mind had recovered enough to throw her back into its imagining of the Chaos Realm, dark shadows and dim lights that offered shape-changing shadows in place of real, tangible, living things.

She moved forward, as she always did, watching the silhouettes of two merfolk move with alarming jerks and twitches. What grim tortures did they endure? But deep within herself, she knew. Because the dream never changed.

She would swim closer, into the shadows, eyes adjusting to the dark until the two merfolk were all she could see, the blue shadow-light playing with her eyes to augment the terror in their eyes.

"Celine!"

"*Celine!*"

It was always her father who cried out for her first, but her mother's scream pierced through her ears with a spine-chilling soprano.

"Celine! Go!"

"Get out of here!"

But there was no out, not until consciousness returned.

"Celine!"

Her eyes opened, the library still dark. The fire had reduced to embers, but she could see Owen's shape on the floor in front of her. They'd fallen asleep, the book still open beside Owen's extended arm. But something was odd about the color of his sleeve.

Celine reached a hand toward him, sight adjusting to the dark.

Something was wrong.

"Owen?"

She blinked, moonlight flooding the room, covering him with bright blue-white light, illuminating the red that stained his clothes and the black that discolored his veins.

Owen was there, poisoned with Hell's Touch and covered in blood, eyes and mouth open. He'd reached for her as he died.

"Owen!"

She bolted awake, panting, eyes open in fear before blinding white forced them closed again. Sunlight poured in from the tall library window, stabbing her eyes. She blinked through it, eyesight adjusting.

Owen was on his back beside her, book open page-down on his chest. He groaned as he stirred, his expression the definition of serenity before his brows furrowed. "Celine?"

She pressed her palm to her clammy forehead, staring at him, forcing her brain to reconcile that Owen was alive and well. *Alive and well.* "Sorry. Bad dream."

He opened his bleary eyes. "Are you alright?"

She managed a half-smile. "You ask me that a lot."

He hummed a laugh, closing his eyes again, and she could sense him drifting off to sleep once more. She looked around the brightly lit library and half wondered if anyone had stepped in to find them sleeping.

Or if someone had slipped in to *watch* them sleeping...

"Sorry I didn't wake you. You looked so peaceful." He stretched his long frame along the rug, arms and legs out in nearly a straight line before he sat up. "Are you hungry?"

She blinked away memory flashes of the dreams. *Dreams*, for they were two, one within the other. "You have Sir Tyrion and Sir Liam with you at all times, right?"

A drowsy eyebrow rose. "Yes."

"I don't think you should be left alone." She worried the edge of her blanket with her thumb and index finger. "What if someone tries again?"

"You mean what happened in the village? The Moonblade assassin?"

She read the intensity of his stare. Was he trying to read her? "With the merfolk and Sudor, and your father's health…" She let her thoughts dangle unfinished, then said, "Being alone makes you more vulnerable."

"I'm alone with you," he said, his voice low, his eyes unblinking. "Am I not vulnerable?"

She stared, eyes wide and lips parted, all words failing. Heat bloomed within her chest, watching the playful tug of a smirk on his mouth.

"You even brought a dagger to a dinner party." A light flush swept across his cheeks. "As you wish. I won't be alone."

"How did we manage this evening without Liam or Tyrion?" she asked.

"Liam is experiencing his reprimands for wrongfully imprisoning you," he said. "I tried to convince Tyrion to take the day off, but I would sooner get a magical weapon from Anya herself before that would happen." He hesitated, meeting her eyes with a careful look. "I didn't want Liam to make you uncomfortable. I can assign him elsewhere."

She looked down at her hands, fingertips worrying the edges of her thumbnails. "I appreciate that, but this will make it difficult for them to guard you."

"Liam acted in haste, and his actions have yielded consequences." But it was much more complicated than that, and the weight of it bore down on him.

He stood, offering his hand to help her up, which she accepted, her body glad to move beyond the floor.

He didn't release her hand right away. "Let's change and meet in my chambers for breakfast."

"Your chambers?"

"Yes. I'm intrigued by this alliance we've forged, and I'd like to discuss plans and resources. And perhaps looping in your teacher." He hummed to himself then as a thought occurred to him. "I wonder if our teachers should meet? Two mentors are better than one."

Something within Celine resisted the idea. Keeping this from Kasindra was easier, though she couldn't pinpoint why. But Owen was right. Kasindra was a valuable resource, and having a magical human prince on their side may help their cause considerably.

He released her to reach for the door but stopped. "I've been thinking about something. When you spoke to my mother before, when she was in your chambers, before any of this happened…"

At his pause, she asked, "You know about that?"

"One benefit of your guest chambers being close to mine." His blue eyes were bright in the morning sun as he studied her. "When the two of you spoke, does she—" He stopped. The words were hard to say. "Does she know I have magic?"

Confirming it felt like betraying Adella. This conversation should happen between mother and son.

"It stands to reason, doesn't it? You can sense those with magic, and they can sense you." Celine tilted her head, looking up at him. "You mean you've never talked about this with her?"

"No, I haven't." He bit his bottom lip. "I've known she and I were different in the same way. But I…" He didn't continue.

"Talk to her," she said. "You're both having to hide in a very public way. That's easier done with someone at your side."

"It'll certainly be easier having you."

The flutter of her heart made her more aware of the warmth emanating from him. He stood close, the rhythm of his breathing caught by the steady rising and falling of his chest.

Owen opened the door, and they stepped forward, moving closely together, though the corridor had space enough to spare.

Sunlight cascaded in through the tall windows, brightening the blue of his eyes and the cool tones of his skin. In this light, his dark hair was more brown than black.

"When you arrive, knock like this." He tapped on Celine's door with two quick knocks, paused for a beat, then knocked a third time. "Then I'll know it's you."

Celine nodded slowly. "A special knock. Very inventive."

Owen bowed, pleased with himself, and turned for his own chamber door. Then, after performing the knock again, he stepped inside.

Celine called for the maid to help her dress, but Miss Helen showed up with a pleasant smile and demeanor.

"Did you rest well?" she asked, looking Celine over.

"I did," she said, saying nothing of nightmares. "I would like to change for breakfast."

"Of course. And—" Miss Helen reached for Celine's hair but recoiled. "May I? It's a bit...*ahem*..."

Celine moved to the mirror and stared at the wavy mass of chestnut brown hair around her head and shoulders. She missed the teal, though the shade of brown was warm and pleasant.

"Oh, my." She touched a section, feeling the tangled strands with her fingers. "This has never happened before."

"Not in the sea, I'd wager. Here—" Helen went to the wardrobe and pulled the dress. "Let me help with this, and I'll set your hair like I do her majesty's."

Celine sensed a gentleness in the head lady's maid that hadn't been there before. Was it kindness in light of what happened? Iron sickness was a harrowing sight, even for those without magic. But something nagged at Celine's intuition, something unknown and unsaid...something that disquieted the otherwise peaceful mood.

But asking could turn Helen's pleasantness sour, and making the head lady's maid happy was a priority. She held power and sway, and Celine needed her trust.

With Helen's help, Celine dressed, and the process was much faster than before with Celine learning how clothes worked. Helen pulled one chair from the table and waited for Celine to sit.

"Brushing out the tangles will hurt a bit, but I'll be gentle."

Celine closed her eyes as Helen began, the tugging and pulling slightly uncomfortable as her experienced hands worked. Tingles danced down her spine with every pass through her hair. What an extraordinary thing, to have one's hair brushed.

Soon, Helen had Celine's long hair twisted and bound, resting over her shoulder in an attractive plait.

"There, my lady." Helen stood back, proud. "That should do you for a while."

The hairstyle was comfortable and didn't hinder her movement. "Thank you. I—" She blushed. "I admit, I feel quite special, Miss Helen. Borrowing your clothes, having you style my hair."

"You're our guest," Helen said, taking one of Celine's hands. "Soon to be Queen Consort. I meant what I said before. Owen means a great deal to us. And you two are to be wed."

"I hope I can gain your esteem too, Miss Helen."

"By taking care of our prince," she said with a kind smile, "I'm sure you will." Then, quietly, she added, "I'm sorry for what happened, my lady. Sir Liam is usually one to act with thought and caution. I cannot fathom what he was thinking."

He was thinking of his prince, Celine reasoned. *He was thinking of his kingdom, protecting it against a stranger.* But Celine kept her thoughts to herself as she readied to leave for breakfast with her betrothed.

When Celine approached Owen's door, she raised her hand to knock but stopped. *What was the rhythm again?*

The door swung open, causing her, and then Owen, to cry out.

"By the gods, Celine!" He pressed a hand to his heart. "You startled me!"

"I startled *you*? Can you see through the door?"

"I was about to come searching for you." But now he took in her appearance, his expression softening. "I see you took your time for a good reason."

She touched the back of her head, hand tracing down the plait. "Miss Helen did it for me."

"You are lovely." He stepped aside, arm gesturing wide to grant her entry into the room. "If you please, my lady, breakfast is served."

A delicious array of meat, eggs, and fruit filled the table in his chamber, and he'd already pulled the nearest dining chair for her.

"If I may, my lady." Owen stood behind it, hands ready to push it in.

Seeing the space in daylight, his room reminded her of the library. Two large bookshelves took up the wall on the right, leading to a table in front of one window, covered with papers, books, quills, and inkwells.

"What work is there?" She pointed at the table.

"My studies, I'm afraid. I'm haphazard, at best, when organizing my work."

"What are you studying?"

"Currently, it's the magical strengths and properties of arcana crystal." He cut into the meat, something red and savory smelling, and poised his fork for a bite. "Its alchemical properties are fascinating, but I keep hitting my head against a wall."

"Alchemical?" She reached for a piece of fruit before remembering to use her fork. "Is that magic?"

"Of a kind. It's interesting to see how organic materials are affected by heat, other materials, or chemicals." He took a bite, looking over his shoulder at his work. "Smithson has been vital in that research, even though he doesn't enjoy looking at magic like a science." He chuckled. "As if curating blends of medicinal teas *isn't* a science."

"Science. *Alchemy.*" She chewed a delicious piece of fruit and immediately went for more. "Magic on land is *very* different."

"Tell me more." He leaned forward, eagerness brightening his expression. "What sort of magic are you familiar with?"

"The same as you, I think—arcana crystal, plants and *organic materials*. But what about singing?"

He tilted his head, confused.

"Do you sing?" she asked. "When you're casting?"

"I'm afraid if I sang, the magic would backfire." He chuckled. "I have a poor voice for music."

"Then how do you cast?"

He shrugged. "There are some spells I've cast by speaking—reading the words aloud, following the directions with any reagents needed. But singing?" He shook his head. "Never singing."

"I wonder if that influences the spell's efficacy?" She took a bite of meat this time, finding it well seasoned, though she would have preferred her protein *raw*. "You're not afraid of someone finding this? All those papers with notes about spells? And that new crystal from the assassin?"

"They're usually put away in the drawers, but—" He looked at her with a bit of chagrin. "I wanted to ask your thoughts on all of this. Arcana crystal, casting." He took a piece of fruit. "I never imagined *singing* would factor in."

They ate a few bites in ruminating silence, Celine considering magic *without* singing. As her eyes traced the objects around his room, she found the painting by his bedside. Before, it was still a vague outline of the view from his window, but now, details and color had enhanced the image. He'd done well capturing *light*.

"You paint?" It matched the landscape visible from the angle of his window, the rolling hills of Estilon in the distance beyond the castle wall with a parapet and tower in view.

"I try." Shyly, he looked at his plate, gathering the remaining bits of food for one bite. "I don't read *all* the time."

"You read, you paint, you fight. Is there anything you can't do?" She smiled, teasing, but was genuinely curious.

"Music, I'm afraid, much to my mother's chagrin. I can't carry a tune to save my life, and I was never patient enough to learn an instrument."

"I could sing for us both," she teased.

He smiled, amused, then asked, "Your voice magic. You have such control over it."

She lifted an eyebrow, taking another bite of meat. "Did you think simply speaking would enchant you?"

"I did." He leaned back, watching her. "And I was intrigued by the idea. Your very existence is power and strength, especially in the way you maintain control."

She stared, flattered.

"I don't mean to embarrass you." His dimple appeared as he

smirked. "But it's true. You're powerful, Celine. And a damn good fighter."

"As are you." Warmth flooded beneath her skin. She was desperate to change the subject, worried with the perspiration in her palms and how she held the utensils. "Don't worry about music, your highness. It's a relief to know you're not good at everything."

"Why?" He leaned forward, mischief bright in his eyes. "You think I'm good at everything?"

"Let's just say that I'm pleasantly surprised."

"Pleasantly surprised?" He took a sip of water. "What about me is the most surprising?"

"That you can walk through a door with that massive head of yours."

He burst out laughing, the sound deep and genuine. "Well done, Celine." His eyes and smile were radiant.

Two sharp knocks prompted both to look at the door.

"Enter."

The Queen stepped in. "Good morning." She smiled at Owen, then Celine. "I trust you both slept well. In the library."

Owen cleared his throat. "Yes, we rested well."

"I wanted to discuss your wedding," she said. "Perhaps we can meet in the butterfly garden? There are still some details I'd like to iron out."

"Of course." Owen looked at Celine, eyes scanning her face. "How does that sound?"

"That sounds lovely." Even though the butterflies swirled in Celine's stomach with such fervor that her balance was in question.

The queen clapped her hands together, their plan formed. "We'll meet when you've finished breakfast, then."

Owen laughed, looking at his mother with surprise. "You're enjoying yourself, aren't you?"

"If you mean preparing my only son's wedding," she smiled, her own dimple appearing, "of course I am."

After the queen left, Owen looked at Celine, spinning the tines of his fork in his eggs. "About our marriage."

Celine waited, her swell of nervous energy finding a new target in wedding planning.

"We can continue to keep separate rooms, if you wish," he said. "We are still getting to know one another, and I don't want you to feel uncomfortable."

He raised his water cup for a drink.

"What about you?" she asked. "Would you be uncomfortable?"

He coughed quietly, a few drops of water escaping his mouth before he raised a hand to both shield and dry.

"I've read about royal marriages," she said. "There are...*expectations*." She chose delicacy over bluntness. "Would the decision to keep separate rooms bring you trouble from the court?"

"I will take care of anything if it comes to that. I should think that *our* wishes are paramount, where this is concerned."

"Especially when this arrangement was done *for* us."

"Precisely."

"But those in power may not see it that way. Royals serve the people first." That was the biggest lesson her father taught, both in word and action. "We don't exactly have the luxury of total autonomy."

"Human and merfolk kingdoms aren't so different, after all. But I'm fairly decided on the matter, if you are."

She considered, seeing no downside. "Separate rooms, then."

He rose, breakfast done. "Shall we go to the butterfly garden and see what awaits us?" He offered his hand with a teasing smile. "I'm sure Mother has already put several things in motion. It's best just to agree."

Celine sighed, relieved, taking his hand. "Merfolk don't have weddings."

"No weddings?" He tilted his head at this. "Do you have mates? Partners?"

He walked her to the door, and the pair stepped out. Tyrion was already waiting in the hall. "To the garden then, your highness?"

"Yes, Tyr." Then Owen urged Celine to continue.

"We have life partners," she said. "And bonds are lasting."

"But no ceremony for the couple? Vows exchanged in front of family and friends?"

She shook her head, then stiffened her hold. "In front of..."

He read her face, likely seeing the panic that manifested. "Don't worry. Our ceremony will be quite small. I don't think Mother will have time to ring in all of Sheraton."

CHAPTER 18

The butterfly garden was a magnificent display of color with a perimeter of the rainbow of flowers drawing Celine's gaze. Her eyes followed butterflies and pollinators as they patronized each well-tended bloom. The serenity of their buzzing and birdsong was almost as calming as the sea. If not for the knights of Estilon standing guard with the queen, Celine would have imagined this place from a magical garden where fairies would appear, glad for the colorful offerings of fruit and flower.

"This is beautiful," she said. "How do you not spend all day here?"

"My mother would, if she had her way," he said with a quiet laugh. "The library is more my terrain."

"Bring the books here."

He grinned. "Perhaps a small library? A little cabinet with doors? Something to protect them from the weather."

But they stopped, seeing the table where the queen sat. Papers already filled the space, as well as pieces of fabric.

"Brace yourself," he whispered, squeezing her hand. "And remember: you're not alone."

As soon as they sat down, the whirlwind of conversation began, from the time of day for the ceremony (midday) to the location (the chapel on the castle grounds). But as soon as the queen said *vows*, Celine blinked.

"Vows?"

"Your promise to one another," the queen said. "There are some traditional vows you could follow, or you can create your own."

Celine looked at Owen, confused.

"We'll go with traditional," he said. "Did you know, Mother, that the merfolk don't have wedding ceremonies?"

Surprised, Adella reached for Celine's arm, her touch delicate and warm. "Is that true? This must be a lot to take in."

Celine smiled through the grimace, though the queen wasn't wrong.

"We cannot simply be married?" Celine asked. "There have to be so many things in place?"

"An excellent question." Owen reclined in his seat, looking at his mother with a smirk. "A simple ceremony, traditional vows exchanged, and we are husband and wife."

Without blinking, the queen pulled a piece of paper from beneath the stack, passing it to Owen. "Simple? We'll need to pare this down, then."

"Mother, by the gods." Owen stared at the list of guests Queen Adella had set to invite. There looked to be a hundred names. "There isn't time."

"Of course, there's time." She set out samples of fabric. "Cynthia dropped off the fabric samples this morning. We could have a dress made, or you could wear something of mine."

"Would she make it in time?" Owen blurted, eyebrows askew as he still read over the names of potential guests. "What *is* our timeline, Mother?"

"After the dungeon incident," Adella said, her words punctuated with distaste at the mention of it, "I should like you both married as soon as possible. That said, I don't want to forego any elements of the ceremony that are expected of us, or expected of me. I think we can get everything together rather quickly."

She smirked at that, tracing her fingers over the fabric samples. "It occurs to me, Celine, that you've only just started wearing human clothes. Do any of these samples feel more comfortable to you?"

Celine touched each square piece, not sure what they expected of her answer. Nothing would be as comfortable as her merform in the sea, but Adella was kind in considering her.

"The dress will be simple but elegant," Adella said. "Cynthia is also working on your other clothes."

But choosing *fabric?* "I'm sure whatever you think is best…"

"If you're sure," Adella said. "But it's not my skin, dear. I wouldn't want to choose something that itched or irritated."

Celine touched one square of fabric, the texture soft. "This one."

The queen smiled, a bit of reassurance softening her expression. "That is a favorite of mine. Excellent choice."

Oh, sweet relief. So much of Celine's time in Estilon had been *wrong*. At least one thing was right.

And Owen. Owen was right, too, wasn't he?

"Ah." Adella sat up straighter, clearing a few things away. "The tea's arrived."

The rest of the afternoon was a blur, with Celine listening to Owen and his mother plan a ceremony that, in Celine's mind, would only last for a few minutes. After their vows, then what? A meal among guests Celine didn't know?

The traditions of humans were strange.

"I think we have the important things covered," Owen said, looking at Celine. He reached for her hand, his palm and fingers covering hers completely. "Are you still with us? You look far away."

She blinked and smiled, as though stirred from a light sleep. "I'm sorry. I was just thinking about how all of this is going to look."

"Let's end things here," the queen said. "I have everything I need for the ceremony next week."

"*Next week?*" Owen nearly toppled from his chair. "Mother!"

"This needs to happen as soon as possible, especially with your father so ill." The queen looked at Celine with a sympathetic smile. "And you, my dear, will have duties and responsibilities that will need to begin. And the knights will defend and protect you, especially as Owen's wife."

Especially as Owen's wife. Her stomach tightened, but she said nothing. Better to be underestimated.

Quinn. Zander. She wondered if her thoughts could reach them.

"Let's abscond to the library," Owen said, rising. "We need to finish that book from last night."

Celine smiled at the idea. "*Abscond.*"

"Shall you have supper sent there as well?" The queen said, teasing. "Will you both be finding rest there again?"

"That's a brilliant idea, actually," Owen said with sarcasm, winking at Celine.

The queen pinched the bridge of her nose with a sigh. "You are my son and I love you."

Owen offered his arm to Celine to lead her back inside.

"Before the library," she said, "could we visit the water?"

He looked down at her, curious. "Of course."

"My friends." She looked down as he laid his hand over hers, securing it in the curve of his arm. She liked its pressure, the gentleness of his warm touch, the calluses on his palm and fingers. "I haven't seen them since I arrived."

"You must miss them terribly," he said. "I would be bereft without Tyrion."

They walked together, exiting the butterfly garden and walking through the courtyard toward the main gate. The guards nodded to Owen and Celine, their eyes lingering on her.

"Tell Tyrion that Celine and I are on the shore," Owen said. "He should be on the training grounds."

"Yes, my lord." And one guard jogged away.

Their steps were slow and measured, neither of them speaking beneath the warm afternoon sun and cloudy sky. Celine looked up, the puffy white masses overhead taking on various shapes that slowly changed as they floated lazily through a blue sea of their own.

"I hope your friends will not be too upset with me for keeping you away this long," Owen said with a hint of playfulness. "I wonder if they expected you to check in sooner?"

"Dathan's instructions were clear," she said. "It made it seem like any sign of me in or near the water was enough to charge me with treason."

It was a relief to speak of it freely, knowing that Owen would understand.

"Perhaps my presence would cause further trouble," he said, "if they suspect you won't follow his orders."

"They don't know what's in store," she said. "They only know I'm here with instructions to work with Jesper's son before betraying him."

"And that is another point of contention. *Jesper's son*. He has a daughter, Elda, who, I'm sorry to say, may not live to see the year's end. Quite sickly and frail. You'd think that Jesper would train any offspring to take his place. But a secret son?" Owen shook his head. "Something's off, Celine. Something is *off*."

She didn't disagree, but she knew so little of the human kingdoms. What would Jesper's end goal be in keeping an heir hidden? What kind of surprise did he have in store?

Celine reached the shore with Owen, her hand still on his arm, and she sent her thoughts through the water.

Quinn. Zander. Are you close?

Silence met her, the steady stretch of the sea reaching up the shore to the toes of her boots and the hem of her dress.

"Maybe I need to—"

"Celine!" Quinn's voice reached her. *"Celine! We're here!"*

"Celine!" Zander. *"Celine, finally!"*

She beamed at Owen. "They're coming."

Quickly, she pulled off her boots and waded into the water.

"You're not leaving me for the sea, are you?" He chuckled, but she could hear the tinge of worry in his voice.

But when she spotted blonde and red hair, she abandoned all other thoughts. She waded in waist-deep and embraced her beloved friends, their wet bodies soaking her clothes and hair. They spoke quickly, their voices overlapping one another's.

"Oh, Celine!"

"Celine, we've been so worried."

"We didn't think we'd ever see you again."

"I'm here," Celine said, holding them tightly with her arms around their shoulders. "And I brought Owen."

"I can see that." Quinn wiggled her eyebrows. "He's cuter up close. *Have you kissed him yet?*"

Celine punched Quinn's shoulder. "We've only just met. We're not even married."

"Don't waste time," Quinn said with a devilish smirk. "Those lips are begging to be kissed."

"By the gods, Quinn." But Zander was smiling. "*I'm right here.*"

Celine stared, wonder-struck. "You mean, you two...?"

"*Finally.*" Quinn exaggerated a sigh, snaking her arm around Zander's.

"You could've asked, you know." He pulled her closer, the two of them remarkably comfortable with touch and proximity. "And I'll have you know, Celine, *she* kissed *me*."

"Well, what else was I supposed to do? *Keep waiting?*"

Peace and joy surged in Celine's heart. Even as she was away from them, separated by land and body, they had each other. And they were *home*. Praise the gods that they have that much after losing her.

But they haven't lost me. They'll never lose me.

And where would she be without them? She hoped to never learn the answer.

But the merfolk turned quickly at the sound of another human approaching—Tyrion, jogging toward Owen with his eyes lingering on the three in the water.

"That's Owen's guard," Celine said. "And his best friend."

"Another tall and handsome knight," Quinn said. "Careful you don't bewitch them all."

"I have no intention of bewitching anyone," Celine said. "The arrangement of one human husband is enough of a responsibility."

"How is that going, by the way?" Zander asked. "Are the humans treating you well?"

Celine didn't want to speak of the iron prison cell, of Liam's accusations and fear. "I am alive and well," she said. "And Owen and the queen are very kind."

"We'll rain the seven hells upon them if they're cruel to you," Quinn said, still watching Tyrion with Owen. "They will regret ever looking upon you, if you so wish it."

"I appreciate your loyalty and violence." Owen approached with Tyrion, and Quinn and Zander straightened. "You must be Celine's friends. She told me how much she misses you."

"Quinn," Celine introduced, "and Zander."

"It's a pleasure to meet you both." Owen's smile beamed with the rising sun, the golden light highlighting his dark hair and bright eyes.

"*Handsome,*" Quinn said with merspeak. When Celine looked at her, she smirked. "*He looks like a good kisser.*"

Celine splashed water at her, Quinn and Zander laughing.

Zander considered both humans. "*The knight looks anxious.*" Then, with his voice, he said, "We should probably go."

Celine hugged them once more, the salt water soaked into her dress. "I'll return as soon as I can."

Celine waited as Quinn and Zander swam off, each of them waving until the finned pair dove beneath the sea.

Carefully, Celine waded back onto shore, her skirt and stockings clinging to her legs. As Owen smiled at her, a strong sense of peace passed between them, almost a mutual understanding and need that they could sense and share with one another.

"My lady," Tyrion said with a bow. "I trust your friends are well."

"They are."

Owen held Celine's discarded boots, but, rather than pass them to her, he offered his arm. "Or I can carry you in like last time."

She looked down at her sand-covered stockings. Walking wasn't troublesome now. "I will manage." She slipped her hand into the crook of his arm, a thrill of warmth surging through her core as he gently pressed her hand against his side.

"To the library, then," Owen said. "I think Mother's idea of having food brought was stupendous."

"Really, your highness?" Tyrion scoffed a laugh, jovially shaking his head. "I'll never understand the allure."

"I'm glad you do," Owen muttered to Celine, his side-glance almost conspiratorial. "Hours together, surrounded by books. By the gods, how marvelous."

Celine couldn't disagree.

CHAPTER 19

The library was just the distraction Celine needed to wait out the day. After they'd finished the book started the previous night, it was Celine's chance to choose another. She took her time, running her fingers along the book spines, fascinated with how they felt when dry.

"May I ask a personal question?"

She looked over her shoulder at Owen, his posture relaxed as he leaned against the frame of the window, arms crossed. Behind him, dusk had settled, and the dark purple sky was steadily reaching its final deep blue. Her stomach fluttered, eyes following the line of his silhouette, meeting eyes that light always touched.

She would meet Kasindra in a matter of hours, and Owen would be there. How would Kasindra react? How would *Owen*?

"Of course." She hoped she masked her nerves well enough.

"How did you learn how to read?"

Surprised, she dropped her arm from the bookshelves, giving him her full attention. "There was a book we found in one shipwreck—*Primer for Young Learners*, I think it was called. There were pictures of mouths and how to shape them around each letter." Celine demonstrated a few, making Owen chuckle. "Zander, Quinn, and I helped each other sound out letters, then words, then sentences." She shrugged. "We enjoyed it. We speak your language well enough, but recognizing it in print was a challenge. Quinn is especially fond of poetry."

"*Poetry*, huh?" At this, Owen went to the shelves and pulled a book from above him. "Poetry is one of my favorites, too. Here." He paused on a page and read aloud,

I have lived
Ten thousand lives,
But none so rich,
So fulfilling,
As the one lived with you.

He looked at Celine through his lashes, his smile broad. "It's exceptional, to say so much in so few words."

"Songs without music," Celine said, echoing Quinn's own sentiment.

"Which is excellent for someone like me."

"Though skills in music are ones you can learn." She raised her eyebrows. "Have you ever been interested?"

"Yes, but not enough to devote the time it deserves. I enjoy learning *everything*." He looked around the books in the library, then at her again. "I look forward to learning about you."

The palms of her hands tingled, and for the briefest moment, she wondered if he would reach for them. She wanted him to slip his fingers across her palm and weave their fingers together. But she looked away, her heart beating like a pair of bird's wings within her ribcage, eyes finding the gold lettering on several cloth-bound spines. "Merfolk culture differs greatly from yours, your highness. There will be many things to teach."

"Your culture has me fascinated." He stepped closer. "But I meant *you*."

He stopped when her back touched the bookshelf, the light in his eyes a strong contrast to the shadows that brought out the sharp angles of his cheekbones and jawline.

She swallowed, the muscles in her throat tight. "Why?"

Finding her courage, she looked up at him, watching his eyes study her face. What did he see? How did he see her?

"You're brave," he said, "coming here after a king you despise treats you like a traitor and sends you here as punishment."

"I don't view this as a punishment," she blurted. "I'm grateful for your kindness. You and the queen." With a bit of a laugh, she added, "Everyone except Liam."

He chuckled at this. "I know. But that was *Dathan's* intent, and you met the challenge, even though it side-railed your own plans against him."

She tried to read him, seeing layers yet unnamed. "Plans that we now share."

"Which is quite fortunate, for a husband-and-wife team to join forces against the same threat." He flicked one eyebrow up. "It makes the task much easier."

"And that surprises me," she admitted, standing straighter, moving closer. "Are you sure, Owen? I've known for so long what I wanted to do, what I was working toward, but this has to be so new for you."

He didn't answer right away, a half-smile flattering his mouth and eyes. He reached for the shelf behind her, his arms grazing her shoulders as they caged her in. He stepped closer. If Celine were to take a deep breath, they would touch.

"Ask me again."

Her eyes flicked to his lips as he spoke. "Are you sure?"

"Are you sure, *Owen*?" He beamed, as though he'd won some kind of game. "You called me Owen."

She moved to shove his shoulder, thinking better of it as she remembered a secret revealed in the stone alcove days before. Her fingers touched his sides, and she struck quickly before he could stop her, tickling him. His arms recoiled, shock widening his beautiful eyes.

"You don't play fair." But he grinned, his dimples deep.

"I work with what I'm given." She raised an eyebrow, pleased with herself. "But I mean what I say. I've been studying from Kasindra since Dathan and Santus took my parents from me. It's been my life."

"Kasindra. Is she the Sea Witch?" When Celine nodded, he pursed his lips, thinking. "And the magic you learned from her..."

His open-ended statement gave Celine room to say it, though she knew the answer wasn't necessary. "Dark magic."

"Dark, like *necromancy*?" His eyebrows rose.

"Why? Are you interested in resurrecting the dead?"

"Of course not." Still, his shadowed grin betrayed his interest. "But the taboo magics are always the most fascinating, aren't they?"

"Well, I hate to disappoint you, but I refuse to go near it. I may learn how to use the powers of Chaos, but I love and respect Shanna too much to debase the dead."

"Certainly." But the spark of curiosity was in his eyes. "I don't wish to treat the dead disrespectfully, either. But the *knowledge*..." He let the statement remain there, glancing toward the window. "We still have a bit of time before we're to meet your teacher. Are you hungry?"

She nodded, touching her stomach. "I should tell you. Kasindra will realize you have magic if she meets you."

He blinked. "Is that a bad thing?"

"Information is valuable. And I'm not sure what she would do if she knew. She may already know."

His eyebrow rose. "Is her magic that powerful that she can sense us from the sea?"

"She has ways of seeing."

Her cauldron, her scrying...how much of Celine's life was already under the Sea Witch's watchful eye? Celine's insides twisted. She hoped the iron within Estilon Castle provided an unexpected barrier.

"Let her learn the truth, then. And we should have some supper before moving this conversation outside." He smirked. "You can teach me some magic while we're waiting."

Leaving the castle grounds was much easier with the prince and his personal bodyguard going with her, and on the shore, Owen asked Tyrion and Liam to give them a bit of privacy.

"As long as I can see you," Tyrion said before he groaned. "By the gods, I sound like my mother."

"Just as wise," Owen said, "and just as lovely."

Liam glanced up at Tyrion, smiling but saying nothing with his hands clasped behind his back. He knew he was still on probation for jailing Celine, but he had yet to apologize to her.

Tyrion chuckled. "Aye, that's the truth, and thank the gods for it. My father's side of the family was *not* so lucky with their looks."

Leaving Liam to stand guard by the gate, Owen and Celine walked slowly down the sand, the sweeping of the water whispering its welcome. Clouds shielded the moon, but the night was no less vibrant. Tyrion stood guard up the shore, giving the couple requested privacy during their evening stroll.

"I can try to call her," Celine said to Owen, her voice low, muffled by the gentle waves reaching up into the sand. "Perhaps she's already close by?"

"How would you do that?"

"Merspeak." She tapped her temple. "We communicate with one another through a telepathic link."

"Doesn't that invade privacy?"

"Only if you let it. We're taught when we're very young how to control our minds and our voices. But powerful magic can break in."

Like the shadows she'd conjured for Santus and Dathan.

Her palms tingled. Did the shadows miss her?

She looked at Owen, the itch in her palms begging her to conjure. And here was the prince of Estilon, an eager student.

"Have you ever conjured shadows before, Prince?" She raised an eyebrow, standing to hide her hands from Tyrion's watchful eyes.

"Conjure *shadows*?" He leaned closer, their shoulders touching as his eyes studied the movements of her hands.

The first few tendrils wrapped around her fingers before the others joined, swimming in the air around her hands, embracing her.

"How do you reach your magic?" she asked.

"You mean through my will?"

"Your will." She nodded slowly, letting the darkness touch his open palm.

He shuddered. "It's cold."

"Use your will to summon your own. You'll pull from the cold, from the parts of the world that are the opposite of light."

She watched him concentrate, fingers taut as magic flickered around them. She brought his hands closer to her, shielding them from Tyrion.

"Good. We don't have the chance now, but when you practice, reach as far as you can. The shadows will meet you when you do."

"The shadows will *meet* me." He looked at her, the night doing little to darken his eyes. "I feel as though a new world has opened up."

"It has."

A silent moment passed between them, the shadows still swirling, their hands still held between them. She had but to lift her head a little higher to touch his lips with hers.

But the shadows swirled, eager to do her bidding.

Owen's warmth staved off the cold from the night and from the conjured dark, and Celine sent them discreetly toward Santus and Dathan. *Catch them by surprise.*

"Where did they go?"

"I sent them to the king and his first commander." Celine fought the urge to smirk. "Remember what I said before about magic affecting someone's mind, if left unguarded?"

His smile broadened. "I see." Something occurred to him. "Dathan's successor..." He left the statement open-ended, studying Celine.

"His daughter, Jessa." Celine said. "She has a good heart. She's been good to me, at least. I can see her making a strong leader."

"Good. Then here's to Jessa inheriting the throne." He mimed a toast with an invisible glass.

The water pushed further up the shore, touching Celine and Owen's feet. They looked down, then out, finding the shape coming toward them from the water.

"Is that—"

"Hello, my dear." Kasindra smiled, her teeth glistening even in the partial light. "And you've brought a guest."

"He was interested in meeting you," Celine said. "Prince Owen, meet Kasindra, the Voice of the Deep."

"It's a pleasure to meet you." Owen bowed his head toward her.

"Charmed," Kasindra said, eyes darting from Owen to Celine. "May we speak freely, my dear?"

"We may," Celine said. "Have you learned any more about Santus?"

"He is just full of surprises," Kasindra said, her tone different— *guarded*. She didn't want to speak in front of Owen.

Using merspeak, Celine asked, *"Magical guards?"*

"*Very good ones,*" she answered, her voice gentle in Celine's mind. "*You and the prince seem to get along quite well.*" Her eyes darted again, this time to Tyrion further down the shore. "*Is his knight comfortable with an evening visit from the Sea Witch?*"

"*They understand that I have those in the sea whom I miss,*" Celine said. "*Wanting to visit wouldn't be anything out of the ordinary.*"

"*Of course not.*" But Kasindra's smile was one of cunning. "*Still. Perhaps we should postpone our meetings until you have more... authority?*"

Once more, Celine asked, "*Anything else from Santus? Or Dathan?*"

"*Quiet as clams, my dear.*" She swam back, looking from Tyrion to Owen. Using her voice, she said, "It was nice meeting you, Prince. You two have a lovely evening."

Then she swam away without another word, leaving Celine with the heavy aftermath of wrongdoing. Bringing Owen was *wrong*. But it didn't feel wrong until Kasindra looked at it and touched it.

Celine stood, and Owen was at her side, his hand warm against her back. "Is everything—"

But a panicked voice interrupted. In seconds, Prince Graham raced down the shore with Tyrion and Liam in his wake, their boots kicking up sand with every step.

"Owen!" Tyrion cried. "*Owen!*"

"It's your father," Graham panted. "He's—"

But Owen knew, by his uncle's pallor. "He's dead."

In Celine's head, she heard Kasindra laugh, quiet and distant and cruel.

When he nodded, they raced back to the castle, up the stairs, and into the king's chamber where Queen Adella waited, crying at the king's bedside.

Owen's approach was slow, and Celine watched him kneel beside the bed, reaching for his father's hand. The black veins had reached far, climbing over the king's jaw. The marks likely stretched along the length of his entire body, every inch a poison that slowly siphoned the life from him. Just as it had done to her father.

Celine didn't expect to feel a swell of emotion at the demise of the human king of Estilon, he who'd made life for her people a living hell.

She knew of the burn of the iron-laced nets on his royal ships. She knew of the cruelties his men would exact upon captured merfolk. But Owen's grief humanized him. Owen's grief mirrored her own. The same cruel hand had taken their fathers, and the ache in her chest tinged from the wound long closed but not fully healed.

Helen appeared at Celine's side. "Allow me to take you to your chambers, my lady."

Celine wanted to argue, wanted to remain by Owen's side to offer her genuine sympathy as he grieved. But Owen turned to his mother, the two who'd cared for the king in life. She agreed, letting Helen take her hand on her arm and leading her to the other side of the grand staircase to her familiar corridor.

Upon entering her room, Helen asked, "Do you need anything, my lady?"

Celine could think of nothing, the weight of Owen's loss letting her thoughts reel. He would have his coronation, they would be married, and they would be the king and queen consort of Estilon.

Alone, Celine undressed and laid across the bed, burying herself beneath the blanket and hugging a pillow to her chest.

From quiet time spent in the library to dark magic casting on the beach, to Kasindra's cold reception and the king of Estilon's death.

How quickly everything had changed.

CHAPTER 20

Owen's eyes were red rimmed when they placed the crown on his head.

His coronation was in the afternoon following his father's death, with every leader and adviser determined to maintain Estilon's leadership in times of war. But Celine could see that none of this reached him—the vows he recited, the ceremonial garb he wore—all of it was a scene unfolding in someone else's life, by the distant look on his face.

The cloak draped over his shoulders was a rich crimson with white and gray fur trimming and gold thread embroidery. It was the same cloak Rolf had worn, just as his father had before. The legacy of the Estilon throne now rested on Owen's shoulders.

"*I, Owen, son of Rolf the King and Adella the Queen, swear to uphold righteousness and justice for my people, for my kingdom, until my dying breath.*"

Polite applause resounded from those in attendance, but Celine watched with an aching heart as Owen bowed his head to receive his people. A single tear fell, splashing on the edges of his robes.

Now, it was Celine's turn to stand at his side, dressed in a borrowed gown to recite vows in the presence of strangers.

"You look lovely," Adella said, smoothing the sleeves. "It fits you rather nicely."

"Thank you, your majesty." Celine's voice was barely audible, the swirling emotions almost too much to be borne.

All the plans they'd hastily made, only to move even faster. Celine ascended the dais beside Owen, who finally looked up to see her.

"Thank you, Celine," he said, taking her hands with a delicate touch. "I can't imagine that this is easy for you."

She tightened her grip, imagining her strength pouring into him. "We are the brave ones, Owen. You and I. We are the brave ones."

They stood before the priest, ready to recite their vows. Owen leaned toward her and whispered, "You look beautiful."

"You do too, your highness. Oh—not *beautiful*. Or maybe beautiful?"

This made him smile, even chuckle, and he kissed her fingers. The watching crowd sighed, pleased, reminding Celine that they had an audience.

She faced the priest, and their wedding ceremony began.

"We have gathered to unite this man and woman in a marriage most holy and sacred. Blessed by the gods, fortified by the strengths of their peoples, they stand ready to bind their lives together."

Owen faced her, prompting her to do the same. He squeezed her hands and nodded, his eyes full of courage.

"Repeat after me," the priest instructed. "First Owen, then Celine."

I will give you that which is mine to give.
I will honor and respect you above all others.
I will guard and nurture your spirit.
I will share your joys and your sorrows.
Together, we shall pass through this life as one.

Owen bowed, kissing Celine's hands before pressing her knuckles to his forehead.

After Celine recited the words and kissed his hands, Adella stepped forward and presented a ring to Owen, nodding slowly as he took it and placed it on Celine's finger. A stunning blue sapphire, the gold band a little snug.

"Now, with the swearing of vows," the priest said, his arms wide and hands open to the crowd, "I present husband and wife, King Owen and Queen Consort, Celine of Estilon."

Owen pulled her close and gently kissed her. Even with the pure, chaste kiss that united their marriage, Celine's heart raced.

Those in attendance gave applause and congratulations as she and Owen stood on the dais, on display in what should have been a moment not shadowed with grief.

"May we present the young couple to their wedding chamber."

Owen and Celine shared a look, each blushing, but they bowed and descended from the dais without objection.

"Congratulations to you both." Adella passed Celine a modest collection of flowers from the garden. She dabbed the corner of her eye, smiling at her son. "Let's get you both to your room and give you some peace."

Owen exhaled, and Celine held his arm tighter as they walked down the aisle toward the exit.

The procession was painstakingly slow, their steps measured as they passed through the castle grounds, up the large stone steps, across the courtyard, and into the main entrance. At the foot of the grand staircase in the castle foyer, Owen turned and bowed to the gathered assembly.

"Thank you all for your attendance, for your well wishes, and for your condolences." He paused. "Today marks a significant change for the kingdom, and for me. As I said in my oath, I promise to lead my people to the best of my ability, and I am grateful for all who offer their support, their wisdom, and their insight."

He bowed again, and the crowd applauded.

"On that, I wish you all well." He raised a hand in farewell, and Celine did the same. Then both turned and ascended the stairs.

"They expect us to go into my chambers," he said, holding her closer to whisper. "I'll see you to your rooms before they notice we're separated."

"We don't have to separate," she said. At his surprised look, she added, "This has been a very difficult series of hours. *Hours*. And the world has changed." She brought her free hand to rest on his bicep, the two of them reaching the top of the stairs. "Losing one's father is hard. Especially—" But she stopped herself. The details were still too fresh, too difficult to give a voice. "We don't have to separate. Unless you want to be alone?"

He didn't let go of her hand, taking her into the corridor. "No. I don't want to be alone."

"That settles it, then." She gestured ahead. "Lead on, husband."

"As you say, *wife*."

Husband. Wife. And the way he smiled as he said it, even with the weight of kingship burdening his grief.

It wasn't until they were in his chambers that he finally removed the crimson cloak and ceremonial crown. He placed them on the dining table where, only yesterday morning, they'd had breakfast. Within hours, Owen had gained a wife and lost a father.

Celine set her flowers beside his crown.

"What do your people say in times such as these?" he murmured, opening the window, the cool breeze coming in from the plains ahead. Celine could smell a hint of salt and seaweed. "How do the merfolk philosophize the dead?"

"*As shells hold their secrets, so do we,*" she recited, "*Our loved ones return to the cosmic sea.*"

"Cosmic sea," he said. "I like that."

She stood beside him, leaning against the wall near the window, admiring the way the sunlight brought out the brown in his hair. "What do humans say?"

"A great many things," he said, crossing his arms. "Mostly about ashes begetting ashes or all life transitioning to something new."

"We don't have ashes in the sea."

He turned his head, amusement brightening his otherwise saddened eyes. "We bury my father, and in minutes, I'm placed on his throne." He shook his head, returning his gaze to the land outside. "I wasn't sure how I felt about being king, Celine, but this? Having it thrust upon me because of my father's murder?"

His fingertips whitened as he gripped his arms. Celine placed a hand on one, feeling him relax. "A murder that we will avenge."

He faced her then, taking her hand in both of his. "I am yours. Completely." He tightened his hold. "Teach me everything. Show me what I must do."

"Don't give yourself so freely, Owen."

"He will suffer as my father suffered." Owen's lips trembled. "As your father suffered. As we suff—"

Emotion choked him, and Celine caught him before he crumbled completely to the floor, weeping. Kneeling together, she held him as he cried, chest heaving, voice muffled as he buried his face in her shoulder.

"We will kill him for what he's done," she said, her palm drawing circles against his back.

They used the wall for support, Celine resting against it as Owen rested against her, crying until he could breathe again, holding her to keep him tethered in his grief and his rage. The breeze continued to carry in, making loose pieces of paper and open book pages flutter.

"What of our plan?" he whispered, his voice hoarse. He leaned against her shoulder, head tucked in the curve of her neck. "After all this, after the way he died, I can't let Dathan rest."

"He won't." Celine held him tighter. "We will haunt his every hour, waking or sleeping."

He sat up to meet her eyes, his red-rimmed and angry. "He will pay for what he's done."

She wiped his cheeks and held her hand open for him. He took it without thought or question.

"The shadows will go where you tell them," she said. "We'll conjure them together."

He nodded, kissing her fingers. "Help me begin."

"Feel for the dark, as you did before," she said. "Channel your magic in the best way you know how."

"How do you do it?"

"I sing magic into being."

"Well, *that* is out of the question."

She hadn't meant to, but she let one light chuckle escape. He looked at her amused face, the steel anger in his weakening as a hint of a smile entered his eyes.

"Are you making fun of me, wife?"

"I wouldn't dare, husband."

He shook her hand, clearing his throat. "What, besides singing?"

"How do you typically cast?" She asked. "What about when you're with your teacher?"

"Smithson hums sometimes. It's obnoxious. He's a *very* good singer."

She couldn't keep her laughter suppressed.

"*Celine.*"

"I'm sorry, but I didn't expect you to be this upset about singing."

Owen and Celine spoke quickly, one trying to explain while the other tried to console, all while their growing amusement made it impossible to bear the seriousness of casting.

"I've always been jealous of those who could."

"We don't have to sing. We'll do something else. Magic is magic."

"I've just never had time to learn."

"You could learn now, you know. Singing is muscle memory and training."

"As is everything we've ever had to do, from fighting to politics."

She stared at him, unabashedly grinning.

He sighed, his breath cool against her skin. "Alright. Casting shadows. *Conjuring.*"

"Relax. Let your magic work." She sat up straighter, urging him to do so, too, and she took his other hand. She closed her eyes. "Relax," she repeated, this time softer. "Let your magic work."

Cold surrounded her hands, cold that she didn't conjure, and she opened her eyes to the shadows surrounding them.

"They will follow your will," she whispered, thrilled at his progress.

He opened his eyes and looked at the swirling dark, lips parted in awe. He stared at them, studied them, and whispered his command:

"Find Dathan. Make him live my father's final nightmare."

The shadows soared from their hands, sailing out from the open window and off to where their eyes could not follow.

Owen stared at their hands, holding Celine's tightly. "That was incredible."

"It was only the beginning." She longed to touch his face, to soothe the grief that still weighed heavily on his brow. "How do you feel?"

"Exhilarated. *Tired.*" He tilted his head. "Is that normal?"

"From dark magic, yes. And grief." She moved to stand, but he beat her to it, getting to his feet before helping her up.

"We should eat and rest," he said. "There are enough expectations awaiting the both of us soon." Then, shyly, he glanced at the bed. "I'm sorry the accommodations aren't more conservative."

"What's the difference between this or the library floor?"

"Connotation."

She pressed her lips together to keep from laughing again. "As you say, husband."

"It doesn't make you uncomfortable?"

"Surprisingly, in the short time we've known one another, I trust you. And you know full well that I am a mermaid skilled with blades and dark magic."

He nodded slowly, his eyebrows rising. "Yes, I do."

"I didn't want to be alone, either, when my father died. And then my mother." Her expression softened. "We'll trust each other. We'll help each other."

"We're the brave ones." He held out his hand as though to seal an accord.

She took it. "We're the brave ones."

CHAPTER 21

She heard her parents screaming.

It always had the same as the dream began, the same dark silhouettes with familiar shadows, but this dream was the first where she saw their faces.

"Mother!" Celine reached, but she wasn't close enough. "Father!"

The seaweed that swayed around them surrounded their fins, their arms, climbed up their bodies, reached for their throats.

"Let them out!" Celine pulled at the seaweed she could reach, her fingers like claws, but it wasn't enough. "Let them go! Aishlin!"

She sat up in bed, sweating, her breath coming fast, and Owen was up beside her.

"Are you alright?" He looked her over. "By the gods, Celine."

"It's my parents," she confessed. "They're in the Chaos Realm."

"The pit of the seven hells?" He blinked. "Are—are you sure?"

She closed her eyes, still seeing their faces twisted in agony, still hearing their voices echoing in her mind, reverberating off her skull. She grimaced, touching her forehead, almost certain for a moment that she could pull the images out.

"I see them there almost every night." She took a deep, steadying breath, but her heart still raced. Her body was weak as she leaned forward, resting her head in her hands. "It's almost always the same."

"Dathan," he said.

"Kasindra said I can get them out. Trade in Dathan and Santus for my parents, and I can free them."

He put his hand on her back, and she leaned into his touch, remembering the same soothing motion she'd done for him hours before when he wept over his father.

"I'm sorry," she said, wiping her face. "You shouldn't worry about this now."

"Why shouldn't I? We're in the same place, Celine. Who else could comfort us, if not each other?"

She didn't fight the natural motion of her body as she leaned toward him, letting his arms surround her.

"Is that why you studied with the Sea Witch?" he asked. "To learn how to free your parents?"

She nodded, almost shivering, as he ran one hand through her hair. "I was going to kill him before he sent me here. His arrangement with your father threw off my timing."

"Lucky for me," he said. "Otherwise, I wouldn't have a friend to guide me." Then, after a moment, he said, "And this Santus. The green merfolk?"

"Yes. Dathan's first commander. He's the one who poisoned my father."

"Santus did?"

She sat up, wiping her face again. "He has some skill with magic and potions."

"Would he have been the one who poisoned my father?"

"I'm not sure." Seeing the thought process behind Owen's eyes, Celine added, "Santus wouldn't act without Dathan's order. It isn't like him to take that kind of initiative on his own."

"There's plenty of room for another target in my revenge."

She almost smiled, something reminiscent in his words. "Who did your father contact when he and Dathan reached their agreement? Did they have a go-between?"

"I wasn't present for it. He kept it a secret until he announced the deal was done."

"But isn't that strange?" She shifted his arms slightly, resting more comfortably with him. "To keep a secret meeting with your sworn enemy with no rumor or suspicion? Someone would have known."

"My uncle may know something." Owen took one of her hands and laid it open in his. He traced the lines of her palm. "I overheard my parents arguing about it. My mother was furious. She said something about my father going among the magic folk alone to discuss the future of their son, and he thought it wise to leave her behind?" He paused. "Now I understand why. She's magic folk."

She watched Owen flatten her fingers gently with a smoothing motion. Relaxed, she let them naturally curl again so that he would apply gentle, warm pressure. The sensation was pleasant.

"Your father taking your uncle would make sense," she said, trying to imagine Rolf and Graham meeting with Dathan. How could they have met without her knowing? *Where* would they have met? There is no privacy among the merfolk. "Why go in secret when he would make a public announcement, anyway? Why would Dathan keep this from us? What if something had happened?" Celine shook her head. "Something doesn't add up."

In the dim firelight, Owen's crystalline eyes were almost amber. He laid his hand over hers, extending his fingers at their full length. They reached past hers enough that he could almost bend the tips of his fingers over them. "What are you thinking?"

"Dathan doesn't trust anyone, not even his own daughter. He would bring the entire merfolk army with him if he'd met with a human king. Which begs the question: why the secret meeting? And how could Dathan have done so without anyone's attention?" Her brow furrowed, trying to make sense of it.

His hand stopped. "Celine. What if—"

When he didn't speak up right away, she squeezed his fingers. "What if?"

"What if he didn't meet the merking? What if someone else was there in his place?"

"But Rolf would have known, wouldn't he? He'd have known if it wasn't Dathan keeping their arrangement."

"Unless he *didn't* know." Owen stared. "Unless someone else had taken Dathan's shape."

Celine blinked, imagining someone taking Dathan's form and posing as the merking to fool Rolf.

"I shape-changed and became Charlie," he said. "It stands to reason that another magical being—a merfolk—could pose as their king."

"But that's—"

That would explain why the deal passed unnoticed by every other merfolk who weren't in on the secret.

"By the gods. Do you really think…"

"Someone met my father and poisoned him," he said. "The deal for our marriage is the only time that makes sense. An assassination attempt while they broker peace." He scoffed. "Of course."

"Santus in disguise?" Celine asked quietly, turning the idea over in her head. "Someone who would tell Dathan that the human king wanted an alliance, something they could exploit." She ran her fingers over her bottom lip, thoughts racing. "Why did your father agree? What incentive did he really have to see our kingdoms unite?"

"Arcana crystal," he said without hesitation. "Because, apparently, Sudor has found a motherlode of some kind of resource underground, one that is quite similar to arcana crystal farmed from the sea. My father is desperate to gain whatever he could that compared to what Jesper had gained."

"Arcana crystal." It was Celine's turn to scoff. "If only he knew how scarce it is."

"I tried to tell him. He still thought this was a viable plan. Resources from the sea kingdom to help strengthen those of ours that remain." He leaned back against the headboard, heaving a sigh as he stared blankly at the ceiling. "I'm sorry if that upsets you, Celine. My intentions are to bring peace between our people, not to exploit the sea for what we can gain."

She rested her head on his shoulder. Their hands remained together, fingers entwined. "I don't imagine you endeavoring on a fool's errand after arcana crystal. But I am interested to know how we can access Sudor's new treasure."

He shifted closer, his cheek pressed against her crown. "What are your thoughts, wife? Dig underground?"

"That's an idea. Create a secret tunnel that leads right to whatever you said—a mother's load?"

He chuckled. "A *motherlode*. It means that the resource they've found is in a location where it's very abundant."

"And it's underground? Buried in stone?"

"Yes. Sudor's primary exports are mined resources, like copper and tin. Sudor finding a precious material in their mines, especially an abundance of it, is unfortunate for us."

"Why?"

"Our primary exports are textiles and crops. Artisan goods. They rely on *weather* and *seasons*, things we can't control. And the seasons have been harsh, not to mention raiders have been wreaking havoc. Our yields have been thin. That, and dealing with a conflict on two fronts has made things more difficult. Financially, Estilon is in trouble."

Celine raised their held hands. How small hers was compared to his. His, warm and calloused, nearly enveloped hers. The length and shape of each finger, the broadness of his palm...she could study his hands for hours. "Shall we send some shadows to Jesper? Feed him some nightmares?"

"Upon your wish, wife." She could hear the smile in his voice. "It shall be done."

"What is he afraid of?"

"Losing," he said. "I pray I live to see the day he loses everything."

He jolted then, eyes wide as he stared at Celine, grinning. "We have a precious gift from the Moonblade assassin. The time might be right to see how effective it is."

He leapt up, nearly pulling the top drawer of his bureau free from its tracks. He lifted a false bottom, a sly smirk as he side-glanced at Celine, and showed the blue-green crystal retrieved the day of the village raid.

"You haven't used it yet?" Celine asked, impressed.

"Not without you. I–" A touch of shyness flushed his cheeks. "I was thinking of a way we could cast together. A romantic evening, getting to know one another."

Flattered, Celine tried to control her mouth to keep from grinning. "You were saving it for me."

Owen settled on the bed in front of her, their knees touching. He held the crystal out to her in his cupped hands. "What do we do?"

She shaped her hands over his, wrapping them around the crystal. "Use the power you feel within the crystal to strengthen whatever spell you're going to cast."

"Together." He moved one hand so that they could both hold the crystal between their palms, hands alternating as they held one another's. "Shadows, together."

Celine liked the sound of that. *Shadows, together.*

And the arcana crystal met them when their power surged through, the magical reagent eager to do their work. She sang, her voice magic reaching through the crystal shell to touch the magic within. The strength of her shadow casting coursed through her blood like never before, the thrilling rush making her light-headed. She focused on her breathing, on her magic, on the strength of the shadows as the arcana crystal helped her conjure forth.

"Go to Jesper," Owen said. "Show him what it means to lose. Let him feel the chilling touch of fear."

His shadows soared to the window, seeping out through the cracks. Celine's lingered, waiting for her command.

"Dathan and Santus," she whispered. "Show them what chaos awaits them."

Dark joy surged through her blood as her shadows left, their cold touch lingering in their absence before the warmth of Owen's hands melted it away.

The crystal held between them still had power left.

"Amazing." Owen studied the magical gem. "I've never felt anything like it."

"Neither have I." Celine met his vibrant gaze, her heart throbbing against her sternum. "That power–"

His eyes held her, a spark of lightning behind the crystalline blue.

He raised her hand to his face, forming her palm and fingers across his cheek.

"Dathan may have sent you as a punishment," he said, his voice low. "But I am so very glad it's you." He leaned into her touch, kissing the heel of her palm. "So very glad, indeed."

"As am I, Owen."

He took the crystal and set it on the sill of his painting easel, the iridescent blue-green shimmering slightly beneath the unfinished landscape painting of Estilon. Owen returned to his spot beside her, and the pair laid back once more. The nightmare had long faded, and the night was more peaceful than before. Her smile remained as she closed her eyes, feeling him gently sweep a lock of hair from her face before rest took her.

CHAPTER 22

Dark storm clouds loomed overhead, casting gray over the verdant land as though nature itself held its breath in anticipation. Celine stared out of Owen's bedroom window, wishing his room had a view of the sea.

Quinny. Zander. Celine crossed her arms, resting a hand over her heart, willing her thoughts to reach them. *I love you. I miss you.*

Owen stepped inside, closing the door quietly behind him. "Breakfast will be here soon." With quiet steps, he closed the distance between them. For a half-second, Celine expected him to put an arm around her and found herself disappointed when he didn't. "You look wistful, wife."

She half-smiled at the playful nickname. "I am, husband. I've been away from the sea for—" She did a quick mental count. "How long has it been? Five days? I never imagined I would miss my scales."

"I'm afraid I haven't been keeping track of time," he admitted. "So much has happened."

"Worlds have changed. Kingdoms. People." She traced the wood grain of the windowsill. "I feel as though I've stood still while everything has swirled around me, finally stopping to show me I'm in a place I no longer recognize."

"What would make it better?" he asked. "Would you—Do you—"

He was oddly vulnerable as he leaned against the wall beside her, studying her face, drumming up the courage to say the words. She waited, patient, willing to listen.

"If it is your wish to return to the sea," he said at last. "I will help you."

But she could see something in his eyes that betrayed his words. She touched the shell charm of her necklace.

"You were forced from your home, Celine." He tried to smile in sympathy, but whatever was unspoken in his eyes flashed across his face. Pain? Fear? She couldn't be sure. "I won't force you to stay. We've married and met the terms of the deal. If you—"

"I want to stay," she said. "I don't feel forced."

Relief smoothed the lines around his eyes. "If you ever feel differently—"

She took his hand, her other still holding the shell charm. "I can return anytime with this necklace."

She held it out, extending the full length of the chain, and he held the charm between his fingers.

"I have to break it," she said, "but it'll change me back."

"You haven't used it yet," he whispered. "Even after the dungeon."

"I don't feel forced to be here. Even though Dathan is a bastard who likes to think he can control our lives."

He chuckled. "I admire how you speak the truth so candidly, Celine."

"I miss my friends. I miss my home." She squeezed his hand. "It isn't your fault or mine. It simply *is*." She studied his eyes, bright and clear and piercing. "But I'm glad I'm here, Owen. I'm glad it's *you*."

He embraced her, pulling her close so that her cheek rested against his shoulder. He cupped the back of her head with his hand and smoothed her hair, his fingers curling slightly to comb through and send shivers down her spine.

What surprised her more than his show of affection was how electricity surged through her, as though lightning spidered outward from her heart, through her bones and blood.

She brought her arms around him, hands resting against his back, allowing herself this embrace, this connection. One soul similar to hers in its aching and its need for revenge. One that, like hers, had been punished for loving.

Their bruises would heal, and they would do so together.

"I am quite taken with you," he said, his breath sweeping across her hair. "If you'll permit me the honor of courting you, Celine."

She smiled, nearly laughing, heart racing with a surge of excitement. "It's not many husbands who want to court their wives."

Abruptly, he spun her, arms tight around her as he held her against his chest. She cried out in laughter as three sharp knocks broke through.

"Breakfast, your majesty," came the maid's voice from the other side.

"Enter," he said, setting themselves right, even as they grinned at each other.

Breakfast entered with the maid with Helen on her heels. A sensation carried over the air, a sense of uneasiness. Something was amiss.

"Her majesty would like to meet with you after breakfast, my lady," Helen said. "And after, we'd like to review courtly duties."

Owen groaned. "*Queen School.*" He chuckled, pulling out a seat for Celine to sit. "You have my sympathy, wife."

"What do you mean?" Celine looked from Owen to Helen. "What is Queen School?"

"Lessons on how to be queen," Owen said. "The ruling partner of a human kingdom."

But Helen added quickly, "I'm sure there are differences between the kingdoms of land and sea. You are now our king's wife, and there are responsibilities and expectations."

Celine winced, looking at the table instead of Helen. Owen chuckled behind his hand. "I see."

"You will be present too, your majesty," Miss Helen said to Owen. "Celine has to learn quite a lot, I'm afraid."

Owen poured Celine a glass of water and helped her to select food for her plate. "I'll be with you at every step. I'm sure a lot of things will make sense from where you're from."

But Celine wasn't so sure. Court training from her parents comprised alliances and grudges between the merfolk enclaves across the many and varied seas surrounding Sheraton. There was still so much she didn't know, especially from the distant lands where her people were not likely to venture to.

Thunder rumbled from the distance, the low reverberating thrum harkening the storm to come.

"A perfect day to stay and read," Celine said. "When I was in the sea, I would swim close to the surface to hear the thunder while reading. There was one story in particular, a house full of ghosts. It was perfect."

Owen stared at her, mischief bright in his eyes. "Are you flirting with me?"

Helen coughed a laugh, turning away to gather herself.

Celine grinned with a surge of confidence. "Maybe I am."

Breakfast continued with lightness despite the dark outside, and once they'd finished, Helen escorted Celine to the queen's chambers.

"I'll be right outside," Helen said.

Celine wanted to ask why but missed her chance as the door closed behind her.

Queen Adella's room was stunning, filled with ornate wooden furnishings, lush fabrics, and delicate objects that shimmered in the sunlight. Celine's eyes traced every inch of the space as the queen sat on the sofa by a long table and gestured to the cushioned chair near to her.

"Join me," Adella said, adjusting her skirts across the cushions.

Celine did, only now aware that she was still not wearing shoes. She tucked her stockinged feet beneath her chair.

"Everything has happened so suddenly," the queen said, regarding Celine with empathy. "How are you feeling?"

"Fine," she said automatically. Then, with more poise, added, "Yes, things have moved quickly. But I'm alright."

"There are a lot of changes in store," she said. "I'm sure Helen told you what will come today."

"She did. Queen School."

Adella blinked. "Queen School?"

"That's what Owen called it."

Amusement broke through her otherwise calm expression. "That sounds like something he'd say."

The queen's hands relaxed in her lap, the morning gray complementary as it poured in from the windows in contrast with the firelight. But there was something there, similar to Owen's hidden emotion when he reassured her. Mother and son were similar in the way they carried their feelings, right on the surface so that, with the right pressure, it would reveal itself.

"Something has you worried," Celine said.

"You mean other than the rising audacity of the Sudorian king?" Adella managed a quiet chuckle. "Something strange killed my husband, and I've been wracking my brain, trying to figure out *who* and *how*."

"You suspect murder, too."

Adella nodded. "Even Kedran was perplexed by the malady, though he knew its source." Her crystalline eyes fixed on Celine. "Do you know anything that could help solve this mystery?"

"I suspect the merking," Celine said with a half-shrug. "Or his first commander. I can't be sure. I don't know how, unless he has a human agent working with him. Or there was merfolk who reached land with no one knowing."

"We're no closer to a solution." Adella reached to the back of her neck and smoothed her hair there. A similar gesture to Owen's. "I admit I feel under-prepared to keep him safe."

"He is the king," Celine said. "That comes with its dangers, as well as its protections. He has Graham and Tyrion."

"And he has you." Some of the worry softened from around her eyes. "I admit to feeling immense relief, knowing you are by his side."

"I will make sure Owen is safe, your majesty. We have sworn our lives to one another."

"It's not only Owen I think of. But Rory." She smiled. "My daughter. My beautiful girl."

Celine studied the queen, understanding what she'd had to sacrifice for the political gain of her people. A husband, a daughter, a home.

"And of my people," Adella went on. "The magicborn have a human throne. This deal is finally met, and I—" She took a breath, emotion showing through her practice royal veneer. "I should like to return to them."

"Return?"

"For a short while to Melia, to see my daughter. Then to Alvar, to see my childhood home."

"Alvar? Home to the elves?"

Adella smiled at this. "The merfolk also call us elves?"

Celine paused, sensing more from the queen.

"The earthborn of Alvar are the sons and daughters of Rhiann, much like the merfolk are the sons and daughters of Shanna. Seaborn. Earthborn."

Celine understood. "I've never seen skyborn or fireborn."

"Nor should we, I imagine. Wings of radiance on one, blood made of fire within the other." She paused with a serene expression. "Humans have taken to calling us elves, much after their own legend and folklore, because of our magic. Illusions, healing. We're not like others who worship Rhiann and can be gifted with shape-changing. The wolfkind."

"Wolfkind." Celine had never heard of such magic folk. "I didn't know the magic of land was *this* different."

"Well, I can't imagine wolfkind needing to use the sea, which would explain why you've never seen one. They are guardians of Rhiann's creations, tasked with maintaining order and balance." The queen cast her eyes down at her hands, her look serene. "Living in a world increasingly accepting of magic folk—increasingly *ruled* by magic folk. My heart races at the very idea of it, doubly so to see it one throne closer."

"Your majesty," Celine prefaced, unsure if she should ask. But she did, sensing the moment as the only right one for it. "Was it your idea to have Owen marry a merfolk?"

"No. And yes. *Magic folk* was what I urged of my husband. I was unaware he'd colluded with the merfolk king." The queen lifted an eyebrow. "But magic is magic." She gave Celine a small smile. "And the result is better than I expected."

"I'm grateful, your majesty. Truly." Celine met the queen's gaze with more confidence than she'd had since arriving. "The command of my king came as a shock. But Owen is right." She said it again, slower, stronger. "He is *right*."

"I'm sure he feels the same about you."

A feeling of closure swelled with the after-touch of relief. The queen, grateful, rose and gestured toward her chamber door.

"Thank you, Celine," she said. "There aren't many I can speak with about these things."

"I am honored, your majesty," she said. "Please, speak with me anytime." Then, with a spark of inspiration, Celine added, "And to Owen. I know it would mean a lot to him to know how you feel."

"I was considering that very thing."

I am quite taken with you, Owen had said earlier. The echo of his words spread warmth through her chest.

"Now." The queen sat up straighter. "We should go to the Solar. The lessons to cover today will be most easily done there, I think."

"The *Solar.*"

"Something of a war room," she said. "Documents, maps, papers, whatever the king needs to keep organized with the political and military runnings of the kingdom." She stood, gesturing toward the door. "You have a lot of ground to cover, I'm afraid. Visual aids are a must."

They stepped out, Miss Helen waiting. But Celine stared at Liam, who waited with her.

He bowed from the waist. "Your majesties."

"Liam?" Adella tilted her head. "To what do we owe this visit?"

"An apology, my queen, to her majesty." Liam kept his shoulders straight as he regarded Celine. "I am late in giving you the apology you deserve, your majesty. I pray for your forgiveness for my actions."

My queen. Liam's behavior was to be expected, as Celine's status and power had changed. Even with the superficial apology, she accepted it.

"I trust we can work together to keep Estilon safe," Celine said.

"Yes, your majesty." He bowed again and remained with the three women as they walked down the corridor. "I should like to personally see to your safety, your majesty, to earn your trust."

"A kind thought, Liam," Adella said. "Each knight of Estilon will see to the safety of this kingdom and its leaders. Any personal attendance should remain Celine's choice."

Celine appreciated the chance to refuse Liam, but Celine felt ill-equipped to do anything but agree. "I appreciate the consideration from both of you," was all she could think to say.

Entering the Solar was a reprieve from the pressure to choose or not choose Liam. They'd walked to the other side of the castle to the large room where she and Owen had hidden from Graham and Rolf, eavesdropping. Now, she stopped in front of the closed door on the left, where Rolf had cursed Jesper and Sudor with each shuddering breath. Liam dutifully knocked three times.

"Enter." It was Owen's voice that bade them entrance. His eyes alighted to Celine, his smile appearing instantly. "Ah, the student has arrived. And with an entourage." He looked at each face, lingering on Liam's. "Bravo, wife. You can certainly draw a crowd."

"Gracious, Owen," Adella said. "Where is Tyrion?"

"I've sent him on an errand," Graham said. "Reinforcements for a nearby outpost. There are rumors of raiders circulating, your majesty."

"Sudor?"

"It's likely." Graham stood beside Owen, each of them leaning over the center table filled with maps and papers. "I've prepared what you've requested, your majesty."

"Excellent." Adella moved to a chair, and Owen helped her to sit.

Thunder rumbled overhead before the pattering of rain filled the room with its soothing ambience. The gray cast outside was a cool contrast to the amber light within, the fire low and the candles and wall sconces lit around them.

Celine looked at the papers covering the table, transfixed by the intricately crafted maps with carefully drawn topography. She leaned close, tracing her fingers over the mountain range that crowned Thurin, the northernmost kingdom of Sheraton. She'd heard stories of how cold those waters were, where ice didn't melt and only certain fish and merfolk could thrive. Merfolk with thicker skin and scales, with sharper claws and teeth.

"The queen's duties typically start with the diplomacy of Estilon," Adella said, presiding over the meeting. "She and the king work together to build relationships with neighboring kingdoms and visiting dignitaries. Alliances are vital."

Celine remembered her mother having similar responsibilities to varying merfolk traveling through the Sea of Kings. Any territorial disputes were handled with peace first, and, most of the time, a conversation was enough.

"We are allied with Melia and Thurin," Graham said, pointing to those regions on the map. "We are, of course, at odds with Sudor. And Runa bears no alliances."

"They seek opportunities," Celine said, reciting what she'd heard. "Pirates always do."

Graham nodded in approval.

"They have a strained relationship with the merfolk," Celine said, pointing to Runa's name on the map, tracing the R with her index finger. "My father didn't trust them but understood their strengths. Trading and bartering happened relatively easily during his rule. But I can't say the same now."

All eyes were on her, absorbing her every word.

"Dathan is technically my stepfather," she clarified with a tinge of disgust at the familial term. "Any diplomatic dealings, if they can be called that, I had no part in. Which was probably for the best."

"I remember King Janis," Graham said. "Well before the war. Probably well before you were born." He regarded Celine with a touch of kindness. "He was a fair leader."

"And Queen Elynda," Adella said, reaching to touch Celine's hand. "I met her only once, when I was a young queen. She was lovely."

She didn't expect her eyes to itch and sting, and she blinked quickly to stave off any emotional display, tightening her lips to keep them from quivering. "Thank you."

The meeting continued, with alliances explained alongside the varying customs across Sheraton. Hours waned to midday, those gathered growing restless with hunger.

"Trust that we'll help when visitors come into the kingdom," Adella reassured. "For now, let's leave the lesson in favor of some of Cook's fine cuisine."

"Praise the gods." Owen was the first to stand. "Shall we all dine together?"

Thunder rumbled again, the rain falling steadily.

"That sounds lovely," Adella said. "We can take the parlor."

"I'll have everything arranged, your majesty." Helen bowed and left.

Celine sat awkwardly silent, eyes scanning the maps and documents on the table. But she looked up from the inked parchment, feeling Owen's eyes on her.

"Are you alright?" he mouthed.

She nodded.

"After lunch," he went on, staying silent, "we can sneak out—"

He made a walking motion with two fingers on his palm, at which point Adella looked at her son.

"What are you two whispering about?"

"Nothing," he blurted, his eyebrows slightly lifted. "Nothing at all."

Graham smirked. Celine didn't look over her shoulder at Liam, wishing that he'd had some other duties to attend to.

But Celine was grateful that, once the midday meal had begun, the conversation was much more casual and light. There was nothing said of war or alliances, no talk of economy or diplomacy. Graham took up most of the conversation, bragging about the newest falcon he was training.

"Remarkable creatures, falcons," he said with reverence.

Owen grinned, looking at Celine with an expression that read, *Here he goes again.*

The rain continued, the scene outside captivating for Celine to watch. She'd only ever watched storms from the sea, whether it was from beneath the surface or while perched on a sea stack. But from an upstairs view within the castle, the landscape stretched far, with wind and rain covering everything up to the horizon.

Change. That was what rain always reminded her of. Change, and something waiting on the horizon.

"Your thoughts are as deep as the sea, wife," Owen said quietly, sitting closer to her. "Do you have words for them?"

"I do." She broke her line of sight from the storm to look at her husband instead, reassured by the warmth in his gaze. "What story do you feel like this time? A pirate story, since we spoke of Runa?"

The dimple in his right cheek was deep as he grinned. "You *are* flirting with me." He took her hand, entwining their fingers. "What did you and my mother talk about? Am I allowed to know?"

"She asked how I was doing." She covered his hand, her fingers brushing over his knuckles. "I think you should talk to her."

"About how you're doing?"

"About you. And her." Celine blinked once with intention. "You two should talk."

Owen exhaled through his nose, his cool breath sweeping over their skin. "I suppose we should."

"You both have sacrificed a lot," Celine whispered, her voice barely audible among their mixed company. "You owe it to yourselves to finally be honest. About everything."

He kissed her forehead, at which point all conversation stilled. Embarrassed, they looked around.

"What?" Owen asked, breaking the awkward silence. "She's my wife, isn't she?"

Graham cleared his throat, stifling a laugh, and Adella allowed a light smile to peek through. Celine didn't bother looking at Liam.

"Perhaps this is the point to conclude our gathering." Adella stood.

"Mother." Emboldened, Owen rose with Celine, still holding her hand. "May we talk before you retire to your chambers? Perhaps in mine?"

"Certainly." She looked from Owen to Celine. "I trust everything is alright."

"Yes, of course. I— *We* would like to speak with you."

Celine looked at him, but he didn't meet her gaze. She watched him swallow and step forward, still holding onto her.

"We are the brave ones," she whispered.

He squeezed her hand. "We are the brave ones."

CHAPTER 23

Once Owen closed his chamber door, Adella turned to her son and asked, "Should I sit down?"

"That's a good idea." Owen helped his mother into one of the wooden chairs at his table.

"Pray, tell me quickly." Adella's eyes darted from Owen to Celine. "How bad is it?"

"It isn't bad." Owen arranged two more chairs, taking the one in front of Adella. Celine sat, wishing she could slip out of the room and give them privacy. "This is a conversation you and I should have had a long time ago."

Adella's hands smoothed her skirt. "Is this about the two of you?"

"No," Celine said. "I can wait outside if—"

"Please stay." Owen rested his hand on her arm. "I can do it if you're here."

"By the gods," Adella whispered.

Owen took his mother's hands, worry deepening on her face. "Mother, we need to talk about our magic."

The queen nearly deflated with relief. "By the gods, Owen. I thought something was wrong." She squeezed his hands. "You have a flair for the dramatic, son."

He leaned back, releasing her, amusement doing little to detract from the seriousness of his expression. "Why haven't we talked about it before now?"

"When was it ever safe?" Adella took a deep breath. "I wondered for a time if you'd had magic at all."

"But you knew I did."

"Yes. Likely the same way you know I do. We can sense others like us. But I knew for sure when Kedran came to see me about your lessons."

Owen groaned, though there was mirth mixed in. "Smithson told you?"

"Of course he did. Which—there is something I should tell you."

Celine didn't physically react, though her insides were endeavoring somersaults. She wouldn't leave Owen, even as her stomach tightened.

"Is it about why you married my father? I have wondered how it happened—an arranged marriage like mine?"

"It was," she said. "Rolf's father was not the king of Estilon then. He'd heard of deals made with the earthborn of Alvar. Old magic."

Owen stared for several seconds, not expecting this turn in the conversation. "A deal? Grandfather wasn't king?"

"The throne of Estilon was in a—" She paused for the word. "—a state of transition, we'll say. War-torn. Rolf's family was powerful but bore no royal connection. So, he made one. All the while, his brother fell deathly ill with a virus that plagued most of Sheraton. That would leave Rolf's father as the primary bearer of a royal line, should he lay claim to the throne."

"What you're saying—" But Owen stopped himself. "I'm sorry for interrupting. Please, continue."

"Rolf's father came to us very eager. He wanted power and knew of the old magics that could seal such a fate. So, he made a deal."

"You said *us*." Owen shifted in his seat. "'He came to *us*.'"

"Rolf came to me and my husband." Adella didn't blink, her expression nothing short of loving and hopeful. "He'd heard of our power and sought our help."

Owen's brow furrowed as he stared, open-mouthed. Betrayal. Disbelief. "You had a husband."

"Have," she clarified quietly. "I *have* a husband."

Owen breathed heavily in and out, his torso inflating and deflating. Celine pressed her hand between his shoulder blades, running small circles there, grounding him in this moment beside her.

"Were you ever going to tell me?"

"Yes." Adella's fingers worried the edge of one sleeve cuff. "I couldn't think how to approach this with you. There has always been unrest in Estilon, and I wanted to protect as much of your youth as I could."

"Royals don't have the privilege of youth." He ran his hands through his hair. "Your husband." He paused, wrapping his words and his mind around what he wanted to say. "Is he still in Alvar, or did he make the trip to Estilon?"

"He's in Estilon." Then, after a beat, she added, "Your sister also did, until recently. She is now in Melia."

"Sister." He rubbed the fingers of one hand, thinking. "You've lived another life, Mother. One I never knew existed."

"I am quite old," she said with a tinge of humor. "Nearly twenty years older than your father. My life with my husband had only just begun when your grandfather met us."

"Twenty years older?" Owen blinked. "The way we age—"

She nodded slowly. "Much slower than humans."

His eyebrows lifted briefly as a shrug. "Father must have been jealous."

"He knew everything, Owen." Adella leaned forward here, everything about her words and her body language insistent. "He knew absolutely everything and followed the deal his father made." She let her desperation show how deeply she wanted him to understand. "He knew about my family. He knew about my magic. Your father and I had no secrets, and we harbored no love for one another. Not in that way."

"But it must have been hard," he said. "Married to a king who fought against magic, separated from your husband and daughter who love you. Wasn't Father bitter?"

"I'm sure he was," she said, "but he also knew the deal gave him power. And the deal gave him you." At this, she smiled, tears glistening in her sky-blue eyes. "My beautiful boy."

Celine's feet tucked beneath her chair, pushing into the floor to fight the urge to flee.

Owen leaned forward, hands clasped together. "Do you miss your family?"

"*You* are my family." Adella wrapped his hands in hers. "My daughter knows and understands, and I miss her terribly. The magic of our people makes demands that can be quite cruel. But I wouldn't change a thing." She reached to brush strands of dark hair from his eyes. "This deal gave me you, and I thank the gods every day that I'm your mother."

This quiet moment shared between them was serene, and Celine breathed more easily.

"What is my sister's name?" he asked.

"Aurora. *Rory*." Maternal warmth filled her teary eyes. "And you should know, Owen, my husband—"

"It's alright, Mother. You don't have to—"

"It's Kedran."

He froze, staring. "Smithson?!" His mouth opened and closed as he looked past Adella to the wall behind her. "He's your *husband*?"

"Learning of your tutelage under him was one of the happiest and scariest moments I lived through." She wiped her eyes. "I was thrilled that he was teaching you, thrilled that you liked and trusted him. But I was terrified about your magic coming out. Terrified that you'd learn the truth about us before I could tell you."

He stared at his mother, mouth agape. Celine quietly prayed that he would understand, but she acknowledged the corner of her heart that harbored empathy for his frustration and anger at such a secret. What if it had been Celine's parents hiding something so significant from her?

A small ache caught in her chest. At least they would be alive.

"So much makes sense now," he said. "Smithson, as your trusted physician. And I thought it was because you are both magic folk."

"Which was not an incorrect assumption." She gazed at her son, worry still in the tightness around her eyes and mouth. "I love you, Owen. Tell me what you're feeling. Spare no detail."

"I hardly know." He combed his hair with his fingers. "I love you, too. I suppose..." He shook his head. "I hardly know."

"Ask me anything," she said, her eagerness and her happiness pouring out of her. "About our magic. About Alvar."

And he did, with Celine listening to every question and answer. Adella even showed her power as she explained their abilities in illusion and enchantment. She held out her arm, a glamor shimmering with her skin shining blue and purple iridescence.

"We are capable of extraordinary wonder." Adella beamed, her joy palpable. "I can't wait to show you everything."

Mother and son spoke for a while longer before parting, and Celine, though an outsider in this very private moment, was honored to have seen and felt how tender they were with one another.

When Adella left, Owen stood at his window, silent, for a long time. Celine went to him, lifting a hand to touch his shoulder but hesitating to make contact. What would she disrupt? Would words be easier?

But Owen turned and wrapped her in his arms without a word, burying his face in the bend of her neck.

"Do you have the words yet?" she whispered, bringing her arms around his neck. He held her tighter. "Talking can help make room in what I imagine is a very crowded space."

"Being magic folk isn't the shock," he said, his voice mumbled as he spoke into her skin. "I've known for as long as I can feasibly remember. Though, I'm not very adept at using it. But having a name for it. *Earthborn.* That—" He stopped, standing up straighter, looking her in the eye. "It's real now. It's not some strange, abstract secret I'm figuring out when no one's looking. And it's far bigger than I imagined."

"You mean because of your mother and her husband?"

He nodded.

She smoothed his hair back, an excuse to touch him, to soothe him. "How can I help?"

He looked at her for a prolonged silence, lips parted with words to be said. But he only sighed, his cool breath escaping through his nose in a rush. "I don't know. I don't know where to start."

"What do you want to start? Understanding your heritage, or understanding magic?"

"Yes?"

She chuckled quietly. "Start where it's comfortable."

"Illusion magic." He thought for a moment. "Inward focus, manipulating my appearance. I've been doing that for a long time."

"As Charlie."

"More than that." He turned his head, closing his eyes. "Look at my ear."

Celine watched as the slightest point appeared. She gasped, touching its peak.

"I've hidden them since I noticed," he said. "I thought they were a birth defect or something odd that would get me made fun of. As a prince, everyone scrutinizes you. So, ever since I was young, I masked myself."

"You don't have to wear that now," she said. "You don't have to wear it with me."

His eyes roamed over her face, over her hair. "Can you—" He hesitated, vulnerability in his eyes. "Can you show me yours?"

What would it take to try? Dathan's magic changed her. Kasindra's magic waited in the necklace to bring more change when she wished for it. But what could she do to change herself?

"I don't know," she said. "I'm afraid to try. What if—" She looked down at her legs, running a hand over her thigh. "What if the tail returns, and I can't change it?"

He shook his head. "Best not to try. I wouldn't know how to help you."

But she wanted to. The way he'd looked at her in the water, with her markings distinctly her own...

She wanted him to see her again.

"There might be a way."

"I don't know," he said, retreating.

"I trust you." She brought his hands to her face. "Do you trust me?"

His thumbs stroked the length of her cheekbones. "Implicitly."

"Use your will. Focus it here." She guided his index and middle fingers down the sides of her face. "Do you remember what I looked like?"

"Of course. Am I—" His brow furrowed as he struggled. "Am I *dispelling*?"

"No," she said. "Rather, you're *seeing*." She pressed her hands against his, forming them to the shape of her face. "Let your magic show you the truth. It won't dispel the magic affecting me, but it will let you see what's really there."

He swallowed, bracing himself. Then, slowly, his fingers ran down her face, from hairline to chin, and Celine watched the awe come over him.

"By the gods," he whispered, continuing down her neck. "Incredible."

Shivers cascaded down her spine, her hands gripping the sides of his shirt to keep herself still.

His hands moved to her hair, showing its true color. "I'd almost forgotten how rich—how *vibrant*. Just like the sea."

Their eyes met, Owen's full of reverence. Celine's body moved of its own volition, without conscious thought or motivation, as though kissing him was the most natural thing in the world. The touch of their lips was gentle at first, curious. With a breath, she sought more, parting her lips and coaxing his tongue to meet hers. His hands pressed her closer. The way he held her, the way their mouths moved, the rhythm steady as the waves climbing the shore, slow and sure and *strong*. Her heart raced, the euphoria exceeding anything she'd ever known before.

"Owen," she whispered, breathless.

He rested his forehead against hers. "I've wanted to do that for a long time."

He kissed her forehead, her eyes, her lips, his worship in every touch.

"With what lies before us," he said. "With everything that's happened, I couldn't do this alone."

She'd never known safety in one's embrace. Not like this, when the reality of the world bore upon her its full weight.

"Celine, I..." He exhaled, fingers combing her hair. "I couldn't imagine having anyone else by my side."

"I feel the same." She nuzzled his shoulder, relishing how perfectly she fit. "Though it's far from over."

They parted, arms still around one another, Celine looking up into his bright blue eyes.

"Kasindra may have news," she said. "Shall we pay her a visit this evening?"

"Will I be welcome?" he asked with a half-smile. "I don't think she likes me very much."

"She'll have to be alright with it, or she'll have to do without me."

He smirked. "I feel quite special, being held in such high esteem."

"We'll see if she has anything to say. I'm not sure if anything we've done has reached Santus." Then, on a more pleasant note, she added, "I could see my friends again."

Thunder rumbled quietly, the storm passing to the distance, and Owen glanced over his shoulder to the window. "There's still time to read in the library by the fire. We can pretend the storm is still heavy outside."

"An excellent idea."

And they went together, hand in hand, their hearts full of one another.

CHAPTER 24

When night fell, Owen and Celine crossed the damp courtyard, the mist of rain lingering like a fog around them. Kasindra didn't know they were coming, but perhaps her cauldron would tell her. Celine didn't expect the Sea Witch to miss an opportunity to see Owen again.

"I rather like these secret meetings," he said, holding her hand in the crook of his arm. The afternoon storm had swept over Estilon, leaving a chilly overcast behind.

"The thrill of a secret," she said. "A secret worth keeping."

"What sort of secret qualifies?" He tilted his head back as he looked down at her. "Few are truly worth keeping from someone close to you. Someone you care about."

An interesting approach to the question. She waited to answer as Owen unlocked the back gate and offered his hand.

"Why are we going out this way?" she asked, repulsed by the closeness to iron. "We went through the front last time."

"*Secrets*," he said with a grin. "Now, tell me, wife, about secrets worth keeping."

"A secret where the person will not get hurt in the absence of knowing?" But she hummed to herself as she considered. "An example fails to come to mind."

"A secret shared with the other person," Owen concluded. "Secrets are hard to bear alone."

"Like your magic."

Owen stepped through the gate and closed it behind him. Celine moved further from the reach of iron. "How different would I be without such a secret? If I still had magic but didn't grow up having to hide it?"

"Probably much the same as you are now, though perhaps more practiced."

An eyebrow rose as he rejoined her, placing her hand on his arm again. "You have that much faith in me?"

"Magic didn't make you a good person," she said. "Magic didn't make you kind."

He stopped, and she met his gaze in fleeting concern. His growing smile made her face warm, her own smile blooming.

"What?" She tugged on his arm. "Why are you looking at me like that?"

"I'd very much like to kiss you," he said. "It would be beneath the moonlight, if the clouds weren't in the way."

"The moon is still above us." She bit her bottom lip, the sensation of him lingering in memory.

"And the sea is before us." He stepped closer, cupping her face in his hands. He opened his mouth to speak, but the words didn't pass his lips. Instead, he let his eyes travel over her face. "I still think about your hair, your scales."

"I wonder what you would look like as a merman." She rested her hands at his sides. "Would your scales be as blue as your eyes?"

"What would it take to find out?"

"Crystal," she said, simply. "And the will to see the magic through. It's a powerful spell, and it hurts like the seven hells."

He flinched. "Don't sugar-coat it, please."

"And you'd have to do it twice." She winced, apologetic. "You'd need your legs back to rule your kingdom."

He kissed her, his lips touching hers with such a quick motion that she almost wondered if it had happened at all.

"With all this talk of pain and transformation," he said, resuming their walk toward the beach, "I thought I'd better kiss you before the moment faded."

"Then let's reach the water before we're caught." She took his hand and moved, playacting in haste. "This secret we share."

They jogged, trying not to laugh aloud as the moment swept over them and through them, the thrill and excitement of existing swelling in Celine's heart until it threatened to erupt from her in a cackle of glee. She'd never felt like this before, like her feet didn't touch the ground as she pushed through the sand, as though her body was lightweight enough to be carried by the wind. One perfect gust, and she would soar to unimaginable heights.

They eased onto the wet sand, and Celine reached with her hand and her mind, dipping her fingers into the water as she sent her thoughts toward Kasindra. Would the Sea Witch hear her, unannounced and unexpected? Did she already know of Celine and Owen's presence on the beach?

"My dear." Her voice crooned in Celine's mind. "You brought him to me again? Do you wish for us to get along?"

"He's an ally," Celine answered. "We can trust him."

"Trust the son of Rolf?" But Kasindra didn't pause or laugh. There was too much interest in her voice.

Kasindra emerged from the water, her head and shoulders breaking through the surface, and she regarded Owen with her keen, lavender eyes.

"Something about her feels familiar," Owen whispered to Celine. "I can't put my finger on it."

"Hello, newlyweds." Kasindra smiled, her teeth vibrant even in the dim night. "I trust all has been well since your marriage."

"You've heard?" Celine asked, both pleased and unsettled that her suspicions were confirmed. Kasindra was always watching.

"Word travels." Kasindra edged closer to the shore. "I have news for you, my dear."

Celine squeezed Owen's arm, stepping closer. The wet sand sank beneath her feet. "Oh?"

"Santus's magic is stronger, and I think I've figured out why."

From the water, Kasindra produced a blue-green iridescent stone, almost identical in color to the one they found on the Moonblade assassin.

"Is that—"

"A new arcana crystal," she said. "One that grows *on land*."

Celine took it carefully in her hands, feeling Owen leaning closer against her to see it in the dim light.

"Is it the same?" Celine asked. Feigning ignorance to its existence felt like the wise choice to make. "Arcana crystal can grow on land? That seems..."

"Too good to be true?" Kasindra finished for her. "I thought the same, but here it is. It's more powerful and works the same way as the crystal we grow in the sea." She leaned closer and played at whispering, "I found it in one of Dathan's secret stores. Well, what he *thinks* is a secret." She cackled. "That is my gift to you both. A wedding present."

"A mighty gift." Celine presented it to Owen. "I've seen nothing like it."

He didn't even flinch or flutter at her insinuation, playing along. "Nor have I. Not even a *rumor* of such a thing."

"Humans may not know what it's truly called." Kasindra smoothed her wet hair away from her face and shoulders. "There's tell of an underground source for it somewhere in Sheraton."

"Thank you," he said, touching the edge of the crystal while Celine held it. "I don't know what to say."

"Just take care of Celine, your highness." Kasindra bowed her head in a gesture that was almost convincing in its reverence. "She means a great deal to us."

"I fully intend to." Owen held her closer, his closed-mouth smile emphasizing his dimple.

"You have my condolences, your highness," Kasindra said. "For all our differences, I am sorry for your grief and your loss."

"Thank you." His tone was no less appreciative, though not nearly as warm. "I appreciate your kind words."

Owen the Diplomat, and how quickly he could switch demeanors! Where he would like to learn dark magic from Celine, she would like to learn that from him—magic of a different kind.

"What of Dathan?" Celine asked. "How is the merking?"

Kasindra's grin widened, appearing more wicked in the darkness. "The king suffers."

Emboldened, Celine leaned in. Owen tightened his hold, his own excitement tangible. "It's working?"

"Of course, it's working." Kasindra clicked her tongue, amused. "The shadows will never fail."

"Tell me everything." Celine nearly kneeled on the wet sand, so eager she was for the news. "What's happening to him?"

"Sleepless nights," she crooned, a dark song in her voice. "Listless days. May I ask—" She hesitated, eyes going from Celine to Owen. "What are you showing him?"

"Our parents' nightmares." It was Owen who answered. "Celine's magic is incredible to behold."

She cackled, her wicked laugh echoing off of the heavens above them. "Beautiful! Absolutely marvelous!" Her voice resounded in dark glee. "Sending him Chaos and darkness. No less than he deserves!"

Celine looked up at Owen, her own pride reflected in his eyes. It was working. Their magic was *working*.

Kasindra parted not long after, the married pair standing on the wet sand in the cold sea breeze.

"That magic I felt from her," he said, "what I thought I recognized." He looked down admiringly at the crystal. "I wonder how much more is down there in Dathan's pocket."

"This is how Dathan made his deals," Celine said. "Whatever Jesper wanted, in exchange for this crystal."

Including Celine's own exile. Flashes of her transformation returned to her, knowing then that they were powered by this very crystal, this precious gem from an enemy king.

"Incontrovertible proof that the merking is working with Sudor." Owen grinned in the dark. "Sufficient reason, I think, to act without kick-starting another war."

"Though this complicates the manner of our marriage as a political healing balm to mend our kingdoms," she said. "The merfolk may not see it as justified."

"I don't intend to wage war against the merfolk for colluding with Sudor," he said. "I do intend, however, to reach Dathan, personally, however I can. Through magic. Through iron."

She winced.

"I'm sorry." He took one of her hands and kissed it. "All I mean to say is he will not get away with what he's done. But I will not compromise your people."

"Your highness!"

They both turned to Liam calling for Owen, coming down from the main road to Estilon. Tyrion was not far behind him.

"We've been caught," Owen said with a laugh. "It was fun while it lasted."

"Where the blazes have you two been?" Tyrion stomped in the sand toward them. Celine waited for him to rest his fists on his hips like an angry mother. "We looked everywhere for you!"

"Just out for a bit of night air," Owen said. "Sorry to cause worry. We escaped for a private walk, just the two of us."

"You don't have the privilege of private walks," Tyrion said, still perturbed. "Your private walks will always have guards in attendance. Is that clear?"

Liam looked at Tyrion, alarmed. "He's our king, Tyr."

But Owen laughed, the sound deep and genuine, bringing a smile to Celine's lips as well. "I understand. Thank you both for prioritizing our safety."

"We'll escort you back," Liam said, making eye contact with Celine and bowing his head.

"Thank you." Getting used to Liam's presence was likely in her best interest, especially since he'd taken the time to apologize.

Owen and Celine proceeded back toward Estilon Castle, with Liam and Tyrion walking several paces behind them.

"They're likely expecting to escort us back to my chambers," he whispered. "Would you prefer that, or your own accommodations?"

She tilted her head, looking up at him. "I hadn't really thought about it."

"It's just that I would like to court you properly." He paused, a touch of nervousness coming through. "We've only just met, really. It's been almost a week, if I have my days straight."

One week. Such a brief amount of time for so much in her life to change.

"Let's get to know one another," he said. "Let's take our time."

She stopped, facing him properly, her smile warm. "I would like that very much. *Husband*."

He chuckled, kissing one of her hands. "As would I, *wife*."

CHAPTER 25

In her chambers, waking up tangled in the blankets, the first thing Celine thought about was Owen.

The second was Dathan.

Kasindra had told her Dathan was unwell. With sick merking creating worry among the merfolk, some of them may take steps toward the throne themselves...

What about Jessa? What about Quinn and Zander? If there was any unrest because of her, because of the shadows she sent to the merking, she would have no way of knowing if her friends were alright. She was far from them in this manmade structure of stone.

Helen had come and gone, ordering breakfast and helping Celine dress. She was glad for her solitude, her thoughts far too loud.

"The queen may come and go as she pleases, right?" Celine considered the question as she chewed a bite of food. "I can go to the sea as often as I wish."

But no one trusted her, save Owen and Adella. How many waited, watching her every move for proof of her intentions toward Estilon?

She needed insight.

Rising from the table and stepping out, she found Liam at his post by her door. Helen was not far, darning a sock near the window.

"Perhaps one or both of you would know," she said without additional context or preamble, "how I could monitor the Sea of Kings?"

"My queen?" Liam asked, confused.

"There is unrest among my people," she said. "I'm worried I won't know anything until it's much too late. Having eyes on the water would ease a lot of my worry."

"The harbormaster is your best bet," Liam said. "As well as the admiral or a captain."

"Brilliant idea," Celine said, making Liam turn a light shade of pink at the compliment. "I trust they'll be forthcoming in reports?"

"They shouldn't have any reason to lie to their queen," Helen said.

Celine wished she had her optimism.

"A letter from the king would probably go a long way," Liam said. "They wouldn't dream of going against a direct order."

So, when Celine met Owen that afternoon to enjoy the midday meal, she breached the subject.

"A fine idea," he said, reaching for the roasted meat on the table. They dined in his chambers while Tyrion and Liam waited outside. "And Liam's right about the letter. Something official to make sure they tell you what you've asked of them."

"I don't blame them for their limited trust," she said. "I'm a merfolk, in their eyes, and still quite new to Estilon."

Owen opened his mouth to say something but withheld whatever thoughts were about to surface. Instead, he said, "You're my wife and the queen consort. That's as far as their reckoning should go."

"In an ideal world, perhaps."

The door burst open after the briefest knock, and Graham appeared, exasperated.

"I sincerely apologize for the intrusion," he said, "but we've just received word of a raid on the Southern outpost." He took a breath, chest heaving from his haste. "It's completely destroyed."

Owen stood, wiping his mouth. "How long ago?"

"The messenger just arrived. The other outposts had more success in remaining intact, but there were no less than three other attacks."

Celine rose and followed them out, the group joined by Tyrion and Liam while crossing to the other side of the castle toward the Solar.

There, Owen and Graham inspected an unrolled map while Celine, Tyrion, and Liam waited patiently. For what, Celine wasn't sure. A plan of action? Owen was quick to respond to a village raid before. He didn't seem willing to let this matter rest, either.

"I'll send pairs of knights to each of the other outposts," Owen said. "Graham, take a team of at least four men to the southern outpost. Bring medical supplies and food with you."

"And perhaps a way to bring men back," Tyrion said. "In case they need Geoffrey's care."

"It may be better to take Geoffrey along," Owen said.

"And leave the castle without its physician?" Tyrion shook his head.

But Owen spoke up before he could object further. "We are not without medical means. The local apothecary is more than capable to assist, and Geoffrey's expertise is needed elsewhere."

There was no further argument, and the plan was set. Tyrion rubbed his hands together, something in him anxious.

"Would you like to join Graham, Tyr?" Owen asked him.

"Not at the risk of leaving you, your majesty," he said, and he meant it. "Wild horses couldn't drag me away."

The resolution in his voice bloomed comfort and even warmth in Celine's chest. She remembered the way he'd carried her out of the prison and reassured her. Knowing Owen had Tyrion—and she, too, by extension—made her feel that much safer.

A gentle knock at the door preceded Helen's entry. "Your majesty," she said to Celine, a pair of dark brown leather boots in her hands. She made way for Lady Cynthia, folded garments in her arms. "Your clothes have arrived, your majesty."

"Oh, excellent." But she looked at Owen, knowing that the conversation wasn't over.

"Go." He kissed her hand. "I will follow as soon as I'm done."

Celine stepped out and walked with Helen and Lady Cynthia back toward her chambers.

"Thank you for working so quickly," Celine said as they walked. "I truly appreciate it."

Stepping into her chambers, Celine led Cynthia and Helen to the center table, where they placed the folded clothes. Helen passed her the boots.

"If these don't fit, your majesty, we can have the cobbler make adjustments."

Celine removed her borrowed boots with relief, and when she slipped into the new pair, everything held her feet and legs in all the right places. "Oh, these are lovely."

She walked a few paces in them and stopped at the table, touching the colorful fabric of the dresses—beautiful rose pink with one, sea blue with the other, both with white accents.

"The shirts and trousers were nice to make," Cynthia said. "May I ask why you wanted trousers?"

"Moving is much easier," Celine said, remembering the raid at the village, trying to hurry in a dress with the fabric heavy around her legs. "I'm not used to staying still, and dresses are more cumbersome than I thought they'd be."

"Oh, I'm sure. There's a lot more freedom in the sea, I would imagine."

"Yes," Celine said, a tinge of homesickness pinging her heart. "Quite a bit more."

"There are some new small clothes matching your measurements." Cynthia smiled. "I hope I can help you with more clothes, your majesty."

Celine placed the dresses on the bed and admired the shirts, one white and the other deep blue. The fabric of the trousers, one pair black and the other dark brown, was light yet durable. "They are beautiful."

"We shall leave you to try them on," Helen said. "If anything is amiss, simply let me know."

Cynthia agreed. "I'll take care of anything right away, your majesty."

When they left, Celine laid out the shirts and trousers on the bed, admiring the shapes and colors, wondering how they would fit on her. The clothes she'd arrived in had been large and shapeless, meant for a man's rectangle body rather than her curves. Eager to try, she reached to undo her clothes when a light knock interrupted her.

"May I come in?" It was Owen. "How do you like your new clothes?"

She opened the door. "I haven't tried them on yet."

"Oh. Is there a problem?"

"Privacy."

His eyebrows rose as he blinked several times. "Ah." He floundered, visibly flustered. "I see."

From the hallway, unseen, Sir Liam snickered.

"I'll be a moment." But before she closed the door, she asked him, "White or blue?"

"What?"

"What color? White or blue?"

"Blue."

She nodded once and closed herself inside. She was careful of the borrowed clothes as she removed them, folding them neatly on the bed as she dressed in her new small clothes, exhaling at their luxurious fit. The trousers hugged her skin, unlike the other pair she'd worn, and walking in them felt almost natural.

"Because they were made for me." She smiled to herself, pleased to have something that was hers. Truly hers.

She pulled the blue shirt over her head, adjusting her bound hair as she set the collar. The cross-ties at the front were dainty threads of leather, a lovely walnut brown that complimented the blue and matched the brown of her boots, which she slipped on last of all. She tucked her shirt into her trousers before she opened the door to grant Owen entry.

He stood in the doorway, his back to her at first, hands clasped behind him. He was in a quiet conversation with Liam, and she caught the end of his words, telling Liam about the crisis with the outposts.

"Hopefully, we'll know more soon," Owen said. "I'm going to go as soon as I hear back from the men."

"Do you think that's wise?" Liam asked. "You're a target, your highness. Jesper—"

"Jesper is a coward," Owen interrupted. "He resorts to attacking someone from behind rather than facing them, head-on."

Liam cleared his throat. "Yes, your highness."

"Forgive my harsh words, Liam," Owen said. "That fool of a king has quite gotten under my skin."

At this, he at last turned to Celine, surprise smoothing the perturbation from his face.

"Is everything alright?" she asked, stepping back from the doorway as he moved in, closing the door behind him.

"Yes." He cleared his throat, cheeks flushing. "Everything is alright. How do—how do *you* feel?"

He rubbed the back of his head, but Celine couldn't pinpoint what had him nervous or unsure.

"They feel *wonderful*." Celine spun, trusting her feet as they moved perfectly in the boots, as her body moved perfectly in her clothes.

"May I—" Owen paused, a curious look in his eyes. "May I try something?"

Celine raised an eyebrow. "You may."

He approached her, his hands going to the tie that kept her braid in place. Undoing it quickly, he worked his fingers through her wavy chestnut hair, gentle with every touch as he combed the braid free. Then, at last, with his fingertips against her scalp, moved the hair to freedom, bringing it to fall over her shoulder. Tingles danced down her spine.

"By the gods," he whispered, eyes taking her in.

She watched him in silence, heat blooming beneath her skin.

His hand cupped her face, his thumb barely tracing the arch of her cheekbone. "You are lovely."

"I can't tell you what it means to have something here that is mine." She took a breath. "Thank you. I will thank your mother as well."

"You may have your heart's desire, Celine," he whispered. "You only need ask."

"There is one thing," she said. "The outposts. When you go..."

He waited patiently as she read his expression, discerning how he would take her request.

"I will go with you," she said.

"Celine—"

"You have your knights, and you have your sword." She clasped his hand. "And you have your wife."

He squeezed her fingers. "My warrior queen."

Warrior queen. The title suited her. "Liam is right to worry about Jesper, and you are right to call him a coward. He works in ways that aren't straightforward, much like Santus, sneaking in the shadows, out of sight until he strikes."

Owen said nothing, his expression thoughtful. Then, "We should go soon. I find it difficult to wait for my men to return."

"I find it difficult to wait for anything."

He chuckled. "Is my wife as impatient as I am?"

"It does well to know something of what we're about to face," she said. "Time is the essence. If Estilon's outposts are compromised, Jesper is creeping his way in, closer and closer."

He furrowed his brow, smirking. "Have you been studying the maps in the Solar?"

"There's a reason merfolk patrol the shores so heavily." She paused for effect. "Humans don't get very far into the sea."

"Alright," he said. "You will join me when I leave for the outposts."

"And you will wait for your men to return." Her tone was firm. "We both are impatient, but we have to be smart."

"Smart, not impetuous. And I have a request, as well."

"And what is that?"

He pulled her closer, gently tugging her hand until they were inches apart. "Conjure with me."

She smiled. "That is easily done."

He raised their joined hands and entwined their fingers, concentrating on their touch as his magic prickled against her skin. She met his request with her own, their shadows spinning and dancing together as their energies gave them life.

"Go, my lovelies," Celine urged. "Give Dathan and Santus my regards."

"Go," Owen whispered. "Give them both their darkest nightmares."

The shadows flew faster around their hands before sailing out the window, slipping through a tiny crack before disappearing from sight.

"I hope the merking cannot find rest," Owen said, looking toward the window in the wake of the shadows. "I hope his dreams are tainted with darkness."

Celine rested her head on his shoulder. "May he be driven mad, in waking and in sleeping."

He brought his arm around her. "And may our rest be full of peace."

CHAPTER 26

Revenge against Dathan wasn't what she'd expected. She'd always imagined more violence. More blood. But conjuring shadows with Owen, sending them to the merking...that was revenge that tasted sweeter. With each shadow, Dathan's mind spiraled further, and she and Owen grew closer.

And Santus? Did the shadows touch him? Did they make him linger in confusing darkness?

The idea spread warmth from her core through to her limbs, the sense of satisfaction lifting a weight she'd grown accustomed to bearing.

But her parents remained in the Chaos Realm. They suffered while Dathan and Santus lived. Breaking their minds was a pleasant plan, but it was still far from the outcome she wanted...the one she *needed*.

She led Liam and Helen to the docks, her mind flooded.

"The new maid is taking well to her training," Helen said. "I should expect she'll be in your employ soon, your majesty."

"That's wonderful news." But she could see the tension in Helen's brow. "Are you not pleased?"

"Well." She hesitated before saying, "It's only that I've quite enjoyed our time together. I admire how proactive you are in your queenly duties."

Celine didn't feel very proactive, not when she can do much more with a pair of daggers and a target. But navigating this very new, very human world left few options.

The harbormaster saw Celine almost immediately, even with the busyness of the ships and workers and the cargo they carried.

"Your majesty," he greeted with a bow. "I hope you've been well."

"Yes, thank you. And you?" These niceties were necessary, but Celine wanted to dive into the real reason for her visit. Small talk only delayed the inevitable.

"Yes, ma'am, and I have news. I'm not sure what to make of it, though It's strange."

She waited patiently as a dock worker briefly redirected his attention asking about cargo placement.

"Three ships were spotted traveling up the coast, likely from Runa." Someone passed him a curling piece of paper, which he skimmed. "Yeah, that's alright."

"What's so strange about three ships from Runa?" Liam asked, his tone more rhetorical.

He passed the paper back and returned to Celine. "What's interesting is that their captains hate each other. Harris, Alden, and Brennan. Notorious feud. They put other ships at risk because of their violent tendencies."

"Where do you think they're headed?" Celine asked.

"Hard to say. Ghostlands, maybe? I'd be surprised if they were headed to Ileden."

"That far north?" Liam's tone drew Celine's attention. The term *Ghostlands* was new to her, but the lands north of Estilon were bereft of fortune, from what she understood. She'd seen enough to know the humans who lived there struggled to do so.

"What could the three of them be up to?" The harbormaster shook his head, his expression worried. "Nothing good, is my guess."

The three left the harbormaster to his work, walking back to Estilon Castle while speaking in hushed voices.

"What are the Ghostlands?" Celine asked her companions.

"Jesper's curse upon Melia," Helen said. "They resisted his attempt at conquering them, and he retaliated with a hateful blight that made desolate the lands north of Estilon."

"Cursing the land." Celine glanced from Helen to Liam. "How did he manage that without magic?"

"Chemicals and blends of various substances," Liam said. "That would be my guess. More alchemy than magic."

"Some say it was a deathwitch," Helen said. "Though I'd be curious to know what he used to convince her."

To hurt the land so deeply that it stole away its *life*...

Celine didn't believe that chemical blends alone were the cause. Like Helen suggested, Jesper had likely used magic.

Hypocrite. But she kept her vitriol within.

Back in the castle, Owen and Tyrion were descending the stairs in the foyer, words traveling quickly between them.

When Owen spotted her, his smile brightened his face. "Ah, there you are. We received word from one of the nearby outposts. Raiders were nearly successful at destroying it, but the knights of Estilon won the day *and* captured a prisoner."

"When do we leave?"

Owen beamed at his wife. "Now, if you're ready."

"Your majesty," Helen said, her voice delicate. "I don't think—"

But Celine could not be deterred. Jesper and Dathan were in league, and these raiders would know something that could help—information about their alliance, strengths and weaknesses, *something*.

Celine refused to remain at the castle and wait.

"I'll return once we're finished," Celine said.

Helen bowed her head. "Yes, your majesty."

"First the armory," Owen said, "then the stables."

Celine walked beside her husband, visiting the now-familiar armory and arming herself as she'd done before.

"We should have some chain mail made for you," Owen said, pulling his own chain shirt over his head. "My warrior queen."

Celine beamed at the compliment. "I do love that title, husband."

The tables were teeming with hands, each of them preparing three steeds for the journey to the outposts. Matilda, spotting Owen, trotted over excitedly, even as her stable hand called after her with her saddle in his hands.

"There's my girl." Owen rubbed her long nose, kissing her cheek below her eye. "How is she?"

"Right as rain, your highness," the stable hand said, hoisting the saddle on her back. "Missed you loads."

"Owen used to ride her every day," Tyrion said to Celine. "With everything that's happened, he hasn't had the chance to take her to the fields for a good run."

Celine reached for the mare, touching her nose. "We meet again, Matilda."

The horse snorted, nuzzling Celine's hand.

"Everything's ready, your highness," the stable hand said to Owen. "And we have a steed for her majesty." The stable hand presented a beautiful mare, mane and body matching in their deep copper color. "Name's Nutmeg."

"Nutmeg." Celine extended her hand to the horse, who seemed receptive.

"She's a sweet one," the stable hand said.

"Thank you for working so quickly," Owen said, admiring Nutmeg as he moved to help Celine mount the saddle. "She's a beauty."

Celine stepped into the stirrup and hoisted herself up just as she'd done before, Nutmeg remaining still and calm. Climbing up and sitting in the saddle was much easier, and, this time around, much more comfortable with only one person in the seat.

Owen climbed onto Matilda. "Call for me if you feel you're about to fall."

"I'll be fine." Celine stroked Nutmeg's neck. "Won't I, Nutmeg? There's a good girl."

Then he urged Matilda forward toward the city gate, with Celine, Tyrion, and Liam following behind.

THEY RODE FOR OVER AN HOUR. The landscape outside of Estilon castle was vast and vibrant, with green and brown all over with a speckling of color from flowers growing wild in the fields. Blinking through the sunlight, Celine tried to study what she could as they passed, noticing the different shapes and colors of each flower and plant.

"I've heard tell of Moonblade frequenting this area," Tyrion said from Owen's left. Liam remained at Owen's right, both men eyeing their respective sides for trouble while Owen and Celine watched the front.

In the far distance ahead, trees lined the horizon, their beautiful brown trunks tall and thick as their green tops stretched heavenward.

"Is that a forest?" Celine asked, pointing. "All of those trees together?"

"Yes," Owen said. "Wolfwood, it's called." His voice added playful drama to the second name. "They say it's filled with magical tricksters eager to lead you astray."

"*Really?*"

"Stories parents tell their children to keep them from wandering off," Liam said.

"I've seen them," Tyrion said, seriousness smoothing any lines from his face. "When I was a boy. Mysterious blue lights floating above the ground, lining up into the woods. I almost followed them."

"We must go soon," she said. "When there's peace in Estilon."

Owen nudged Matilda closer to Nutmeg. "We will cross through those trees as soon as we can manage." His voice was confidential with a dramatic thrill in its melody and rhythm. "You shall have your wish soon, wife."

Her excitement morphed as the tingle of expectation warmed, her heart fluttering at his proximity, at the intimacy of his promise.

She hadn't expected to become emotionally close to her human husband, their union arranged by kings she didn't trust. But he'd found his way in. As they rode side by side, she could feel him settling down in the comfortable spaces of her heart.

She was grateful, then, for his wish to court. The partnership ritual she'd read about in books had, in reality, held more excitement than she'd expected. Owen wanting to take time to get to know one another had tempered what could have been an impetuous step on her part. Celine wasn't one to idle when her heart took the lead.

"What you said before," Liam said, conversation returning to more serious matters, "about Moonblade wandering these parts. Could that mean that they aren't with Jesper, after all?"

"Moonblade is only loyal to itself," Tyrion answered. "They follow coin more than any master. Their allegiance to Jesper depends strictly upon his purse."

"If it isn't Sudorian soldiers in disguise," Owen said, "it's mercenaries and assassins-for-hire. Have they connected at all with the Wandering Order?"

Wandering Order? But rather than ask, Celine listened.

"That, I know," Liam said with a snap of his fingers. "Moonblade is quite adamant about freedom for all folk, including magic folk. Unless they have members secretly aligned with that *cult—*" The word from him came out like a curse. "—Moonblade doesn't tolerate them."

"At least we have that going for us," Owen said. Then, to Celine, he asked, "Do the merfolk know anything about Moonblade?"

"Not to my knowledge," she said. "This is the first I've heard of the Wandering Order, too. Perhaps they know better than to get too close to the water."

Owen chuckled at her dark implication.

Another half hour passed before they reached an impressive encampment surrounded by a tall wooden fence. At one side was a lookout, the window narrow to provide sight for a bowman's shot while protecting the body from fire. From there, a voice called that three Estilon riders approached.

"Oy! One of them's Prince Owen!"

"It's *King* Owen, you halfwit!"

"Oh, apologies, your majesty!" A hand waved. "Long live King Owen!"

Voices echoed the call as they approached the outpost.

Footsteps hurried, and the wooden gate squeaked open, revealing a team of men in Estilon colors and one woman with dark brown hair bound at the nape of her neck. She wore tight, black clothing with a gray wrap covering her shoulders.

"Your highness!" The men bowed, though the woman only nodded her head, remaining behind the gathered group. One man, presumably the leader, spoke up. "What brings you to the outpost, your majesty?"

"Concerns about Sudor." Owen dismounted, reaching for Celine to help her down. His hands braced her waist as her hands held his shoulders, and she descended without issue, though her feet landed below weakened knees. The heat from his hands and the strength of his hold stirred something within her.

He continued. "We've heard of your troubles, and I'm interested in anything you've learned."

Celine eyed the woman, who studied Owen with a smirk and a critical eye. She'd seen an expression like that on Kasindra as she measured someone up.

Owen must have sensed it, for it reached a hand to her. "I am King Owen of Estilon."

"Valera." She shook his head, her soft brown eyes matching her smirk. "Honored to meet you, your highness."

"She's from Moonblade, your majesty," one soldier said immediately. "The Wandering Order's been raising the seven hells to the south in Runa, and she's tracked a band of them this far north."

Owen winced, looking at Tyrion. "I was afraid of that."

"She helped with the raiders," another soldier said. "She captured the one we've questioned."

"With Sudor stirring up trouble," Valera said, "the Wandering Order has a perfect opportunity to feed off of the chaos."

Her voice was a smooth mezzo soprano, though Celine could hear her playing around the lower notes as she spoke.

"My guess is they're heading into Sudor," Valera said.

"Where they'll likely receive a warm welcome," Owen quipped. "I can't expect Melia will be too pleased if they move past Sudor's borders."

"Some assume Melia is still weak in recovery," Tyrion said. "But that is a very ignorant opinion, if I may say."

"I agree." Owen nodded once, looking around at the other soldiers. "What else to report?"

"The one we've captured has said very little," the soldier said. "Even with various methods used to get him to talk."

Celine could only guess what those *methods* were.

"I would like to speak with him," Owen said. He glanced to his knights and to Celine as they assented to follow.

The soldiers and Valera led them into a small shed, likely used for sleeping in shifts. There, tied to a chair in the center of the room, was a man, his head lulled in sleep.

"Nice to know someone's getting some rest 'round here." The soldier nudged the prisoner's leg with the toe of his boot. "Oy! Rise and shine!"

The prisoner stirred, blinking slowly as his eyes focused on Owen and the others. His gaze lingered on Valera, a smile widening as he stared.

Then his haughty gaze fixed on Owen. "Your majesty." He grinned, leaning back in his seat as though at leisure. "I'm pleased to make your acquaintance."

"What was the goal behind your attempted seizure of his outpost?" Owen asked, his tone cold and official.

"No attempted seizure," the man said. He chuckled, looking at the knights bearing Estilon colors. "There was no intention of leaving anything or anyone behind."

"What is Jesper's endgame?" Owen asked. "What does he want?"

"Isn't it obvious?" The man continued to laugh. "You already know the answer, your highness."

"Answer the question," Liam said, stepping forward.

As the two men locked eyes, the prisoner sneered, clenching his jaw. Seconds passed before the prisoner's gaze shifted, internal pain reflecting in the stare he tried in vain to maintain. His eyes lulled back, his body twitching and seizing before it fell limp in the chair. With his hands and legs bound to his seat, his body collapsed in a strange, maligned way.

The head bobbed from side to side, his chest stilled. Something sweet carried over the air and into Celine's nose, something smelling of fruit. "Owen—"

But he'd already suspected what her senses caught. Taking the man by the hair, Owen lifted his head, showing the white foam at the edges of his mouth.

"Damn it all," Owen said, letting the man go. "How did he manage poison?"

"Likely something kept in his mouth," Valera said. "I'm sorry. I didn't think to check for that."

Stepping forward, Valera searched the prisoner's neck immediately, as though she knew what she would find. When she revealed the silver chain bearing the emblem of moon and dagger, she hissed a curse.

"You dare bear the mark of Moonblade, you *liar*." She kicked at the dead man's legs. "Where are the rest of your rats hiding?"

"May Anya's justice be served," Tyrion said, looking with disgust at the dead man as the other knights untied his arms and legs.

Celine's dark thoughts simmered in the bitter emptiness of work left unfinished.

"We should return," Tyrion said. "I can send a pair of knights to help fortify the outpost."

"Good." Owen turned to the men of the outpost and bowed his head. "You have done Estilon a great service. What supplies do you need?"

"Standard fare, your highness," one said. "Though some of Cook's peach cakes wouldn't be unwelcome."

The men chuckled.

"I'll let her know," Owen said. "She'll be happy to make them for you."

"I can ride with you until the bend toward the east," Valera said. "I've heard of a rogue group claiming to be Moonblade when their actions speak otherwise." Her eyes darkened, casting a shadow across her smirk. "I can't wait to make their acquaintance."

The others didn't have any qualms about a fifth joining their party. Valera, with her own horse, followed the party out of the outpost.

Celine shifted in her seat, the relief of standing lost to the return of the saddle's discomfort. The joints at her hips ached.

"Are you alright?" Owen asked quietly.

"I'll be fine. This is new, is all."

"I have some healing balms," Valera offered, reaching into the right saddlebag. "They're essential, with hours of riding."

She offered Celine a jar of medicine, the blend a familiar translucent green. Merfolk medicine.

Celine held up the jar. "How do you have this?"

"I traded for it the last time I was in Runa." Then, with a side glance bearing surprise, she turned the question back to Celine. "*You* know this medicine?"

"The person you traded with," Celine said, though she was hesitant to ask.

"Yes," Valera said quickly, looking from Tyrion to Liam. Because of their Estilon colors, perhaps she knew it best to shield her words. "They were."

"They were merfolk," Owen said. "You may speak freely with us, Valera. We are now allies to the merfolk."

But Valera's side-eye shifted to Owen, this one more suspicious than surprised.

"It's true," Celine said. "I'm merfolk. From the Sea of Kings."

With pride, Owen added, "She's my wife."

"*Truly?*" Valera's eyes light up, the secretive smirk transforming into pleasant surprise. "I must ask, how is life that deep in the sea?"

"Dark, cold, peaceful." Celine smiled as she imagined home. "At least, it is when we're not at war with humans or each other."

"With each other?"

"Merfolk aren't unlike humans in their desire for power," Celine said. "Whether their methods are the same or different, we are well matched in motivation."

Valera smirked conspiratorially. "What power do you want?"

The question surprised Celine, and for a moment, she wondered at Valera's intentions. "The power to live my life in a way that makes me happy."

And it was true. To live unbound and limitless.

"A desire that I respect." And she did, her smile of approval reaching her eyes. "It is an honor to meet you, Celine of the merfolk."

Her look was one of reverence, or something close to it. Heat bloomed across Celine's cheeks. But there was no way out, nowhere to hide. She wasn't in her watery home, where kelp and coral provided convenient hideaways. She was on horseback in the middle of a field heading east, the world vastly different and foreign and *open*.

"I can't blame her for being fascinated," Owen whispered. "It's a completely different world there, in the depths of the sea."

Valera parted ways not long after, venturing eastward. She lifted the gray wrap over her head, the hood forming as she pinned the front to become a mask. Valera waved farewell and rode on.

Celine, soothed by the quiet afternoon, hadn't expected rest to come easily while traveling steadily on horseback. She nearly dozed until Nutmeg cantered, escaping a rustling in the brush by the main road.

"Steady," Owen whispered. "Nutmeg's spooked. I didn't see what it was."

Celine remained secure in his hold, which he loosened when Estilon Castle was in view on the horizon.

"There and back in time for supper," Tyrion said. "I only wish we'd have learned more from that wastrel they caught."

Liam chuckled. "*Wastrel*."

"Shall we dine in my chambers?" Owen asked her quietly. "Are you hungry?"

"I am. Supper would be nice."

He shifted, holding the reins with one hand, the muscles and tendons of his forearm taut. "I wonder what Cook's made today."

The guards at the main gate prepared to grant them entry, but Celine could form no coherent thought as her eyes traced the lines of veins and tendons in Owen's forearms, her heart racing.

CHAPTER 27

Supper was an array of roasted meat and vegetables, fresh fruit, and two small individual cakes, which smelled heavenly.

"Cook likes you," Owen said, nodding at the cakes. "I made sure she knew how much you liked them, and now she's determined to keep you in cake."

"She's very kind to think of me." Celine smoothed her hands on her trousers, the pair of them sitting at the table in Owen's chambers. The room was mostly lit by firelight, from either the fireplace or the candles all around the room, and the hue did wonders for Owen's eyes.

"She was flattered to know that the soldiers at the outpost wanted some, too." He cut into the meat, pairing his bite with a bit of cheese. After chewing for a few seconds, he added, "Cook will be busy for a while, I wager."

"As will we," Celine said. "Sudor, raiders, Dathan."

She took a sip of water as he studied her. "The tasks ahead keep multiplying, it seems."

"Though meeting Valera was an unexpected turn of luck."

"How do you mean?" With a hint of mischief in his crystalline eyes, he asked, "Because she's fascinated with the merfolk? She may have a crush on you, wife."

Her cheeks warmed. "I mean her devotion to Moonblade, what it's supposed to stand for." She paused before asking, "Those men from the village raid. They weren't really Moonblade, were they?"

"That's my guess, if Valera's any indication," he said. "If there are those going around claiming membership to the guild, expecting a specific type of reception, that could be how they've made it this far into Estilon otherwise undetected. If they're Sudorian or simply blades-for-hire..." He shrugged. "But you're right. I have a feeling Valera will deal swiftly with any frauds. Moonblade's reputation depends on it."

"Moonblade, the raiders at Estilon's outposts, and three ships sailing out of Runa, seemingly together." At this, she remembered the news to share. "Have you heard about them?"

"I have," Owen said. "The harbormaster saw fit to share the details with me." He chuckled. "I think he's still taken aback but your proactivity."

She rolled her eyes. "Yes, I'm sure that's it."

"It's strange that those captains would sail together when they'd as soon sink one another's ships. Especially Captain Alden." He popped a grape into his mouth and chewed before saying, "I know their activity isn't good for us, but with Sudor very much at our doorstep, I'm afraid the Runan sailors will have to wait until it becomes more pressing."

But she could tell he wasn't satisfied with that idea.

"Our navy men will be our eyes and ears." He knew the truth of it, but he remained unsettled.

"Runa doesn't have allies," Celine said. "They have *opportunities*."

Owen nodded slowly. "And that's what makes them dangerous."

They ate for several silent minutes, the food delicious and the quiet comfortable.

"I meant what I said before," Owen said with a slight smirk as he poised his water cup to drink. "About fitting you for chain mail."

"*Chain mail*." She considered what it would feel like. "What a strange idea, having been born with scales."

"I will have the smithy work on it right away." He took a draught and set the cup down, taking another bite of meat and cheese. "Cynthia has your measurements, so it shouldn't be a problem."

"You're certain?" she asked. "I got the impression from Miss Helen that my fighting wouldn't be appropriate."

"That's because she's never seen you fight." His summation illustrated his own admiration for her skill. "You are Estilon's warrior queen, and the warrior queen should have her own chain mail."

"You know," she prefaced, "something I haven't tried since coming to land…" She didn't explain as she held her hand up, calling to her magic to summon one dagger. "I'm not sure if it'll work, being out of the water…"

Owen stayed silent, watching as magic pulled at her beckoning. Steadily, her power coalesced to craft blade, hilt, handle, and pommel. She smiled, pleased, as the barnacles wrapped around her creation, just as they'd always done.

"Remarkable." He breathed the word, leaning closer before finally standing. "Can you teach me?"

She dispelled her dagger, standing. "I can." He offered his hand, and she posed it as hers had been before. "Magic is tactile, as you know. Pull from the air. Tell the power what you need it to become. Form it with intent."

He stared at his hand, eyes locked on as his fingers and palm mimicked her movements. But nothing happened.

She took his hand. "May I?"

When Celine stood, Owen followed, moving close to her. She placed his palm and fingers in her hand, palm up, so that his would take her shape.

"The most important thing is using your will to pull with your mind and body." She tightened her hand's muscles and tendons, and without coaching, he copied well. "Think about the weapon you want to conjure. Think about how you're going to use it."

Her hand moved slowly, the weaving of magic as important as the intent, and he followed well, with brow narrowed and mouth pressed in a firm line, but no weapon appeared.

"Close your eyes," she said. "That may help."

"How? Is sight a problem?"

"It could be," she said. "You could be distracted by what you see or don't see."

He closed his eyes, hand still posed to summon.

"Feel the power in the air." She brought her other hand to his, feeling the tightness of his clawed fingers. "Every inch of the world possesses magic all its own. Kasindra would tell me that the ocean is like our blood, full of power."

"The sea is blood," Owen said, almost as a joke, but the words landed as he said them again. "The sea is blood."

"The world has power," Celine whispered. "Just like we do."

Air shifted as he cast. Celine held her breath, afraid that any sound or stirring would disrupt his concentration. As the seconds passed, a pommel appeared, then the handle, the hilt...

...Then the partial weapon disappeared.

"Damn." He laughed off the disappointment, but the focus remained tight around his eyes.

"If you did it once," she said, "you can do it again."

He closed his eyes, perturbed, and exhaled slowly to force his body to focus. Much like before, the hilt manifested slowly.

"Keep going," she whispered.

And he did, pushing his magic until the long, wide blade sprouted from the hilt. In his hand was a broadsword.

"Not my first choice," she said, the weapon seemingly much clumsier than her own preferred daggers. "But to each his own."

He studied his creation in awe. "Not as balanced as I would like, but it's a start."

"It's a start."

"And dispelling it," he said, the phrase open-ended for her instruction.

"Just as you command your magic to end, follow the same push of your will to dispel the sword."

Concentrating, the sword disappeared.

"With practice," he said, his eyes bright with excitement, "I can summon this at will."

"You can." She couldn't help but match his excitement, his *glee*, with a beaming smile of her own. "Imagine being in battle, your weapon knocked loose from your grip. You can summon another one while you fight."

As he stared, she could practically read the scenarios passing through his mind, and his elation didn't waver as he took her and spun her. She cried out, the sudden motion thrilling, and he laughed even as he stopped, holding her steady as she regained her feet beneath her.

But he didn't let go, not as his eyes flickered from her eyes to her mouth and back again.

"I would very much like to kiss you, Celine of the merfolk, Warrior Queen of Estilon." He brushed her hair from her face, tucking it behind her ear. "Would that be alright?"

"Yes." The barest whisper, as she looked up at him, nearly breathless.

Owen's hand curved around her face, his fingers reaching into her hair as his mouth met hers. Her hands rested on his back, feeling him breathe.

They parted too soon, even as Celine breathed deeply to fill her deprived lungs. She pulled him closer, resting against his shoulder. With his cheek against her crown and his hands in her hair. Even as the slithering guilt threatened to shame her into remembering her parents suffering in Chaos, she held him even closer, willing the moment to overwhelm any darkness.

He responded in kind, the pair of them tightly bound, together.

CHAPTER 28

Zander. Quinny. There is so much to tell you. Owen. Their plan. Their magic. Her heart ached in missing them.

She changed into the white shirt and black trousers with little thought about her intentions. It was not yet dawn, the first light of morning teasing the horizon. She would see Quinn and Zander, even if she had to sneak through the entire castle to do it.

Owen would want to come.

And the truth of it made her heart soar. He wanted to join her, to be as much a part of her merfolk life as her human life.

Would he be awake yet? She hesitated, guilt tingling at the idea of waking him too soon. He bore so much as the new king of Estilon, with conflict raging at every turn. Rest was a precious, rare commodity.

She slipped her feet into her boots and, when she opened her chamber door quietly, peeking out to see what knight guarded her door or patrolled her hall. There was no one in sight, and she stepped lightly down the soft, carpeted path toward the stone foyer and stepped down.

"Your majesty?"

She gasped, spinning as Liam walked from the hallway beneath the stairs, the one that led to the kitchen.

"Is everything alright?" he asked.

"Yes." She cleared her throat. "I only wanted some air." The reasoning felt untrue, so she added, "I miss the sea."

"Please, allow me to escort you."

Somehow, this surprised her. "You're not going to stop me?"

"How could a knight stop the queen consort when she's made up her mind?" He took one step toward the entrance, his demeanor almost casual. "The knight's job is to protect, your majesty, and I aim to do just that."

Still struck by his compliance, Celine followed him to the main entrance, rather than through the back gate.

"Tell Tyrion we're headed to the sea," Liam said to one. "He should be leaving the barracks any minute."

The guards agreed as they continued on.

"Don't you sleep?" she asked. "I didn't see Tyrion in the hall. Or any knight, for that matter, save you."

"Shift change, your majesty. But I do sleep. I woke up early this morning and didn't see a reason not to start my duties. Another knight is watching over his majesty." With an amused, breathy chuckle, he added, "Tyrion's a heavier sleeper."

Reasonable enough, she decided. And he was keeping his word about keeping watch and protecting her.

"I mean to call for my friends," she said candidly, as he was so accommodating. "I've missed them."

"I should imagine so," he said. "I can't imagine being separated from my loved ones. That is a difficult thing to bear."

"It is. But Owen and the queen have made that easier."

They walked on quietly, the birds stirring in their morning songs. The horizon gained highlights of deep and golden oranges, the flames of the sky kindling the dawn.

"Have you thought about going back?" he asked, but then backtracked. "Forgive the impertinence, your majesty. I'm only curious, is all. Being from such a different place as this, having to live where you're not used to..." He let the statement hang.

"No," she said. "I haven't thought about going back."

And the confession activated the tinge of guilt that touched at the fringes of her core, the sensation reaching further to the pit of her stomach. No, she hadn't thought about going back. Not in the way Liam meant when he asked. She'd been focused on how to use this forced turn of events to still get at Dathan, to burrow beneath his skin even from land, but her friends...the people who loved her...

She walked faster toward the shore, apology in her heart, urgency pushing her feet even as they sank into loose sand. Her vision had tunneled, and she'd moved forward without so much as a second glance.

She knelt by the water, the sea sweeping up to the edge of her knees, and she reached her hand into the frothy brine.

Quinn, she thought, reaching with merspeak. *Zander. Are you awake? Are you close?*

Their answer was almost immediate. *Yes! We're close! Celine!*

Their voices mixed in her mind in joyful unison. The days between their separation had passed quickly for her, but she could hear eagerness and longing in their words. The guilt stabbed deeper.

Celine!

"*I'm here.*" Emotion swelled in her throat.

The blonde head of Quinn appeared first, but Zander's red wasn't far behind. "Celine!"

Tears flowed freely as Celine pulled off her boots and walked into the water.

"Your majesty!"

But she didn't look to Liam as she reached for her friends, arms open. She embraced them both, water soaking into her clothes, the sensation the closest to home she'd been since arriving in Estilon.

"We've missed you," Quinn said, pulling back to look at her face and hair. "We've been so worried!"

"They've taken great care of me," she said, touching Quinn and Zander's faces.

"Are you safe?" he asked. "Who is that man with you?"

"That's not Owen," Quinn said. "Aren't you married?"

"We are married," Celine answered, "and that is Liam, a knight who agreed to escort me to the sea."

"Escorts and knights and kings." Quinn smiled. "*Queen Celine.*"

Celine scrunched her nose. "Just Celine, please and thank you."

"How is Owen?" Quinn asked. "Are the humans treating you well?"

Celine said nothing of the brief time in the dungeons. Instead, she recounted learning queenly duties, trying to help with the threat of Sudor, and adjusting to life with legs.

"Boots and trousers that fit," Zander said. "Scales of a different kind."

"I miss my scales terribly."

"*What you said before,*" Quinn said, switching to merspeak, "*about Sudor, with Dathan's orders about the Estilon and Sudor kings...*"

"*I will be killing no one,*" Celine said, resolute.

"*I'm glad you're not giving Dathan what he wants,*" Quinn said. "*But you were to have met Jesper's son, right? There was supposed to be someone to help you...*"

Celine shook her head. "*No one ever came.*"

"*Dathan's information must have been false,*" Zander said. "*Which doesn't surprise me. Leave it to a human king to mislead the merfolk into some superficial alliance.*"

"*From what I've learned of Jesper,*" Celine said, "*he isn't to be trusted.*"

"*What if he intended to kill you,*" Quinn said, gripping Celine's arm, "*and wanted to make it look like Estilon did it?*"

"*Sudor would benefit from more conflict and war,*" Celine said. "*They have a strong arcana crystal in their land that grows underground.*"

"*We've heard,*" Zander said, excited. "*It's rumored that one crystal is as strong as three of ours.*"

Curiosity played at the back of Celine's mind, picturing the crystal gifted from Kasindra. "*Dathan apparently has a hoard, likely gifted from Jesper. If he has access to that kind of power—*"

"Ah," came a voice from the sand. *Owen.* "There she is."

She turned, seeing Owen walk toward them with Tyrion in his wake.

"Your highness." Liam bowed at the waist. "She asked to visit her friends at the sea."

They watched as Owen approached with Tyrion.

"He looks different," Quinn said, squinting at Celine. "Come to think of it, you look different, too."

"I thought the same thing," Zander said.

"What do you mean?" Celine touched her face and looked down at her hands and arms. "I feel alright."

"It's the way he's looking at you." Quinn glanced at Owen, then studied Celine's face with teasing scrutiny. "And the way you look at him."

"We should have known," Zander said. "It was only a matter of time."

"What are you both talking about?"

Zander and Quinn touched shoulders, crossing their arms. "Are you two in love?"

Love? The idea seemed far too much far too quickly. "Not love."

"Not *yet*."

Celine splashed water at Quinn.

"You both definitely like each other." Zander narrowed his eyes. "And you both have definitely kissed."

Celine stared, powerless to deny the accusations.

"He's a good kisser, isn't he?" Quinn smirked.

"I should go," Celine said, embarrassed to the brim. "I'll return soon."

"Promise?" Quinn and Zander hugged her tightly. "Soon"

"I promise."

"*Before you go,*" Quinn said, her voice quiet in Celine's mind. "*You should know that Dathan is...different.*"

"*What do you mean?*"

"*Sleepless,*" Zander said. "*Anxious.*"

"*He talks of shadows taunting his dreams, showing him nightmares.*"

"*He speaks freely of that?*" That was the most surprising thing of all, that Dathan would admit to anything resembling weakness. "*Isn't he afraid of being seen as vulnerable?*"

"*He doesn't seem concerned with much else.*" Quinn's gaze was specific, filled with intent, with *knowing*. "*Whatever you're doing, Celine...*"

But she stopped. Celine wondered how Quinn would have ended her sentence.

Whatever you're doing, Celine, it's working.

Whatever you're doing, Celine, please stop.

But Celine wouldn't stop. Not until she freed her parents from Chaos.

"I love you both." She kissed each of their faces, their arms enveloping her. "I'll return soon."

Slowly, Celine waded out of the sea, taking Owen's offered hand as she set her bare feet into the sand beside him. They waved to Quinn and Zander before her friends dove into the water, disappearing.

"I have a meeting with Graham after breakfast," Owen said, stroking the curve of her hand with his thumb. "But after, maybe we could ride out to Wolfwood?"

Celine beamed with excitement. "Really?"

He kissed her temple. "Maybe you'll see a forest sprite."

CELINE CHANGED out of her wet clothes before electing to join Owen in his meeting with Graham in the solar.

Helen was gracious enough to attend her, rather than sending the new maid to practice her training.

"Things are going well," Miss Helen said after Celine asked. "She's learning quickly."

Helen's deft hands were quick and sure as she helped Celine remove the wet clothing and change into a dry dress. Celine missed her trousers already, but the dress was soft and fit well.

"Shall I dress your hair as well? A few strands have come loose, your highness."

Celine sat dutifully, sitting up straight against the back of the wooden chair as Helen's hands unbound and loosened the braid. But a clatter outside stilled her movement, and she and Celine turned toward the door.

"What on earth?" She patted Celine's shoulder. "Stay here, your majesty. I'll return in a moment."

Celine obeyed, though curious, relaxing in the seat as she faced the bed in front of her. The afternoon sun poured into the room, augmenting the rich pinks and blues of her bedclothes and the soft gray of the stone walls.

She wasn't alone long. Hands took her hair and continued to undo the braid.

Celine jumped, the touch unexpected. "Miss Helen! I didn't hear you return!"

Fingers carefully combed through the wavy strands, tingles cascading down her spine. She closed her eyes, the motion slow and relaxing. A warm hand rested on her shoulder.

She nearly whispered his name—*Owen*—but stopped, a flash of embarrassment sending a slight flush to her cheek, should the hands actually belong to Helen. But the touch was different. The *intention* was different.

"Miss Helen—"

"Miss Helen will be occupied for a moment."

Terror bloomed beneath her skin. She jumped up from the chair, spinning on her heels and nearly toppling onto the bed.

"Liam?!"

"I apologize for frightening you," he whispered, hurrying to close the gap between them. Celine backed up further, nearly sitting on the bed as the edge almost buckled her knees. "It's just—after seeing you today with your friends, after you trusted me to escort you—"

"What are you talking about?" she snapped, not letting him finish. "Why did you come in here? Why did you—"

She couldn't say *touch my hair* because it was more than simply *touching*. It held expectation, longing. Her scalp was too tight, shifting slightly over muscle and bone as though to remove any trace memory of his hands in her hair.

"You must feel it too," he said, edging closer, his boot scuffing against the floor. "This isn't just in my imagination."

Without a second thought, Celine summoned one dagger, the magic tingling in her fingers as they wrapped around the barnacle-laced handle. She raised the blade to the level of his throat. "It is *entirely* in your imagination."

He narrowed his eyes, a flicker of anger betraying his expression before he took control. "Celine—"

"If you touch me again," she said, her voice low, her teeth bared, "I will kill you."

"Even a queen cannot touch a knight of Estilon." He nearly scoffed in boasting.

"It's a pity you believe yourself invincible."

"What in the blazes—" Helen gasped from the doorway, eyes wide, blinking from Celine to Liam.

"Get out." Celine aimed her sharpened words at Liam with violent intent. "Stay out of my sight."

Liam turned on his heel and left without another word, brushing past Helen in his exit.

"I will see Owen immediately," Celine said, offering no explanation as she dispelled her dagger.

"What happened?"

Celine didn't answer, rushing out of her chambers and through to the other side of the castle, her hair wild around her shoulders. But Owen, Tyrion, and Graham had already left the solar, talking animatedly about gathering soldiers and arms.

Owen's smile flashed at the sight of her, only to dim as he took her in. "What's happened?"

"I need to speak with you," she said, her gaze sharp as her eyes met his.

"We have to go," Owen said, glancing at Graham and Tyrion. The two men stepped away to give them privacy and waited for Owen to finish. "There's been another attack on a village, simultaneous with one on an outpost."

"I'll tell you on the way," Celine said.

Owen reached for her hair, the waves wild around her face, but she recoiled, gasping.

"Forgive me." She set her jaw to keep her lips from trembling. Anger and shame swirled dangerously in her core. "I will explain everything."

"Celine," he whispered. "What happened?"

He offered his hand, giving her the freedom to take it, and when she slipped her fingers across his palm, he brought them to his lips, pressing a kiss that lingered long after it ceased.

"I will tell you." She swallowed, her saliva like shards of glass.

"Your chain mail isn't ready yet, I'm afraid."

"I'll meet you in the armory," Celine said. "Don't leave without me."

"I wouldn't dream of it."

"Owen." Her throat was tight. "Don't bring Liam."

Worried curiosity furrowed his brow, a touch of anger lining his eyes. "As you wish."

Owen left with the others as Helen waited, worried eyes following Celine as they hurried back to her chambers.

"Do something with my hair," she said. "And please hurry."

"Yes, your majesty."

Helen's hands were quick, even as Celine grimaced and shivered at the sensation of her hair being twisted and bound.

Damn Liam to the seven hells.

"Trousers and shirt, your majesty?"

"Yes, please."

Just as Helen helped her dress, she helped her undress, and Celine was soon running out of the castle toward the armory. The haste, the mission, the action all propelled her forward, helping her body and mind shove the unpleasantness away. Was Liam truly so delusional to believe that a spark of any kind existed between them? Or did he simply want another excuse to throw her in the dungeon to suffer and die by the iron?

I will save one shadow for him. The dark promise soothed the seething rage in her chest. *Perhaps more than one.*

CHAPTER 29

This raid was closer to the sea, the smell of salt and seaweed strong over the gentle breeze as they rode. Nutmeg snorted as her hooves pounded against the earth in rhythmic thunderous beats.

She heard the sounds of the fighting before she saw the men, armed and bloody, fending off the raiders dressed in black. Clanging metal competed for sound against the shouts and grunts as each hit landed.

Tyrion urged his horse faster, his grimace full of anger as he leaned forward in his saddle. Graham wasn't far behind, calling out commands to his horse. Their hoofbeats were thunder across the landscape.

Somewhere, a woman screamed.

"They'll wish they'd never been born," Celine swore, hands itching to summon blade and shadow.

"Stay safe, wife," Owen said, their horses nearing the edge of the village. "Stay alive."

"You too, husband."

Nutmeg stopped, and Celine jumped down, landing hard against the earth, the sensation jolting through the stretched muscles of her legs.

After dismounting Matilda, Owen kissed Celine's hand before

drawing his sword and shield. "Meet me in the center of the village when the fight is over."

"I will."

And it was a promise she would keep.

She summoned her daggers and hurried to the nearest house, eyes scanning for the safest place to send any women or children she found. There was only the field she had just crossed, but it was better than nothing.

The first house was empty, so she hurried to the next. A pair of children huddled next to a cabinet, an older brother protectively hovering over his sister.

"Outside," Celine said, nudging her head toward the door. "The king has arrived. Run out into the field where the horses are and wait."

The children stared at her, wide-eyed, not moving.

"You're not safe here," she said, moving to them. But as she did, the girl screamed.

"I won't hurt you." Celine glanced around quickly, hoping for something to help guide them out. They were far too vulnerable. "The raiders will come in and ransack this place. Don't let them find you in it."

"We'll go," the boy said, his tone sharp and brave. "But not with you."

Ouch. But Celine didn't blame them for not trusting a stranger.

The boy rose, taking his sister's hand, and hurried out the back door. Celine glanced through the window to see them following her instructions, going to the horses to hide and wait.

"Where are their parents?" she muttered to herself. But with the sounds outside, she feared for the answer.

Men and women cried out, and Celine hurried from this house to enter the next one.

"By the gods!" someone shouted. "They have magic!"

"They'll kill us all!"

Celine turned, eyes scanning the rush of the miniature battlefield before her. Trace flickers of magic shimmered in the air, hints of iridescence that faded as soon as her eyes caught them.

Magic folk among the raiders?

She saw him, then. His broad shoulders and piercing gaze. Only, his eyes and hair were dark brown instead of green, changed to human shades much like her own.

Merfolk had come to land, and Santus was leading them.

"For Sudor!" one of the merfolk cried with a cruel laugh. She recognized him as one of Santus's lackeys. "For Sudor!"

Santus and his men had dressed crudely, just as she'd done when she first emerged from the water. Tattered trousers from shipwrecks, and Santus bare-chested among them.

But Sudor would do nothing for them. Jesper would just as soon string them up and dry them out on land, cackling at their withered demise. No, this was for something else. Santus wouldn't be here if it wasn't out of great need.

Celine hurried, her boot heels sinking into soft earth as her hands gripped her daggers. He didn't see her rush up behind him, didn't see the blades poised to strike down into his back. But he spun, meeting her blades with his, a broadsword similar in shape and size to Owen's preferred weapon. The clang of metal reverberated in the air, piercing through her ears while the sounds of fighting continued uninterrupted.

"It's good to see you again, Celine." His broad grin was sinister. "You look well among the humans."

He pushed against her daggers, trying to make her kneel before him. She pivoted on the balls of her feet, letting his blade fall as she stepped around him, forcing him to spin.

"What are you doing with Sudor?" She sneered at him. "What do you hope to gain from this?"

"You seem to have forgotten the task before you." He chuckled, moving with surprising confidence, given the newness of his legs. "The merking will be disappointed when he hears of your disobedience."

"Disappointed or vindicated?" She strangled the grip of her blades. "He has to know I wouldn't follow through with his ridiculous request."

"Request?" An eye twitched. "It was the command of your king!"

"Not my king." She smiled, proud of how angry she made him. "Never my king."

Santus rushed forward, hands bracing the broadsword to strike. His ability to move this well made her wonder if he'd been human long before this fight, wandering the land and passing as one of them. But she didn't have time to question him as she deflected another blow.

"You're good with legs," he taunted with a laugh. "I'm still getting the hang of them."

"You seem pretty balanced to me." She quirked an eyebrow, watching for any twitch of movement. "It's almost as though you've done this before."

They side-stepped slowly, neither of them blinking.

"It's like wearing a costume for you, isn't it?" she asked. "Playacting with people's lives?"

He rushed in, raising his broadsword to strike down. She countered as she'd done before, but the broadsword was a distraction for the real strike. His fist collided with her side beneath her ribs, but her breath didn't catch until he pulled away. Muscles convulsed as the unseen blade left her, blood blooming fast in the threads of her shirt.

"You're focusing on the wrong thing, Celine." He ran his tongue across his bottom lip as he grinned. "But you always have. Narrow sight to suit a narrow mind."

She pressed her arm against her side. "What are you talking about?"

"Oh, I'd hate to spoil the surprise."

He charged for her again. She dodged and lashed out with a dagger, her blade meeting the flesh of his shoulder. He howled in pain, rounding to meet her again, but she didn't relent. Another swipe of her dagger drew an angry red line at his side, curving across his chest. Blood flowed freely from both wounds.

"This flesh is softer, Santus," she said, panting through the pulsating pain. The wound at her side burned, and she remembered the toxin that kept her from healing.

Santus growled, lifting his sword in an upward swing, knocking her off her feet. She called to the shadows, summoning them as a reflex and sending them straight to his chest. He staggered backward, blinking in slow realization.

"*You.*" He narrowed his eyes. "I should have known."

She clamored to her feet, pushing more magic into her daggers to make the blades longer and wider. "Have any nightmares lately?"

"Your weak magic does little," he said, but there was an additional layer of anger in his eyes. Whatever the shadows had done had been enough to garner his attention, but she suspected they'd done more than simply raise curiosity. "But it's nice to know what pest is responsible for them."

Celine feigned emotional hurt. "You mean I'm not the only one?" But her mocking faltered as she struggled to breathe through the pain at her side. "I don't stand out among your admirers?"

A knight of Estilon was knocked toward them, the distraction enough to pull Santus's gaze, opening a window of opportunity for Celine to strike. She aimed to give him a wound that matched hers, the dagger nearly meeting his side as she was almost successful. Her blade sank through flesh and muscle, but Santus pivoted, slamming the pommel of his broadsword against her thigh. She crumbled to one knee, the pain and shock of the blow reverberating through her.

"I end this now!" Santus lifted his sword higher, the veins in his face and neck protruding beneath his skin.

Celine lunged up, sensing the nearness of death, and buried both daggers into his gut. *If I die, you die.*

His breath shuddered, abhorrence in his eyes, his lips pulled back from his teeth. Just over his shoulder, Celine spotted the fletching of an arrow. Someone had shot him as she struck.

Glee filled her as she twisted her daggers. "Give Aishlin my regards, Commander."

"Fall back!" Santus staggered back, his breathing wet and ragged. "Fall back!"

"Sweet dreams, Santus." Celine didn't take her eyes off him as he retreated. A few other transformed merfolk followed their leader back to the water.

Her body disobeyed her as she tried to stand, instead collapsing to the earth, soft and welcoming. The metallic scent of blood was sharp. Her side and thigh throbbed.

She wasn't healing. He'd laced his blade, and she was so far from merfolk remedies. Could Smithson help? Would he reach her in time? Did Owen have any skill in healing?

She was untethered as her breathing continued in its quick, shallow pattern, floating blissfully between the waking and dreaming spaces. Had she lost enough blood to make her consciousness wander? Or had Santus injected her with something else to rob her of reality?

Her name was a distant alarm, the cry tearing through the air to reach through the growing fog in her mind. It came to her again and again until hands turned and lifted her. Owen's voice was louder and clearer.

"Celine!" He touched her face. smoothing strands of hair away from her eyes. She blinked, the sunlight blinding. "Who did this?"

"Santus was here." Her voice sounded far away. "He changed into a human. There were others."

"Merfolk on land."

"By the gods." Was that Tyrion?

Owen stroked her face. "That's how they've made use of those crystals from Sudor?"

Crystals from Sudor. Of course. Santus and his minions, coming to land easily and painlessly with a more powerful conduit.

Owen lifted her in his arms, holding her close as he carried her. The horses nickered, and Celine tried to take a fortifying breath, reaching for the fringes of consciousness.

Breathing was a labor. She forced her eyes to focus, forced her body to work.

"The wound in your side," Owen said. "It doesn't look right."

She almost laughed. *What does* right *look like when you're nearly run through?* "A toxin, is my guess. Santus's specialty. Brewed with the crystals?"

She didn't like the thought of that.

"I've never healed a toxin before. Cuts and bruises, but nothing like this."

"I haven't either." She swallowed, her throat remarkably dry. "Quinn and Zander always took care of me."

"Tell me what you need," he said. "Should I try to reach your friends?"

She nodded. At least, she intended to nod. But her body was floating boundless, untethered…

"Give her to me, your majesty." Tyrion, his voice sure. Celine could see his colored shape, his form bleary, as he approached on horseback. "There's no time to waste."

Celine reached for help as Owen lifted her, and Tyrion was careful as he sat her in his lap.

"Hold on, your majesty," he said. "We must ride quickly."

"I will follow." Owen was already climbing on Matilda's back. "Go."

"Nutmeg…"

"I will have someone take her back to the castle," Owen said.

Tyrion clicked his horse to turn and raced off. Celine grimaced and groaned, her leg and side aching deeply, but she inhaled the rich scent of salt and sea, the breeze sweeping across her face to welcome her.

Tyrion slowed as his horse navigated down to the shore, bypassing the wooden stairs with careful steps.

"I'm here." Owen nearly jumped off Matilda and reached for Celine.

She almost fell as she moved toward Owen, his arms catching her. Tyrion's horse whinnied at the jostle and shock, stepping away from them even as Owen hurried to the water.

"What do I do?" he asked. His voice was frantic. "Put you in?"

"Yes. They'll know what to do."

Owen was careful, kneeling first before he laid Celine into the shallow reach of the Sea of Kings. The salt played hell with her wounds, but as she reached with merspeak to call for Zander and Quinn, relief swelled in her heart.

"*Celine?*" Quinn, the question casual. "*Back so soon?*"

"*Couldn't get enough of us?*" Zander chuckled. "*We're pretty irresistible.*"

"*Santus was on land.*" Celine took a deep breath. "*Can you come to shore?*"

"*What!*" Their voices in shocked synchronicity echoed loudly in her mind, making her flinch.

"Are they coming?" Owen smoothed her hair. Anxiety radiated from him.

"They'll be here soon," she said. "Santus is a conniving bastard, but this isn't something that can't be undone."

"You're so pale." He kissed her forehead. He was in the water with her, his clothes soaked through. "I will kill him. Slowly."

"That honor will be ours." She laughed, wincing at the pain in her side.

"Was that the merfolk I shot?" Tyrion asked, holding the reins of their horses. When Celine nodded, he said, "She gave him hell, Owen. Absolute hell."

Owen kissed her again. "My warrior queen."

"Celine!"

She turned, seeing one blonde head and one red coming toward her. Their hands reached her next, Quinn's outrage audible.

"No corner of the seas will be safe for that slithering bastard," Quinn swore.

"Owen and I don't know how to heal this," Celine said.

Zander carefully pulled the fabric of her shirt away from the deep wound in her side. "A toxin that keeps you from healing." He cupped his hand over the cut. "This will hurt."

He pressed hard, and Celine cried out. Owen took her hand, letting her squeeze his fingers as Zander hummed a low melody, his magic sinking into her skin. The toxin moved through muscle and blood, slipping back through the wound as Zander's magic drew it out. He didn't stop singing, even as he pushed healing into the cleaned wound, forcing her flesh to sew itself back together faster than if it was left alone.

"My leg." Celine touched her thigh. "A deep bruise. Gods, it hurts."

Quinn passed the same magic through the bruise on her thigh, feeling its depth. "Gods, it's deep. It's a wonder it didn't break the bone."

"Death is too good for him," Owen said.

Quinn reached in with magic and song. Celine leaned her head against Owen's arm, breathing deeply through the dull, aching pull of pain before it left her completely. Relief was sweet, the pain exhausting, and Quinn mended her body with a careful touch.

"You reach in with your magic and find what isn't supposed to be there," Zander said. "And tell your magic to draw it out."

"Is it really that simple?" Celine asked, strength and energy returning slowly.

"Yes, and no." Zander managed a half-smile, worry still heavy around his eyes. "Magic can also push something like poison in deeper, if you're not careful."

"Two objects cannot occupy the same space," Owen reasoned, understanding. "And magic takes up space."

"I read that in a book once," Quinn said.

But they were each startled when a sudden splash came from the water. Celine's eyes searched for the lavender of Kasindra or the dark blue of Dathan but was surprised to see the snow-white of Jessa.

"Tell me what you've done." Her eyes were full of white-hot fury. "Tell me what you've done to my father."

Weak, Celine sat up with Owen's help. "Jessa—"

"He can barely sleep. He's paranoid and terrified." She swam quickly, moving past Quinn and Zander even as they tried to reach for her. "He's having nightmares full of people screaming. I know it's you, Celine. I know it's something you've done."

"Jessa?" Owen asked. "You're Dathan's daughter?"

"Yes, *your highness*," she said with a sneer. "I'm sure it pleases you to hear how the merking suffers."

"You know what he did," Celine said. "What he did to my parents. Owen's father died of the same toxin."

Jessa didn't blink as she looked from Celine to Owen and back again. "The same toxin?"

"Hell's touch."

But rather than glare in justified triumph at her step-sister, Celine's sympathy settled deep in her core. Even as Dathan was a monster among merfolk, Jessa was his daughter. A daughter's love for her father is one of the most powerful forces Celine knew to exist.

"I—" Jessa's lips trembled. "I didn't know."

"I hate that this hurts you," Celine said, reaching for Jessa's hand. "That's the last thing I want."

She let Celine hold her hand, emotion heavy on the mermaid's face, before she yanked it away, her anger restrengthening the lines of her eyes and mouth. "Yet you do it still."

"My parents are in Chaos," Celine said. Giving voice to the words felt vulnerable, but somehow, it was as natural as breathing. She'd lived with the truth of it for so long that the revelation didn't feel as sudden as it was. "They're in Chaos because of him."

"Torturing my father won't bring them back."

"No?" Celine's own anger edged through, her lips twitching as she fought to keep herself level and steady. "What if it will? What if trading your father and Santus will free them from Chaos and give them the peace they deserve?"

Jessa's heartbreak stabbed through Celine's resentment, but Celine held on, pride and stubbornness winning over empathy. Jessa turned and left, her body cutting through the water with impressive speed.

"Celine—" Quinn started, but stopped herself.

"Something I read in a book," Zander said quietly. "*Revenge is the suffering of he who receives as well as he who gives.*"

Suffering. As though Celine wouldn't suffer if she left Dathan alone.

Zander's words had tried to reach her before.

Revenge is a path that doesn't end well. It will take a piece of you that you will never get back.

As though she could move on with her life, knowing the monster who destroyed her family would suffer no vengeance.

"Let's get you back to the castle," Owen whispered, resting a hand on her shoulder. "I'll call Smithson."

Celine embraced her friends, the hug awkward both in position and feeling, but their love soothed her.

"Thank you," she said. "Thank you for everything."

"Take care of yourself, Celine." Quinn's sunshine eyes held sadness in their worry.

"No one can control you unless you let them." Zander's words were heavy with meaning. *No one* meant *Dathan.*

Or *Kasindra.* She and her brother longed for power with such jealous fury that all else faded away.

Celine could understand that kind of tunnel vision, where nothing else could get in the way because of how *badly* she wanted what she'd been working toward. Dathan's soul would fall prey to Chaos, and Santus's right along with it. A two-for-two exchange. Dathan and Santus, for her parents.

They deserved to be free, even if Celine built her own prison to surrender herself into. At least, then, her parents would be free.

Once Quinn and Zander left, Celine let Owen help her to her feet and, carefully, they mounted Matilda and rode for Estilon Castle.

CHAPTER 30

Celine slept through the afternoon. She awoke in Owen's chambers, his bed soft and warm. She didn't want to sit up, to leave the pillow in favor of consciousness, but she heard something scratching in the room.

"Owen?" She blinked, seeing him sitting at his desk, pen in hand.

"Rise and shine." He scribbled something quickly before setting the pen on its rest beside the inkwell. "Smithson left this." He picked up a vial from his desk and brought it to her. "He didn't want to disturb you, since you were sleeping."

The vial was small, the liquid milky white. "That was kind of him."

He sat on the bed beside her, rubbing the back of his head. "He said it's restorative. You've used a lot of energy to heal, which also explains why you slept so much."

"I'm alright, Owen." She took his free hand in both of hers, hearing and seeing his nervousness displayed. "I won't give Santus the satisfaction of killing me."

But her words struck an already raw nerve, and he brought her hand to his mouth, holding it there. She could feel his lips slightly tremble, but tears didn't come.

"I will have the whole of Estilon out for his blood," he said, his voice dangerously low.

"It was strange, seeing him on land. Seeing him with *legs*." The details of him were clear—the human color of his hair and eyes, the power of his body as he brought his blade down. "I almost didn't recognize him."

She looked down at their hands, both of hers touching his fingers and palm. Flashes of the afternoon swirled around, out of consecutive order. Jessa's accusing glare and words echoed as Celine stabbed Santus's gut with both blades.

"Torturing my father won't bring them back."

"Tell me," he whispered. "Something's bothering you."

She traced the lines in his palm with her index finger. "My stepsister."

"Dathan's her father," he said. "It makes sense that she would want to protect him, that she would get defensive over him."

"But she knows what he did."

"She does now."

"How could she not have known?" Still not meeting his eyes, Celine sneered at the memory. "She had to have known, Owen. Dathan has his cruelty on display, like a badge of honor."

Owen covered her hands with both of his, enveloping them in calloused warmth. "Talk to her."

An emotional tide swelling within Celine's chest. *Talk to her*. So simple to say, yet...

"What could I say? *Sorry I'm torturing your bastard father for killing my parents*?"

"Perhaps a bit more delicately?"

This brought her eyes to meet his, confusion dissolving to amusement as she saw the shadow of a smile on his face.

"*Talk to her*," he repeated, his thumbs drawing circles on the backs of her hands. "You care about her."

"What if—" Celine hesitated. Owen's expression looked so calm and assured. She couldn't tell if any part of him would be disappointed. "What if this compromises everything?"

"You mean our revenge." He reached to brush her hair behind her ear. "It seems our shadows have done well, wife. What if we stopped here?"

She stared, incredulous, consciously denying the small, quiet part of her core that relished warmth at the idea. "What if we stopped?"

Her echoed question was a whisper as her mind traveled down the proposed path. Days filled with Owen, with life in Estilon, far away from Dathan and his cruelty. Celine, living happily despite everything he'd done.

"He has suffered," Owen said. "Yes, he still lives, but wouldn't killing him make us as monstrous? Wouldn't killing him destroy your relationship with your step-sister?"

"I thought—" Her lips trembled, every inch of her afraid of letting go. She'd held on for so long. "I thought you wanted this."

"In my anger. But I..." He touched her face, fingers tracing the edge of her jaw. "I have you, Celine. And we have a chance at a life together. I want that now, more than anything. More than revenge on the merking."

Warmth swelled at last. The small and quiet part of her was no longer timid as it stretched to fill her.

A life of her own making, apart from Dathan and Santus.

Living happily would be the best revenge.

She moved the blankets from her legs, relieved to find mobility easy and pain-free. "Let's go."

Owen stood and helped her with her boots. "As you wish."

But she tugged at his hand, pulling his gaze back to her. "Thank you. You understand without needing me to explain, to justify—"

He squeezed her hand. "We're alike, you and I. That makes it easier."

"It does."

She closed the distance between them and kissed him, the gesture gentle and natural. Kissing Owen was easy, as though their lips were always meant to touch. And who was she to stand in the way of destiny?

Owen deepened the kiss, touching her face. She held him closer, his warmth covering her as they moved together in a gentle rhythm.

He exhaled deeply as they parted. "I will never tire of kissing you."

He kissed her mouth again, then her nose, then her forehead. "I will kiss you every day that we're together."

"I will hold you to that promise."

Hands entwined, the pair stepped out, meeting Tyrion in the corridor, standing watch.

"We must go to the sea," Owen said, "to confer with our merfolk friends."

Tyrion only nodded once, taking his king's command and escorting them out of the castle, through the main gate, and to the shore.

"May I ask you something?" Tyrion looked at Owen as they walked down the wooden steps from the main road toward the beach. "Why was Liam reassigned to field patrol?"

At this, Owen looked to Celine, trying to come up with an answer.

"I am ashamed of the details, though I shouldn't be," Celine said. "With the fight at the village, there wasn't time to explain."

Owen stopped. "What did he do?"

The dangerous tone returned to his voice, the one that made Celine imagine Owen tearing the landscape apart as he searched for one man.

Celine told them how Helen was interrupted and stepped out, how Liam slipped in silently. Her scalp tingled unpleasantly.

"He touched my hair—" Her voice was quiet, though her anger was not. "He touched my hair in a way that made me think it was you."

"That bastard," Tyrion swore.

But it was Owen who was devastatingly quiet. Celine would swear that she'd seen lightning flare in his eyes.

"Let's go to the water and speak with Jessa," Owen said. "We'll discuss together what will be done with Liam."

"Short of the earth opening up and swallowing him whole?"

His lips twitched in the shadow of a smirk. "That's not out of the question. I happen to know an earthborn strong enough to see it done."

They walked down the shore, letting the quiet night whisper to them through the wind and sea. Celine looked to the star-studded horizon, wisps of gray-white lining the sky.

She saw her head and shoulders before the others did, the water barely telling of her movement as she swam gracefully toward them.

Celine didn't need to see the lavender of her hair and eyes to know who approached.

"Kasindra's here," Celine whispered. "Give me a moment."

Owen looked down at her, alarmed, but hid his surprise quickly with his signature diplomatic smile. "Take as much time as you need."

Celine walked to the water, standing just out of reach of the swaying waves as Kasindra stopped, her smile full of mischief.

"I was wondering if I'd see you here tonight," Kasindra said. "We need to talk about Jessa."

"What about her?" Celine nearly crossed her arms, suddenly protective of her step-sister. "Has she done something?"

"After what she said to you, child, I was worried you would waver on your plan for Dathan."

Of course, Kasindra would know. That damned cauldron of hers. "It's understandable that she's upset. He's her father."

"And the man who killed yours." Kasindra edged closer. "Both of your feelings are justified, surely, but you mustn't let her deter you from your goal."

"You came here simply to tell me that?" Celine raised an eyebrow. "Or is there something else?"

"You've worked so hard." There was the mask of sing-song in her voice, the veneer of maternal comfort and encouragement. She'd used it often, and Celine could spot its artificiality. She only used it when she wanted something. "You've come so far, Celine. This is no trifle."

Kasindra's eyes glanced toward Owen and Tyrion before bearing into Celine's, and she could feel the question burning through her mentor's mind, though she gave it no voice.

"It's my revenge," Celine said. "I know what I've done and how far I'll go."

"Your revenge with my guidance," Kasindra said, her tone sharpening. "And my—" But she stopped herself.

"Your what?"

She shook her head. "It's nothing, dear. Only I—" The sing-song quality had returned. "I wonder if you've forgotten all I've done for you? The magic I've taught you, the tools I've given you."

The voices of her friends echoed in Celine's mind: *She's using you.*

Celine had known that from the beginning. Kasindra wanted power, and Celine was a way to that power. But Celine, broken, grieving, had wanted Dathan to suffer.

Kasindra reached her hand up, seeking Celine to take it. When she did, power surged through her like lightning, the sensation overwhelming before it was intoxicating. Pure magic laced her blood, threaded through her muscles. She could do anything. She was unstoppable.

Kasindra released her, satisfied. "So much has happened, dear." Celine stood upright, regarding her teacher as her lovely face looked up to her. "Ever since you left the sea, so much has changed."

Echoes of her parents screaming carried on the sea breeze. Celine winced, their agony catching her off guard.

"I wonder if you've forgotten," Kasindra's voice echoed in her mind with merspeak. "And only need a moment to remember what you've set out to do."

Their screams grew louder, joined with flashes of Celine's nightmares, visions of what she'd imagined the Chaos Realm to look like, the silhouettes of her parents seized in agony.

"Kasindra." Owen's voice broke through the growing tumult in Celine's mind. "Lovely to see you again."

"You as well, King Owen." Kasindra bowed her head. "Thank you for bringing Celine to see me this evening."

"She was eager to come," he said. "And I am grateful for her friends and the alliance we've forged." He brought his arm around her waist without applying pressure. It was a reassurance that he was there, a reassurance she didn't realize she needed. "We were surprised to see merfolk on land, attacking innocent villagers."

The last of their screams finally left her mind, Owen's voice filling it instead. She stepped closer to him.

Kasindra's eyebrows rose. "I heard. I hope this doesn't bruise the alliance between the merfolk and Estilon."

"The first commander was leading the charge," Owen said. "Was he acting independently? Or by the order of his king?"

The Sea Witch pursed her lips, considering her answer. Celine tried to peel back the mask, but Kasindra was adept at hiding. "That line of inquiry is justified. Perhaps we could arrange a diplomatic meeting between our kingdoms." Then, tilting her head, she said, "The first commander came back nearly dead. His injuries were severe."

"Would that death had taken him." Bitterness soured alongside her lingering chill of shame. "My daggers, buried deep in his gut, and he *lived*?"

Kasindra regarded that with an upraised brow. "Perhaps his use of magic has extended beyond our reckoning, if he could survive that. Sudor's arcana crystal is likely in play."

"Perhaps."

The silence that passed between them was heavy. The whispering sea was the only voice until Kasindra spoke. "I should go." Her pasted smile was broad, everything about her demeanor a diplomatic show. "I will hopefully hear from you again soon, Celine."

Celine said nothing as Kasindra turned to swim away.

"What happened?" Owen muttered, his mouth close to her ear. "You looked like you were in pain. Was she hurting you?"

"She thinks I'm wavering in my revenge against Dathan," she said. "My parents are still locked in Chaos. Santus and Dathan's souls will free them." She stared out across the water, hating how much Kasindra's words reached her. "Kasindra is as eager for this revenge plan as I am." But she faltered. "As I *was*."

"Think about what *you* want, Celine." He pressed his lips against her temple, holding her there. "Think about what *you* need."

"I want my parents." She took a deep breath of sea air. "I want them to be alright."

"Can they really be pulled out of Chaos?"

"If I don't try," she said, "I'll spend the rest of my life wondering."

She stepped to the water, reaching with her mind, calling Jessa's name. "Can we talk?"

Celine felt her step-sister's presence before she saw or heard her, the telltale snow-white hair coming through the water like a beacon through the dark.

When Jessa surfaced, her eyes flickered from Celine to Owen. "What do you want?"

"By the gods," Tyrion whispered before he caught himself. He cleared his throat and stood at attention.

Celine tried to smile at her step-sister, the muscles in her face tense with anxiety of how this would go. How could she apologize for something she wasn't sorry for?

Shame feathered through her insides like blooming fog, chilling everything it touched.

"Kasindra was here," Jessa said. "I can feel her magic lingering. Did she give you a little pep talk? Encourage you to keep going in this scheme against my father?"

Celine knew well the contempt Jessa had for Kasindra, but not because of the feud between her and Dathan. In some ways, Jessa respected Kasindra—her knowledge and usage of powerful magic, her independence, her tenacity. But Jessa had little respect for those who toyed with the darker magics like Kasindra did…darker, more taboo magics that blurred the lines between the living and the dead.

"I'm sorry, Jessa," Celine said. "I'm sorry that you've been hurt because of this."

"You said that already," Jessa said. "Did Kasindra tell you that your parents could be freed from Chaos if you killed my father?"

"Souls traded in Chaos," Celine said. "Two for two."

"Did Kasindra tell you what's consuming him?" Jessa's lips trembled almost imperceptibly before she hardened herself. "Some strange sickness."

"Hell's Touch?"

Jessa shook her head. "Something else. Something dark." Her accusatory eyes didn't leave Celine's face. "Like a touch of shadow magic that won't leave."

"That—" Confused, Celine tried to process quickly what Jessa said. "That's not what I've done."

"Are you certain?" Embittered, Jessa moved closer. "You learned your magic from the Sea Witch herself. How much do you really know about what you've done?"

"What are you saying?"

"How easy is it to tell someone trusting what they want or need to hear? How easy is it to tell them what you want them to know?" She scoffed. "By the gods, Celine, think. My aunt is the most skilled user of the dark arts among our people. Probably among his, too." She gestured vaguely toward Owen. "She could tell you anything about that kind of magic, and you'd have to believe her. It's not as though we have an abundance of resources at our disposal, explaining every minor detail of deathmagic."

Celine winced. *Deathmagic.* "That's not what I've done, Jessa. I would know."

"Would you?" Jessa blinked, her white eyes vibrant despite the dark. "Would you know what your magic has *really* done?"

I didn't care before. The truth soured on Celine's stomach. *Kasindra was right. So much has changed.*

"What if your parents aren't in Chaos?"

Celine stared at her step-sister, dumbstruck.

"Aunt Kasindra knows how to get what she wants."

What if your parents aren't in Chaos?

"The merfolk, working with Sudor," Celine said quietly. "That new crystal they found underground. Have you seen it?"

Confusion etched lines on Jessa's face. "What are you talking about? What crystal?"

"Dathan and Santus are working with Sudor."

"Yes, that I know. My father doesn't like to listen to reason. You can't trust human kings." Then, looking at Owen, she said, "Sorry, your majesty."

He held up a hand, wordlessly acknowledging that he didn't take offense. But he glanced at Tyrion, whose expression spoke the opposite reaction, even as his eyes lingered on Jessa.

Jessa continued. "What crystal?"

"The new arcana crystal." Celine blinked at her step-sister in disbelief. "You don't know about it?"

She shook her head. "If it crossed my father's path, I would know."

"What about his secret hoard? The stuff he keeps hidden."

"What secret hoard?" Jessa almost laughed, the notion ludicrous. "He wants his wealth on display. He practically dares others to touch it."

Celine took a breath. What did all of this mean?

"Think about everything you think you know," Jessa said, something akin to victory in her tone. "Think about all that fertilizer you've helped add to Kasindra's garden."

"Her garden?" Celine's anger flared. "I've had nothing to do with it. How could you think that?"

Jessa flicked the surface of the water in response, her smirk triumphant. "Good night."

She left Celine stunned to silence on the beach, and Celine watched the white of her tail disappear to the dark.

"What did she mean?" Owen asked quietly. "What garden?"

"Kasindra's garden," she said. "Rich with dark magic. It's an arcane focus, or a conduit for stronger spells. But I would never—"

She took a breath, her chest aching.

"What fertilizer?" His question was quiet, but, by his tone, he already knew.

"It feeds on the living."

"Gods above."

Celine had a dark idea of what Kasindra had done to keep her garden alive. And Jessa believed that Celine was capable of knowingly feeding it.

Of course she does. Bitterness and shame swirled with more fuel in Celine's core. *I'm torturing her father, aren't I?*

"Let's go home." Owen took her hand and squeezed. "I'll have some tea brought."

Celine let Owen lead her away from the beach, his warmth battling against the chill that emanated from within her.

Murderer.

CHAPTER 31

When they returned, Celine and Owen sought solitude. Once the maid brought the steaming array of tea, they drank in his chambers in blessed silence.

Think about everything you think you know.

Celine's mind considered nothing else—Kasindra, Dathan, the Chaos Realm, her parents. She set her tea on the table and went to the window, looking at the star-studded horizon before her, vast in its darkness and sprinkling of light.

How much was the truth? How much was a lie?

"Tell me what you're thinking." Owen held her from behind, leaning his head against hers. "Spare no detail."

"I hardly know." There was too much to find the words for, too much to give voice to.

"Should I guess?"

She rested her hands on his arms, leaning against him. "Go ahead, husband."

"You feel guilty." He gave her a moment before going on. "You don't want to hurt anyone, but Dathan shouldn't go without justice for what he's done. And you don't want your parents to suffer." He paused again. "You don't know how much of this is real. You don't know if you've trusted the wrong person."

He spoke gently, kindly, the words coming without judgment.

"I never trusted her completely," she said. "I always knew her motive. But I suppose I trusted her in every other way. And it's cost me something I didn't realize I was giving away. Or, in realizing it, I didn't care. Not then. Not when all I could think about was Dathan. It was an obsession. And learning dark magic was an addiction. Feeling that kind of power after Dathan had taken so much—"

When she took a breath, it shuddered in her lungs.

"But what if it wasn't Dathan?" Her lips nearly trembled at the swelling emotion within her. "Your father and mine died from the same poison. Why did I believe it was from Dathan? Santus's hand, but Dathan's command?"

After a breath's silence, Owen guessed, "Because Kasindra told you."

Yes. "And I was broken enough to believe her."

"But you wanted to learn from her," he said. "She's powerful, and that was an answer you needed."

"She hates Dathan as much as I do. Maybe more." A moment passed, the pair of them quietly looking across the night-painted landscape. "It was easy to say yes. I had nothing to lose."

"What about Quinn and Zander? They don't seem pleased with the arrangement."

"They're not, but they understand. They know the depth of my rage and hatred."

"Hatred takes a lot out of you." He took a breath, his chest rising and falling against her. "You must be so tired."

She was. Tired of harboring darkness, of having to justify herself to everyone. Owen was a breath of fresh air. Owen was a *relief*. She didn't have to defend herself or explain *why*.

"Would you like to rest here?" He swayed her back and forth gently. "You're welcome to, unless you want to be alone."

She hugged his arms tighter. "I don't want to be alone."

He kissed her temple and loosened his hold, but she held firm, turning to face him as her arms found their way around his neck. He blinked in surprise, having only time enough to steady himself as she kissed him. His broad hands flattened against her back, bringing her closer.

When they parted, Owen rested his forehead against hers. "Celine, I—"

A scream pierced the air, the pair looking abruptly at the closed door.

"What on earth—"

But Owen didn't finish as thundering footsteps grew closer until they stopped outside. The door burst open without ceremony.

It was Graham, with Tyrion looking confused over his shoulder. "Owen, the queen—"

He didn't have time to finish as Owen hurried out of the room, running across the castle to his mother's chambers. Starlight filled the warmly lit suite, and the only open door among them framed a horrified maid, her trembling hands cupped in front of her open mouth. A tray of tea things lay broken at her feet as she backed away, hitting the door jamb with a jolt.

Owen rushed in, Celine on his heels, but he froze at the sight of Queen Adella lying on her back across her bed, eyes open, lips slightly parted. There was no blood, only the queen's lifeless body, but Celine caught a strange fragrance, almost sickly sweet, something akin to spoiled fruit.

With a cry, Owen went to his mother and shook her shoulders. He called her name, touched her face and hands, until the emotional wave took him. He wept bitterly, burying his face in the bed beside her.

"Who did this?" Graham had the maid's shoulders, his voice pointed with authority. "Who was in this room?"

"No one!" The maid squawked her answer, terrified. "There was no one!"

"Did she eat something?" Celine asked, sniffing. "Do you smell that?"

"I didn't bring her any food." The maid sobbed, likely sensing her own doom. "She asked for tea, and I've only just returned."

"You think she was poisoned?" Graham asked, looking at Celine.

She wasn't sure, not seeing any signs on the queen's body. "I'm not sure, but that smell—"

Owen, still weeping, lifted his head, looking at his mother's face and fingers. "There's no trace of poison. What could kill without leaving a trace?"

In the corner of her eye, the curtain fluttered, the waves of the fabric gently swaying.

But the window was closed.

Without a word, Celine summoned a dagger. The maid gasped before Graham covered her mouth. Celine tip-toed across the wooden floor. Owen watched, his expression steeling as he, too, glanced toward the curtain. But Celine didn't break to her gaze from her target, her hand reaching before yanking the fabric away.

The man burst out of his hiding place, arms tucked against his chest and stomach as he aimed his shoulder at Celine, intending to drive her down. But Owen reacted quickly, hands gripping and pulling on the man's tunic and yanking him back against the wall. The glass of the window rattled in its pane.

"*Liam.*" Owen's voice was vicious and laced with murder.

Liam's wide eyes flickered anxiously at the faces in the room. Graham shoved the maid behind him, and she used her chance to flee. Tyrion entered, sword drawn, with Graham at his heels.

Celine raised her dagger, the blade flush against the apple of his throat. "*Murderer.* What did you use?"

"You mean you don't recognize it?" Liam smirked at her. "Think. *Smell.* Smelling's as good as tasting. You know it's familiar."

He wasn't wrong. The familiar scent, rotten fruit mixed with something sharp, acidic...

"A merfolk poison." She blinked at the traitorous knight. "*You're* working with Dathan?"

Liam moved to shove Celine's arm away, but Owen landed a punch hard in the softness of his gut. Liam coughed and choked, doubling over and hugging himself.

"You murdered the queen of Estilon," Owen said. "You traitor."

"The magical queen of Estilon." Liam laughed. "And her half-breed magical son, crowned king."

"You watch your mouth," Graham growled.

"Go on and protect your magic-born nephew, Prince. I know exactly what he is, and I can't wait for Estilon to crumble around him."

"You have such little faith in your own people." Graham shook his head.

Liam laughed, his crazed look as alarming as the sound that came from it. "They're not my people." His eyes darted to the faces around him. "To be a traitor, one has to be a citizen of the kingdom in question." He smirked with arrogance at Owen. "I'm as much a citizen of Estilon as your fish wife."

Owen punched him, giving Liam the motion to brandish a small vial before anyone could stop him. He pushed the cork free and drained the vial into his open mouth. Owen and Celine had no time to react as he consumed whatever poison he'd prepared.

"Kasindra sends her regards." Liam laughed, manic, even as he collapsed to his knees. "She and her little puppet have been very useful."

"*Kasindra?*" Celine would have known if Kasindra had someone in the castle. "What puppet?"

"*Helen.*" Liam laughed until he coughed, a flicker of pain contorting the victory painted across his face. "She made a lovely addition to her garden, she said, and the husk was fun to play with. *Her words*, of course." He managed a slight sneer, despite the joy he took in the horror on every face in the room. "Helen's been dead for a while."

"That's absurd," Owen said. "That kind of control is impossible."

"Impossible for you, perhaps." Liam chuckled. "Magic folk are a bane of these lands, but I have to admit *that* was impressive."

All this time?

Celine's thoughts were rampant, but nowhere among them was any trace of denial.

Kasindra had used her. She'd used Helen almost in the same way that she'd used Celine—a mindless puppet, obeying the command of the Sea Witch.

Even with every step Celine consciously made, she couldn't see the path behind her without Kasindra's signature.

"Why?" Owen demanded. "Why have you done this?"

"Long live King Jesper." Liam gurgled, blood appearing on his lips. "My father will rule Estilon into its golden age."

The stunned silence didn't linger, even as Celine remembered Dathan's command:

You will meet the son of Jesper, king of Sudor, and work together to end the bloodline of Estilon.

"It was you," Celine said, breathless. "You were supposed to meet me. Dathan said—"

"It wasn't supposed to be you." Liam coughed, spraying blood on the floor. He collapsed there, body almost fetal. "I was right not to trust you. You should have died in that cell."

She tightened her hold on her dagger, but any physical retaliation was pointless. Liam's last breath rattled from his blood-filled lungs and out his red, parted lips.

"Get rid of it." Owen's disgust and anger twisted the handsome features of his face as he stared at Liam's body. "Throw him out with the waste." He looked at his mother's face, lips trembling. "We need to take her to the Chapel."

Guards were summoned, and Liam and Queen Adella were taken to their separate resting places, one foul and the other holy. Owen and Celine followed Adella. Graham and Tyrion remained close. A somber procession.

At the rear of the Chapel was a door that led to the royal mausoleum. Celine had passed through that portal only once, at the resting of King Rolf. It was far too soon to pass through it again, as there was no coffin prepared, but the central slab of stone was cleared for those coming to remember. The guards laid her carefully, Owen holding her hand.

Celine remembered holding her own mother's hand after her death. *After Dathan killed her.* Celine had wished and willed for her mother to stir and wake, as though from a magic-induced sleep, but her muscles remained still and her skin cold.

She rested a hand on Owen's shoulder without saying a word, thumb rubbing the curve with gentle pressure.

"To the Solar," Owen said to Graham, Tyrion, and Celine. He kissed Adella's fingers before gently setting her hand on her stomach.

The queen looked like she slept. "We have much to discuss. It was the Sea Witch, not the merking, who—" His lips twitched, a silent snarl passing through him. Controlling himself, he repeated, "There is much to discuss."

He swept from the room, his footsteps hard against the wood floor, against the soft earth outside, against the stone in the castle. He moved with violent purpose, his heels thunder.

When he burst into the Solar, there was no firelight, no candles, nothing living in the space. Everything held in stasis until he arrived, moving through the room like a storm at sea.

Graham and Tyrion worked to start the fire and light candles. Owen went to the large table and shuffled through papers in the dark until he found a map of the eastern coastline. He unrolled it, weighing it with whatever he could find, and spread his hands across the inked parchment, studying the layout.

"Merfolk on land, apparently aligned with Sudor. But the Sea Witch is behind it all, isn't she?" He pointed to the village where Santus and the others had raided. "Celine, where does Kasindra spend her time?"

She looked at the lines that represented land and sea, trying to picture depth and distance across paper. "Here?" She pressed a finger out near the edge. "It could be farther. It's difficult to tell, without swimming there to show you."

"Which I am very tempted to ask of you." Candles bloomed to life, and Owen looked at Graham and Tyrion. "What do we know?"

"That the Sea Witch is working with Sudor," Tyrion said, his lips tight as he spoke through his anger. "And that Liam is Jesper's son, if he's to be believed."

"We'll have to take that on faith," Owen said. "It's a hell of a thing to lie about, if it isn't true."

"I'm inclined to believe it," Graham said. "What does he gain by lying? Deepening an existing war with Sudor?"

"But why my mother?" Celine could see how Owen strove to control every inch of his body, from his muscles to his voice. "Why her, and why now?"

For a moment, Celine blamed herself and the command of Dathan to work with Sudor to end the monarchy in Estilon. Liam was told to expect someone—likely Jessa—but he received her instead. Celine, who was hellbent to disobey Dathan, who wouldn't sacrifice herself for the command of the man she hated.

But she wouldn't make herself responsible for the feelings and actions of others. Not like this, and not Liam.

"Your majesty?" A male voice came from the other side of the door. "A guard reports suspicious activity at a nearby outpost."

Owen set his jaw, an internal debate raging.

"I'll go," Graham muttered.

"No." Owen took a fortifying breath. "It will only take a moment."

He left the door ajar behind him, and Celine studied the map of the Sea of Kings scaling up the eastern Estilon shore.

"I can hardly believe what's happened," Tyrion said. "Liam, of all people, killing our queen."

"Your imprisonment makes more sense now," Graham said, apology in his eyes as he looked at Celine. "I'm sorry I fell for his deception, your highness. I pray you'll forgive me."

"I have—"

But a crash outside interrupted her, followed by grunts and shouts.

"Take the *King of Estilon* to his new throne room!"

Graham, armed, rushed to the door, but Tyrion held him back, peering through the crack in the open door.

"We don't know how many there are," he whispered.

"To hell with how many. They have my nephew!" His whisper was coarse. "They have *your king*."

"And we're captured or dead if we burst out now."

Tyrion peered through the narrow crack and held up six fingers.

"Six men?" Graham whispered.

"Sudor." His brown eyes met Graham's. "They have Owen."

Celine rushed to the door, pushing through Tyrion's protesting arms to see Owen, bound and gagged, dragging his thrashing body toward the stairs.

"Find his wife," one man said. "Check the bedchambers. Let's show him what we think of mermaids play-acting as human queens."

A chill scaled down her spine, Celine's hands filling with her daggers without a conscious thought. "I will enjoy peeling the skin from their bodies."

"We won't let them capture him." Graham stared at Tyrion in disbelief. "We have to go out there."

"We're outnumbered, and they want her." He glanced over his shoulder at Celine. "How many others are already in the castle?"

"How did they get in?"

"How many of our men were really *our men*?" Tyrion's eyebrows rose at the question. "Liam wasn't."

"They're taking him to the dungeon, aren't they?" Celine's sense memory of that place sent shivers across her skin.

"It looks that way, your highness," Graham said. "How do we get to Owen? We'll have to fight our way in."

"We need others," Tyrion said. "We need—"

"Wait." The two vials from Kasindra, one green and one purple, rested in the drawer of her nightstand. "I have an idea."

CHAPTER 32

"A *stealth elixir*?" Graham peeked outside the door, looking left and right before sneaking out, Celine following. Tyrion remained behind her, returning the door to its original position. "How often have you used it, if I may ask?"

"Just once. The night Liam captured me."

"He followed you, even with the elixir?" Tyrion exhaled sharply through his nose, a quiet scoff. "Do we really need to risk our next for something that probably won't work?"

"It isn't meant to hide someone completely from view, but the scent can muddle the senses. Unless you're looking for someone and you're paying attention." She gestured vaguely, meaning, *Like Liam*.

"They're looking for you," Tyrion said.

"But they don't know where I am. Liam did. He had an edge where these others do not." Rage flashed in her eyes. "They don't know what they've done or what they will suffer."

"It's a miracle they haven't checked the Solar yet," Graham said. To Tyrion, he asked, "Have they already checked her chambers?"

Voice resounded from downstairs, and there were a few cries and whimpers from maids.

"It doesn't sound like it," Tyrion said, listening. "We need to move quickly."

"Unhand them, you craven wretches!"

The sound of a fight echoed up the stone, coming from beneath them. The corridor beneath the stairs, near the kitchen? Celine couldn't be sure.

Graham hesitated, his expression tense. Celine wouldn't have blamed him if he raced down the stairs, sword drawn.

"We'll take care of them soon enough," Tyrion reassured. "Let's let our knights serve their kingdom as we go to rescue our king."

Graham nodded curtly. The trio were alert as they crept across the suite toward the grand staircase, eyes and ears open to any sign of an intruder.

With a clear shot, they tip-toed quickly, feet meeting the soft rug path to the corridor of chambers. But they froze at the crash of disrupted wood from down the hall.

"They're in Owen's room," Tyrion said.

Celine hurried to her chambers, but Graham held his arm out to stop her so he could go first. After checking that the room was empty, Graham stepped back to give her and Tyrion entry before he slipped in and silently closed the door.

"They're just here," Celine whispered, going to the nightstand and opening the drawer.

She stared, mouth agape. The vials weren't there.

"What is it?" Graham whispered.

"They're *gone*."

Tyrion smiled mirthlessly, shaking his head. "Of course they are."

"No, I swear, they were here."

"Who else knew about them?" Graham asked. "Who would know what they are and what they do?"

"A maid put them in the drawer for me, but she didn't know what they—"

A maid that was with Helen.

"By the gods. *Helen*."

"Helen?" Tyrion asked. "Dead Helen, who was a puppet for the Sea Witch?"

Celine nodded. "She knew. And if she was really the Sea Witch's eyes and ears, then she would know everything about them. And me."

Tyrion shuddered. "I still don't enjoy knowing that she was here all this time."

"Are you suggesting," Graham said slowly, "that we visit Helen's chambers to search?"

"Where are her chambers?" Celine looked at Tyrion and Graham, reading their tense expressions. "It's impossible, isn't it?"

"They're in the servant's quarters," Graham said. "But, since Helen was the head lady's maid, her chambers are easier to reach from here."

"Easier," Tyrion said, his tone rich with displeasure, "but not by much."

"Servant's quarters are upstairs," Graham said. "And we can reach them from this side of the castle."

Another crash outside silenced them, their bodies freezing as they listened and waited.

"We go now," Graham whispered.

Carefully, they stepped out, and Graham led Celine to the end of the corridor, where she had yet to set foot. Masked cleverly with the stone was a corner revealing a narrow spiral staircase, winding up. With the same formation as before, Graham moved first, Celine second, and Tyrion third, their steps almost silent as they crept up the stone steps.

The floor revealed several closed doors, similar to the royal suite where Adella and Rolf had lived, but the wooden framing and makeup were much more provincial in architecture and design. There were no rugs or tapestries, and the single window was modestly dressed.

One stand held a single vase filled with fresh flowers. A humble allowance for beauty. Enough for a servant, but not nearly grand enough for a royal.

Graham stepped quietly across the stone floor to the last door on the left. There was another staircase there, winding down. Celine mapped the castle in her mind, understanding that they now stood above the royal suite. This staircase provided easy access to either royal chamber.

Easy access to kill a king and his queen.

All this time? Kasindra's laugh echoed in Celine's memory. *Everything was a lie.*

Jessa's hurt and angry expression and the words that followed. Quinn and Zander's worry about Celine's state of mind and her willingness to do dangerous, dark things in the name of revenge.

And the lie she so completely believed would have cost her everything she held dear.

Shame curdled in her stomach.

Graham opened the door and moved to enter, but not before two guards in Sudor tabards raced up from the chambers, colliding with Graham and Celine. A fist collided painfully with her cheek as the man brought her to the hard floor.

"Could this be the queen consort?" He chuckled, the sound making Celine's skin crawl. "Just who we've been looking for."

Tyrion roughly pulled at the man's shoulders, slamming his fist against the man's nose. Graham scuffled with his own target, weapons clanging in their fight.

Celine thought to summon her daggers, but the fighting was too close. Any strike to an enemy could hit Graham or Tyrion.

She had another weapon—one she hadn't needed or considered until now.

Her stomach lurched at the sound of a hit. Tyrion groaned. The look of shock in his wide eyes read more than simply a well-placed punch.

"Tyrion!"

He collapsed to his knees, holding the man who'd stabbed him with a well-concealed knife.

Celine didn't hesitate. Her fingers dug into the assailant's hair, pulling his head back as she held her mouth close to his ear. The song she hummed was a gentle lullaby favored among merfolk. The melody was light, a caress of comfort that could lull anyone to slumber. Combined with the voice magic inherent to her kind, and the ears that captured it wouldn't stand a chance.

Tyrion and Graham suffered some effects, even as she kept the song low and personal for the man she wished to incapacitate. They shook their heads and blinked their eyes back to consciousness once the song was over. The Sudorian soldier fell limp at her feet.

Graham moved quickly to Tyrion's side, hands working to loosen his clothing and reveal the wound.

"I can help some," Celine said, "but I'm not a healer."

"We can't stay here," Graham said. "We need to get out of the castle."

"How?" Tyrion coughed. "Sudor is everywhere."

"There's a way out," he said. "One that only the queen and I knew about."

Celine and Tyrion shared the same confused expression.

"She visited a friend often," he said vaguely, and Celine wondered if *friend* meant *Kedran*. "I would help her sneak out."

"A friend," Tyrion said. "A magic friend."

Graham nodded. "We can take these stairs to the queen's chambers, but getting you downstairs, Tyr—"

"I can manage." He tried to sit up, groaning before his breath caught. He rested his hand on the wound.

Celine moved his hand and pressed both of hers in its place. Humming quietly, she tried to send magic into the wound, just as Zander had said, to help the skin and muscle heal itself. Tyrion growled in pain as it worked, but Celine had to release her hold on him. She panted, breathless.

"Help me get their tabards," Graham said to Celine. "We can use them when we come back into the castle."

"I would rather die than wear their colors." Tyrion looked ready to spit upon the unconscious men.

"I rather like the idea of using their own identities against them," Graham said. "Make a mockery of it."

That perked Tyrion up, who sat up more easily after Celine's attempt at healing. Celine worked quickly with Graham to relieve the Sudorian soldiers of their kingdom's colors, and, after binding their hands and feet, pulled them into Helen's chambers.

Finding the vials was easier than Celine expected, even in Helen's ransacked room. They were in a discarded drawer beneath the window, their corks in place and the glass unbroken. The iridescent green and purple glistened beautifully in the sunlight. She snatched up both before slipping out, Graham closing the door behind her.

"Here." Celine dabbed the green elixir on the sides of her neck and on her wrists. "This will keep the potion from affecting you both."

"The magic and the cure." Graham nodded approvingly.

Tyrion looked at the drops of elixir dubiously on his fingertips before applying it as directed.

They each applied the purple elixir before Celine helped Tyrion to his feet. He leaned on her as Graham, holding the tabards in his arms, took the lead.

The trio eased down the stairs, Celine helping Tyrion keep his balance as he gritted his teeth against the pain. Graham kept watch, eyes and ears alert to any change in the atmosphere. When they reached the bottom of the stairs, Graham peered around the corner.

"One soldier," he whispered, the sound barely audible. "He's outside the Solar."

"Cover your ears," Celine said.

The men obeyed without question, and Celine hummed as before. The guard fell to the floor quickly, a hint of a smile adorning his sleeping face.

They moved quickly, Graham pulling the guard into the solar and securing him inside as Celine waited with Tyrion by the queen's chambers.

"I never knew a secret passage existed here," Tyrion said. "And before anyone says *because it's a secret*, haven't knights patrolled outside where this passage leads?"

"Not if I've directed them elsewhere," Graham said. "The queen's privacy was paramount."

"I know her majesty had her reasons, but…" Tyrion let the statement hang unfinished, though his thoughts were clear.

"The king knew," Graham said. "He knew from the very beginning, even before they were married. There was never any deception, as far as that's concerned. If that's any comfort."

Tyrion shrugged. "I suppose it is."

Graham moved to the left of the wide window, reaching behind the crimson curtain to the hook that held it in place. With a slight twist down, a stone panel released, showing a narrow passage with a hidden stair.

"Impossible." Tyrion stared in wonder. "The stone is far too heavy for hinges."

"It isn't stone." Graham knocked, and the material sounded like wood. "Clever craftsmanship and a lot of magic."

Tyrion exhaled. "How much of my world do I even know is real?"

Celine could relate. "I was asking myself the same question."

Helping Tyrion down these steps was more difficult, with the narrow passage having to accommodate all three of them. They moved single-file, Tyrion's hands resting on Celine's shoulders as she led him with Graham helping from behind.

"Not much farther," Graham said. "The door will open to a small room with a way out. Then we walk to the small village on the other side of the castle lake."

"The queen would make that journey alone?" Tyrion asked. "No escort?"

"Anyone who crossed her majesty was met with a force of reckoning," Graham said, a hint of pride in his voice. "I wouldn't allow her passage unless I was sure she would be safe."

Celine continued until she reached the door Graham had mentioned. But as she reached for the handle...

"There's nothing here." She rubbed her hands on the solid wood. "How do we get out?"

"That stone there. Just about eye level, you'll see a slight bevel on the right side."

Celine followed his guidance and pressed the correct stone to release the latch. The door popped ajar, swinging freely as she pressed it open. They filled into a small room, closing the door behind them, and Graham moved immediately to the next secret panel, using the same latching mechanism as the previous door.

"So many secrets," Tyrion muttered. "But this is impressive."

Tyrion faltered as he stepped forward, Celine catching him under his arm. Blood still oozed from his wound, even as her healing had slowed it down.

"I can make it," he said, slightly winded. "We can't afford to slow down."

"We can afford some rest," Graham said. "Celine, is there anything you can do?"

"I can try." But she didn't have any hope in helping. Healing magic was far from where her strengths lay, but the lack of trying felt too much like giving up.

"Magic is limitless," she said, helping Tyrion to lean against the wall. He had turned a shade paler since they were upstairs. "The only limitation is the user."

She rested her hand on his wound again, feeling the sticky, warm wetness of the blood. She whispered a song, sending magic through her fingers and palm, pushing healing into the depth of the stab wound there. It was weak—the shadows were so much easier and stronger to conjure—but it was enough to help him breathe more freely.

"That's all I can do, I'm afraid." When she removed her hand, blood had seeped into the creases of her fingers and palm.

"It is enough." Tyrion stood straighter, his breathing steadier. "Let's press on, then."

With the last door out of the castle closed behind them, the trio began the quiet trek toward the village where, if the gods were with them, they would find allies with aid.

If not, if Sudor had reached them first...

But Celine would face that terror when it came, and not a moment before. With a bleeding friend leaning on her as they walked, with her husband locked within his own prison, there was no time for *fear* or *what if*.

But there was time for the shadows that she secretly swirled around her hands, mentally commanding them to find the Sudorian king and show him his deepest nightmare. The shadows soared behind her, likely back to Estilon Castle, eager to meet the enemy king.

CHAPTER 33

Celine walked beside Graham, who'd taken Tyrion's arm over his shoulder to relieve Celine. The village was in sight, a modest community of small houses and various resources. It looked like a quiet place to live.

There were quiet spaces in the depths where merfolk didn't pass through. There were quiet days when Celine would read, either above or below the surface, but to *live* in a quiet place? A place of calm and tranquility? What was that like?

She made a lovely addition to her garden.

The husk was fun to play with.

She shuddered, Liam's taunt echoing. *The husk*, as though Helen hadn't been a living thing prior to Kasindra's magic—to her *invasion*.

But her body was in the castle all this time. How—

"It's a powerful conduit, my dear."

Like arcana crystal, but stronger. Lasting. Sustaining.

"It thrives off of living things, and it helps me to maintain even the most powerful of spells."

Thrives off living things...

Her garden, with crystals from Sudor...

Fear pulled at Celine's insides, making them contract and recoil, as though to make her body smaller.

How long did it take the living to die once they're taken by the garden? How did it feed on them? Did it...

She didn't want to think it, but the voice in her mind forced the question:

Did it keep them alive to feed?

Perhaps these were the questions she should have asked, rather than focus so much on herself and her own desperate growth in power.

Graham raised a hand, waving to a villager walking in the distance. Something akin to recognition passed between them, for the villager stopped, stared, and then ran.

"Where are they going?" Tyrion struggled to step forward. Graham held fast.

"For help."

And help came. The villagers brought a wheelbarrow to take Tyrion to their healer.

"They mean Smithson," Graham said to Celine after they hurried with Tyrion. "They're quite protective."

"Understandably so."

Children played near the street and around the houses, screaming and laughing. Women and men looked on, their previously contented faces now furrowed with concern.

"Trouble at Estilon," someone said. "Sudor's finally here."

Kedran Smithson emerged from the house where the wheelbarrow stopped, and the two villagers with Tyrion spoke quickly.

Heartbreak had already found residence in Kedran's eyes. "Adella—"

Graham nodded. "I'm sorry, Smithson."

"Come inside." Kedran stood aside as the villagers helped Tyrion to stand, practically pouring him out of the wheelbarrow to help him to his feet. Carefully, they walked him inside, and Graham and Celine followed.

"The man who killed her is dead," Celine told Kedran immediately. "He was ready with poison."

"The coward's way." Kedran guided the villagers with Tyrion to the dining table, cleared off as though he'd expected them. "We'll work here."

They laid him carefully on the tabletop and stepped out, leaving Celine and the others with Adella's widower.

"I'm sorry, Kedran," Graham said, remorse heavy in his voice.

"He disguised himself as a knight of Estilon," Celine said. "Even Owen didn't know."

"He took advantage of your trust." Kedran worked gently, pulling Tyrion's borrowed tabard and bloody tunic up to reveal the bruised stab wound diagonally up from his belly button. When he touched the red, swollen skin, his brow furrowed. "There's been some healing done already."

"I tried," Celine said. "Healing isn't exactly my strong point."

"The shadow arts." He glanced at her, though with acknowledgement instead of judgment. "Powerful dark magic."

"Shadow arts?" Tyrion stared at her. "The queen consort of Estilon uses *shadow arts*?"

"The last few years haven't been kind," she said. "And now, it seems, the very person who taught me is the reason I learned."

"The Sea Witch taught you?" Graham asked.

"Kasindra?" Kedran stopped, giving Celine his full attention. "She isn't exactly the type to mentor a pupil."

"I've only just learned that truth myself."

While Kedran continued to heal Tyrion with herbal mixtures and a touch of healing magic, Celine explained everything—from Dathan's usurpation and Kasindra's mentorship, to the recent revelation of what Kasindra was truly doing.

"The Sea Witch caused my wife's death?"

"Your *wife*?" Tyrion exhaled, fully relaxing on the tabletop so that his body appeared to collapse. "By the gods, what is happening?"

"And the knight, Liam," Kedran said. "He mentioned Kasindra's garden?"

"Yes. She told me once that it helps her channel her magic, like a conduit."

"And how does she fuel it? What resource does it need?"

How did Kedran know to ask? Celine didn't look at Graham or Tyrion, awaiting their shock.

"Life," she said simply. "It requires things that are living."

"Like—*people*?" Graham asked.

"Anything that's alive." She looked from the knights of Estilon back to Kedran. "That's why Liam said the head lady's maid was a powerful addition to the garden. But her body was in the castle. She's been with us since I arrived."

"The soul is in the garden, while the body remains." Kedran smoothed a healing salve over Tyrion's closed wound, the redness already diminished to a light pink, before helping the knight to sit up. "Hold up your clothes while I bandage this."

The knight obeyed without a word, listening to the two magic folk discuss the Sea Witch and her power.

"Strong necromancy," Kedran said. "Likely fueled by the garden itself—the soul required for the body to remain. Ironic and cruel."

"Do you know anything about the Chaos Realm?" Her question was meek, but the need to ask outweighed any shyness.

"Aishlin's domain," Kedran said, steadily wrapping bandaging around Tyrion's waist. "The gauntlet for the dead to fight for redemption."

"Can magic free a soul trapped within?"

She was far too vulnerable, far too open. But Kasindra had lied to her about everything. Had Celine given up part of her soul for a revenge that wasn't real?

"What do you mean? Like, pull them out?"

Celine looked at Graham and Tyrion, afraid to speak of magic and goddesses in front of them.

"There were stories, when I was a boy," Graham said, his voice kind, "of a trade you could propose to a Chaosborn. Sometimes even to Aishlin herself. A life for a life."

Kedran didn't speak right away, the pause deepening the despair in Celine's chest.

"There isn't a way," she whispered, "is there?"

"There is," he said. "Just as Sir Graham said: a life for a life. But it's not that simple."

"My parents—" Her breath caught in her throat. "Could I save them?"

"They're in Chaos?" Kedran finished with Tyrion, facing Celine completely. "Janis was a good king. Even with the tensions between the merfolk and landfolk, he was always fair and just. I don't believe for a second that Shanna or Anya would allow him into Chaos, unless he kept some significantly dark secrets."

"There were no secrets." Sadness overwhelmed Celine's half smile. "But I see them there. Visions and dreams. And they're screaming."

She had to stop, her lips trembling as hot tears made her eyes sting and itch.

"They," Kedran repeated. "Your mother, too?"

She nodded.

"And you see them there?"

"It's always dark. I only see their shadows." She breathed slowly, collecting herself. "But they call my name. They beg me to leave, but I try to save them."

"Is there a chance that those visions aren't real?" Tyrion asked, regarding her with sympathy. "Would Kasindra be responsible?"

"Why would—" But Celine remembered how Kasindra touched her glass orb, the purple and green smoke churning within until it changed to dark slate gray.

"If she needed something from you," Kedran said, "she would likely use whatever she could to...*persuade* you."

"Talk about cruel," Tyrion said. "Using your own parents as leverage."

"Are they even really dead?" Celine pressed her lips together. "I apologize."

"Don't apologize, your majesty," Graham said. "I would question the same thing."

"What of Helen?" Tyrion asked. "Is she really dead, too?"

"If what I understand is correct," Kedran said, "Helen's body has been separated from her consciousness, which, once it's released from the garden, won't return. The body will decay, and her consciousness will have no magical guidance to do anything but pass on."

Celine's father had died. The toxin had taken him. She watched his final breath shudder before it left.

...Didn't she?

If Celine's parents were in the Chaos Realm...

...Were they in Kasindra's garden?

She doesn't know what to believe anymore.

"I'm going to tear that garden apart," Celine said. "And her, right along with it."

"Whatever is trapped within will be released," Kedran said, "be they bodies or souls. And that will give them the freedom to move on."

That's what her parents deserved: *freedom*. Even if that was to Anya and Shanna instead of to her. Seeing them in the light of goodness instead of the dark of Chaos was the better choice.

Her parents were no longer rightfully among the living. But they would always belong among the light. And Celine would break through Kasindra's cruelty and darkness to get them there.

"So," Tyrion said, looking at each of them. "What happens now?"

"We remove Sudor from within our borders and free our king," Graham said.

"And I return to the sea to deal with the Sea Witch," Celine said. "But only after Owen is safe."

"The dungeon is dangerous for you," Graham said.

"And Sudor is dangerous for you." She straightened, chin raised and shoulders back. "We fight together to free my husband, and then I go beneath the sea."

Graham conceded, though she could tell it was unwillingly done. "As you wish, your majesty."

"Then, we should hurry," Tyrion said. "We don't know what they're doing to them down there."

"I will join you," Kedran said. "I'm no fighter, but you will have wounded. If you'll have me."

Graham extended his hand to shake Kedran's, and the two sealed the accord. "You will be welcome with us."

"Here." He opened a cupboard and revealed two vials of silvery liquid, giving one to Celine. "Drink this. It'll help against whatever iron we encounter."

She drank it without question, grateful for any help against the poisonous metal, only to grimace at its taste of mossy earth and wood smoke.

The four left Kedran's home, letting the villagers know Kedran's intent, and they departed for Estilon.

CHAPTER 34

With Graham's guidance, the secret doors opened without issue to give them easy access back into the castle. Frustrated voices grew louder as they moved through the hidden passage. Celine leaned closer to the stone, listening.

"Where the bloody hell is she?"

"Liam said she was here."

She smirked, summoning her daggers.

Tyrion readied his own blade. "I'll never get used to that."

Graham, already armed, stood ready by the door to Adella's room.

"What should I expect?" Kedran whispered, hands empty. But, with his magic, he was far from unarmed.

"A lot of angry humans," Celine said. "Owen's in a cell in the dungeon."

"And Jesper is one cruel bastard," Graham said. "He won't simply allow Owen to rot in his own cell."

Graham carefully stepped out before waving them in. "All clear."

Moving through Adella's room, Kedran paused by her vanity table, touching a hair comb with a single, gentle finger.

Celine stopped, his gaze passing over her things. But he wasn't seeing objects. He was seeing *her*.

Graham opened the chamber door silently, peering through the sliver of an opening. As soon as Graham held up a finger, a voice asked, "Anyone in there?"

Graham whispered, "In the Solar."

"No," the other voice answered. "But these documents look important."

Graham crept out, the others following, and Celine could see that the guard's back was to Adella's chamber doorway, even as he leaned a little to see further out into the suite.

"Take what's useful and burn the rest."

"It all looks useful."

But the hallway watchman didn't get to speak his witty reply as Graham covered his mouth and ran him through, the blade piercing through the other side. The quiet *drip, drip* hit the man's boot until Graham lowered him to the floor.

"Go and be judged," Graham whispered. "May Anya have mercy on your soul."

The next fight wouldn't be so quiet, but Celine helped to ease the struggle as she entered first, singing a low, disorienting tune. The man's look twisted to a dangerous sneer, even as his eyes bleared with the fog of her song. His body seized as lightning surged from Kedran's fingers. Celine buried one dagger into his shoulder and another in his side, twisting her anger into the wound before releasing him to bleed onto the stone.

"Two down. How many to go?" Tyrion surveyed the other rooms to ensure they were empty.

Kedran looked dubiously at the doorway. "I'm afraid to hazard a guess."

They moved through the suite and crept toward the foyer, voices echoing up the stone from downstairs. "King Jesper requests an audience with his lordship, and he has the nerve to refuse?"

Owen.

Sounds of a struggle preceded those of agony, the groans causing Celine's stomach to stir with worry.

"That'll show you how to respect your king!" Cruel laughter followed.

Boots shuffled and stomped.

"To the throne room, where you will kneel before your king!"

Celine, eyes alight with dark rage, kept her whisper low as she asked, "How much iron is in the throne room?"

"Very little," Graham answered. "And sound carries very well, your majesty."

She grinned.

"You're really scary when you smile like that," Tyrion said. "Thank the gods you're on our side."

Kedran snickered.

The soldiers' footsteps thundered against stone as the doors to the Great Hall opened. Boots scuffled on the floor and fists collided with flesh, then the doors closed once more. They'd forced Owen inside.

She remembered her introduction to Rolf and Adella, their thrones at the end of the large room, the space intimidating even in memory. As she crept slowly with the others, she considered the enemy king sitting where Owen should sit. As her hold on her daggers tightened, it wasn't *intimidation* she felt.

"Hey!"

Someone in Sudorian colors dove for them from the opposite upstairs corridor, landing on Graham and falling with him down the stairs. Another appeared, sword drawn, and jogged down the stairs, casting confused looks at Graham and Tyrion before realizing what they'd done in wearing their tabards.

"You dare wear our colors, you filth!"

He lunged for Tyrion, but the knight of Estilon was ready, as was Kedran. With might and magic facing this foe, Celine made for the soldier fighting Graham. The older knight was beneath the younger, enduring several punches to the face and throat. Celine didn't hesitate, bringing daggers down into his back. He gasped for breath even as she pulled him off of Graham and throwing him to the stone floor. He didn't gasp for long.

Graham breathed heavily, his face bloody and bruised, and one hand cupped his side as he winced in agony.

"They're here!" The guard struggled, pinned beneath Tyrion. "They're here!"

Celine turned away as Tyrion swiped down, spilling the man's blood on the stone. Kedran blinked, breathless, perspiration heavy around his brow. Whatever magic he'd cast took a significant toll. But his gaze found Graham, and he went to him immediately, hands going to the clutched side as he muttered words of healing.

Graham breathed more easily just as soldiers rushed in and surrounded them. Celine sang, the stone carrying her voice, and several of the soldiers faltered. *Several*, not all, and their hands still gripped their weapons.

Frost bloomed in her core. Her magic wasn't working on them.

She slashed her blade toward the nearest soldier, moving to catch him off guard, but he countered with precision, taking her wrist and using her own momentum to pull her into his arms. He held fast, nodding quickly to another.

"She's here, your highness."

A man sauntered out of the Great Hall, hands clasped behind his back. Jesper, the king of Sudor, was taller than Celine had expected. Taller, and more rotund. But there was nothing clumsy in his stride or bearing. A hard, cruel body, with sure footing and a sharp eye.

"Celine!"

Owen's call didn't come from the Great Hall, but from the dungeons below.

The rime in her core solidified to a block of ice.

"My, my." Jesper's smug smile deepened the laugh lines around his mouth. "What a lovely voice you have."

She sneered, readying a string of curses to throw at him, but the man who held her lifted her chin with a harsh pull. She hated that she cried out in pain.

"Celine!"

"The mermaid who would be queen." Jesper met her gaze unabashedly. "The Sea Witch warned me you would rebel. She seemed to regard it with pride—the spirit of the merfolk—but rebellion is an unnecessary waste of energy."

He paced a few steps, hands still behind him. He sucked his teeth, thinking. Celine grimaced at the sound.

He stopped in front of her. "She asked me to return you to the sea unharmed." He tilted his head. "I'm currently weighing my options if I choose to disobey and kill you instead."

"What's the worst that could happen?" Celine asked, as though to offer him counsel. "She brings your kingdom to the ground? But only after she robs you of all your crystal?"

Defensive anger flashed across his face before he laughed, the sound grating as it bounced off the stone walls. "Well, then, it's good that Sudor is landlocked and out of her slippery reach."

The Sudorian soldiers laughed with their king, and Celine smiled, too, though superficially, her eyes unyielding. "Of course. No access to Sudor whatsoever. No lakes or rivers for those pesky merfolk to swim through."

Mirth left him, though the shadow of his smile remained. The shape was more sinister than before. "You speak so flippantly of your own kind."

"Am I merfolk, good king Jesper?"

He blinked, understanding slow to reach him.

"Would access to water be what *really* stops us?"

With a growl, he yanked the necklace from her throat. "Back to the sea with you, wretch!"

He threw the necklace to his feet and slammed his heel against it. The magic left Celine instantly, her body remaking itself then and there with agonizing efficiency. Her captors dropped her as she screamed, blood and muscle shifting and breaking, tearing and stretching. Then came the blessed healing, but only after her heart nearly leaped from her chest. Her trousers ripped to ribbons as her legs coalesced, scales shimmering in place of skin. The fin pushed the boots free before the tail finished, the sunlight glimmering off of shiny teal.

Heavy breathing still didn't fill her lungs. Her gills flapped, desperate, but the pain still hummed in her bones.

He knew. *He knew.*

Jesper grabbed her necklace to banish her to the water.

Betrayal soured deeply in her core, Quinn's words echoing in her mind–*she's using you.* Shame reached to the marrow of her bones.

"A fish out of water." Jesper chuckled as he crouched in front of her. "How long can you last? Will we reach the sea in time?"

Another human, ignorant to the strength of amphibious merfolk. She screamed in his face, using what she could muster to propel her voice magic like a weapon. It did its work, pushing the King of Sudor with enough force that he landed hard on his tailbone. A dagger was in her hand before her conscious mind could conjure it, and she slammed it into his gut, down to the hilt. A boot collided with her face, breaking her nose and throwing her back. Dazed, she blinked through blurred vision and pain as a fight erupted. One man had the laborious task of pulling Jesper out of the fray, but not before Celine dispelled her dagger. His wound flowed freely.

She hummed her shadows to life, sending them to surround Jesper's body. The King of Sudor screamed, and for a moment, Celine wondered what nightmare had wrapped him in its cold embrace. Her nose healed, cartilage resetting as the blood flow stopped.

A hand pulled her hair, yanking her up. The growling face of a Sudorian soldier looked down at her with murder in his eyes. "I don't give a damn what the Sea Witch wants. *You're dead.*"

His sword went through her, right above the navel, and he yanked it free with bloodthirsty victory.

Unseen force slammed into him, knocking him back. Celine collided hard with the floor. She pressed a hand to the wound, hiding her magical flesh as it already began sewing itself together. Kedran nodded to her once, knowingly, and kept fighting alongside Graham.

Only a few Sudorian soldiers remained, and their last moments met them at the lethal touch of either magic or steel. The man who'd tried to save his king faced Tyrion.

"Our king is head," he said. "The mer-bitch killed him. Not even Estilon's finest could defeat him without magic."

Tyrion grabbed the soldier by the throat. "You will not speak ill of the Queen of Estilon and live."

He offered the soldier no chance for a response as his sword ran him through.

With the last of them dead, Kedran worked to heal Graham, who looked the most battered out of all of them.

"Get Owen," Celine said as Tyrion dropped the man and turned to her. "Go get Owen."

Tyrion ran, leaving the man to sputter into his death as his enemies looked on.

"Better this," said one dying man at Graham's feet, "than your rotten prison."

He gasped as he died.

Better this? Celine disagreed. Life was always the better choice. Without it, how could she avenge her parents? Without it, how could she have learned about what Kasindra had done?

"Are you alright, your majesty?" Graham said, stifling a cough.

She moved her hand to reveal the healing wound. Blood still oozed, but, in time, there would be no evidence of it left behind. "For all of Sudor's strength, they know very little of their magical enemies."

She reclined, the cool stone floor a blessed relief against her skin and scales. She turned as Owen thundered up from the dungeon, his face and hands bloodied and bruised.

"Celine." He crashed to his knees beside her, pale with panic.

She touched his face, one black eye nearly swollen closed, his mouth scabbed with dried blood. "Would that I could bring them back to life to kill them all again. What have they done to you?"

"We had our retribution," Celine said.

Owen gingerly touched the healing wound at her side. "May Aishlin have her way with them." He pressed her bloody hand to his face. "I was out of my mind. I heard you screaming."

She noticed that the blood on his hands was fresh. "Did you try to break out of the cell?"

"Through stone and iron." He touched her cheek near her nose, his eyes discerning what had happened. "Their remains will be devoured by wild dogs for what they've done."

"At your command," Graham said.

"How do we change you back?" Owen asked. "We have the crystal."

"I need to return." She moved to sit up, Owen helping by leaning her against him. "Kasindra won't stop."

"Take me with you."

"*Owen.*"

"Your majesty."

"Celine," he said, his crystalline eyes fixed on hers. "Take me with you."

Her smile was sad as she shook her head. "Your kingdom just survived a siege. Estilon needs her king."

"And my wife needs her husband. You come first."

She smiled at that, kissing his hand. "Trust me."

"I do," he said without hesitating. "Only..."

She waited, reading the conflict in his eyes.

"The revenge that I promised for Dathan actually belongs to her." He bore the same look as he did in the library, one eager for reprisal. "I want her to receive it."

"She will. I swear it. But changing your shape will require incredible magic and recovery. There simply—"

"—isn't time." He knew she was right. After a moment, he nodded, conceding. "Give her every layer of hell, wife. And return to me when it's over."

"I will. You have my word."

Graham cleared his throat, glancing at Kedran. "We should see to your injuries, your highness."

"Smithson." Owen sat up straighter. "I apologize. I didn't realize you were here."

"You had other priorities." Kedran smiled warmly at Celine. "I am here to offer my aid, your highness."

"And there are likely other soldiers to face," Graham said. "Soldiers who are as yet unaware of the fate of their king."

"More rats to exterminate." Tyrion wiped his sword on a dead soldier's tabard. "And let's return to Estilon colors, for gods' sake."

Kedran's magic worked quickly on Owen, most of his wounds fading as the others were shadows of what they'd been. Without announcement, he lifted Celine in his arms and. With Graham, Tyrion, and Kedran as their protection, he carried her toward the sea.

"You will return to me," he said. "Or I will bury myself in the Sea of Kings to find you."

He kissed her before he waded into the water up to his waist, and even then, he didn't let her go.

"Ridding the sea of her darkness will bring so much light," she said. "We could do with a bit of that, I think."

"We could." Then, with a chuckle, he said, "Would you like for me to be incredibly sentimental and say that *you* are my light?"

She groaned with a laugh. "Prepare some poetry for my return. Be ready to read to me for hours."

He kissed her, the pressure of his lips and the strength of his arms enough to surge the tidal waves crashing within her.

Then, with a sigh, he loosened his hold and let her go.

The Sea of Kings was colder than Celine remembered.

CHAPTER 35

Celine swam with great speed, the motion of her tail beyond familiar. She's returned to more than just the sea when she swam through the glacial blue of the deep. She returned to her body, to the part of her that had been true for so long.

But the way Owen held her before releasing her back to the sea, the strength of his arms and how she fit against him...

Not that he replaced or changed anything by existing alongside her in the past days. It was that she'd made space for him, and he fit. *They* fit.

It was comforting to return to the world she'd known before, knowing that she could step back into the world she'd discovered. With Owen.

"Quinn. Zander." Celine reached their reef, familiarity and comfort soaking into skin and scale. "Jessa, are you close?"

"Celine?" Quinn answered first. "Where—"

Her blonde head poked up from the coral, eyes and mouth wide open in shock.

Quinn swam fast and crashed into her, her arms and tail colliding in an embrace. Another body crashed in, Zander's arms surrounding them both.

"What are you doing here?" he asked. "*How* are you here?"

"Celine?" Jessa's voice reached her, though the mermaid was nowhere in sight.

"There's a lot to tell you," Celine said, first to Quinn and Zander, and then again to Jessa.

When Celine asked Jessa to come to her reef, she didn't receive a response at first. Shame swirled in her core, knowing her step-sister had every right to still be angry, to still resent Celine for what she'd done.

"What's wrong?" Quinn touched the fluttering ends of Celine's teal hair.

"I have so much to apologize for." Celine rested her head on Quinn's shoulder, her arms still around both of her friends. "So much that I thought was right or true, but it was all a lie."

"Are you talking about Kasindra?" Zander asked. "Has something happened?"

Celine opened her mouth when she caught sight of Jessa, swimming slowly toward their reef with her frosted eyes locked onto Celine's.

"You're back," Jessa said. "Did you tire of the humans?"

"Jessa—"

She held up a hand. "I know what you're going to say. Or, at least, I think I know. And I'm not ready to hear it just yet."

If only the apology would spill out of her. If only she didn't dumbly nod, guilt and shame forging the cage she cowered within.

"Kasindra's working with Sudor." Celine's merspeak only touched their minds, but she kept her voice low. "Jesper's son was one of Owen's knights. He murdered the queen."

"*What?*" Jessa was the first to voice her surprise. "*Kasindra?*"

"I think—" Celine struggled to give the words her voice. They were silent, staring at her. Quinn reached to touch her arm. "The poison that killed my father killed King Rolf." Celine looked at each pair of eyes, from fire to sunlight to ice. "I think Kasindra killed my father."

The suspicion passed through each of them in silent wonder, the questions storming in their minds unsaid until, finally, Jessa asked, "Why?"

"Certainly not for her brother," Quinn said.

"For her garden." Zander didn't waver, convinced as to the former merking's fate. "Janis was one of the most powerful merfolk. The magic he had, all going into her garden…" He shook his head. "That would be hard to refuse, for someone like her."

The flutter of anxiety in Celine's core worsened to a hurricane of raging wind and thunder and freezing rain. "She's stronger than I realized. She had a human thrall in the castle—a lady's maid that everyone trusted."

"A *thrall*?" Quinn blinked. "She controlled it from here?"

Celine nodded. "That's what it looks like."

"We destroy that garden," Jessa said.

"Not destroy her?" Zander asked with a mirthless chuckle.

"It *will* destroy her." Jessa's gaze was glacial. "Her power comes from it. And it requires constant fuel."

Zander gulped. "Do I want to know what it feeds on?"

"Exactly what you think," Celine said. "Life and magic of the living."

He grimaced. "I didn't know about the *living* part."

"So, how do we do it?" Quinn asked. "How do we destroy her garden?"

"We could rip it apart with our bare hands," Jessa said, "though that will probably kill us."

"There's something she always touches when we train," Celine said, "an orb with purple and green smoke."

"Will breaking it make the garden vulnerable?" Quinn asked. "Or will it kill us all as soon as we breathe it in?"

"With Kasindra," Jessa said, "both are likely true."

"Before we get close, we need to know where she is." Zander settled onto the seabed beneath him, laying his hands flat against the sand. "Let's see what I can find."

He closed his eyes, his red hair fluttering around his head as he concentrated on his magic. Then, with a flash, his eyes opened, the red overwhelmed with bright blue as he pushed his magic out into the water.

"There she is," he said. "Harvesting from the Coral Deeps."

"Only Kasindra could go through the Coral Deeps unscathed," Jessa said. "Hells, she probably *made* the Deeps."

"By the gods." It had never occurred to Celine that the Deeps could be made by anything other than either a divine hand or natural biological progression. "What if she did?"

Silence fell over them, *probability* overshadowing *possibility*. Once Zander magically returned, they swam out of the reef for the Sea Witch's cave, eyes scanning all that they could for any sign of her. But there was nothing. Just the four of them swimming carefully through the sea. The absence of the Sea Witch was more disconcerting than the alternative, but Celine kept moving forward to whatever fate awaited her.

"My father's out for her head," Jessa said. "Aunt Kasindra's played her last game."

But Celine knew better than most that Kasindra would never yield, especially to the likes of Dathan. The brother was no match against his sister. Unless his first commander had something incredible tucked away in secret, Kasindra would come out on top. Just like always.

CHAPTER 36

The sea was always quiet when Celine reached Kasindra's cave. The Sea Witch's Lair.

The four slipped inside, navigating carefully so as not to touch a single thing, even the sandy floor or the narrowest stalagmite. Her enchanted touch could be on anything.

Returning to this space, Celine saw every square inch of it with fresh eyes. The dark reaches were still unseen, carrying secrets she'd never discovered. The ethereal light from Kasindra's cauldron was a beacon of dark deeds.

Celine had learned among these artifacts and trinkets, these potions and reagents, all of them used to control her and others. Power in the hands of one intent upon darkness.

Celine hadn't deluded herself to believe that Kasindra was a force for good. But that she'd done such a heinous betrayal after Celine had given her trust...

Celine grieved her older self, the one who'd agreed to Kasindra's tutelage without thought or consideration of consequence. If only...

But that would yield nothing, especially when time was running out.

They stopped at the end of the cave, the cauldron's dim green light casting everyone in a sinister hue. The garden waved and fluttered green, purple, and blue flora that held its curiously dark beauty out for everyone to behold. Aesthetically, it was marvelous. Magically, it was magnetic, fascinating to anyone close enough who could sense its power.

And among it all was Sudor's prized resource, a significant pile of it —enough crystals to fuel Celine's magic for *years*. Small and large pieces of their arcana crystal shone in pure beauty among the dark magic that filled this cave. Celine picked up one shard, nearly the size and length of two fingers together. It was cool against her palm.

"You feel that?" Jessa asked, reaching a hand toward a tall blade of what looked like oversized grass with a gradient pattern that shifted from purple to green and back again. Her hand hovered over the blade, keeping a few inches of space between them. "It's like a vessel of magic, holding steady and waiting to be tapped by its user."

"It's no wonder she could control a thrall all the way in the castle from here." Quinn stared, her wonder laced with fear. "There's so much about this that we don't know."

"Knowing Kasindra, the garden is probably armed with some kind of trap." Celine looked around, eyes scanning the baubles and trinkets, hoping to find the clear orb she always touched. "What triggers the trap, I don't know. But I can only assume being eaten by her plants is the punishment."

"*Eaten by plants.*" Quinn shuddered. "Not how I imagined going."

"I'll keep checking on her whereabouts," Zander said, settling out of the way of the cauldron. "I know you know to hurry, but—"

"We'll hurry," Jessa reassured. "We have no interest in taking our time."

Ah, there it is. Celine reached for the orb, the size and shape fitting perfectly in her palm. Just with Kasindra, the purple and green smoke within swirled to life at her touch.

But Celine didn't expect the whispers.

Tell us, the voices said. *Tell us what you want. What you need. Tell us what we can do for you.*

"Tell me how to destroy the garden."

We cannot.

We cannot.
We cannot.
We cannot destroy ourselves.

"Celine?"

Celine twitched her head at Quinn's voice, wordlessly asking for silence. The voices whispered still. She held tighter to the arcana crystal, as though it had become a tether to reality.

We cannot destroy ourselves.

"Who is in the garden?"

Everyone.
So many of us.
Bound together by root and power.

"I need to break through," Celine said. "Kasindra has used you to hurt so many others."

She hurt us.
So we hurt others.
The cycle goes ever on.

"Is she talking to the garden?" Jessa asked. Celine could picture the quirked brow as she stared at her step-sister.

"The cycle should be broken," Celine said. "It's time for a new chapter. It's time for your freedom."

Freedom.
No such thing.
These bonds will—

Something stopped the voices, a force within them purposefully disrupting them.

"These bonds need to be broken," Celine pushed, sensing a weakening. "You deserve to be free."

Free.
Such a lie
A beautiful lie.

"It's not a lie," Celine said. "Please, tell me how."

Break us.
Let us shatter.
Then you will see.

Celine didn't hesitate, slamming the orb hard against the uneven stone wall beside her. The clear glass turned to dust, fine particles embedding into her palm. She hissed at the sharp pain, feathering strands of blood weaving around her and mingling with the freed purple and green smoke that swirled freely before soaring toward her face, right into her eyes.

"Celine!"

But all Celine could see was a massive landscape, her feet treading over soft, mossy earth around large trunks of very massive trees. The forest that surrounded her left very little room for light. She reached to touch something, anything, whatever she could reach to keep her anchored and aware of movement. But the tree's bark was far too smooth, the texture far too forgiving beneath her fingers.

This...this was no forest.

This was Kasindra's garden.

She looked up, standing beneath the boughs of the massive purple-green blades.

You can see now.

You can see us.

You can free us.

"Tell me how," Celine said. She held the arcana crystal to her chest, afraid that she would drop it and unwittingly feed the garden with its power. "I still don't understand."

"Celine, we have to go." Quinn's hands touched her arms. "Celine, your eyes—"

At Quinn's touch, the vision broke. She was in the cave still, at her normal size, her palm bloody.

But purple and green smoke filled the cave, billowing slowly out of the cauldron and onto the sea floor.

"By the gods!" Jessa cried out. "It's everywhere!"

"She's coming," Zander said, returning to himself. He swam out of reach of one arm of smoke. "We don't have long."

Celine blinked through blurring vision, the cave walls shifting and melting as mud. Her heart raced, the sense of collapse imminent. The walls were closed in. They would be buried alive.

"Celine—"

"This toxin has to come from the Deeps," Jessa said, blinking. "Kasindra, you smart, clever merfolk."

"Oh—" Quinn's voice softened, her hold on Celine loosening. "The lights..."

Celine saw no light, only the melting mud walls. They wouldn't make it out in time.

"Keep going," Zander said, his voice still resolute. "We're almost through."

"The garden reacted to you using the cauldron," Jessa said. How could she focus so well, with the world crashing down around them? How could Celine still hear her through the pounding of her heart? "I can sense something in it. A sentience. But it's hard to read."

"A sentient garden," Quinn repeated, a dreaminess to her voice. "And all these beautiful lights..."

"Almost there."

Zander's voice helped Celine to focus, and the immediate relief of their escape opened her mind and cleared her senses. The world was no longer melting around her, but her body still quivered with the panic still running cold through her blood.

"We need to figure out how to destroy it," Celine said. "The voices..."

You can see now.

You can see us.

You can free us.

"Who were you talking to?" Quinn asked.

"I'm not sure. They said I could see them, free them." Celine rubbed her closed eyes with one hand, the sensation cooling and soothing. The other hand still held the arcana crystal, whole and beautiful and full of potential.

"Kasindra's victims," Jessa said, her voice low. "The souls of everyone she's harvested."

Zander shuddered. "Harvested is a *very* graphic word to use."

A voice came to them, almost satisfied. "But it's accurate."

Then she chuckled, her voice reverberating in their minds.

"Hello, my dear."

CHAPTER 37

Kasindra's lavender hair and eyes were magnificent against the dark blue of the sea, tangled strands undulating in the water as her eyes glowed with magical light.

Beautiful and terrible and powerful. And those eyes stared at Celine with challenge and expectation.

"I regret things ending this way," Kasindra said. "You had such promise, Celine. Such promise."

"They were lies, Kasindra," she snapped. "Every promise was a lie."

"Even so." The Sea Witch smiled, eyeing the others. "And you, Jessa, darling."

"I'm not your darling," Jessa snapped. "You're the reason behind everything. Celine's magic and the darkness she sends to Father—"

"Ah, my dear, I can't let Celine take *all* the credit." Kasindra swam around them, edging closer as she forced them to turn to keep her in their sights. "Dathan has been mine for many years now, well before he took the throne."

Confusion weighed on Jessa's brow. "What do you mean? What are you talking about?"

"Surely you've sensed it. Ever since he became the merking, he hasn't been the man you've known."

"Of course, but—"

Jessa stopped, staring at her aunt, unseen pieces falling into place. "He's—"

"Mine." Kasindra chuckled, far too pleased with herself. "Who has ruled the merfolk all this time? Certainly not my idiot brother. Though he was keen to enlist my magic to help him gain the upper-hand against Janis and Elynda." At this, she looked at Celine. "Things were in motion for a very long time, my dear."

"You killed them," Celine said, her voice almost detached from her body, from her consciousness. "You murdered my parents."

"To be fair, your parents were among the most powerful of our kind. Your father especially." Kasindra looked past them all toward her cave, pride softening the hard angles of her face. "They are magnificent."

"Are?" Rage kindled a wildfire in her core as Celine stared at her former teacher. "They're caged in your garden?"

She imagined Lady Helen as Kasindra's puppet, a husk filled with a foreign entity bent on dark things. What of her parents? Had Kasindra cored them to become shells of their former selves? Were their very essences still survived not in the Chaos Realm but in the hell of her garden?

Celine imagined what horrors she could conjure for the Sea Witch to endure, only to remember that Kasindra had made her. Now, it seemed, she would unmake her. What power did Celine possess to stop her?

"You're a monster," Quinn whispered, staring aghast at Kasindra. "I always knew you were obsessed with dark magic, but never—"

Quinn stopped, something invisible stifling her words. She reached for her own throat, clawing at something that wasn't there.

"Stop it!" Celine watched her best friend struggle. Zander screamed, his magic useless. "Kasindra!"

As the Sea Witch laughed, her maniacal voice filling Celine's mind, Celine bolted, her body cutting through the water with incredible speed, set to barrel into the lavender mermaid. And she nearly did, but for Kasindra's readied strike to slam Celine into the waiting fronts and leaves of the garden.

"Away with you!" Still cackling, she waved her hands through the water and pulled the remaining three merfolk toward the garden that gently pulled Celine in.

The harder she thrashed, the stronger the garden's arms pulled, as though to match the power of the one who resisted.

"I may have lied about a lot of things, but I feel I should reassure you." Kasindra swam closer, lavender eyes flattered by the blue-green light. "I never lie about strength, my dear." She wove her hands in circles, eyes locked onto her garden with passionate reverence. "And you have it. My garden will be sustained for a very long time." She smiled, the sinister edge stretching wide. "You have my gratitude. Oh—and before you go..."

Kasindra touched Celine's cheek, with Celine bound and powerless to pull away. Flashes of Estilon filled her mind, the massive castle shadowed by storm clouds, the vision guiding her to the foyer where she'd been earlier.

Jesper, alive, had Owen on his knees, a sword pointed at his throat.

"No." Celine, eyes wide, stared at the Sea Witch with chilling horror. "He's dead. I killed him, myself."

"Did you, my dear?"

Celine wanted to rake her fingernails down Kasindra's throat and claw out the arrogance in her voice. "Even his own soldier—"

"And no soldier would ever lie to protect his king." Kasindra's quiet laugh echoed quietly. "Oh, Celine. You trust so easily. You take things at face-value."

"Why should I believe you?" Celine's words held more conviction than her body, her heart and stomach competing for which could fail first.

"Because when the truth hurts," Kasindra said with a grin, "I tell it."

The sound of Celine's parents screaming...

That was the truth, then. The horrible, unfiltered truth, laid bare for Celine with purpose and intent.

"There is strength in pain, my dear, and my garden is starving."

With a flourish, Kasindra waved her hands once more, holding her hands and arms taut as the garden finished consuming them, the final shred of light covered, the magical dark engulfing them.

CHAPTER 38

Voices. So many *voices*. And the world was so dark. Celine brought her arms in, holding herself as she trembled in the miserable cold as her mind swam with visions of Jesper holding Owen at sword point.

Owen.

"Celine?"

"Quinn!" She blinked through the darkness, hoping to see shapes or shadows. "Zander? Jessa?"

"Here," Zander said, then Jessa after him.

"Do you hear that whispering?" Zander said. "What *is* that?"

"I think *who* is more correct," Jessa said. "This is Kasindra's garden. I think those voices are all of her victims."

Celine's stomach curdled. How many had Celine helped find their way to this prison...this living death?

I didn't know. She told herself again and again. *I didn't know.*

But she knew what Kasindra needed to fuel her garden.

She wasn't ignorant. She wasn't innocent.

"Celine! Jessa!" Quinn called. "I have Zander. Where are you?"

"I hardly know," Jessa said, speaking Celine's own thoughts. "Is this hell? By the gods, I expected it to at least have *light*."

Celine hummed a merfolk lullaby, glad to hear Quinn and Zander pick up the melody, then Jessa. Minutes passed—long, confusing minutes—before Celine finally found Jessa, with Quinn and Zander close behind. Sight was so limited by pitch darkness that they could only feel for one another's hands and arms, holding one another close.

"This is a nightmare," Quinn said. "How could Kasindra even dream up a thing like this?"

"How much of this is Kasindra's imagination," Celine said, "and how much of it is the magic itself?"

"Sentient magic." Zander shuddered. "I never want to think about that ever again."

"We're swimming in it," Jessa said. "Thinking is the least of our worries."

Saying it aloud helped to ground Celine in the notion that the dark magic Kasindra who heavily relied upon was, itself, a thinking entity. It learned its user, gained their trust, embedded itself into their consciousness to force them to thrive on *need* rather than *choice*.

Hadn't the same happened to Celine? Though she'd considered herself conscious of dark magic's tempting pull, she'd been resistant to giving herself over completely...so she thought. But how different was she from Kasindra? She may not have had a garden to feed to fuel her magic, but the shadows that were eager to see her were the same that itched her palms, begging her to cast. They were the same that tickled the back of her mind, begging her to torment.

Kasindra had taken everything from her, and she'd let her. Including *herself*.

"I ignored everything important, all to side with my anger." Celine closed her eyes, the gesture comforting, making her confession easier. The pitch darkness was still too open. She shut her eyes to shut herself in, even as her words revealed it, anyway. "I'm just like her."

"No, Celine." The dark absorbed Quinn's voice. "You're nothing like her."

"I'm *something* like her." She breathed in, acknowledgement settling in her still churning core. But, even with the unrest and anxiety, she was taking responsibility. That helped.

"*Celine. Celine.*" Whispers, voices reaching her through the pitch, cacophonous voices melding together in disharmony. *"Celine, my love. Celine."*

She fought the urge to press her hands over her ears, to block out the sound of their incessant hissing. Was this how the garden fed? Did it drive its victims to madness and force them to use magic and try to escape or fight?

Owen. Her fists tightened around the crystal, the edges hurting the soft flesh of her palm. Her heart was heavy beneath a promise she was forced to break. *I'm sorry.*

"Call for us," the voice said.

"Call for us, Celine."

"The garden will show you. Call for us."

"Call for you?" Celine asked aloud, so that the others could hear. "How?"

"Ask for us by name."

"By name."

"Ask for us by name."

"Ask for who?" Celine tightened her hold on the hands that held hers. She wasn't sure if it was Quinn, Jessa, or Zander, or some combination therein. "What name do I say?"

"You know what to say, love."

"Call for us."

"Celine," Zander said. "Do you think..."

He let the question hang, the quiet as palpable as the darkness.

"Do you think they're your parents?" he asked at last.

Against her will, her face contorted with the tears that welled in her eyes, with the emotion that swelled in her chest and tightened her throat.

"Mother?" Her lips trembled. "Father?" She took a breath. "Are you here?"

"Yes."

"Yes."

"Tell the garden to show you."

"Show me!" She screamed it, pushing her voice and her will into the tangible dark. "Give us light and show me, gods damn it!"

They each had to blink as the world brightened, the shades of purple and green now visible in the stalks and leaves that surrounded them.

There, appearing between the stalks in front of her, their silhouettes slipping into the light. They were unchanged but for the ethereal quality that made them almost ghostlike.

Her parents. Janis and Elynda, once king and queen of the merfolk.

She was in their arms with her next breath, surrounded by their strength and their warmth. Their *warmth*, when everything else around her was so cold.

"Oh, my love." Elynda kissed her hair. "I'm so sorry, Celine."

Janis had embraced them both and tightened his arms around them. "My darling girl."

"All this time, you were here." She was grateful for merspeak. The words would have been too big to speak, with the tension in her throat. "I'm sorry I didn't know."

"How could you know?" Elynda leaned back, cupping Celine's face with her hands. "How could you have known?"

"The Sea Witch is skilled at lacing her lies with the truth," Janis said, pressing his lips to her temple. "We saw how cleverly she dressed falsehood with truth."

Celine looked at her parents, realization dawning. "You saw?"

"Everything." Elynda stroked Celine's hair. "We already know, love."

"Everything." The darkness she learned to harness. The attention and trust she'd given to her parents' killer.

Celine—daughter, *betrayer*.

"We love you," Elynda said, then Janis echoed.

"I'm sorry." Emotion tightened its hold, strangling her, suffocating her. "Gods, I'm so sorry."

"We love you."

"We love you."

The world silenced, the voices of the garden stilled.

Then the stalks groaned, the ground shifted, the air changed.

They each looked around, eyes wide.

"Celine—" Zander struggled to give voice to the words they were already thinking. "The garden. Is it—"

"Shrinking?" Jessa touched the nearest stalk. It partially disintegrated where her fingertips made contact.

"I thought pulling us in would strengthen it," Quinn said. "But this looks...*frail*."

"Is it molting?" Jessa asked. "Shedding skin for new growth?"

"No, this..." Janis eyed the withering stalks. "This is new."

"How?" Elynda asked. "How is this possible?"

"How does the garden consume its victims?" Jessa asked.

"Consume?" Janis shook his head. "It doesn't consume, not like that. Not like a predator."

"Like a parasite?" Celine wondered how much of them it had already taken.

"It absorbs," Elynda clarified. "At least, that's what we've found."

"*Absorbs.*" Zander touched another stalk, the flesh of the vegetation breaking as his fingers trailed down. "Magic? Life essence?"

"Yes," Janis said. "Life and magic are the same. They are power. And power can move mountains."

"And create a garden of chaos and hell," Quinn said. Zander laughed.

"So, it's absorbing...what?" Celine considered the darkness receding, the tangible manifestation of Kasindra's shadowy power withering to nothing. "We haven't used magic."

"No," Jessa said. "But you found your parents."

Quinn's quiet gasp matched the tremor in Celine's heart, connecting her father's philosophy on magic with Jessa's observation.

"Love?" The world around Celine nearly shuddered at the world. The air was almost reactive with the lightning energy of it.

"How do you defeat darkness?" Zander asked, but it was more of a statement than a question.

With light.

With so much light that Kasindra would go blind.

Even a single candle was bright in the dark, but Celine wanted to set the world on fire. No corner would have any shade, least of all Kasindra's depraved garden.

Zander reached a hand to a disintegrating stalk, magic tingling from his fingers as he hummed. They watched as the stalk healed, the purple and dull green replaced with verdant life, rich and vibrant.

"Healing magic," Janis said. "Light, shaped into love."

"Sentimental, if you ask me." Jessa smiled. Her snow-white eyes met Celine's. "But you can't argue with the results."

Celine had little skill with healing or conjuring light. Her hands were adept at calling forth shadows, enjoying their swirling dance before they went about their dark business. How could she bring out light when the dark felt like him?

Her father took one of her hands in both of his, his smile warm and eyes kind.

"My darling girl." He kissed her fingers, even as shame soured on her stomach. "There is light in you."

"How?" She tightened her hold on him. "So much darkness..."

Her mother hugged her from behind, her hands on her shoulders, her head leaned against hers. "No amount of darkness could overshadow your heart."

But it had. Celine knew it, felt it. She relished in bringing out the dark and sending it to those who'd wronged her.

But her parents saw her goodness. Owen saw her goodness.

Owen.

Her heart soared with urgency. They had a way to remake the garden, to destroy its darkness and strip Kasindra of an incredible source of power.

I hope I'm not too late.

Warmth spread through her like liquid sunlight, her heart pounding as each stalk transformed.

Thunder roared overhead. Kasindra. Her precious garden, changing from the inside out, out of her control. Celine was almost giddy with excitement at the thought of causing Kasindra even a modicum of distress.

Voices whispered, voices called, and the captured spirits within emerged with the full force of their power.

Escape. Freedom. The chance to finally pass on.

Ice formed in Celine's core. Passing on. Her parents. As soon as she found them, they would leave her again.

But they deserve to move on. They deserve so much more than this.

What of Celine and the others? Would she leave the garden and kneel at Anya's holy feet? Would she still have her life as she'd known it?

So much was still unknown, but Celine took courage from the truth that anywhere was better than this, that she could help her parents and the other victims find their peace at last.

We cannot change who we are, nor should we.

But we can change what they've turned us into...

What we've turned ourselves *into.*

The crystal warmed in Celine's tight grip. The crystal, whose potential was ripe for what they were destroying, for what they were building.

Love in place of *hate.*

Light in place of *darkness.*

And Celine, even without the crystal, was strong enough.

The garden's hold was weak. Nothing stopped them as they broke past unseen barriers, the contest of wills overwhelmingly in their favor by the sheer number of magical souls pushing against Kasindra's dark magic.

The solution was so simple, even sentimental, as Jessa had said. Why should magic be complicated? But Celine was lucky. She could give love, only because of the love she'd received. Not every soul could say the same.

Make the love you deserve to have, she thought, wondering if that philosophy could reach souls long imprisoned. *Love the fight you've endured all these years, surviving everything to make it this far. Love the pieces of you that remain despite everything.*

The notion struck, the words reaching a deep place in Celine's heart that hadn't known touch in a very long time. Not by her friends, not by Owen. A place that only she could reach. A place that she had to heal for herself.

The garden shuddered, the air easier to breathe.

More thunder overhead, and the sound of things crashing.

"It's time to go," Celine said. "Get ready for a fight."

The others moved quickly, the space in the garden shifting with their action, the garden itself helping them in their escape as Celine tapped into the crystal's power. The sensation of something breaking preceded a relieving exhale, as though the garden was at peace at last, and Celine found herself on the cave floor with Quinn, Zander, Jessa, and her parents.

And her parents.

But any surge of jubilation froze at the sight of Santus gripping Kasindra by the throat, murder in his vibrant green eyes.

CHAPTER 39

"What have you done, Sea Witch?!"

Kasindra didn't seem worried by the first commander, even as his grip held fast to her throat. Though it was difficult to offer her signature smirk, she quirked an eyebrow. "Took you long enough, Santus, dear. Years, in fact."

He threw her across her cave, sending her crashing into a shelf of glass jars and bottles. "I should have killed you when I had the chance."

"I never expected Santus to seek retribution for Dathan," Zander said, unable to mask how impressed he was.

"I did," Jessa said.

"And what chance was that, my dear?" Lavender eyes alight, Kasindra retaliated with shadows already forming behind him, the gray tentacles reaching for his arms and wrists. With teeth bared in a snarl, he jerked free of them and slashed his arm toward her, unleashing some kind of magical attack.

"While they're busy..." Zander continued to dismantle the garden, Janis and Elynda working quickly beside him.

"The others," Celine said. "We can help get them out."

Jessa and Quinn understood immediately, reaching with whatever magic they could muster to guide the remaining souls out of the garden.

Celine tapped into the crystal still clutched in her palm, but the brilliant iridescence had diminished to an ordinary opalescent blue-green. She cast the crystal aside and pulled from her own reserve of magic.

"Come on," Celine urged the souls through merspeak. "Come on, come on."

But she didn't feel her voice reach any living consciousness. Still, the spirits seemed alive enough to understand the cage they were in and the prospect of freedom right before them. Souls surged toward escape, the garden slowly diminished, and Kasindra was fairly matched with Dathan's own first commander.

Santus has been toying with magic again. Was this why Kasindra was worried enough to mention it before? Did she know he would seek her out one day to exact his own retribution?

She must have known. No action was devoid of consequence.

One soul whizzed past Celine toward Kasindra, its hungry anger near to gaining its fill. The blow landed hard against Kasindra's chest, forcing the Sea Witch to take a breath. Then her lavender eyes alighted on Celine and the others, on her precious and once beautiful garden, now reduced to a fraction of its former self.

Her scream reverberated off the walls of their skulls, making them wince and close their eyes against the sharp stabs of sound.

But more souls surged forward, dealing blows that Kasindra couldn't dodge. Santus's cackling laugh gave sound to triumph, wielding more magic while Kasindra was compromised.

If only Celine could attack Santus, distracted that he was...

Kasindra screamed, a shockwave of magic pouring out of her as she raged. The attacking souls shuddered, and a few of them scattered. But most of them stayed. Santus, close to the blast radius, sailed through the water and slammed against a stalagmite, breaking it in half.

Breathing heavily, eyes wild, Kasindra stared at the remains of her garden, verdant and healthy and powerless.

"You will regret every second you're alive." Her ominous threat rumbled in their minds, within their chests. "You will beg for death for what you've done."

Zander scoffed. "All this for some plants?"

"Such talk from a wisp of a witch." Santus laughed, arrogance and cruelty framing his demeanor as he rose from the stone rubble and edged closer, hands and arms poised to cast. "What will she do, pray tell, without her precious garden?"

Kasindra lifted an arcana crystal, its blue-green iridescence brilliant in her hand, and she unleashed a magnificent billowing wave of shadows toward Dathan's first commander. But Santus had shielded himself, an invisible wall forcing the shadows to cascade around him.

If Celine didn't loathe them both, she'd have been impressed. But, with the last soul released from the garden and its shadow-touched flora returned to its beautiful, natural green, there was little left to do.

"We should go," Celine said. "Let them kill each other."

"We can't leave her alive," Jessa said, darkness shadowing her white eyes to a silvery gray. "Not after everything she's done."

"It won't bring you peace," Celine said.

And she hadn't wanted peace. She'd wanted chaos. But in this moment, understanding the breadth and weight of *action* and *consequence*, it was a peace that her heart had ached for, the kind that comes with love.

She hadn't allowed her heart and mind to move on, hadn't allowed the love and companionship from Quinn and Zander to be enough.

A mistake she wouldn't make again.

Celine held tighter to Jessa's hand. "You still have me."

Conflict warred on Jessa's face as she tried to remain stoic.

"She won't stop." Jessa watched Kasindra and Santus fight, her fists trembling to enter the fray. "What we tore down, she will remake."

Her father's hand was gentle on her shoulder.

"Owen is in danger," Celine said. "I fear I'm already too late."

"Go," Jessa said, resolution steeling her gaze and her posture. "You have a family to protect."

"I do." Celine reached for Jessa's hand, curving her fingers around the tight fist.

Jessa brought her other hand to cover Celine's. She held her eyes for several seconds, giving her a half-smile before letting her go. When she moved her hand, a fresh piece of arcana crystal laid there beneath her knuckles. "Go to your king, Queen Celine of the Merfolk." She placed the crystal in Celine's hand and curled her fingers around it. "See you on the other side."

Quinn pulled on Celine's other hand, Zander already leading with Elynda as they swam out of Kasindra's cave.

Shanna, if you can hear me, if you're listening, please keep Jessa safe. Keep her alive.

They moved quickly, their first instincts taking them to their reef.

"There isn't much time," Celine said, her heart dividing itself between land and sea. She looked at her parents, alive and breathing and smiling.

She'd helped to free them from Chaos, after all.

"You said his name is Owen?" Her mother's smile was serene, even content.

"My husband. Dathan—" But Celine corrected herself. "Kasindra arranged our marriage to unite the merfolk with Estilon. I know now her intentions were something else. But he's—he's wonderful."

"And you love him." Janis held her hand, his thumb stroking her knuckles. "You said he's in danger?"

"An enemy king that Kasindra allied with. He's—" Celine recalled the vision of Owen on his knees, how close the sword blade was to his throat, Jesper gloating with his haughty gaze. "If what Kasindra showed me is real. Gods, I can't even be sure."

"But you can't rest until you know," Elynda said. She rested a hand on her husband's shoulder. "I would do the same, Celine."

"He won't let Owen live. Not for long."

"Go," her mother said, kissing her forehead. "Help him."

"We'll take care of them here," Quinn said, already helping Zander prepare various healing blends to administer. "Your mother's right. You won't be able to rest until you see things for yourself."

"Return when you can," her father said. "When everything is safe and your husband is by your side." His smile was the same as it had always been, and seeing it again made her heart ache. "I can't wait to meet him."

"We'll be here when you get back," her mother said.

At this, the tears freely fell. They wouldn't disappear. They were with Quinn and Zander, and they were all right. Even if Kasindra tried to retaliate, she was only a fraction of her former self. And Jessa wouldn't let the Sea Witch get very far.

To be rich in such friendships. Love overflowed from within her, courage coming with it.

"Don't forget the clothes," Zander said. "Humans don't gallivant around without clothes."

"At least not in polite company." Quinn cackled at her own quip, and, to Celine's surprise, her parents chuckled.

She gathered what she needed—a similar outfit to the one she'd debuted in and remembered to include a belt. With their blessings and the fresh arcana crystal from Jessa, Celine hurried to the surface, going to the edge of the beach not clearly seen by passers-by. The sun had waned to late afternoon, sunset close at hand. Hours in the water, and so much had changed.

Bracing herself against the sandy incline, and prepared for incredible pain, Celine moved her magic through the arcana crystal and changed her body, scale by scale. She bit into the soaking wet tunic to muffle her cries and screams as bone and muscle stretched and shifted. By some grace, likely from the arcana crystal, both pain and process were easier, and, when it was over, Celine rested, breathless, on the edge of the shore before dressing herself and crawling up the sand. She walked more practiced ease, even with the throbbing aches in her back and hips. Small favors, indeed, as there wasn't time to rest and wait for her body to recover.

I'm coming, Owen. Hold on. Please be alive.

She knew the path to the rear sewer gate and slipped inside easily, though she shuddered at the iron gate and key. Her magic worked as before, her technique and gestures careful to remain soundless. How many Sudorian guards were outside? If Jesper had truly lived and was still a nightmare within the castle, how many more of those men also remained?

Celine held her breath as she stepped across the castle lawn toward the hidden doorway Graham had shown her, exhaling slowly as she struggled to find the correct stone to press, fingers frantically searching and pressing until, finally, the correct switch gave beneath her urgent touch. She slipped inside, securing the door behind her, and passed within the castle walls unheeded.

Where would Jesper and the others be? The throne room? The dungeon? Did they leave Owen's body in the foyer?

No. She forced the thought from her mind as ice-cold fear stole the heat from her blood. *Owen isn't dead. He isn't dead.*

She forced herself to blink, to cool her dry, hot eyes, to focus on seeing and listening with the magical strength her seaborn blood afforded her. But the world was far too silent to leave much room for hope.

When she reached Adella's room, she peered through the slight opening before proceeding into the empty space. She did the same when leaving for the suite. These spaces were alarmingly empty. Had Kasindra lied again?

When the truth hurts, I tell it.

Oh, how she'd smiled at that.

There is strength in pain, my dear, and my garden is starving.

No, she hadn't lied. She'd shown Celine what she'd planned, down to the moment where she'd wanted Celine to lose hope. But hope wasn't lost. Not when she could bring the world to its knees if anything had happened to Owen. Hope could thrive, even in chaos, even in shadow, because hope was a way forward. Even in darkness, hope could thrive.

Laughter, low and rough. She edged toward the archway leading to the grand staircase, eyes and ears open.

"His majesty, the king." More laughter. "Iron suits you, your majesty."

Celine's core tightened, wishing she had Kedran's elixir.

"Your apothecary doesn't look so good. It isn't contagious, is it?"

Her heart quickened. They were in the dungeon, Owen and Kedran, and likely Tyrion and Graham, if they yet lived.

Her steps were silent, the pads of her feet touching before her heels. She checked the hallway of rooms first, avoiding the mistake of hours previous. But it was devoid of any soldiers, just like the royal suite.

Jesper didn't see any threat. He and his soldiers had accomplished what they'd wanted and rested on their victory.

Such hubris would cost them.

Her hand clutched the banister as she descended, her body all too aware of the iron pit she would reach. She could almost smell the toxic metal as she reached the foot of the stairs, its reach stronger than she remembered. But fear could make shadows taller, corners darker. She wouldn't let fear win.

With a deep breath in, down she went. Bodies shuffled, boots scuffed against the floor, something small clattered against wood. She readied shadow magic, the tendrils swirling around her palm and fingers, and peered through the archway to see two men sitting at a wooden table, rolling dice.

The man with his back to her slumped forward. "Best three out of five?"

"Come on, you lost, fair and square." His partner grinned, leaning back in his seat with the haughtiness of winning.

"Let me try again. I want to hit him this time."

"Then get better at rolling dice."

Wooden chair legs scraped against stone as the winner stood, his smug eagerness highlighting the ridges and peaks of his athletic face. Even through his garb, Celine could tell his build was muscular. Hands gripped the iron bars as he pressed his head between them. Celine seized the chance to send her shadows in, guiding them to the two guards. The smoke was subtle, unnoticeable to the untrained eye, and it slithered around their boots, crawling up their feet and ankles.

"Hear that, your majesty? I have the pleasure yet again."

Owen chuckled, and Celine's heart ached. "You sure those dice aren't loaded?"

"Oy!" the other man exclaimed, turning in his seat. "He has a point!"

The shadows rose higher, sinking into the fabric of their trousers to touch skin. Their change in demeanor was almost immediate, their bodies stiffening in sudden alarm and anxiety. They looked to one another, eyes wide, pupils pinpricks.

The sitting guard cried out, hands trembling even as his arms rose to protect his face. He fell from his seat onto the floor, curling in on himself. The standing guard threw punches at the air, though his shoulders had curved forward and his head ducked close to his chest.

"What in the seven hells..."

Celine crept down the stairs, eyes trained on the hallucinating guards. She recoiled toward the stone wall behind her, the iron far too close, but she pasted a stoic look of control on her face as she came in view of the cell.

Kedran was on the ground, his head supported by a bundle of fabric filled with straw. Sweat poured profusely from him as he gently shivered, gripped by iron sickness.

Tyrion and Graham sat on either side of Owen and Kedran protectively, their bodies leaning forward as they stared at her.

All of them were battered and bruised, with dried blood on their faces, clothes, and hands.

Owen nearly called her name, relief and elation brightening his abused face. But he stopped himself only as he looked at the panicking guards. "Your handiwork, my love?"

Your handiwork, my love?

My love?

My love?

She could sail heavenward on the strength of her heartbeat, alone. Such was the surge of power within her. *My love.*

"Keys?" she asked, pointing from one guard to the other.

"Hook." Owen reached through the bars and pointed. "It's iron, Celine."

"You humans are your obsession with *iron*." She played at nonchalance, unrolling her sleeves to use the fabric as a makeshift glove. But her fingers tingled and burned still. She handled ring and key as quickly as she could, hurrying to pass them to Owen and free her hands from the toxin.

He moved deftly, working the lock from behind. "What about them?" His eyes darted to the guards. "How long will that last?"

"Long enough for me to run them through?" Tyrion sneered at them.

"I should say so," Celine said. "They'll be hallucinating for a while, depending on how strong their minds are."

"Not very strong, I'd wager." Graham moved to Kedran, taking his arm and laying it across his shoulders. "Can you move, Kedran? Can you stand?"

He groaned, moving with Graham's help. Owen went to Kedran's other side and helped Graham get him to his feet.

Celine kept her distance from the iron cells as Owen and Graham helped Kedran walk. Tyrion dispatched the two guards quickly and without ceremony, the dark bruises on his face deepening his scowl of hatred.

Without another word, the group gathered their confiscated belongings and made for the stairs to freedom, away from the iron and the blooming smell of copper and death.

"Jesper is in the Great Hall," Owen said. "Taking up residence on the throne of Estilon."

"We need to get Kedran somewhere safe," Graham said. "The iron almost killed him."

"I'm feeling," Kedran said, wheezing. "Much better already."

"Any hidden passages on the ground floor?" Celine asked.

"No," Graham said. "The nearest place out of the way is there." Graham pointed to the corner by the grand staircase. "Access to the tower."

"It's better than staying out in the open," Owen said.

Together, they slipped through the narrow door, careful of Kedran as the three men side-stepped in, and closed the door as they set Kedran to sit on the wooden stairs. The space was cramped, but they were safe from prying eyes.

"I'll climb up and see if anyone's there," Tyrion said.

Owen squeezed his friend's shoulder in response, watching as Celine took Kedran's face in her hands.

"I have little skill in healing," she said, "but I can ease some of this discomfort."

"The medicine helped some," he said with a weak smile. "Still, being so close to it—"

She pressed her palm to his forehead, closing her eyes as she tried to do as Zander had instructed, but she faltered against the oppressive presence of iron sickness within him. Even with the prepared mixture to ward against its effects, Kedran was very sick.

Shanna, Celine prayed. *Give me the strength to help him. Guide me, please. What do I need?*

"Help Owen and Tyrion," Kedran whispered. "They were beaten so badly."

"I'll survive, Smithson," Owen said, standing beside Graham to give Celine more room with the apothecary. He reached down and picked up Kedran's hand. "How can I help, Celine?"

She pulled the arcana crystal from her pocket, the lingering magic still shimmering faintly beneath the surface. "I think we can do it with this."

He nodded, relieved. "My beautiful, clever wife."

"All clear," Tyrion said, coming down the steps but stopping short with Kedran in front of him. "What's going on?"

"Could we heal everyone with this?" Owen asked.

"I used it to transform, so it doesn't have its full strength." She looked at Kedran, remembering how iron sickness felt, how it continued to slither beneath her skin even after she was freed from the dungeon. "I think we'll need all of it for him."

Owen didn't question it, taking her hand with the crystal between their palms. "Deep breath, Smithson. This should help."

With each of them holding one of Kedran's hands, Celine began the delicate process of healing the areas inside of him that were under attack. Owen's magic soared through with hers, each working in tandem to pass through the apothecary and push out as much of the toxin as they could. The power of the arcana crystal magnified their casting tenfold, the rush of it bordering on euphoric. Celine understood Kasindra's hunger for the crystal. The sensation within her was incredible, and her magic was strong.

Minutes passed before Celine exhaled at the release of sickness, the hold on Kedran loosening before the hand of iron disappeared completely. But, rather than breathing through the relief of healing, Kedran rose and immediately laid hands on Owen's face, his torso, his hands, healing where his fingers touched.

"Those men were cruel," Kedran said, finishing with Owen before moving to Tyrion. The knight almost hesitated before nodding his consent. "May my strength help you defeat the depraved king of Sudor, once and for all."

"I think Kasindra had some kind of magical connection with Jesper," Celine said. "He should have died, but for something she held over him."

"Necromancy?" Kedran asked. "He seemed very alive and well to me before we were thrown into that iron hellhole."

"I don't think he's a thrall. But Helen didn't look strange before, either."

"He's already a dead man walking," Tyrion said with a low growl as Kedran finished his healing. "How do you still have the strength for this, Mr. Smithson?"

"I'm afraid I don't, young knight," he said, "but what I had left has to go to those who will protect this city to the very last."

He turned to Graham, the captain's injuries less severe than the others, and healed his bruises and abrasions. Sweat gathered at Kedran's brow, and when he stopped, his breathing was deep and labored.

"You should stay here," Celine said. "Or anywhere other than the castle. Can you get back to the village?"

"I wish to see the demise of those who took Adella from this life." Kedran's jaw set. He pulled a vial from his pack and downed it. "We were all robbed of something beautiful, and I still seek recompense."

No one objected, and, with weapons ready, they walked the short distance to the Great Hall.

CHAPTER 40

The hinges squeaked to give sound to their arrival, the booming voice on the other side belonging to Jesper, barking orders at one of his men. Blood stained his clothes—blood Celine had shed—but it hadn't been enough, by the lively look of him.

"Ah, we have guests!" He laughed, and his men readied sword and shield. "How on earth did you escape?" His eyes traced Celine, a hint of confusion narrowing his eyes. "How did you manage that? Has Kasindra double-crossed me?"

"Your first mistake was underestimating me," Celine said. "Your second was hurting people I care about."

Tyrion hummed, pleased. "I'm touched."

"It's lucky you're here, actually." Jesper grinned, walking around the throne and bending to pick up something secreted behind. He lifted a very large, shimmering arcana crystal, the blue-green iridescence lighting up his face as he held it close. "I was going to use this on his majesty, but *two* for the price of *one*?" He chuckled lowly, almost to himself. "It's too good to be true."

"Use it?" Celine looked from the crystal to the smug-looking king. "How?"

"This," he said, holding the crystal out as though to display it for an awe-inspired audience. "This will rid Sheraton—maybe even every continent in our realm—of magic folk. Every single one. *Gone.*"

"Rid?" Owen stared. "He can't be serious."

"Oh, I'm quite serious."

"What does it do?" Tyrion asked. "What *is* that?"

"Anti-magic." Jesper's glee was close to maniacal. "And we're going to start with the two magic folk in this room."

The guards with Jesper smirked with evil pleasure in their eyes, eager to watch.

Celine glanced at the others. "It will destroy us."

She looked specifically at Graham and Tyrion, both nodding once.

"How did you discover this power?" Owen asked, narrowing his gaze on the Sudorian king.

"I watched it happen," he said. "The magic folk withered to a husk right in front of me."

"What magic folk?" Graham asked, understanding without exactly knowing. "Elf? Godborn?"

"Merfolk." Jesper grins at Celine. "As demonstrated by one of their own."

Kasindra. Lying to the human king about the treasure he'd unearthed, fooling the hate-filled human to misuse his own resource. If there was any good to come from her selfish deceit, at least it was this.

Celine met Owen's eyes, each of them sharing a significant secret that brought a smile to their faces.

"Let's finish this," she said.

"As you wish, my love."

"It will be finished." Jesper moved closer, as though he held the key that would end their lives. "At least you have each other. At least you will go together."

Tyrion made a half-step forward before Owen stopped him. Jesper's guards moved as though to strike, stopping at Jesper's command.

"My king—"

"Trust me," Owen said.

"With my life."

"A wise move," Jesper said. "We don't want this to get ugly."

"Too late for that," Celine said, looking up at the king of Sudor. "You're here, aren't you?"

Graham couldn't hold back the sputter to keep himself from laughing. Even one of Jesper's guards had to press his lips together.

"You first, then."

"*No.*" Owen, with feigned urgency, moved in front of her. "Don't you touch her."

"Owen, don't—"

"Celine—"

"*Enough.*" Jesper gripped the crystal with both hands and commanded, "Both of you, lay your hands on the crystal. Do it *now*."

They looked up at Jesper. "Your highness..."

"Do it *now!*"

Owen kissed her, and she could feel him smiling against her lips. They raised their hands to the crystal, making a show of their slowness before slamming their palms and fingers down with a flash, conjuring their shadows with ease. Gray-black smoke filled the room, surrounding the soldiers and king of Sudor before any of them could react. They screamed as the tendrils of smoke slithered up their bodies, coiling around legs and torso, up chest and neck, before the darkness smothered each soldier and their monarch.

The men screamed and flailed, and Celine pushed harder, the crystal making it easy.

"This feels incredible," Owen said, breathless. "It's like this was always meant for me, for my power to move through."

"How?" Jesper cried, hands uselessly wiping at his face to wipe away the smoke. "How is this possible?"

Celine and Owen didn't relent, with Celine humming voice magic to augment the destructive power of the smoke. Tyrion and Graham braced their weapons and struck quickly, taking down each enemy swiftly while the magic held them.

They let Jesper live, and when Celine and Owen released their magic, he collapsed to his knees, shivering and shuddering, wide-eyed with fear.

"To the dungeon with him," Owen said. "I want to take my time figuring out his sentence."

"He may have it," Celine said, regarding his trembling form with pity. "Reduced to madness...that's no small thing."

Owen embraced her then, burying his face in her hair. "I was worried I would never see you again."

"That fear nearly came true," she said. "Kasindra's garden was a devastating place."

"Was?" He pulled back, tucking her hair behind her ears. It was far too thick and slipped out of place, but his hands and fingers didn't relent. The touch was soothing and loving. "What happened?"

"My parents were there." She smiled, fatigue settling into her muscles and bones as the urgency of the moment ebbed. "They're alive. We destroyed the garden together."

"Celine—" He blinked. "I—"

"We need to take him to the dungeon, my king," Tyrion said. "I don't wish to leave you alone, and Graham can't manage him by himself."

Owen looked as Graham tried to pull the still-trembling king of Sudor, who was mumbling unintelligibly to himself.

They followed the knights to the dungeon, where they locked the king of Sudor in a cell.

"Celine." Owen took her by the shoulders. "You came back for me."

A series of emotions passed across his face, with Celine trying to see and read each one.

"And I want to ask you to go back." His thumbs stroked the curves of her shoulders, and he didn't meet her gaze. "You came back for me when you have your parents."

She reached her hands to his sides, feeling his ribs expand and recede with each breath. "Kasindra showed me, before throwing me in her garden."

"And you knew it was true?"

She nodded. "She wouldn't keep the truth from me because it hurt me. Pain fed the garden."

He controlled his expression, his jaw flexing and his lips pulling back from his teeth before he relaxed. "Is she dead?"

"I don't know. Jessa and Santus will likely make sure that happens, but I had to get my parents out."

"And you still came back for me," he said, "after getting them back."

"I still have them," she said. "They survived the garden, and they're safe with Quinn and Zander. But I may not have had you."

He rested his forehead on hers. "I thought he rose from the dead. That was the most scared I'd ever been. How do you kill something already dead?"

"But he is only a man, after all."

Their silence carried only slight discomfort, a concern between them left unsaid.

After Jesper was secured in the dungeon, Owen and Celine gifted Kedran the rest of the arcana crystal.

"Heal yourself," Celine urged. "You've done far too much."

"There is so much power here." Kedran stared, moving the crystal over and over in his hands. "Even after healing myself, it will barely tap into what's here."

He was quick to do so, returning the crystal to Celine.

"Kedran—"

"Trust me." He held up his hands, surrendering the crystal to her. "You'll need what's left."

"You will." Owen touched her back, standing close. "He's right."

She looked from one to the other. "What are you talking about?"

Rather than answer right away, Owen took her hand and laid in the crook of his arm.

"Let's go outside," he said. "I don't know about you, but I need to get out of these walls."

She walked with him to the butterfly garden, its serenity and calm natural music to soothe their nerves. He took up one end of the stone bench, guiding her to sit beside him, and there they remained in the quiet for several lovely minutes.

"You're not saying it," she said, her voice quiet. She tightened her hold on his arm. "It must be serious."

"You want to go back." His voice was low, relaxed, though she knew the calm was the aftermath of a torrential storm that they both survived, the debris scattered inside them both. "Don't you?"

"I do." And the truth of it ached in her chest. "Would that I could be in two places at once."

"You've missed them," he said. "And, at last, they've returned." He pulled her to lean her head on his shoulder, wrapping her tightly in his arms as they both watched the butterflies. "I would want to spend every second with my mother, and I've only just lost her."

She took one of his hands, cradling his fingers as they curled into her palm. "You haven't even had time to grieve her."

Or your father, she wanted to add. Life had given him so much to carry in such quick succession that Owen only knew the briefest touch of grief. It would burrow further into his heart and stomach, affecting him more deeply than he could be ready for. She wanted to be with him through it all, as Quinn and Zander had been there for her. Grief in solitude is its own thorn in an ever-winding vine.

"I will." He exhaled, his breath cool as it swept through her hair and over her forehead. "I imagine it will hit me when I least expect it. The hole in my heart hasn't made itself known yet—too much has happened too quickly."

"In the quiet moments," she said. "In the moments that are the most mundane. You'll hear their voice or see their shadow and swear they were just next to you. You'll say something for them to hear, forgetting for a moment that they haven't been there, but the place where you lived together still feels like they're close by."

"Like they're in the next room."

His voice trembled slightly, and she held his hand tighter.

"I would love to meet them," he said. "When you're ready, of course."

"They want to meet you, too. When *you're* ready."

He kissed her hair. "When do you want to go?"

She didn't answer right away, wanting the quiet of them together to linger, with only the sound of birds and the gentle touch of wind to fill the silence.

"I don't," she confessed. "I want to be there already. I want to stay here. I want—" She gripped his shirt, leaning more into his shoulder. "I want what cannot be."

"I will do whatever you wish." He kissed her hair again. "I will agree with whatever choice you make. My love. My Celine."

"I will return to them." She looked up at him, her eyes sad to have to leave so soon after defeating Jesper, after finding peace in Estilon since arriving. "And I will return to you."

"And I will wait."

She kissed him, the shape of his mouth perfect against hers, her heart torn between two places that she could call home.

"I love you, Owen."

"And I love you." He pressed her hands to his face. "Say my name again. Please."

"Owen."

He kissed the heels of her hands.

"Owen."

He kissed her forehead.

"*Owen.*"

He kissed her lips.

CHAPTER 41

Kasindra was dead. Santus and Jessa relieved her of her remaining magic, which ended her life before either of them could.

"Pity," Santus supposedly remarked as her merfolk body withered like a dry husk, floating on the current like pieces of sea flora. "I wanted to be the one to end her."

"Let's say you did," Jessa had said, and in her retelling, she seemed as nonchalant as Celine would have imagined her to be with the first commander. "It makes no difference to me, as long as the plague is ended."

Referring to Kasindra as a plague stung in a way Celine didn't expect. Hours spent learning from her, believing her to be caring and sympathetic, to want Celine to have power and agency against those who took so much from her...

But that had been Kasindra all along. It would take Celine a very long time to rectify that, but she was glad to have time with those she loved.

Santus had fled, suffering severe weakness in his magic after defeating Kasindra. Celine didn't blame him, especially with merfolk rallying behind Jessa to become their next leader. Janis's resurrection had brought some favor his way, but he was quick to refuse any placement in merfolk hierarchy.

"I want to live," he'd said, and he'd looked kindly upon Jessa. "If you wish to lead, they would welcome you. And so would I."

It was a positive change from Dathan—from *Kasindra*—who had ruled the merfolk with fear. Jessa had already proven her battle prowess and commitment to her people each time she stood up to who they thought was her father.

"I can't imagine what that poor girl is feeling," Elynda said as she farmed for fish and oysters with Celine. Her delicate hands worked through the seabed with precision in seeking her quarry. "She was led to believe her father was here with her all this time. She's been robbed of the chance to properly grieve him until now."

Celine had gone through the years without her parents steeped in anger and the want for revenge. Was it the same for Jessa?

"She was kind to me," Celine said. "And I always felt guilty for wanting to hurt her father, for the way my shadows affected him."

"You were split in two," she said, touching Celine's arm. "The want for vengeance, at war with your goodness."

"What goodness?" Celine stared at a patch of seaweed waving in the water, gentle shifts and tremors in the current. "There has only been darkness for so long."

Her mother embraced her without word or warning, stirring a tightness in Celine's chest that reached up her throat. Her eyes welled with tears, her lips pressed tightly together, but her mother's hold didn't waver.

"You are good, Celine. And your heart was broken."

She gently cried against her mother's shoulder.

"The merfolk have a saying about the darkness trembling at the sight of goodness armed for war. That was you, my love. Armed for war."

"I let the darkness in, Mama." Celine couldn't help but feel small, as though she were a child confessing to wrongdoing that left her ashamed. "And I liked it there. I enjoyed it. I felt *powerful*."

"When they made you feel power*less*." She stroked Celine's hair, her fingers gentle combs through each strand. "That doesn't mean your goodness diminished."

Her words soothed, but Celine still felt marked, as though the touch of darkness cast her as *other* among her own people, among anyone who would know what the sign meant.

"How do we fare, my loves?" Her father swam up, kissing Celine's crown before kissing his wife. Reading their faces and sensing the mood, he asked, "Is everything alright?"

Celine's mother looked at her. These were her words to say, not her mother's.

"I trusted Kasindra," Celine said. "I was hurting, and I trusted her, and I wanted to hurt Dathan. And Santus, for obvious reasons."

Janis couldn't help but stifle a laugh. "Santus has that effect on practically everyone he meets."

"But what light is there left in me?" She looked at her parents, desperate for an answer but afraid of what it would be. In her heart, she knew that the shadows had blocked out a lot of the light she'd had before Dathan struck and the entire world changed.

But it wasn't Dathan, she reminded herself yet again. *He's become the face of my anger, but that isn't right. It's the mask Kasindra wore, the vessel for her magic.*

Celine clenched her fists, her body remembering her painful transformation to human, remembering the trauma and fear and seething hatred. None of that would find Kasindra now.

It doesn't have to find her. She's faced judgment, and Anya and Aishlin are fair. Trust them.

But trust was elusive when it had failed her before.

"Darkness itself isn't inherently evil," her father said. "It's only what we make it out to be. It exists, regardless of us and our actions. The same goes for light. We laud light's goodness because we see by it, but light also creates dark. Without light, there would be no shadow."

Without light, there would be no shadow.

We each have light and dark within us. They cannot exist separate from one another.

Soothing relief helped her heart to beat more steadily, more freely. Breathing was easier.

"I miss Owen," Celine said. "I feel ashamed for wanting to return."

"Shame and guilt, my love?" Her father pulled her into his arms and pressed her against his chest firmly. Almost too firmly. He chuckled, playful, swaying her back and forth. "Why should you feel guilt and shame for wanting your parents safe? Why should you feel guilt and shame for wanting to be with the man you love? My love, you must be kinder to yourself."

He kissed her crown three times before tugging her hair.

"Father!"

Janis beamed, his smile widening as he watched his wife shake her head, amusement flattering her lovely features.

"I've only just gotten you back," Celine said, guilt still heavy in her core.

"And we are with you always," her mother said. "Your life is beginning, my love. *Your* life."

"Be with him." Her father took her hands and kissed them. "It must not have been easy for either of you when you returned to the sea."

"He visited the shore every night to see her," her mother said. "Their reunions were heartfelt and heartbreaking."

Celine's face warmed, but boldness made her smile, excitement flowing through her.

"Your mother and I were talking about traveling around the waters of the realms," he said. "There are still corners of the world we haven't seen."

"And after being in that garden, there is so much we want to do."

She embraced her parents. "I love you."

"I love you, too," they each said. "To the farthest reaches of the sea."

Celine carried hope with her as she returned to the reef ahead of her parents. Her confession left her lighter, but there were still two loved ones who needed to hear the truth from her.

She wanted to return to Estilon.

She wanted to return to *Owen*.

And she feared that Zander and Quinn would think she was leaving them behind.

She found them working together with what they'd gathered for the meal. They looked up at her approach, seeing her satchel laden at her side.

"Looks heavy," Zander said with a smile. "Where are your parents?"

"They're on their way." She ducked out of the strap of her satchel and passed it to Quinn, whose waiting hands immediately looked through the gathered clams and seaweed. "I wanted to talk to you both before they returned."

Quinn looked up as Zander turned, both of them slightly alarmed.

"Those four dreaded words," Quinn teased. "*We need to talk.*"

"No," Celine said immediately. But, as the words sank in, they weren't exactly wrong. "It's about me." She paused. "About going back."

Zander and Quinn shared a look. He said, "We wondered how long it would take."

Celine blinked at them.

"You miss him," Quinn said. "I would, too, if Zander was on land and I was here."

Zander kissed Quinn's temple.

Quinn's shyness peeked through before her confidence took over. "You're my one, Zander." She half-shrugged. "Always have been."

"You're *my* one."

Celine moved backward slightly, feeling like an intruder in a beautiful, private moment.

"You will still have us, Celine," Zander said, moving closer to Quinn, his fingers extending to reach for hers. She took his hand without hesitating. "The beauty of magic is that you don't have to choose one or the other. Merfolk or human. You can be both. You can *have* both."

"I'm sorry for everything I've done." Her beautiful friends, who'd been there for her, who'd stayed with her, despite everything she did that fed her guilt and shame. "Please, forgive me."

"There's nothing to forgive," Quinn said. "Your heart was broken, and you were trying to mend it."

"I should have listened to you."

"Yes." Quinn grinned. "You should have."

Celine embraced her beloved friends, content that this wasn't *goodbye*, relieved that she had their blessing to return to Owen. This wasn't a chapter ending, but a strong, fresh branch on the tree of her life, one that would hold her weight as she ventured toward her future.

Kasindra's hoard of arcana crystal was protected, the precious and powerful commodity monitored by Jessa's guard. With the merfolk queen's permission, Celine took a small sliver. It held plenty of power to fuel her transformation.

"Be well, Celine," Jessa said, handing her the small shard of crystal. "You deserve happiness."

"So do you."

The step-sisters embraced, so much behind them and between them, so much ahead of them.

When Celine reached the shore, Owen stood there, waiting. He smiled at her tattered garb, the recurring wardrobe choice still effective even now.

"Just as I found you before," he said with a smile. He kissed her, lingering, holding her close. "I've missed you, Celine."

"I've missed you."

She breathed him in, the rich smell of book paper and coffee mingling with the salt air of the sea. She smiled as they walked the beach, Owen holding her close even while still soaking wet.

Such was happiness and peace, surrounded by the calm of sea and sky.

EPILOGUE

The Storyteller's fingers grazed the final page, the inked words vibrant on the parchment.

"Your story is done." She smiled kindly at the volume in front of her, the life thriving in the pages.

There was a note of sadness from the book, newly filled and finished, but such was the way with every story that reached its end.

For a moment, the Storyteller could almost hear the voice of the book call out to her, its soul still eager for more, the melody of her magic still strong.

"What's done is done," the Storyteller said, taking the closed book and sliding it in its place on the shelf. It was the first of many to come. "Rest. You've earned it."

A pulse thundered through both page and cover as the Storyteller released the book, and she clutched her hand to her chest. "So full of life, even still. I hope I've done your warrior's spirit justice."

But she knew she did. She captured every moment, allowing the soul to move through her, bleeding words from her fingertips onto the page. The story was complete with all of its sadness, joy, and hope.

She could still hear her singing.

Satisfied, the Storyteller turned from her bookshelf, the other story spirits reaching out to her, whispering their tales in voices all their own.

She would revisit them soon, but for now, there were other stories waiting to be told.

ACKNOWLEDGMENTS

This book wouldn't have happened without Jesus and coffee. Thank you, Heavenly Father, from whom all blessings flow. This book was only possible because of all that You have given. (Especially the coffee.)

Thank you to my family for your patience and support. Mom, you're the best cheerleader a writer could ask for. Kelly, you're a great soundboard for ideas. Dad, you get ALL my jokes. Ariel, you're a rockstar beta reader. Savannah, you post the best memes.

Thank you, Kandi, Elissa, Lawrence, and Hannah for the hours of venting and co-op video games. Thank you, Emily, for taking me to get ramen and boba so I could see sunlight, touch grass, and breathe fresh air. Thank you, Misty, Bridget, Sue, Laura, and Terry Anne for all of your support and hype. You are all the best friends a writer girlie could ask for. <3

I knew I could do this—write a series, start my publishing journey—because everyone in my life believes in me. Words cannot express the depth of my love and appreciation for all of you.

And finally, thank YOU, dear reader, for taking a chance on this debut. I hope to see you in the next adventure.

ABOUT THE AUTHOR

When Morgan's not writing, she's playing video games. Find her on social media @morganreallywrites (except X, which insists on being DIFFERENT — @morganrlywrites).

Find all of her stories on Kindle Unlimited:
   amazon.com/author/morganreilly

Stay up to date by signing up for her newsletter at
   https://subscribepage.io/gQ6p2Z

Website: https://morganreallywrites.com/

   facebook.com/morganreallywrites
   instagram.com/morganreallywrites
   tiktok.com/@morganreallywrites
   threads.net/@morganreallywrites
   goodreads.com/morganreallywrites
   amazon.com/author/morganreilly

ALSO BY MORGAN REILLY

Short Fiction

Secrets of Northanger Abbey

The Dark Library Series

Book One: The Book of Water

Book Two: The Book of Dreams

Book Three: The Book of Light

Newsletter: https://subscribepage.io/gQ6p2Z

Website: https://morganreallywrites.com/

www.ingramcontent.com/pod-product-compliance
Lightning Source LLC
LaVergne TN
LVHW010308070526
838199LV00065B/5483